TRAITOR MAGUIRE

C R DEMPSEY

CRMPD MEDIA LIMITED

For Mena and Maya

CONTENTS

CHAPTER ONE

HOW DOES THE WIND EMBRACE?

ORMAC O'CASSIDY LOOKED AT his chapped hands and the small torrents of blood pooling in the ridges of his knuckles. How could he have fallen so? A malignant curse must have possessed him. Was it sin that lodged itself as a black tumour upon his soul? Had God heard he toyed with the heretic religion from across the water? He looked to the sky for answers and all he got were drops of rain in his eyes. Neither God nor man nor beast had sympathy for him, a victim of the cruel torments of Eunan Maguire. Melancholy possessed his very bones.

"I am but a destitute man, shorn of the trappings of wealth and both the burden and pleasures of family and responsibility. They cut respect and love for the world from me and tossed them to the wayside alongside my honour and dignity. How does the wind embrace these cursed bones?"

The wind embraced the trees, from root to branch, its cold torrents climbed and shook the bare limbs and bowed them into submission until they would spring back and bend in the other direction when another gust would subdue them again. The wind embraced the land, from soil to sky, chilling plants and animals alike and forcing those who could to seek shelter. The wind embraced the water, moulding its still form, as it huddled for respite at the bottom of gorges of mud, the residue of the frozen footprints of weary travellers. The wind embraced the road, it chilled the mud and froze the stone, driving back anyone foolhardy enough to travel it. The wind embraced

Cormac O'Cassidy. It blew through his thin layers of clothing, now reduced to rags, but he did not care. The wind embraced his bald head, freezing his brain and howling in his ears, but still it could make his life no worse than the misfortune he had fallen into. So he trudged on. One foot went before the other, forming those gorges of frozen mud. A weary traveller, lost but not directionless. He bowed his head into the wind, and each hair contemplated greying or deserting. The wind whistled in the trees, the spindly bare branches bowed into the path and grasped at the air, testing the resolve of the man to continue his journey. Their leaves had long since abandoned them in the fairer climes of autumn, and they embraced the wind as skeleton bones, trying to grasp onto life once more.

He tore at his clothes, undeserving of even their meagre protection. Should the cold take him and cast him in a ditch to become at one with the bog, he would surely end up in hell, a suitable punishment for the destruction of his family under his watch. Cormac cursed himself for not taking care of Eunan Maguire when they had the chance and he cursed his dead son for projecting his failure upon his family and ensuring their downfall during his brief, miserable existence. He staggered forward each foot without a destination, but the memory of his daughter drove him on. He could save her. If he made it to Dublin, he could save her.

The road became full of creatures fleeing war and the famine in the north. They dragged their possessions behind them, and Cormac felt the pang of jealousy for whatever had cast them into such a maelstrom, they had the time to gather necessities for the journey. Cormac joined in behind them and they formed a slow train, plodding towards the Pale. The Pale had a large English garrison that would surely never fall to the rebellion in the north, and even if it did, Dublin port could bring you anywhere in the world you wished.

As they got nearer to Dublin, the ranks of the rabble swelled. The people's supplies ran out. His starving companions saw his tattered rags were once fine clothes and concluded he was hiding something from them and pulled at his sleeves, begging for food or drinkable water. They were a tiller's hands, the skilled hands of a seamstress, the coarse hands of a cow herder or a tanner or a blacksmith. All of those hands would have once poured money into the pocket of the O'Cassidy Maguire but famine and coign and livery of the hired Galloglass living off their lands, compounded by the destructiveness of the war, had driven them from their once plentiful lands and emptied their bellies of food and their minds of hope. But Cormac beat their hands away, for he had nothing to give. They had cast him out of his mansion with only the clothes on his back and the wits and brains in his head. He pulled out the bottom of his pockets to show he shared their emptiness, but the people scoffed and scornfully said he was playing a trick. Cormac sensed danger and told them his men were just beyond the hill and they could either back away and gain the benefit of their protection or persist and feel the wrath of their swords. In the rabble's moment of hesitation, he made his way to the front of the column and declared he knew the way to Dublin and his previous dealings with the O'Reillys meant he could get them through their lands unmolested. The rabble followed him, for no one else had lofted themselves up into such a position and any promise of safe passage would have landed sweetly on the ears of such a melancholy mob. He lifted his arm and pointed towards the dark clouds to the east and the crowd would have eagerly followed him had his words not been snatched away by the wind. He bowed his head and pulled his clothes tight and set off into the wind.

Bogs were as treacle, streams became meandering rivers, rocks grew into mountains, children were baggage and the baggage weighed like rocks of burden as they hauled themselves over the bogs of Breifne. But each of them held some beacon of hope in their hearts to drive them forward, even if for Cormac, it was the burning ember of the hope for revenge.

They reached the muddy path to Dublin. Its distinctiveness from what they had travelled on before was that it was muddier, the road most well-trodden down by the English army. Some from the crowd pointed forth and hailed the masts of the port of Dublin, but Cormac's judgement was not so clouded. He only saw the rainbow of swirling clouds of grey fighting for the privilege to pelt them with rain. He did not tell them that a lifetime poring over ledgers had filled his pockets but reduced his long sight to a blur. His precious glasses, imported at great expense, he presumed had perished along with the rest of his valuables when they set his house on fire. The column gained more stragglers as it weaved its way through lands devoid of hope and its ranks swelled. They attracted attention from the locals, who would brave the weather and stand by their houses and stores, pitchforks at the ready to protect their skinny pigs and bony hens. They sent their sons to warn the local chieftains of the trail of destruction coming their way. The men of the local clans took to their horses and shadowed the column to escort it off their lands. Cormac felt life become more precarious. A spark in his soul ignited. He wished to live, if only to free his daughter and gain his revenge.

The next day jubilation seized the masses at the front, but Cormac, for all his endeavours, could only see clouds. But rumours spread quickly, and the crowd continued with renewed vigour. However, they soon found their path blocked.

"Turn around and go back to where you came from!" shouted a grizzled English sergeant who commanded a bristle of musket barrels.

The English soldiers had positioned themselves in front of a bridge, a fragile piece of masonry held up more by moss than mortar. Its last action was likely to be to bear the weight of this wretched horde. There was no way across the river than via this well-defended bridge. The column broke into huddled groups to discuss their limited options. After a few moments of mass inaction, Cormac made his way to the front for his former cowardice had deserted him. He felt his destiny lay ahead and as long as the musket ball did its damage with haste, it would be a blessed relief. He stood an execution's distance in front of the wall of guns and addressed the sergeant.

"You would run out of bullets before we would run out of men. Step aside! Let this gorge not be the burial ground for all of us!"

The clarity and forcefulness of his call surprised even him.

The sergeant looked behind him and over the bridge. He ordered his men to step aside, but it was not Cormac's demand he obeyed.

Across the bridge rode a one-armed man, but his lack of an arm did not diminish his authority. The soldiers parted and reassembled their ranks on both sides of the road with a precision that gave a motivational combination of fear and respect. The captain's face was a sheet of granite, and a lack of bullets would not be an obstacle should he have to clear the road. In his wake marched another twenty men with another rider at the rear. It was clear he was not here to negotiate. He rode up to

Cormac and pulled his horse to a halt. He spoke both to Cormac and over his head to the rabble behind.

"Clear the way now or face the lead of the Crown. My name is Williamson and I am on a mission from Her Majesty. If successful, it could lead to land for you to settle. But if you persist on this march to Dublin, let you account to God for any fallen souls this day, not I!"

Cormac looked up at Captain Williamson and saw a resolve that could not be reasoned with. He had cast off his normal cowardice, which acted as a restraint on reckless actions that could have a consequence of physical pain, but he considered he should have died under the old oak tree alongside his son. He let his mouth wander where it may.

"Curse you and your wretched whores from the Pale who serve the Crown. Curse Eunan Maguire and Seamus MacSheehy and may my brother Donnacha wreak my revenge upon them. Go on! Do your damnedest and let's see who is still standing when the bullets fly!"

Captain Williamson reached for his pistol, cocked it, and aimed at Cormac's face. Cormac closed his eyes. The expanding wet patch on his breeches gave way to a feeling of inner tranquillity in both soul and bladder. He gulped, for his cowardice had not wandered far. At least if it was to the face, it should be quick and relatively painless.

Captain Williamson lowered his gun, his curiosity piqued.

"Say, you cursed Eunan Maguire and then Seamus MacSheehy. Who are they to you?"

"They are my nemesis, a curse on my soul for all the evil I have done in the world. My daughter was due to be betrothed to the son of Connor Roe. It was to be the making of the O'Cassidys and a victory to all those in Fermanagh who wished to bring this wretched war to an end. Alas, I am to die a pauper on the windswept road to Dublin and my failure will be complete," and he once more closed his eyes and awaited his bullet.

It did not come, for the captain paused momentarily, bringing the lines around his eyes together.

"You look like a man who likes a bargain. Your life is forfeit, for the bullet from my gun will smash through the front of your head. Take it as a given that I will fire without hesitation. But I can give you the chance of revenge, a chance to get your life back. All you need to do is swear allegiance to the Crown and do what I say until Her Majesty's order is restored. When the spoils are shared, you can share them with the winners."

Cormac opened his eyes, for he could not believe his luck.

"My loyalty to the Queen never wavered. I always supported Connor Roe even when I had to do so in secret." Cormac grabbed Captain William's boots. "I swear loyalty to the Queen! I swear loyalty to the Queen! But my loyalty never wavered!"

Captain Williamson gave a grim smile.

"Cross the bridge and don't look back. Take it as your first test of loyalty. Follow my instructions to the letter to prove your trustworthiness. Follow the road over the hill."

"Thank you, sir! Thank you for your kindness!"

"Be gone with you for I have the Queen's work to do whilst you will get some rest before the Queen calls on you!"

"Yes, yes! Thank you, sir! I will set off at once!"

Rejuvenated, he ran across the bridge and set off up the gentle slope of the hill on the other side. He was so elated with his reprieve that he barely heard the volley of guns from behind him on the other side of the bridge. He held his nose to the whiff of gun smoke and he did not look back. He was now a Queen's man from the Pale.

CHAPTER TWO

HOW THE DAWN GLISTENS

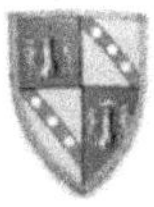

CORMAC'S ONCE GRAND HOUSE, whose architecture marked the no-man's-land between the English Pale and the Gaelic hinterlands, was now a blot on the landscape, another charred monument to the low-level violence that bubbled under the surface in Fermanagh only to burst through occasionally in great fissures. Where once there was the activity of commerce was now the activity of war, for Seamus and Eunan had converted the surrounds of the house into a great shabby camp for their undisciplined men.

Eunan was nervous for he knew not what it took to be the O'Cassidy Maguire but searched endlessly for clues or advice. He fumbled through the charred remains of the once opulent corridor of the grand entrance to O'Cassidy house, searching for anything of value, be it perhaps a book or an ornament that had survived the flames. The tapestries and furniture had all gone up like a tinderbox as Óisin's men had bombarded the house with flaming arrows. The blackness of the soot and smoke had damaged the house as completely as the plague would damage any body. Eunan had berated Óisin for such a callous act of vandalism, for what was the point in him being the O'Cassidy Maguire if his men had destroyed everything worth having?

Suddenly, the back of his head throbbed. There was blackness and then stars in his eyes. His new wife had not been afraid of making known her objections, both verbally and through whatever items of value she could lay her hands on to aim at his head. Her objections were plentiful but could be summed up as: why did you destroy my house and lands, why did you kill my only brother, why did you steal my family's title and why did you force me to marry you? There were not enough potential projectiles in the house with which to express her rage, but she searched and hoarded the most deadly for an opportune time to ambush him. Eunan did not have the verbal dexterity to populate his powers of persuasion to placate his wife, and usually had to rely on her fear of Seamus to get her to stop.

The cause of Eunan's pain today was a beautiful vase which was filled with an abundance of flowers from the surrounding fields, and purchased by her father on one of his trips to the Pale. The smoke had dulled its beauty and a stray arrow had taken a chip off the rim, the fury upon sight of this multiplied the force with which Caoimhe propelled it towards Eunan's head. It left a swollen lump and a trickle of blood as it smashed into a thousand pieces, but even that was not enough to express the depths of Caoimhe's rage. Books, combs and whatever else was in immediate reach clattered against the back of the door that Eunan pulled behind him to make his escape. He fled and descended to the less damaged parts of the house, and sat in the empty kitchen. He dabbed a corner of cloth into a bucket of water and soothed his fresh wound. But the anger and violence combined with Caoimhe's beauty excited him. She would be a ravishing wife if she could be tamed. The kitchen door scraped as it opened.

"Still mad, is she?" said Seamus.

A chilly breeze snuck in behind him and stole the heat from the room and the daydreams from Eunan's head.

Beads of sweat rolled down Seamus's face, defying the cold. His beard appeared whiter, as the season rolled on his cheeks bore a winter rouge, and he had the air of a man for whom things were going his way. Such a jovial entry jarred with Eunan and he threw his hands in the air.

"It's like you threw me into a bag with a cat and then married us!" said Eunan.

But Seamus was used to Eunan's negativity and did not let it dent his mood.

"It's always me, isn't it? No matter what I do, if anything bad ever happens to you, it's always me!"

Eunan looked at him incredulously.

"Do you expect me to say anything other than yes?"

Seamus closed the door behind him, gaining both privacy and shelter. He took off his coat and dusted it down before casually throwing it on a table.

"Enough of your tales of domestic bliss. It'll be a long time before she calms down, if ever. I don't know why you bother paying attention to her. Now that you have achieved your dream of becoming the O'Cassidy Maguire, get yourself a mistress and be done with it. Now we have business to attend to."

"Some dream!"

Seamus ignored him and carried on, something Eunan was used to. He leant on the large table in the centre of the room and searched the surfaces for food, for he was ravenous but was quickly disappointed. He got down to business.

"The O'Reillys have pledged to the O'Neill."

Eunan looked confused at Seamus's serious tone and shrugged.

"Well, it's good if you are the O'Neill. If you are the newly incumbent and very unpopular O'Cassidy Maguire, then it's not," said Seamus.

"If anyone made me unpopular, it is you! Why can't we get Desmond and bring him here? We could get your wife too. I'm sure you'd be a lot happier!" Eunan gave Seamus a knowing grin.

"You're the last person I'd take marriage advice from given the state of your two marriages! If you can't stand on your own two feet, you'll never last as the O'Cassidy Maguire! I can't stay here forever, the O'Donnell wants me back. Remember, for as long as the O'Donnell needs me, you are safe."

"So what do we need to do about the O'Reillys?" asked Eunan.

"John Roe has always been a scourge to south Fermanagh, raiding, looting, destroying crops and demanding black rent. The last thing the people want to see is you coming in as a naive pup and cosying up to him."

"But what can we do about it? He has the protection of the O'Neill! The Maguire would never tolerate us threatening his alliance with the O'Neill."

"You forget the golden rule of Irish politics. Every alliance, every election creates an enemy. I'm sure there is someone else that would be a little more to our liking that could be the new O'Reilly and if we get lucky, ingratiate ourselves to the O'Neill at the same time."

Seamus grinned, expecting appreciation for his sound advice.

"Do nothing without my specific instruction! I am the O'Cassidy Maguire!"

Seamus sneered and got up to leave.

"Go visit your wife again. Get her to throw something heavier at your head this time. Your brain has gone lopsided. You are getting delusions of grandeur. Leave the politics to me and you tend to the farm and deal with the locals."

"It is you who is delusional if you don't think I'll retaliate if you undermine my position!"

"Get dressed. It's time for training. The men are waiting outside. We'll talk again when you have more sense," and Seamus closed the door behind him.

Eunan went to his room and searched through his meagre collection of clothes he had thrown over the back of a chair, so he could dress appropriately to train the men in deep winter. He had a room nestled at the back of the house on the ground floor, barely licked by flames but it stank of smoke and had been ravaged by both the ransacking of the house and Eunan's untidiness. Occupying the room for all its discomforts was a vain attempt to save face, to at least be in the same house as his new wife, where he could pretend to the outside world that they were together. However, everyone knew that Caoimhe just used his head for target practice while he could not get within range of an old flying boot, never mind lay a marital hand upon her. Only Seamus was brave enough to say, for Seamus knew a frightened little boy lurked beneath the thin warrior visage.

When granted cover by any convenient distraction, Eunan would search whatever parts of the house time and opportunity would allow for the remnants of his uncle's possessions. He searched for his clothes, for he considered they would, when properly sized, bestow upon him a certain authority that would impress the villages and farms of south Fermanagh and help persuade the people to love and respect him. He found little except fire-damaged scraps, but plenty of shoes his wife threw at his head. It was a pity for none of them fitted when he was granted the peace to try them on.

He hoped to find the papers and ledgers that would reveal the means by which his uncle had achieved his success. However, he would have to find someone suitable to read and decipher them. He dreamed of Desmond coming to live there and his uncle's notes may prove just the lure to get him there. But his uncle's drawing room was one of the first places to be hit and its fires, fuelled by his uncle's mounds of paper, consumed half the house. There appeared to be nothing of value that Caoimhe had not already hoarded in her room. Eunan had strongly resisted calls by Seamus to force her from there so they could search it. Eunan still harboured the belief that he could win her over, so remained fiercely protective of her.

But something upon which he placed a value caught his eye. He found himself a cloak on a hook by one door with no apparent owner nearby to claim it. Eunan had restricted who could enter the house and his wife and what maids he had allowed her had not left their room. It was a brilliant scarlet, a colour so pure that even though it had been worn, for it bore the gentle mould of a body, it had resisted the continuous assaults of the Fermanagh weather and kept its colour and shape. Eunan put it on. Tight at the shoulders and generous on the hips, but nothing a belt could not fix. The only obvious previous owner of such a fine garment was his uncle, so Eunan thought no better a symbol to show the men in training who was the O'Cassidy Maguire now. He pulled the cloak around himself and went to survey the area over which he was now lord. The cloak gave him an assurance, a warmth he never felt, shivering in a bog as a Galloglass apprentice.

He opened the door and the rush of damp air startled him; nerves jangled and on edge, the pressure of having to impress and live up to his image of his uncle weighed on his hemmed-in shoulders.

"I must look strong and in control. I must look strong and in control."

Due to his preoccupied mind, an indecisive foot stepped straight out into a puddle.

The men were busy training, the clashes of steel and the thunder of muskets providing enough distraction for most not to notice Eunan's embarrassing entrance. But Seamus did.

"Get back to work!" he growled at the men in his vicinity whose eyes and smirks bore witness to Eunan's folly.

Seamus walked over to Eunan, trying to ensure the hulk of his body shielded the conversation from prying eyes.

"Get that cloak off you now! You're not at some fancy dress party at the Pale!"

As scarlet was torn from Eunan's shoulders, it was replaced with scarlet on his face.

"Fancy dress does not work with fighting men or men from the field. They just think their leader wasted the blood of their fallen brothers or the sweat of their labours using it to become an Englishman."

"I have been around the court of the Maguire long enough to know what impresses!" hissed Eunan.

But that limp bravado was not enough to gain much dignity back.

"Sorry to ruin your illusion, but you are not there now and these men's efforts are your best bet to get back there. Now come and inspect the men and let's have no more of this folly of trying to be your uncle!"

Seamus cast aside the cloak, and it fell to decorate the rim of another puddle in the shadow of the house, the red seeping into the muddied water, an echo of the wedding day massacre.

Eunan had come out to inspect the grounds of the house and the men training there, but his humiliation at the hands of Seamus blurred his critical eye. He saw nothing of what had previously impressed him so much: the order of the fields before the house; the neat lawn out front and the gleam of success and money in the well-maintained facade of the building. The ousting of his uncle had meant that the world of Eunan Maguire now imposed itself on the land. Eunan first observed the churned-up lawn, where his men and farm boys had their drills and engaged in single combat practice for the brutal future fight for Fermanagh's fair soil. Where once were orchards were now shooting ranges under the supervision of Arlo. Fruit, which had once been sold around the country and recently graced the merchant ships of the Pale and been sent to England, was chipped away as it hung on the trees by boys eager for target practice. When the remains fell, they were fit only for rats and crows. Fields once fallow and waiting for the spring crops to be sown were now reduced to mud as the men cut down the surrounding trees, stripped them down for pikes, and paraded across the ground. The sheds beside the old oak tree that once housed the carts that brought the labours of the O'Cassidys to markets across the island now lay idle, awaiting orders for their new usage as transport for war. All that had been said about Eunan was true. All he brought in his wake was destruction and death.

He felt a shiver emanate from the chill of the wind on his shoulders, amplified by the light drops of rain. But without the fancy cloak, he appeared closer to the men who shivered before them. The older men bore a look of steel in their eyes, yet they seemed distant, as if asking Eunan to make their efforts worthwhile, to improve their lives, to give them something to live or die for. The young farm boys' eyes contained the giddiness and naivety of youth, an enthusiasm yet to be blunted by the pain and misery the blades of their axes, points of their pikes, edges of their swords and round leaden bullets could inflict on those who would receive them – if they had time to use them before being struck down by their foes. But to them Eunan was an unproven hope, a young man whose real influence only lay in his powerful allies. For no matter the tales that Eunan or any of his lieutenants could tell, Eunan could not live up to the stories. A young man trapped in a shadow, as long as Seamus remained.

"They are doing well, some of them," said Seamus, breaking the silence of Eunan's entrance, an attempt to cover the lost opportunity that Eunan should have taken to address the men. "Arlo has done especially well," and Seamus drew attention to the Spanish captain who had come from the nearby field when he was told that Eunan wished to inspect the men.

"Yes, sir," said Arlo. "It is not long until you'll have the finest shot in all of Fermanagh. I will be reassigned," he said, hinting at Eunan's promise of his release.

"It is one thing shooting at apples, another to be shooting at a body of men charging at you. I wouldn't be packing your bags just yet," and Seamus cut off Arlo's route to undermining Eunan. "Pick up your axe, Eunan, and show these men what you can do."

Forgiveness had been in ample supply as Seamus had hoped to incorporate as many of the O'Cassidy men into their ranks as he could. As long as Eunan could impress them, show strength as the new warrior leader of the clan, rather than a mercantile lord waiting to become an Englishman as his uncle had been, then their loyalties would pivot. Seamus knew Eunan would not do it with his feeble and hesitant words but could with his prowess with his axe. Seamus pushed forward the first O'Cassidy man to take Eunan on.

The sound of clashing metal was as unwelcome as it was uncommon before Eunan arrived in the grounds of the O'Cassidy house. An uncouth method of allocating status by unsophisticated brutes not familiar with the power of the word, the pen, the allocation of monies and, above all, politics. Caoimhe was done crying, done mourning and done with this puppet boy who had ruined her life. She had gone through every scene of her tragic wedding that she had borne witness to in a seeming distant haze, cross-examined every witness account the remaining house servants had recounted and attributed blame and reconsidered and assigned blame again until she ran out of tears. Caoimhe had torn her clothes, her tapestries and thrown her ornaments and prized possessions against the wall until her room, which had mainly suffered smoke damage, resembled the other rooms, devastated by fire and destruction, in her mind at least. She had banished the oafish brute who had forced her to endure the ceremony to save her father's life and now insulted her by calling himself her husband. Every time he uttered the word, it was if he stabbed her in the ear. But that boy, that wretch from the lake, would be easily controllable if it were not for the puppet master, his uncle Seamus. If she could separate the two, she could surely manoeuvre Eunan into an untimely death, or at worst get him to do her bidding.

She dried her eyes and looked out the window. They were destroying her father's once magnificent fields with their war games. It looked as if they had gathered all the men outside to watch some single combat. She knew what she must do. She ran to her table, but it was bare. Her latest tantrum with Eunan had cleared it of its contents. She scrambled around the floor and found a prized quill from her collection, a beautiful gift given to her by her father after one of his trips to Dublin port. Paper was harder to come by, for most of it was torn and soiled, victim of her various tossings of the room. Caoimhe found a piece, untorn but stained, though she considered the stains would add drama and help her express the peril that a learned young lady was in where her words would not. She had appointed herself a spy, a vital spoke in the wheel of all those who opposed Hugh Maguire, Eunan, Seamus and all those traitors who brought the Maguires and Fermanagh into jeopardy. She would stand for peace and freedom, so a man and his family could trade with who they wished so they could prosper, and not be beholden to whatever gang of thugs might come over the hill and lay some ancient unproven claim on your lands at the blade of an axe. She would fulfil her father's wishes and marry into the senior Maguire clan. Connor Roe had some spare sons, even though she may appear to them a big sister rather than a lover, but that would make them easier to control. But her chief hope was Donnacha, who she had always called uncle for he had always acted so, if technically he was not. So it was 'uncle' that followed the word 'dear' that appeared in her letter.

She had composed an elaborate plan, a scheme that would unite all the dissident elements against Hugh Maguire and begin the search for her father, bathed in the optimism that he was still alive. But as the quill broke the skin of ink, she thought better of it. She had no messenger except for her trusted handmaids and would die of guilt if her foolish words were to endanger them. She re-evaluated and wrote a simple letter to her uncle, telling him she was still alive, a prisoner of Eunan Maguire, and asking him to write to her via her messenger and assist in her rescue. She reckoned it was a letter that would express her situation best but would not raise undue attention or provoke suspicions of her true intentions. Once a safe route to communicate was established, then they could plot and scheme.

She waved the letter in the air to assist the drying of her words and called her most trusted handmaid to attend.

A young woman answered her call. She bowed her head. Her tousled chestnut hair was a familiar sight to Caoimhe.

"Lasair, I am sorry to ask you this, but I have an important mission for you."

"Whatever you wish, ma'am. I am here to help."

"Take this letter to my uncle Donnacha in Enniskillen and it is for his eyes only. Will you do this for me?"

"Of course. Your father was always good to my family and the sooner he is restored back here the better."

"Thank you for this, but go now, while the men are distracted by their silly games. May God speed you on your way."

"I will bring you back a message from your uncle. May he have hope and good tidings for us all!"

Lasair closed the door quietly behind her, went down the back stairs, and exited by the unguarded back door. She was soon in the woods on the way to Enniskillen.

The comfort Eunan felt leading with an axe in his hands almost matched the ease with which he knocked the O'Cassidy men to the ground. The hired Galloglass were dead or long since on the horizon in search of a master with as deep pockets as Cormac O'Cassidy but with a much greater chance of survival and success. A swift thump of an axe butt to the side of the temple was enough to erase the memories of Eunan's follies with his red cloak and imbue the levels of respect Seamus wished the men to have for Eunan. Seamus studied the faces of the O'Cassidys and decided that enough was enough. A display of Eunan's martial prowess rather than the physical pain of losing to him was enough to convince most to concede. Eunan wiped the blood and sweat from his forehead and braced himself for the next bout.

"Enough!" cried Seamus. "All you men willing to fight wait over there by the oak tree. Our terms will be generous to those who are loyal and willing to fight. There are plenty of cattle in the fields, as you have seen. Eunan and I have also filled the paddocks of the Maguire in what will be merely a skirmish compared to what is coming. Those wishing to slink off or change sides had better beware of the wrath of the new O'Cassidy Maguire."

Most of the men went over towards the oak tree whilst some men attempted to slip off. Óisin grabbed a bow from one of his men and hit one of the unwilling square in the back and stopped him in his tracks.

"Don't doubt what Seamus said," said Óisin.

Those who once turned to flee picked up their comrade and hurried to the oak tree.

Seamus sat behind a table. One of his veterans appropriated one of Cormac's ledgers and he began making notes about who pledged, for how long and for what wage. The pledger would then make a mark in the ledger to signify agreement once they had been reassured that what was agreed had been correctly noted in the ledger. Family units and fathers pledging sons were more complicated and even involved Seamus getting off his seat if the negotiations got heated. Soon the line was finished and Sean O'Toole came to review what had been agreed. He flicked through the pages.

"You're not planning on doing much harvesting this year?" he said to Seamus.

"There's two ways I see this going. Either the peace talks fail and we are back to war, or the peace talks succeed and there is a Maguire civil war. No matter what the outcome, the Crown will not tolerate friends of Spain ruling the clans of the north."

"A famine is no way to endear Eunan to the people."

Seamus smiled and gave Sean a knowing look.

"We'll steal our way into their hearts, don't you worry about that."

A rider came and dismounted his horse. The caking of mud on his breeches warned of bad weather coming from the west. The letter handed to Seamus gave news of a different type of storm brewing. Seamus read the letter and stuffed it in his pocket.

"Óisin! Sean! With me! We need to speak to Eunan in the house."

They convened a meeting of the new military heads of the O'Cassidy clan in the pantry of the O'Cassidy merchant's house. The walls were thick, giving the illusion of privacy. Eunan arrived from another part of the house, where he was busying several men with restoration and repair. He opened the door to grim faces and Seamus pointed to where he wanted him to sit.

"Why do you summon the O'Cassidy Maguire to a conference in a food cupboard in his own home?" said Eunan.

Eunan's voice quivered with nerves, allowing Seamus the excuse to ignore him.

"Our enemies have moved quickly. Donnacha has complained to Hugh Maguire about the ousting of his cousin. He has petitioned for your removal. Connor Roe has also complained about the death of his son. We need to act fast. Eunan, go to Enniskillen and see how the land lies. See Desmond, for he will know how to negotiate that vipers pit better than most. Sean, go with him and if necessary go to Tirconnell, see if we have the support of the O'Donnell and also what men we have there. Óisin will come with me and take care of the O'Reillys."

"What if I want Óisin to come with me?" said Eunan.

He stood up from his assigned seat.

"Don't puff your chest out to argue because you feel belittled. You know I am right. Sean has the discipline Óisin hasn't. Óisin needs to stick with me and prove he can be a reliable commander if he wishes to stay with us."

Óisin snarled, but kept his comments to himself. Sean wished to break the standoff and got up and slapped Eunan on the shoulder.

"Come, lord, we have Enniskillen politics to master, something you have shown yourself to excel at."

"We all have our jobs to do if we are to succeed," said Seamus. "We must deal with the O'Reillys before I am summoned north again."

"Then I bid you good day and let us all succeed before we meet again!" Eunan said.

Eunan shut the door behind him, and Sean went ahead to the stable.

Eunan paused and considered saying goodbye to his wife. He then thought better of it. But the scarlet cloak caught the corner of his eye and looked cleanable since anyone living in Fermanagh would soon become proficient in cleaning mud from clothes. He went and retrieved it and brushed it down. It would require a good soaking to bring it back to its former lustre. He slung it over his shoulder and then smuggled it into a bag before Sean could see and comment. They set off at a trot towards Enniskillen.

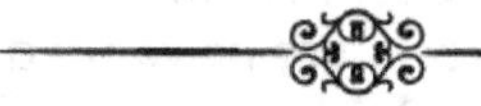

Caoimhe knew all the secrets of the house since she had grown up in it and many a time her father had retired to the pantry to have a secret meeting away from suspicious ears. Her father's meetings had mostly been boring, for a child would not fully understand them or know everyone mentioned in the discussion, for her world was once limited to the lands of the O'Cassidys. But the adult Caoimhe was infinitely more worldly and the conversation she overheard definitely worthy of a note to her uncle. She ran to her room to pen another note, for she still had another handmaid willing and trustworthy enough to make the journey to Enniskillen. She may not get there before Eunan, but she would arrive before too much damage was done.

CHAPTER THREE

DARK CLOUDS SURROUND THE CASTLE

HUGH MAGUIRE PACED THE room. The roaring fire reflected in his eyes as he stooped to throw on a couple more logs. Anything to distract himself from this tense negotiation. Plumes of smoke floated towards the ceiling, diverted from their former path by the casually thrown logs. The Maguire realised his mistake and looked up to see if he had done any damage to the family heirlooms above his head.

The tapestries of his ancestors looked down upon him and added to the weight on his shoulders of the trappings of being the Maguire. He hated politics. His father eclipsed him in the art of negotiation, of looking the other man in the eye and assessing what was important to him and what he was willing to give up to get what he wanted. Hugh was more a man of action, wielding an axe in his hand, leading the nobility of the Maguire in a cavalry charge, planning and co-ordinating raids.

However, he understood politics and knew what made his lesser Maguire lords tick. But he did not like it. His father had, as all the elders liked to remind him, been able to suck the distasteful in his mouth, with the vision not to be distracted by that same taste and steer a steady path for the Maguires even though his individual decisions may have been unpopular and seemed irrational. His father had made plenty of agreements with the English, smoothed out the edges of quite a few, openly broken some, but had the patience to wait until circumstances favoured him once more.

However, these skills had bypassed Hugh. He would have preferred single combat with these representatives from across the water. He would even have considered a duel if it was more to their liking. But after hours of talking in circles, he grew tired. He left the politics as much as he could up to Donnacha.

Donnacha had set aside his recent family issues and planned this set of talks meticulously. He knew that the O'Neill and the O'Donnell were conducting face-to-face talks with the Irish Council that would cover the current truce and any subsequent extensions to it. He also knew that each of these leaders was negotiating a settlement for all of those lords that were subservient to them. The lords of the north had also arranged various back channels to the Irish Council so that more controversial potential compromises could be tested out away from the public eye.

Donnacha saw this as an enormous opportunity to break away from the lords of the north and the old ways that meant that the Maguires and the O'Cassidys were always subservient and constricted, victims of constant violence and war. His cousin Cormac had led a second-rate sept to prosperity when he switched the direction of their attention to the embrace of the Pale and the prosperity that trading with market towns could bring. He had been a shining example of the new way of thinking, breaking out of the submissive chains of the clan structure and striking out on your own where wealth and titles were passed on to your own children, where you could build something and not have everything constantly destroyed in low-level civil war. Connor Roe felt the same way, or so he insinuated in their private discussions. But Connor Roe was not the Maguire, and he had the boot of the O'Neill on his head. Donnacha had Hugh Maguire to deal with, and he knew Hugh hated politics. Hugh had yet to realise that putting your axe through someone's head only got you so far and the art of politics was the path to genuine power, and Hugh had left that up to him.

Donnacha was determined to grasp this opportunity he had been given. He imagined it was like a play on the English stage, stories of which the merchants from the Pale would bring. He was to be this play's author, the determinant who would control what happened and the outcome to suit his own desires. Donnacha employed the finest tailors in Enniskillen to use materials imported through the port of Dublin to create a special outfit for

Hugh for this series of meetings with the representatives of the Queen of England and the King of Scotland. He had told him that an air of wealth would be something that the representatives could both respect and relate to and would elevate Hugh's negotiating position. Hugh wanted to appear in chain mail and undershirt, similar to what he would have worn on the battlefield to show the strength of the clan. Donnacha had persuaded him otherwise, for he said that every small-time chieftain with a pot to piss in would try to intimidate the English negotiators and all they would do was give away how weak their forces were compared to the regular English army. Hugh relented and let Donnacha orchestrate the meeting, playing along with his plan. But now he was having second thoughts.

"The basis for a deal is there," said Hugh. "We all know that we are going to reach a compromise, for the famine does not pick sides. However, what you ask is too much. Ask for some other show of loyalty. I cannot turn on the O'Neill and the O'Donnell for fear of what has passed for supposed resolutions before. The forces of the Crown may defeat the lords of the north, if they can catch them, but if I join the assault, they will surely exact a bloody revenge when the Crown retreats once more to the Pale."

Hugh looked around to see where his pleas had landed. Captain Williamson's face was unresponsive, a sheer face of stone with a rhythmic wheeze to show he was alert and calculating behind his veneer. James Fullerton sat and sipped his wine. He was the secret envoy of James VI of Scotland with the mission of ending the rebellion of the Irish and securing support for his King to unite both the thrones of England and Scotland. James wore unflattering clothes, ones that would make him melt into a crowd, not clothes to exude power or to give away his true standing. He was relaxed as he sat and sipped his wine, for he knew he was towards the beginning of a negotiation rather than at the end. If he stayed silent, he expected Donnacha to come running to him, for out of everyone there, he was the most motivated to make a deal. Once he found out why, then the advantage would fall to him.

"Gentlemen, we are all men of reason," said Donnacha. "Why do we dwell on what prises us apart when we have so much in common and so much to lose? We realise the Crown cannot be seen to give away pardons as if they were free. But we can show loyalty by the way the Maguires conduct themselves. By our conduct we can show loyalty and distinguish ourselves from other perpetual rebels in the north."

Donnacha smiled at the other three men, trying to bring them together once more.

It was Captain Williamson's turn to take a slow sip from his wine, to build the tension, to get Donnacha to make the first move and to make a concession that he could not move away from. But he needed a little more coaxing.

"You can't just move in and out of being a dutiful servant of the Crown, then a rebel, then an obedient servant again and keep Her Majesty's trust. Trust has to be rebuilt. There have to be consequences to prove oneself worthy of forgiveness."

He went silent to gauge Donnacha's reaction and slowly sipped his wine once more.

Donnacha looked to Hugh to see what move he could make and Hugh turned away and looked into the distance. For all of Donnacha's knowledge of Hugh's mannerisms, he interpreted this as giving him the floor.

"What other ways can we show the Queen that we are truly loyal?"

"She'll always accept a contribution to her coffers," Captain Williamson replied, "but her forgiveness does not come cheap. No matter what we agree, there will always be a fine, for she doesn't like to be left holding the bill for putting down rebellions. I fear that the fine alone will make you howl, never mind any additional amounts to pay for forgiveness. But we have fined you before, yet here we are. It'll have to be something else, something that shows you are truly sorry and wish for a genuine reconciliation."

Donnacha paused and shook his finger in the air, as if being torn in two by some inward debate.

"What if we could show that English law is supreme in Fermanagh despite what has happened in the recent past, and we show where we follow the Queen's laws to the letter even though it may be painful to us?"

"Is this not the same ground you just covered?" Captain Williamson said. "Isn't following the Queen's laws something you are supposed to do, anyway? You refuse a sheriff nominated by the representatives of the Crown, so you would need to show you can govern yourselves better than a sheriff could govern you."

"You may not know it yet, but we are on the same page!" and Donnacha's face illuminated at the joy of a meeting of minds.

"Tell me before you burst with excitement. Tell me of your scheme."

"The resumption of tanistry, elected succession, has led to chaos in the land."

Hugh glared at him, for he did not like this new direction. Donnacha had raised such sentiments in the past, but they had withered upon Hugh's disapproval. They had not pre-agreed to this as a line of negotiation.

"Except for my master, of course. His father was the Maguire so it can be said that he inherited it from him, with popular support."

"Of course," Captain Williamson replied. "But many a great man has borne the title of 'sir' and the Maguire would be no less the man for it if he also bears it. In fact, he would be more of a man in the eyes of the Queen, the one he is beholden to and with whom he wishes to make amends."

"To douse the flames of rebellion, we must tread carefully and not provoke anyone any more than we have to in order to achieve peace. Once peace is embedded in the land, we can make such semantic adjustments so that everyone can live happily within the new circumstances. The Maguire or sir must make little difference to the Queen in the present circumstances."

"Let us not get bogged down in a maze of words arguing about their meaning. Continue with your scheme," said James Fullerton.

His frustration was clear as he waved the previous arguments away.

"My family and that of Connor Roe have been victims of tanistry, a usurper having murdered members of both families and taken my brother's title. If we gave the usurper a trial under English law, we would surely find him to be an attainder and my family and that of Connor Roe would receive suitable restitution."

Hugh turned away, for he did not want his guests to see his reaction. Donnacha had complained vehemently about the usurper and Hugh thought he had accepted that something would be done at a more opportune time, but apparently not.

"That is a story we hear, no matter what clan we speak to," said Captain Williamson. "The clans are split by this wave of rebellion, but all will be restored by the Queen's peace. If you side with us, we'll give you the power to defeat your enemies. But our previous offer still stands. You need to openly side with us."

"What if I were to tell you the usurper's name was Eunan Maguire?"

Captain Williamson's eyes lit up.

"Then that would be a different story. Were you to sacrifice him for the Queen's rule of law, I could persuade her to accept that as a suitable gesture. But would you accept it, Hugh? Donnacha has done all the talking, and you have kept quiet. Would you give up Eunan Maguire?"

Hugh was silent, deep in thought. Donnacha had outmanoeuvred him, but still he knew that if he let the insult to Connor Roe stand it would divide the Maguires and shatter the fragile peace. On the other hand, would siding with the English empower Connor Roe, their traditional ally in the Maguire?

"If it were to save the clan, Eunan would sacrifice himself."

Captain Williamson could not hold in his grin.

"A noble choice, Hugh. I will give you my full assistance with the arrangements. We must ensure that nothing can reflect badly on the Maguire. Come Donnacha, we have much to discuss."

CHAPTER FOUR

THE COMPANY OF STRANGERS

EUNAN PULLED ON HIS horse's mane as they reached the edge of Enniskillen town. Sean O'Toole pulled up just behind him. The rain pelted down and soaked Eunan to the skin. He shivered in the pangs of a bitterly frosty night, his arms alight with goose pimples. As they speculated about the reception they would receive, the rain relented. The street became a line of sparkling white, as rain dripped to merge in the many gathering puddles and the shimmering moon rested upon them. A moonlit procession welcomed them into Enniskillen town. Eunan smiled, for he read that as a good omen and waved Sean forward. Sean pawed at the grip of his axe as the empty streets made him nervous.

The resolute Maguires had rebuilt parts of the town after recapturing it back from the English, in order to breathe back life and commerce. Eunan thought this premature, for if he was to toss his uncle's axe and place a bet on the future, it was far more likely that all that had been rebuilt would be swept away once more in a tide of destruction. The next toss of the axe would probably show that Eunan would not be alive to witness said destruction, but he banished those thoughts from his mind, for his mission meant that he needed to be a resolute Maguire, too.

They should have arrived several days before, but they had taken a detour to Desmond's island to consult with him before going to Enniskillen. Eunan had committed Desmond's advice to memory, repeating it word for word lest he forget. Eunan was to contact him within a week, or else Desmond would fetch Seamus.

They rode through the town and reached the gates of the castle. It looked foreboding in the moonlight, especially with Eunan's decidedly mixed experiences there. He smelt the waft of roasting deer on the wind, which increased his hunger and his hope for a warm reception. At the gate, they immediately recognised Eunan. He asked for an audience with the Maguire and they let him in and directed him to the tower. Eunan and Sean dismounted their horses and gave them to the stable hand. They went to the tower door and were met with a familiar face.

"Sorry, the Maguire is in conference. Can you find lodgings in the town and I will send word to you when he wishes to see you?" said Caolán, the MacCabe Galloglass constable.

His men intertwined their axe heads to block the entrance and pushed their chests out to make themselves look bigger.

"Has he no lodgings for one of his greatest friends and allies in all of Fermanagh?" said Eunan.

He was here to show off his status and curry favour, and no better place to start than the door to the tower to show that he was part of the Maguire favoured few.

"There have been some pretty vicious rumours being spread about you. I hear you call yourself the O'Cassidy Maguire these days?"

"South Fermanagh calls me the O'Cassidy Maguire. It will please the Maguire to know that I have vanquished his enemies from the region, and where once it was a bastion of discontent, it is now the region of his greatest support."

Eunan expanded his chest, almost in mimicry of the guards, daring Caolán into disloyalty and deflate it. Caolán smirked but declined.

"I am merely a constable and not a man of politics. I admire your skills with an axe, but I would watch your back here in Enniskillen. Certain parties have it in for you."

"As have I for all traitor Maguires!"

Caolán was in no mood for bravado and put his arm around Eunan's shoulder and led him away.

"Rest, for you'll need all the energy you can muster. The Maguire may see you tomorrow, call back in the morning after he has eaten. He has left word that the O'Flynns will take you in. You can leave your horses here, for it is only a short walk. He says that you are well acquainted with them from Seamus's drinking days in the town."

"Seamus has many a friend that keeps a tavern. I bid you good evening and will see you bright and early when the Maguire is ready."

Eunan saluted him, tapped Sean on the shoulder, and walked towards the gate. They went into the town and walked through the remnants of a rainy night. Hardly anyone was awake, and the streets were still empty. The lights of O'Flynn's tavern spilled out onto the street like a glowing welcome mat and Eunan knocked on the door. The landlord recognised Eunan as the young man that chased after Seamus and invited him in. A wall of warmth enveloped the guests. He showed Eunan to the room out the back and told him his possessions and weapons would be safe there. The landlord offered some fresh clothes and the two men peeled off their wet garments and threw them in a sopping heap on the floor with unreserved joy. With his guests refreshed, he invited Eunan and Sean into the main house for some food and mead.

They entered a large tavern where the shadows clung to the ceilings and dust sprung from the floor as they arranged the tables to give access to the large mature fire. The whiff of hot food tortured their nostrils, converting once dormant stomachs into cavernous holes. The landlord proudly escorted them to the best seats in the house, through sparsely occupied tables where lone figures and the odd couple huddled around the dregs of their mugs of mead. Enniskillen's decline was obvious to any visitor who had been there in the past. They seated themselves near the fire, and the landlord called for his wife, who laid out quite a feast considering the famine.

"Deer from the forest? How come such luxuries are being given to me?" said Eunan.

"These are straight from the kitchens of the Maguire. His way of apologising for not being able to take you in, I suppose," said the landlord. "Tuck in and keep warm, for it is cold outside and you'll need all the good food inside you can get!"

Eunan smiled and accepted the invitation to eat. The more he ate, the more the room emptied.

"Where are they all going at this time of night?" asked Eunan of the landlord when he returned. "Is there a holy festival that I don't know about?"

"They are retiring for the night for there is little food, except for those with the favour of the Maguire."

"Nothing would cheer me more than to see the people eat as I, but there is much politics to be had and blood to be spilt before they can."

"More's the pity we can't start by spilling yours!" came a voice from the doorway.

Burly armed men led by a man in a mask blocked the front door. Tables and chairs flew as everyone except Eunan and Sean fled for anything resembling an exit.

"The Maguire wants you for the murder of one of his chieftains!" said the man in the mask.

"I'm sorry, Shea Óg forced me," mumbled the landlord to Eunan and Sean before he fled towards the kitchen.

Eunan grabbed the table and tossed it into the air. He reached down to his belt, for he had the foresight not to be parted with his throwing axes. He took aim at the masked man, released and ran for cover in the crowd. The axe landed squarely on the nose of one of the armed men, and his shrieks of pain only heightened the commotion. Pandemonium ensued. There were only two exits, the front blocked by Shea Óg and his men, and the rear entrance clogged up with the fleeing locals. The slots in the walls that were the windows were too tight. But another of Shea Óg's men replaced every person who escaped. Two of the men rushed Sean O'Toole. Sean lashed out with the fork he kept from dinner and shoved it into one man's eye. The man howled in pain and dropped his weapon. Sean stooped to pick up the sword.

"This one's for my boy!" cried Shea Óg, and his axe descended upon Sean's bent head.

Shea Óg struggled to dislodge his axe while his men surrounded Eunan. Eunan went for another throwing axe, but he would not have survived the swords pointing in his face before he retrieved it.

"Give it up whilst you still have your life," said Shea Óg as Sean's blood dripped down from the axe head and onto Shea Óg's sleeve. "Unfortunately for me, the Maguire wants you alive."

"Since when do you speak for the Maguire?" said Eunan.

"Since you murdered one of his chieftains. His own men were too cowardly to do the job. Now come on. Enough innocent people have died because of you."

"You'll never take me! Never!" and Eunan crouched down into a defensive ball, swinging his axe, ready to take on all comers.

A candlestick swung down from behind and left Eunan sprawled out cold on the floor with a trickle of blood from his head.

"I hope you haven't killed him," moaned Shea Óg. "I may get that deducted from my pay and then I'd have to claim it back against you."

The landlord stepped back, the candlestick over his shoulder, ready to swing again.

"There's your man, now go. There's been enough killing here tonight. I wanted no part of it, but was forced into it. I'll have to live the rest of my life looking over my shoulder to see if Seamus MacSheehy is there. Go and never darken our door again!"

The front door opened and the wind and rain swept in. The one-armed man standing in the doorway made even Shea Óg afraid.

Captain Williamson looked around the room and saw the still-armed landlord. He took some coins out of his pocket and placed them on the only remaining upright table.

"That's for the damages and for your trouble. No ill will come to you because of this. The Crown always looks after those who have served her well."

The landlord raised the candlestick a little higher.

"Pick him up," said Captain Williamson, pointing at Eunan. "The Maguire has somewhere reserved for him in his jail."

The men lifted Eunan out of the tavern and back out into the pouring rain.

CHAPTER FIVE

OPENING ARGUMENTS

E UNAN WOKE UP WITH a throbbing in his head. The pain seared into his mind, preventing him from thinking straight. His clothes seemed to stick to him, creating a blanket of cold. Eunan's senses gradually returned. His whole body was wet, and he shivered. He rolled over onto his back. The room was dark but penetrated by a weak shaft of light which showed him it was daytime.

He tried to think back to what he could last remember. Arriving in Enniskillen. The rain. Sean O'Toole was there. The rest was a haze. He sat up and looked towards the shaft of light. It was broken up by metal bars. His head ached so much that Odin himself would not have bothered to show up to torture him, for there was no room for further pain.

He huddled by the wall. He was starving and also bursting for a piss. Eunan searched the nearby hay for he did not want to soil his own bed. He found a modest pot, decrepit and seared with yellow and green stains. As he relieved himself, it soon overflowed, and the contents spilt onto the floor. Eunan shook and swayed his head in a storm of pain and blackness. He tried to cast the remaining warm yellow liquid out the window and into the castle courtyard. But he should not have bothered, for he tripped and fell and a little of the offending liquid troubled the courtyard but most sullied his shirt. He took some dried straw from the floor and tried to brush himself clean.

"Step back from the door!" came a voice from the other side.

Eunan attempted to focus on the door and staggered backwards.

"I have. Has the Maguire seen sense?"

"Step back, I am coming in."

Constable Caolán Maguire stood there, wearing his stony face, the one he reserved for traitors.

"They have summoned you to stand before the Maguire Council."

Eunan fought the pain in his head so he could appear coherent.

"Is this to receive an apology?"

Caolán sneered.

"There have been some serious allegations made against you. So serious that some are suggesting you should be handed over to the forces of the Crown."

"The Maguire would never stand for that. Even if he did, the O'Donnell would immediately oust him."

"Times are changing. There are some serious negotiations going on."

Eunan stood and looked confused.

"Come, they are waiting for you."

Eunan held up the arms of his wretched clothes.

"Am I to go like this, like a common thief?"

"Some say you do not even deserve the dignity awarded to you now. Come as you are, for only by appearing before the council may you have hope of a reprieve."

"Am I to be in chains?"

"The Maguire has at least spared you of that."

Caolán held the door open as his men rushed past him to seize Eunan.

Four armed men dragged Eunan from the dungeon at the bottom of the tower up the stairs to the great hall of Enniskillen castle. When the guards let go of him, he stood and tried to compose himself whilst staring at the back of the great hall's door. His head spun. He could barely remember the day before, never mind defend himself in a room full of accusers. He tried to recall Desmond's advice, and gradually his memory clicked into place.

The Maguire eventually called for him. Eunan was glad of the wait, for his nerves had a restorative effect on his wits. The guards opened the doors with an ominous creak. For some, the packed great hall was a stage where they could dress up and both play to the gallery and wield power with one theatrical swoop. For others, it was an oppressive weight which slowed the senses and played on the nerves. A den of intrigue to be avoided. Eunan had seen both play out here during his time as Desmond's assistant, but had yet to determine how he himself would cope when he was the centre of attention.

Eunan was confronted by a murmuring, amorphous mass of faces with all eyes fixated upon him. His head hurt and he struggled to concentrate on his predicament. He heard the mutterings of various crimes, all of which had his name attached. They marched him to the other side of the hall through two lines of guards who protected the prisoner on one side and the gentry of the Maguire from him on the other. The guards made faces between themselves when they noticed Eunan's stench. They brought him to the top of the room to stand inside a circle of guards to the left-hand side of the Maguire. The guards tried to edge away from Eunan to get out of the range of his odour, but the prying eyes of Donnacha defined the perimeter's extent.

Hugh had donned his finest robes, designed to inflate both his confidence and authority. The Maguire was unlike his father, in that he was a man of action and only suffered the court when he was obliged to. When he entered and saluted the well-to-do men of his clan, he did not look at Eunan and stared straight forward at the far wall, above the heads of all the Maguire gentry. He nodded when the court greeted 'the Maguire' in unison. He could not have looked more uncomfortable or reluctant to be there if he tried. Donnacha was on the far side, with a pile of papers, and consulted with his clerks, ensuring that everything was prepared.

Eunan positioned himself between the heads of the two guards and searched the room for friendly faces. He could not find any. He recognised the main arbitrators of law and justice in Fermanagh, alongside several priests of the islands who kept records of legal decisions. The rest of the hall was filled mainly by men he did not recognise, though he guessed they were merchants or nobles from the south and east of Fermanagh. All cronies of Donnacha. Low-level murmuring circulated around the room as rumours and counter-rumours spread about why they were there and what Eunan had done. Donnacha lifted his head from his papers and nodded to Hugh to signal he was ready.

Hugh looked at the floor and muttered something regretful to himself. He raised his hand.

"Silence," said Donnacha. "The Maguire is about to address you."

Hugh stood and signalled for the room to be silent.

"Gentlemen of the Maguire. Thank you all for coming today under the circumstances. I bring to you an update on the troubles in the north. We are currently engaged in talks with the Irish Council, with the O'Neill and the O'Donnell acting as intermediaries. I have no progress to report as the lords of the north are exerting most of their energies in combating the famine that grips us all and the Council is not pressing us for a resolution. So it is not for those reasons that I bring you here.

"No, it is because there are grave allegations made against Eunan Maguire, for if they were true, it would be difficult for him or his family to provide recompense under Brehon law. Therefore, the issues concerning Eunan Maguire are twofold. One, did he do what is alleged, and two, should we try him under English or Brehon law?"

The room exploded with shouts of derision.

"Please! Silence, please! Donnacha will explain the details of what Eunan is accused of."

Hugh invited Donnacha to take the stage. The Maguire sat down and looked to the sky. The matter was no longer in his hands.

Donnacha hurried across to stand in front of Hugh. He looked to ensure he had his audience's attention and began.

"It is difficult for me to find a point where to begin for Eunan's crimes affect the rule of the Maguire to the very core. It is a heinous abuse of his position, family and standing with the Maguire."

Eunan regained his composure and positioned himself behind the heads of the guards to counter Donnacha's allegations.

"What is it you accuse me of, for if it is what you just said, I could accuse you of the same!"

Donnacha grimaced.

"Be quiet Eunan, you'll get your turn."

"How can I get my turn? Who is here to represent me in this tangled web of courtly matters? You sent English soldiers to get me from a tavern in Enniskillen town! We are supposed to be free! Free men under Brehon law! We don't go calling on the English to resolve our disputes! They beat me unconscious and dragged me to this trial without even telling me what I am accused of! Where is the justice in that? How can you have brought the Maguire so low?"

The room erupted into shouts of anti-English slogans and discontent with the actions attributed to the Maguire.

"Silence everyone, please! Eunan will get his turn. But we should all know what events have brought us here. Upon that, we must agree."

Donnacha waited until the murmurs had died down.

"Let me explain. Eunan Maguire is a relative of mine, a distant one, but importantly, a relative on the female side. As I'm sure you all know from what the Maguires stood for through the ages, that means he has no claim!"

Donnacha paused and, with a wave of his arms, invited the audience on a tour of the historical Maguire tapestries on the walls and how eligibility to be the Maguire always came from the male side.

"It was on this basis, from his mother's side, that Eunan O'Keenan came to my brother's dwelling, claiming to be an O'Cassidy."

Donnacha pointed over to Eunan Maguire behind the armed guards.

"When he came to my brother's house, he abused his hospitality and had to be removed! I was there and witnessed everything."

"That is because he is a traitor!" cried Eunan.

He punctuated each word but emphasised 'traitor'.

"We will see who is the real traitor as we work our way through the evidence," came Donnacha's retort. "It all culminated in a despicable crime I also had the misfortune to witness. This man disrupted the lawful wedding of my niece, Caoimhe O'Cassidy to Art Maguire, the now deceased son of Connor Roe Maguire, brutally struck down at his own wedding, and took the bride and title, O'Cassidy Maguire, for himself!"

The mood in the room soured at such an accusation.

"They were traitors in league with the English! I demand the right to defend myself against my accuser!"

"It is such an abominable crime I cannot see any recompense that would satisfy either the O'Cassidys or the senior line of the Maguire family. The attender should be sent to the Pale to be hanged, so none of his crimes may sully the reputation of the Maguire to either his allies or the Crown. What do you say? Let us condemn him and send him in a cage to Dublin!"

The room erupted with shouts denouncing Eunan, the occasional slogan against the English and cries for and against sending him to Dublin. The onlookers seemed evenly split.

Then a familiar face struggled his way through the crowd and to the front. It was Arthur.

"Eunan Maguire deserves the right to be tried by his own clan," Arthur said.

He stood and looked directly at Hugh Maguire.

"Silence! Let him speak!" said Hugh.

"We should give Eunan a hearing in front of the elders of the Maguire when he knows what he has been accused of and has had time to prepare a defence. At that stage, if any of the accusations still stand, the elders should decide to try Eunan under English or Brehon law. Desmond MacCabe has agreed to represent Eunan. He will come to Enniskillen and discuss the matter with the Maguire, but only if he is given a bodyguard of MacCabe Galloglass and is guaranteed safe passage. What does the Maguire say to such a proposal?"

Hugh rose from his seat.

"He will have his bodyguard, who will first escort you back to the islands. I will meet him here in a week."

Hugh turned to the crowd.

"I have urgent business to attend to, so this session is over. Eunan Maguire will remain in prison until I speak with Desmond. Donnacha, make sure that Eunan is in better condition for his next appearance than that of which you dragged him here today. Good day."

Hugh Maguire left. The room disintegrated into shouts and arguments. The guards took hold of Eunan, fought their way through the throng of onlookers, and dragged him back to his cell.

CHAPTER SIX

DIPLOMATIC RELATIONS

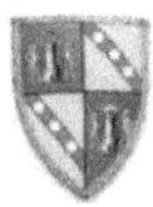

S EAMUS FIDDLED WITH HIS collar in front of the shard of a mirror placed on the mantelpiece of his room. The shard was the largest piece of a once great ornament that used to decorate the hallway, an adornment that formerly declared status and wealth to any guest that entered the house. But it was shattered into many pieces and now resided mainly under Caoimhe's bed, with other pieces taken as trophies by men under Eunan's command. It had a new role, a new symbolism, that of the destruction of the house and lands of the O'Cassidy Maguire. Seamus fiddled with his matted and grey hair.

"Helmet or no helmet?"

He toyed with his morion, wishing his wife were here to make such a decision. He normally did not care for such things, but on this day, appearances mattered.

Anticipation floated with the dust on the half-repaired former drawing room of Cormac O'Cassidy. Seamus had taken it as his quarters and used it to both sleep in and as his office. It was almost like the old days when the MacSheehys had their castles and lands in Munster in the Earldom of Desmond and the Earl was coming to inspect the Galloglass. But times were different now. It was a big day. An important guest was coming who he was keen to impress.

Óisin knocked on the door and entered when given permission. He stood behind Seamus as he got ready, silently absorbing his instructions.

"Lock her in her room and make sure she doesn't come out," said Seamus. "As much as I loath to do it, I am leaving you in charge whilst I am away."

"I won't let you down," said Óisin.

"You'd better not. You are no Eunan. I would have far less patience with you. Let you take heed!"

Óisin was keen to press his abilities, including that of reliability.

"The house repairs will continue along with recruitment. You'll have a new fresh batch of fighting men waiting for you when you return."

"Good, now when the O'Neills arrive, be polite and don't get yourself into trouble."

Seamus was no less reassured by Óisin's promises.

"I'll be the perfect host," said Óisin.

He smiled to himself for he thought the conversation a success.

The Kern arrived first. They scouted the area before them and only sent messengers to the main body of men when Seamus reassured them that the area was secure. Cormac MacBaron was clearly leaving nothing to chance.

Seamus ordered his men to line up in drill formation on the front lawn of the house. The pride of his men were Arlo and the south Fermanagh shot, fifty men who had shown enough ability to be singled out for this unit and trained by Arlo. The unit had come together quickly and consisted mainly of ex-Kern, who were especially proficient in their aim and those with a proven ability with the bow and arrow. It took much wrangling and expense for Seamus to assemble the guns and powder for the men to practise with, but Seamus thought it was a wise investment for Eunan to make with the riches that came along with his uncle's title. The men even dressed reasonably similarly to make the inspection even more impressive for their esteemed guests. Taighe Maguire, who had led the villagers to kill Eunan that fateful night, and not been killed in reprisals after Eunan became the O'Cassidy Maguire, had made it to being a captain in the new unit. The fear Seamus inspired in him had motivated him to be one of the best shots in the unit, but also one of the best recruiters.

Eunan had not ordered the normal taking of hostages or killing of his rivals when he became the O'Cassidy Maguire. Instead, he had taken to his room to hide his remorse, which he feared they would interpret as weakness. Seamus had laughed off Eunan's instruction but saw how unpopular Eunan was and if such restraint brought a little peace and respite, it may win them some support. Anyway, Seamus did not need to inspire any more fear for rallying men to his cause. Plenty wanted to sign up anyway for the promise of food, a wage and a share of the loot, as it was better than sitting on your farm and starving. They soon had over one hundred and fifty men rallied to their cause, a respectable number for south Fermanagh.

Óisin was in charge of the Kern, the Irish skirmishing troops. A riotous rabble, surly and undisciplined, like their master. The place where the young boys of Fermanagh would first gain battle standard weapons and get their first taste of blood. However, supply fell short of what money could buy, so they had to do with javelins, bows and swords donated by the O'Neills and O'Donnells. Seamus could not resist the nostalgia of creating a unit of Galloglass. Ten men in chain mail and six-foot axes drawn from men he saw in his image comprised this unit. They became his personal bodyguard and his most trusted men. Eunan could sort out his own bodyguard when he returned.

The south Fermanagh shot lined up in front of the house in a nice neat row with their guns slung over their shoulders. Seamus stood on the road to the north of the house, waiting. About thirty minutes later, twenty O'Neill horsemen thundered down the road and pulled up in front of Seamus. The man in the middle of the horsemen rode up to Seamus. Cormac MacBaron was tall and thin and sat comfortably on his horse as if he belonged there. He looked every inch the soldier in his breast mail and morion, and recognised Seamus immediately.

"Seamus MacSheehy! I've heard a lot of stories about you, most of them bad, so I'm glad to have you on my side."

One of his men helped him dismount. Cormac approached Seamus and shook his hand.

"That's what you get with old MacSheehy Galloglass, the job done, no matter how dirty. We are re-establishing ourselves here, in south Fermanagh, in the safety of the north. Many good fighting men are coming here from my various connections in

Munster, the Netherlands, Tirconnell and soon Leinster. We can be good allies to the O'Neills if you be so willing?"

Cormac dusted himself down and gestured to his captains to join him.

"I see parades of men in every town and village we enter, who have polished up the best weapons they can find, and stand with their chests puffed out pledging to the O'Neill. My brother takes them all in and embraces them. It is I who have to witness their swords and axes either abandoned or turned upon us when they receive a better offer. Why are you different?"

Seamus laughed.

"You must hear some grand stories to disregard a reputation such as mine so easily. I have long been employed by the O'Donnell and my nephew, the O'Cassidy Maguire, is one of the Maguire's most trusted men. If the O'Neill was here, he would definitely embrace me!"

It was Cormac's turn to laugh. He slapped Seamus on the back and Seamus took this as the signal to embrace.

"Come, let me give you as much hospitality as I can in this broken-down house. Óisin! Have the men prepare food."

Cormac gripped his arm.

"Let it just be the two of us. My distrust makes me weary but still burns. We must plan the campaign ahead."

"I will have my most trusted men guard the doors."

Seamus smiled to himself for here was a man he could understand and do business with. He invited him into the house.

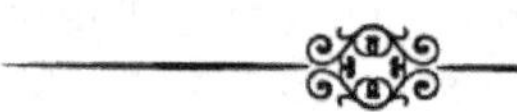

Seamus led Cormac into the drawing room, made some space on the table and dusted down a couple of chairs.

"Excuse the mess. Some of these transitions of power can be chaotic," he said.

"I have seen far worse. The O'Neills have been in almost perpetual conflict since my youth so I have seen it all, in both their states of glory and destruction."

Seamus nodded.

"We tried to destroy as little as we could since only the head of the snake had to be cut off. The body was sound."

"Have you any wine? I thirst from my journey."

"We have wine, mead, water, whatever you wish."

Seamus invited Cormac to sit and went to the door.

"Óisin, bring us wine and mead, and then the dinner!"

Óisin nodded from the corridor and set off for the kitchen. Several minutes later, the kitchen staff brought the victuals and spread them out on the table. The feast began with the eyes for a tired traveller.

"Deer? I am impressed. A fine feat while the peasants starve!" said Cormac.

"We only keep the best for such esteemed guests. South Fermanagh is a bread basket that must be protected for the good of the Maguire and the other lords of the north alike."

Cormac reached out and filled his plate.

"You seem to have an agenda, Seamus. But first, we must talk about the forthcoming campaign."

Seamus turned towards the door and the unwanted Óisin standing in its shadow.

"Óisin, we need privacy. Ensure my Galloglass surrounds the house and there are no spies. Then attend to the O'Neill's men."

Óisin sneered.

"These are important tasks. Leaders also have to lead in the mundane."

Óisin slammed the door behind him. He stomped down the main corridor of the house and ushered everyone out. Caoimhe stared down at him through the banisters and smiled. Óisin could not help it, but a smile slid back from the side of his face. With the house cleared, Caoimhe could do what she liked.

Cormac sat and ate.

"You need to protect those cooks. They are certainly a prize worthy of any raid."

Seamus smiled back.

"I can see why the previous incumbent fell into decadence and became a slave to the Crown's investment of the Pale. 'Tis a fine jail that serves food such as this!"

Cormac laughed, coughed, and took another swig of wine. Several minutes later, he pushed his empty plate into the middle of the table.

"You have won me over! The O'Neill himself would embrace you after that and demand your cooks as part of any bargain struck!"

Seamus laughed and pulled his chair closer to Cormac.

"Now that we have eaten, we can speak frankly. The O'Reillys have long been a thorn in the side of the Maguires. We have suffered constant raids, and then when John Roe capitulated to the English, they used his castles as the bases for their raids. If we are to become allies to the O'Reillys, the new O'Cassidy Maguire needs to show the people that they have gained something from placing their faith in him."

"Even though you may be neighbours, I may have the superior source of information."

"How so?"

"John Roe is dead. Philip O'Reilly, his brother, has kept it a secret. He wants to declare himself the O'Reilly but Maelmora O'Reilly, John's son, has been rallying support amongst the Irish Council and those who still have a fondness for the English, even after the cruelty of their appointed sheriff."

"Ah, the regret of co-operation with the Crown. Yet, it is Galloglass who have the terrible reputation."

Cormac eyed Seamus to see if there was the body language of support before he made his proposals.

"The O'Reillys were once great allies of the O'Neills, and we stood by each other for years before they sold out to the Crown. But the O'Neill has given me instructions to make Philip the O'Reilly and reinstate both tanistry and Brehon law. Your help could secure your southern flank and also make you a friend of the O'Neill. A new O'Cassidy Maguire would be untouchable with such powerful friends as the O'Neill and the O'Donnell."

Seamus smiled by far his largest grin of the day.

"When do we leave?"

Caoimhe tried to shake the pain from her hand. It was seldom that she had to write so fast. She far preferred calligraphy to note taking, and her collection of paper pens and ink was a testament to that. But she wrote because it was her way out, her form of revenge, her sense of doing something worthwhile. Her faithful maid, Lasair, stood dutifully by the door, barely back from Enniskillen from delivering the last letter. Her pocket had been weighted down by Donnacha's reward for her good work and she was promised plenty more as long as she remained discreet.

Caoimhe finished the last of her scribbles and sealed the letter with the wax seal of her father, which she had retrieved from his office.

"Here, Lasair, take this to my uncle. They will well reward you when you get there."

"Yes, ma'am." She curtsied, took the letter and snuck out the back door when she thought no one was looking.

She ran across the fields as she had done before and stopped for breath when she was safely in the woods. She looked up when she heard a twig break.

"So where do you think you're going?"

She thought of screaming, but kept her wits about her.

"For carrying this letter, I am well rewarded and meant you no harm. I willingly give it up to you if you spare my life."

He smiled and stuck out his hand.

"Let's see what her ladyship has to say first, shall we?"

CHAPTER SEVEN

NEW MAN OF THE HOUSE

THE NEXT DAY SEAMUS dressed for battle. He had carved out a space among the debris of the once magnificent drawing room, reduced to ash and cinder by Óisin's recklessness, a constant reminder to Seamus that Óisin could not be fully trusted. Seamus had made the most of what was left, what over-exuberant arrows had not punctured, what pilfering hands had not stolen. This room would make a fine command centre for the estate and the soldiers of the O'Cassidy Maguire. These lands could be great again, like the great Desmond estate he defended in his youth. He smiled to himself and remembered himself as a young horse boy, setting out with his father and uncle, the pride of the MacSheehy Galloglass. His mind became clouded with other, less pleasant memories. He shook them off. He was back, buried in Óisin's destruction.

"Where is that useless boy, Óisin?" he shouted.

The words reverberated around the house.

Caoimhe snuck out of her room and listened by the banisters. That useless boy Óisin had neglected to post guards at her door. She smiled to herself and pondered whether this was deliberate. Óisin rushed through the front door with tousled hair, an unbuckled belt, a dangling sword and a brow of sweat. Caoimhe laughed to herself as Seamus inspired the same amount of fear in Óisin as her father had in his farm foremen when he used to call them in.

"I need to leave this morning. Where are the O'Neills? Are the men ready? Do you know what you have to do when I am gone?"

Óisin struggled to fix his belt. The fog of having just woken up still clogged his brain.

"Yes, yes, and yes," replied Óisin.

"What are you saying yes to?"

Seamus slapped him around the head.

"I have given you a lot of responsibility. Don't give me a reason to regret it, for you are no Eunan and I will not hesitate, no matter what he thinks."

Óisin scowled and pulled the bottom of his shirt down and stuffed it in his pants. He straightened his belt and sword.

"Good. You look like they have only dragged you through one haystack, which is an improvement on being dragged through a field full of them. Now, what have you said yes to?"

"Yes, the men are ready. Those that travel with you are lined up in the front garden. Yes, I know what I have to do when you are gone. Yes, the O'Neills have already left."

"What! Why didn't you tell me?"

Seamus bent down and picked up his bags and made for the door.

"Get my horse! My horse!"

He turned to Óisin, who had kept a swing of Seamus's arm distance away.

"Now, if you have destroyed everything when I get back, I'm going to string you up from the old oak tree. This is your big chance to impress me and make something of yourself. Don't screw it up!"

Seamus's horse arrived, and he threw his bags at the horse boy and mounted his steed.

"If you've not heard from me within the month, come looking for me." Seamus bent down upon his horse and tried to look in the windows of the house. "Keep her inside and locked up. Don't let her barbed tongue lock itself to your ear. I don't want any mischief from her. I'll hold you responsible."

The tip of Seamus's finger in his face made sure that Óisin knew who would be to blame in the event of any mishaps. Seamus dug his heels into the sides of his horse and ordered his men to march south. Óisin stood at the front of the house and waved until Seamus was in the distance. He turned and admired the once great door to the O'Cassidy house, ignoring that it was his orders that caused the scarring there upon it. Óisin laughed off

Seamus's instructions and went inside. He was now the man of the house.

Óisin turned to go down to the kitchen to see what food he could find. He ran his fingers along the walls of the hall. This was all now his, the beggar boy from Enniskillen. All he had to do was fix everything from his previous rush of blood. He heard a snigger and saw Caoimhe pushing her face through the bars, her long black hair dangling down, framing her face as the only surviving picture of beauty left in the house. Óisin scowled at her and she ran away, laughing. Óisin had had enough of being humiliated that day and with muscles tensed, he strode straight past the kitchen and to the outhouse.

He had locked Lasair in there waiting for his opportunity to lord it over herself and Caoimhe and to let them know he was now in charge. Lasair had cried herself dry, convinced that she was going to hang. A certain bitter pang gripped her heart, her the lowly servant girl, an entangled knot of tears and regret and her mistress inside untouchable, an unending gift of her birth. She hid in the corner behind the pigs, waiting, imagining Óisin reading the letter and storming outside to string her up. Or worse, Seamus could come! Óisin threw open the door, but no joy came as the light flooded in, just the anger of a humiliated man.

"Where are you? I know you're in here!"

The pigs scattered and bolted for the door. Óisin did not care as they knocked past him, for the light revealed Lasair, who had found new tears and crawled up the wall, wishing she was a minuscule spider able to crawl through the holes in the wall to make her escape. But there was no escape from the fury of Óisin. He grabbed her by the arm and walloped her with the back of his hand. He dragged her out of the pigsty and across the yard. No stone was too large or puddle too deep to make Óisin change course. She screamed as he dragged her along in the mud and Óisin turned and kicked her to make her get up. He threw open the back door and went into the study and picked up the letter. He stomped across the hall dragging Lasair behind him and climbed the stairs.

"Caoimhe! You may be a rich trader's daughter, but you are going to feel the back of the hand of lowly ol' me for disobeying me!"

The door to her room was closed, and Óisin pounded it with his fists. The door shook, but stood firmly closed.

"Let me in!"

Lasair trembled behind him. He kicked the bottom of the door. A sweet voice cooed from the other side.

"If you press the handle down, the door will open, just like most doors in the house that survived your fire."

Óisin stopped pounding. There was no fear in the voice from the other side.

"You can come into my room any time you want. You don't have to break down the door to get in, but you can if you want to get in that bad," said the voice.

Óisin let go of Lasair and pressed on the handle. He opened the door to a waft of perfume, something he had rarely smelt before. He was far more familiar with the stink of dried mud. Óisin stood, closed his eyes and inhaled. He tried to remember where he had smelt it before. It reminded him of Enniskillen castle. He saw his mother there. The smell was so sweet it lifted him wistfully away. He stared at Caoimhe, the source of this wonderful smell. The forgotten Lasair snuck in behind him and hid behind Caoimhe's bed.

"Now you know how to open the door. What do you want with me?"

Óisin stood and stared as if in a trance. The perfume, the long curls of black hair, the porcelain skin of Caoimhe's oval face, the feeling of joy it triggered within him. A new image sprung into his head. He was a boy being snatched away, the waft of perfume, the long black hair growing distant. His childhood arms grasped at air.

His adult hand scrunched the letter he had confiscated from Lasair. The memories were extinguished.

"What is the meaning of this?"

Lasair poked her head above the other side of the bed and mouthed 'no' to her mistress.

"Can a young maiden who has been through such a trauma not write to her uncle to tell him she is well and not to send soldiers to fetch her for she has such a brave and handsome man to protect her? You wouldn't want soldiers from Enniskillen to come and spoil our alone time together now that you have got rid of Eunan and Seamus?"

Words did not reach Óisin's mouth, for his brain froze. The smell of the perfume was up his nose again. The room was still, yet the air trembled. Óisin's mind raced, fixated with the curls of long hair, Caoimhe brushing it slowly, the curves of her body beneath her thin green tunic, barely enough to cover herself, but his body was frozen still. Frustration collided with lust. He deployed anger to reassert his authority.

"Call me the next time you write to your uncle, for I wish to censor it!"

"I can but try, but my fair hand writes what my heart feels. Come tomorrow and I will try to calm my feelings and we can write to my uncle."

Frustration rose from the pit of Óisin's stomach, and he wanted to scream. He looked from Caoimhe to Lasair and back to Caoimhe. Caoimhe batted her eyelids. Óisin threw the remains of the letter on the floor and stormed out. Caoimhe and Lasair held in their laughter until Óisin was out of earshot.

CHAPTER EIGHT

ANOINTING THE ENEMY

T DID NOT TAKE Seamus long to catch up with the O'Neills for their pikemen trudged along the paths of the countryside burdened by their weapons and the O'Reilly mud, which stuck to their feet and slowed the main bulk of the army down. The O'Neills were fanned out across the countryside and plundered and interrogated the farmers and townsfolk unlucky enough to be in their path. Those that pledged allegiance to Hugh O'Neill, Hugh Maguire or Philip O'Reilly were spared. Those that expressed indifference had a levy of their livestock placed upon them. Those that were deemed loyal to the Crown had their houses burned and were set upon the road to the Pale where the O'Neills said they belonged. The judgements of the O'Neills appeared arbitrary and easily swayed by a paddock with some healthy cows or the nod of an O'Reilly guide with a grudge or a glint of greed in his eye. The horde crawled across the landscape like a giant slug, leaving a patchwork of destruction draining the lands of all foodstuffs, with all chattels directed northwards.

Seamus rode alongside Cormac MacBaron in front of the main O'Neill column made up of shot and pike, determined to cement their alliance, leaving his men to march behind the O'Neills under the recently appointed constables. Seamus watched Cormac from a distance, studying him to see what made him tick. After a few minutes the worm had caught the trout for Cormac was not a man mystery paused to possess. Swords were swords, an axe an axe and most men were traitors ready to stab you in the back or steal your land with the stroke of a pen. Seamus had met many a man like him and knew how to befriend them. He rode up alongside Cormac's advisors and supplanted himself into their conversations with Cormac and was quick to link events that had unfolded before them to stories from his time in the Netherlands and lace them with a bit of humour, name-dropping leading O'Donnells and flattering the prowess of the O'Neill army at any opportunity he got. Cormac laughed along, for he was far more soldier than politician and enjoyed black-humoured tales about his craft. But scouts approached from the south and rudely interrupted Seamus. The tales from the past would have to wait. One of the O'Neill scouts rode up to Cormac.

"Lord, the O'Reillys have sent a contingent to greet us."

The messenger pointed at the gap between the woods to the south and the black specks moving towards them.

"They're keen to meet us, the pace they're riding at," said Seamus.

Cormac kept his eye on the advancing riders. His bodyguards halted the O'Reillys outside of hand gun range and one of the O'Reillys dismounted and ran past them. The O'Neill men went for him.

"Leave him!" said Cormac.

The man shook himself free of the bodyguards and came to grovel at Cormac's feet.

"Why does the man we are about to anoint the new O'Reilly cower so? If your kinsmen see you act thus, you'll have called us south to fight a civil war."

Philip O'Reilly composed himself. He took off his helmet to confirm to Cormac who he was: a greying man, who looked a little lost, his beard plumped from taking his helmet off. A little plump and at least in his fifties, he was not the usual renegade who had taken to the hills and lived off the proceeds of theft and murder that had flocked to the O'Neills and O'Donnells in the past. He was an old patriarch, trying to relive past glories that reverberated around his head. He reminded Seamus a little of the broken, faded Fiach MacHugh O'Byrne, attempting to rejuvenate his alliances after giving up his son. An air of foolishness hung around Philip's shoulders as he fell over himself in his enthusiasm to show his martial prowess to his new allies. His armour scraped as he stood up proudly.

"There'll be a civil war all right, as we fight over cinders and ash after the destruction you've left. All my people have known for years is pain. They are prepared to rise to remove it. Please don't inflict more upon them and drive them back into the arms of the English."

Cormac was well practised in ignoring the pained expression of a less powerful lord attempting to invoke sympathy. Nothing would divert him from pursuing the O'Neill's agenda.

"My men have orders and they are following them. We have to show the population there are consequences for supporting the Crown. We have spared those who support us. I have heard of the hardships you suffered when you came northwards with the late John Roe to pledge to the O'Neill. Our sympathies go out to you and your brethren who share the same allegiances. However, the ancient Kingdom of Breifne has long been shired, and the lands swept clean of good Papist Irish forced to move out to make way for English settlers. We're here to give the people their lands back."

"That is a most commendable aim and one that has my wholehearted support. However, let me direct you, for I know these lands and its people and have long struggled against the English. Once I am the O'Reilly, we will send them back across the seas!"

Seamus sneered. Was this the great Philip O'Reilly he had heard so much about? How could a small man with a retinue of ten strike such fear into the Maguires?

"Where are your men?" said Seamus. "If we wanted to take the lands unsupported we could have just invaded and taken all your cattle, just as we are doing now."

"Who's this?" said Philip.

His rouge cheeks told of anger and embarrassment.

"One of the Maguires," said Cormac. "I hope riding together will not cause friction, Philip?"

"As long as he remembers the past is in the past. We would be better combining to defeat a common enemy rather than pursuing historical grudges."

"I'm a MacSheehy, and I have no grudge against you. But I'm not here to do good deeds. We need a capable ally, or else we should treat the land as hostile, given its history. You've come here more a beggar than a chief."

Philip puffed out his scarlet cheeks and did battle with his scabbard to pull out his sword. Seamus casually aimed his axe at Philip's head.

"If I were here as an aggressor, my axe would have been long through your head by now. But I take the word of the O'Neills and wish to be faithful allies to them. We will come and assist you as long as it is to the benefit of the Maguires."

Philip pushed the top of his half pulled out sword back in its scabbard and turned and walked back to his horse without another word.

Cormac chuckled to himself.

"I wouldn't like to get on the wrong side of you, Seamus MacSheehy! I'll leave the hostile negotiations up to you."

It was Seamus's turn to laugh, and Cormac waved his men forward.

Philip led the O'Neills and Maguires through the fields of the O'Reillys to Cavan, the principal town in East Breifne, the traditional capital of the O'Reillys and the centre of English dominance in the region. The army marched at a brisk pace and, by order of Cormac MacBaron, the surrounding lands and its occupants were spared its wrath. He had noticed the scars on the land which indicated that the internal power struggle to replace John Roe O'Reilly had already started. The aftermath of burning here was less intense than that created by his own orders, but the smell long lingered in the nostril. The tang of brother on brother, son on father destruction defeated the efforts of several swigs of mead employed to remove it. In moments of contemplation Cormac wondered if he had backed the right horse, judging by the small number of locals that joined their cause as they marched past.

Cavan town was lightly defended and any token resistance fluttered away in the wind to their coop in Cavan castle to join their comrades in the small English garrison posted there. The civilian occupants of the town had long since taken to the woods for their own safety. The rebels set up camp on the outskirts of the town in a position which enabled them to throw a cordon around the castle to prevent free movement by its occupants. They reconnoitred the town and its vicinity and, having found the commercial heart of the town empty of people and victuals, began scouting the land for provisions. Philip and his men made camp beside the O'Neills, with the Maguires on the other side, with a large tent for Cormac MacBaron in the middle of the campsite. Philip sent his messengers across Breifne to call the local chieftains to arms. Events were not moving fast enough for Seamus, so he sent out his own messengers too. Philip was more heartened by the responses he received back and an inauguration at Finn McCools Fingers, an arrangement of ancient standing stones that comprised the traditional initiation ground of the O'Reillys, was organised.

The day of the inauguration came, and the O'Neills surrounded the site and controlled who came in and out of the circle to ensure the safety of Philip and the distinguished guests. Seamus dressed up for the occasion, ordering his horse boy to wash his armour and lay out his least tattered set of undergarments, for he saw it as important that the representative of the Maguires had to be seen as more powerful than the O'Reillys, even though it was their event. Seamus left his tent with a gleam in his helmet not seen since he last met with the O'Donnell himself. He stood with Cormac MacBaron and the O'Neill constables, a constant flow of O'Reilly dignitaries coming and introducing themselves and attempting to gain favour with the would-be liberators. Cormac nodded politely to them all and Seamus shook hands with those who would shake hands with the representative of the Maguire and sneered at those who would not.

The ceremony switched now to connecting the new O'Reilly to his ancestors in the hope they would lend him an air of legitimacy.

Seamus could not help but laugh to himself.

"Shh," said Cormac. "You're supposed to be representing your clan."

Seamus covered his mouth to whisper in Cormac's ear.

"I've been to many inaugurations over the years, but this one is the most pathetic. High Kings of Ireland, my arse! If the O'Reillys ever were a force, it's buried deep in the past. This lot are a bunch of frightened rabbits too used to hiding in their holes when the big bad sheriff comes to relieve them of their goods. This can't be all the O'Reilly chieftains here, can it? They'd barely half fill a decent hall!"

Cormac, a veteran of many an inauguration himself, smiled a wise smile.

"You've got to go through the play no matter how few people are watching. I think you'll be the witness to many more an inauguration before we have freed this island, then you can measure this one on the scale of patheticness. We should talk afterwards. I understand the antipathy felt by the Maguires toward the O'Reillys, but you need to see the bigger picture. I didn't and felt much like you until I spoke to my brother."

"Philip O'Reilly has too much baggage, turned coat too many times to be trustworthy. There's no point in giving him all of this support just to have him change sides mid-battle."

"We need him to cement an alliance in the middle of the country."

Seamus winked at him.

"I knew that's what you'd be wanting, so I have sent forth my men to my contacts. You'll soon have your alliance of good, trustworthy, hard fighting men."

Cormac slapped him on the back.

"I look forward to your scheming but you should stop your whispering as you are drawing attention to us."

Seamus smiled and stood a couple of yards away. He was soon bored, for they had reached the prayers and blessings part of the ceremony.

They had commandeered several large houses surrounding a tavern in Cavan town. The O'Neills were careful in their selection to ensure that the site was easily defensible. Philip O'Reilly made his court in the tavern and the various O'Reilly chieftains came and swore loyalty to him. Cormac and Seamus were guests of honour and had to listen to the many drunken brags of farmer chieftains telling tall tales of their battle exploits or lying about how many men they could raise.

Seamus sighed and felt the curve on the back of his head. His welted hands offered little comfort.

"I don't know how you do this, Cormac. I really don't. I hear a lot of drunken nonsense from them but at least I can tell them to shut their mouths."

"We'll be back on the campaign soon, don't you worry. If you are tired of diplomatic relations, we can find somewhere quiet to talk. I have received some intelligence which we need to discuss."

Seamus rose from his seat, and Cormac invited him through the door that led to the street. However, Philip O'Reilly blocked their way. His rosy cheeks and involuntary swagger gave away what a half-filled bottle of whiskey would confirm.

"Where are you two off to? We're only getting started here!"

Cormac bowed his head and placed his hand gently on Philip's shoulder.

"It's getting late and there is much soldiering to do tomorrow. We would not want to impose our weary faces upon the O'Reilly celebration anymore."

"Sure, have it your own way. We are grateful for the O'Neills' help. But why don't you stay, Seamus? You never know, we may even spare your master's land the black rent when the O'Neills and O'Reillys dominate Leinster once more!"

"I have no master," said Seamus, "and you're in no position to be making threats. Why don't you go back to your little party and dance around like a lord for the evening and then crawl back to the O'Neills in the morning and ask for your next set of instructions?"

"No one talks to me like that in my own lands!"

Philip went for his dagger and was successful this time in retrieving it and posing it as a threat to Seamus's life.

Seamus sized up the tip of the blade and the blaze of red on the face behind it. Years of anger and frustration culminated in the metal point of a dagger.

"If that blade comes near me, your alliance will die and you along with it," he said.

The coldness in his voice matched the frigidness of the blade pointing towards his face.

Cormac stepped forward, for he sensed someone would die if he did not intervene, and he did not know O'Reilly politics well enough to find an adequate replacement for Philip.

"Let's all calm down and get back to the party. There's no point in fighting amongst ourselves."

But Philip did not calm down.

The blade edged nearer Seamus's face.

"Don't do something you may not live to regret," said Seamus.

The tone of his voice was steady.

A crowd had started to gather and the swirling of alcohol and pride in their bellies and brains stirred a fit of anger in their guts. The door of the tavern slammed shut. Seamus and Cormac now had no means of escape.

CHAPTER NINE

THE VISITOR

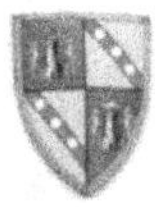

E UNAN'S CELL WAS A dank, dark hole that swallowed him body and soul. The walls were sheer, covered in a green slime most visible in the late afternoon when the fading sunlight shone through the bars in the narrow slit at the top of the cell. The visitors were rough and abusive, and the food was a punishment all on its own. They had given him plenty of maltreatment but no clean clothes, despite the Maguire's instruction. His stool and bed of hay sat in pools of water and soaked in the moisture and the odours of the cell no matter how many times the guards came in to change them.

Eunan had taken to shouting under the door of the cell about 'respect' and 'revenge' but if he ever thought he got a reaction, it was the sound of distant laughter. They normally housed the noble prisoners on the islands of the lake. Devenish Island was a pleasant prison for those of the greatest prestige. Those prisoners normally did not dwell there for long, as they were too valuable for both Maguire and foe and soon bartered their freedom. But the cells of Enniskillen castle were for the lowest of criminals and those who were the greatest escape risks. Their conditions matched their status.

It was by this act of casting him into the most inhospitable dungeon in the land that Eunan realised how much sway Donnacha had over Hugh Maguire. Hugh would never have done this of his own accord, Donnacha must have lied to him. He looked at the damp patch of green slime on the wall to tell the time of day, for he was not tall enough to look out of the slit through which came the only source of light apart from the narrow slit under the door. He thought of all the prisoners that must have died in this cell, fixating on those imprisoned during the English occupation. Maybe this was some heavenly vengeance for all the sins he had committed, none of which he wished to remember, no matter the time granted to him or the crushing humdrum of boredom he was subjected to.

He looked to the slit of light, dulled by the lashing of the winter rain. It was cold in here and one guard who he knew from when he was held in esteem in Enniskillen in an act of kindness threw him a blanket. He wondered who would come and save him. Would Desmond come back from the islands and oust Donnacha and become the advisor to the Maguire once more? Would Seamus come? Eunan's imagination ran away with him, wondering whether Seamus would save him by cunning, subterfuge, or riding in on a torrent of blood. Or else would Donnacha pay off some guard or lowly thief who would steal into the cell and plunge a concealed dagger through his heart? It would be only what he deserved. He threw his hands up in the air and slumped down on the moist strands of hay. But he had been in jail before, sentenced to death, without hope. As the moisture seeped from the hay into his trousers, he resolved:

"I will get out of this hole and be a better man than either that would contest the right to call himself my father."

He crawled over to the slit at the bottom of the door.

"Send me a physician as the Maguire ordered you to."

He heard no response and crawled back onto the hay.

He looked up towards the slit of light and went over Galloglass axe and firearm drills in his mind to pass the time.

A boat pulled up in the small harbour that nestled beneath Desmond's modest house on his island. It picked its way through the jutting rocks that dotted the lake bed upon the approach to the shore. Dervella was the first to notice and also the first to realise the visitor was a stranger. Visitors were few, and those few who came were always known to the islanders. Dervella made sure the axe was still hidden beside the pile of wood beside the fire in the main room. She called for Desmond.

A youthful head peered from the top of the boat. Dervella's concern was relieved when Desmond came from the other side of the island and, when he laid eyes on the youth, broke into a knowing smile. The youth leapt out of the boat and immediately lurched to the side and fell into the knee-deep water.

"Arthur!"

Then he remembered his manservant was on the mainland and he would have to perform any heroics himself. Desmond's bones rattled and a pang of fear jolted from the bottom of his spine. He ordered his body to move, but his over-developed belly and many aches from old battle wounds meant all he could muster was a wobbly wheeze. He felt old and helpless as the youth's head was subsumed by the water and a trickle of red came from the depths below. Dervella saw the struggles of both men and ran from the house and waded into the water, took hold of the youth and dragged him by the arm to the shore. The youth coughed the water from his lungs, and Dervella raised his head. The youth opened his eyes.

"Cúchonnacht Óg! What are you doing here?"

"Don't fuss over him by the waterside, woman! Get him to the house where you can clean up his ankle. He'll have plenty of time to tell us why he's here when he's been tended to."

Desmond came and helped Cúchonnacht Óg up on his good foot and became his crutch, and they hobbled together to the seats in front of the house. Dervella had run ahead and pulled out a chair. Desmond could do little to prevent Cúchonnacht Óg from falling into the chair when he released his grip.

"Careful with him," said Dervella. "We want to give him back with as few bruises as possible."

She turned to Cúchonnacht Óg.

"Now show me this ankle of yours. Oh, that's a nasty gash. You won't be putting much pressure on that for a while."

Dervella tended to and wrapped his ankle with a tenderness seldom seen in famine-stricken Fermanagh that winter.

"Now you sit there and rest. You won't be leaving here for a couple of days, so you may as well lie back and enjoy yourself. I'll make sure Desmond doesn't pester you with questions. Isn't that right, Desmond?"

Desmond made a face behind her back, and Cúchonnacht Óg sniggered.

"Don't you be minding him. I'm the only one who does the cooking in this house, so don't you be giving yourself too far to crawl back from when you're getting hungry!"

Both of them nodded apologetically and then looked at her in silence.

"I know how to take a hint. Now don't you be thinking of taking Desmond off on any adventures. He's an old man, you know. He'll just slow you down if you're lucky, and keel over holding his heart if both of you are not."

"We'll be careful, sure we have your husband to protect us," said Desmond.

"You are way too old to get into any of the trouble Seamus gets into. I'll leave you to your plotting, but make no plans to follow Seamus."

She turned and walked into the house. Desmond's eyes followed her in to make sure she was out of earshot.

"She's got a heart of gold, really," he said. "Now, why did you really come?"

Cúchonnacht Óg leant forward and grabbed Desmond's hand.

"Come back. The Maguire needs you now more than ever. Let it be like my youth when you helped steer my father through the choppy waters of dealing with the English. My brother is lost to that snake Donnacha. He now openly cavorts with representatives from the Crown and the King of Scotland. I fear my brother's folly will be the end of the Maguires."

Desmond tapped Cúchonnacht Óg on the forehead.

"It's all in there," he said. "Many a time we cleared the room when you were boys and your father and I would do deals with the English, the O'Reillys, etc. You name them, we did a crooked deal with them."

"You cannot renege on your duties to the family that made you!" said Cúchonnacht Óg.

"Alas, the two sons did not inherit their father's temperament. That's what people like Donnacha prey on. Pull the right strings, you lose your heads and they manoeuvre you in any direction they wish. What can I do for you, an old man, that you will not quickly undo in a youthful fit of temper?"

Cúchonnacht Óg shook his head. He could not come all this way and fail.

"Eunan needs you!" he blurted out.

"Why does he need me? He has Seamus. As long as he follows Seamus's guidance, he will be all right."

"You obviously haven't heard. I didn't know this island was so isolated."

"I picked this island for good reasons," said Desmond.

"Eunan is a prisoner in Enniskillen castle."

Cúchonnacht Óg paused and waited for a reaction.

"Prisons have never held a friend of Seamus for long. Send for him instead."

"Donnacha wishes to have him killed."

"Eunan has got to stand on his own two feet. An old man like me is no use to him. When he was here I said that I would send for Seamus if I did not hear from him in a week. I sent Arthur to find him and then for Arthur to go to Seamus if needs be. It is best if you send for Seamus."

"But -."

Desmond put his fingers to his lips.

"Why don't you tell me the entire story if it concerns you so? Then I'll be able to discern whether or not I am needed."

Cúchonnacht Óg told the story of Eunan becoming the O'Cassidy Maguire and how Donnacha had rallied the nobility of the Maguire against him and how Donnacha was negotiating in secret with the Crown. He told of how Arthur had spoken up for Eunan and promised the Maguire that Desmond MacCabe would represent Eunan but Donnacha had delayed him so he could not meet the week deadline the Maguire had set for Desmond to come to Enniskillen. He watched the thunder of concern envelop Desmond's face as the story deepened and the lightening of the cracks in his face flourished as the story ended.

"If Arthur has promised on my behalf then we must leave for Enniskillen castle straight away so I may plead Eunan's case."

Cúchonnacht Óg smiled.

"I knew you'd be concerned."

"This is no time to crow, for dalliance will only bring the crows of the English settlers to pick on our bones. We must leave now."

"What about Dervella?"

"I have long since given up attempting to exert any control over that woman. She will do what she wishes and to hell with what I think."

CHAPTER TEN

SECOND CHANCES

CORMAC O'CASSIDY FELT AS if he had lifted a burden off his skin. The bathwater he emerged from had to be changed three times and drained of all its scum before Cormac felt clean again. His wounds had been tended to. They were many, but none were deemed so serious that he would not recover from them in time. They had given him a set of clothes to match the finest he used to own as the O'Cassidy Maguire and a manservant to attend to his every need, though Cormac suspected he also fulfilled the role of spy for his new masters.

He went to the window of his new residence, sucked in the salty air and looked out onto the harbour below. Dublin harbour was full of ships all destined for faraway lands, and those with the acumen and luck to choose a successful ship that avoided the harsh storms of the open sea and could evade the numerous pirate ships would become rich men indeed. Cormac had previously chosen a steady but lucrative path with investments into ships going to England and the continent absorbing the profits of his trading ventures. But now his eye was cast further afield, to those ships that travelled to faraway lands that he only heard tales about from merchants or seamen that he met. For he felt liberated, and he could take more risks for the second chance they had given him meant that his life was not his own, so he was no longer so concerned with preserving it.

"Lord, a gentleman has arrived with whom you are to do business," said his manservant, who bowed when he entered the room.

"I will be there momentarily. Do we have a note keeper available to whom I can call if we mean to strike a bargain?"

"I have the requisite skills you require as a merchant of the Pale. I can take notes, notes that both parties can refer to."

Cormac noted the man's English accent and reckoned he was really his minder, probably an ex-soldier who could not bear to leave the service for civilian life and turned instead to espionage. He followed his manservant down the stairs and towards the parlour. He admired the beauty of the house and the workmanship of the stairs. They had given him a grand house, fit for the finest merchants of Dublin port, from the finest and most loyal families in the Pale. Cormac knew they were going to work him hard to earn all of this and that he would have to sell out many lives to keep himself in such grandeur. But his only thoughts were of living here with his beloved daughter.

"Damn the rest," he said.

His manservant opened the door to the parlour, and he saw his guest.

Captain Williamson sat there alone, by the table wearing not the muck of the road but the freshly cleaned shirt of an English captain, bright yellow with red decorative patterns that Cormac could not make out at a distance. His blue pantaloons made him look like a fashionable well-to-do gentleman, but the stub of his left arm gave him away as a veteran of combat.

When Captain Williamson saw Cormac come in, he looked around the room in exaggerated awe, lifting his right hand to point out the items upon which his eye lingered.

"I trust you are pleased with the accommodation the Crown has provided you with?"

Cormac pulled out a chair and sat on the opposite side of the table.

"You have spared no expense, for which I am grateful. The bath alone was as if it were a gift from the good Lord himself. However, you seem a shrewd man and no doubt you are here to have me earn my keep."

Captain Williamson pushed his mug onto the table and stroked his brown beard.

"You are sharp. I like that. As long as you obey my instructions and repay your debt to the Crown, you could happily live here and be many times richer than you were as a minor Irish chieftain."

"You would give me all this?"

Cormac looked around the room, unsure of whether to be elated or fearful that the responsibility would crush his shoulders.

"Give?"

Captain Williamson moved his face closer to Cormac's.

"There is no give. Only earn."

The wind deserted Cormac's sails.

"Will I ever be free?" he asked.

Captain Williamson sat back and pointed knowingly at Cormac.

"I would expect you to be one of the colony's premier merchants when this war is over. As long as you forget about ever being a Maguire and embrace being as near to an Englishman as you ever could be, having never been blessed to be born on her shores."

"Eunan Maguire smashed the umbilical cord to whatever allegiance I had to my former brethren. But you have breathed new life into me and given me purpose. Now let me fulfil that purpose and please provide me with the opportunity for my revenge."

"Your brother Donnacha -."

"Cousin."

"Cousin. He has proved a most useful ally by which we may lever the Maguires out of the war."

"Don't underestimate the romantic notions of Hugh Maguire and his desire for himself to live forever in the tapestries of his forefathers in Enniskillen castle."

"I know his kind, don't you worry. Many a man blinded by glory has done my bidding, even if it was to his own detriment. He has Eunan Maguire in his prison cells awaiting trial for the deaths of your son and the son of Connor Roe. They have to decide whether to try him under Brehon or Common law, where they decide to break from the Crown or not."

A smile broke across Cormac's face.

"I have just the man for you, a Brehon I know well and who owes me. Tell Donnacha I live, be it a secret or in public, whatever serves your needs the best. Tell him to send for Conchobar MacAodhagáin, in the employment of the Earl of Clanricard. He will tie any man of the law put forth by Eunan or Hugh Maguire in knots. Then pick your own outcome. Whatever serves your purposes best. A public execution under Common law and impose a sheriff, or financially cripple Eunan and Seamus under Brehon law and you may trigger a Maguire clan war. Either or, whatever is your choosing."

Captain Williamson turned and nodded to the manservant, who took notes.

"Can you hire this Brehon for us?" asked Captain Williamson.

"Bring me some writing materials and my seal and I will send him a letter and remind him of the debt he owes me."

Captain Williamson silently mulled over the options.

"Write the letter and I will present it to the Brehon and instruct him myself."

"So be it."

Cormac got up to leave.

"We haven't finished yet. The house you stay in is not so shabby as to be deserving of just one favour."

Cormac took his seat again and gave a business-like smile.

"To undo this rebellion quickly and to save unnecessary bloodshed on both sides, we need the help of men like yourself to help the Crown from the inside of the rebellion, so to speak."

Cormac nodded in acknowledgement.

"We need to establish ourselves a network of sympathisers and spies, those who know who the winners will be and wish to share the spoils afterwards."

"How do you propose to establish that?"

"Through the tentacles of commerce. Nothing shows better a man's soul than offering to put money in his hand and see what he will do to earn it. War and raiding have been terrible for men of commerce. The promise of peace and the opening of the market towns of the Pale to the Irish hinterlands should be enough to entice most waverers. You can send men throughout the north under the guise of commerce and, from their distribution of bribes, build a network of spies. We'll even let you keep most of the money with only a minor cut for the Crown for facilitation, protection and other services."

Cormac bowed his head.

"That is most generous of you."

"The Queen's generosity does not end there. Step this way and let us look out the window."

Cormac was initially hesitant, but the look in Captain Williamson's eye told him he did not have a choice.

"We need to trust each other well enough for the arrangement to function," said Captain Williamson.

They passed through the house and into the front room. Captain Williamson invited Cormac to look out the window.

"What am I looking at?" asked Cormac.

"See that ship to the left on the docks that is currently being unloaded? The cargo is yours to establish your network. The profits are to be split fifty per cent for the Crown, to be taken by me, twenty-five per cent for bribes and twenty-five per cent for you for commission. I have arranged that you join the merchants guild so that you can take part in other trading voyages and establish yourself, and from then on we'll have a fifty-fifty split."

Tears welled up in Cormac's eyes, but he turned away from the Captain and looked out onto the harbour.

"I will repay this kindness many fold. I only ask that my daughter be able to join me here."

"We have a role for her as well. She can come and join you as soon as she has assisted in the demise of Eunan Maguire."

Cormac's tears dried up. He knew the costs of this bargain were not immediately apparent.

CHAPTER ELEVEN

ENLIGHTENMENT

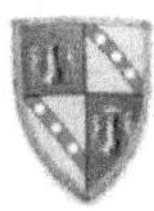

E UNAN SAT IN HIS cell as the light passed across the wall, day after day, night after night. He mulled over what was said in the hearing again and again, for his brain had little else to occupy itself with. His paranoia got the better of him. Why had the Maguire allowed Donnacha to do this to him? Could he not see that he did it all to protect him? A certain bitterness festered in the back of Eunan's mind.

He had taken to sitting on his stool and looking out the slit to the outside world and trying to catch glimpses of sky. In what would normally have been a futile pursuit, for in the winter Fermanagh sky grey is grey and usually in the form of a blanket, Eunan excelled. From even the slightest corner of cloud, he would estimate if it were going to rain and within which timescale, all based on the colour and formation of that same cloud. He would etch the results on the wall to measure his successes and failures and to track his improvements in weather predictions, for he had so little else to do. For instance, an alternative would be to pace the cell. He had developed a cough, for his blanket was light and the cold stone of the floors, walls and ceiling only amplified the cold of winter. Pacing the cell and the inhalation of cold air appeared to bring on the cough, and the cough wore him down and gave him a fever, so he had to restrict that. Estimating that the day had changed and trying to guess the date only took up so much time in the day. The guards would only feed him and must have otherwise been given instructions to otherwise ignore him. He spent much of his time these days wrapped in his blanket, coughing and looking out the slit.

His inner world reflected the turmoil of his outer world. He fought the demons of the past and tried to banish them from his fragile mind. His father, his real father, his mother, Seamus, Odin, the Knights of St Colmcille. He tried to banish them all from his mind, sometimes with success. He was getting stronger mentally now as he left his youth in the past.

He had survived for two weeks, or so said his scratches on the walls, with no one coming into his cell. The weakness of his body and the weariness of his mind signalled to him that his illness was getting worse. He heard a noise from the corridor. His bony knees hurt as he crawled over the uneven, stony floor. He leant on his side, fearing that if he fully committed his body weight to the floor, he would not get up again. He breathed in the relatively fresh air from the slit under the door.

"The Maguire..."

His mouth was dry from inhaling all the cold air. He rolled onto his back to see if he could swallow and generate some spit. Eunan heard footsteps on the other side of the door, so he rolled over again. He knew his opportunity would be slim.

"The Maguire promised me a physician. I have served the Maguire well and always kept my promises to him. Let him keep his to me."

He heard footsteps again, but growing more distant. Eunan waited for as long as he could, but the floor was damp and cold. He crawled back to his hay and his blanket and tried to warm himself again.

Eunan lay on his hay for goodness knows how long, for he was not conscious of making his etchings on the wall.

"Boy! Are you alive?"

He could not tell if he was dreaming or awake, for it had been such a long time since anyone was brave enough to refer to him as 'boy' and the only person who did that was Seamus.

He felt a warm hand on his shoulder. Then a gentle shake.

"Donnacha sent me. He heard you used to see the priests out on the island. They said you may need our help, physical and spiritual. He said you needed some enlightenment. They didn't tell me you were in this terrible shape at all!"

Eunan could only mutter "thank you." His anger only fused a little spark at Donnacha's name and then fizzled out.

The newcomer unwrapped Eunan from the protective shell of his blanket and examined him, placing his hands on Eunan's forehead and chest.

"You won't last too much longer here. Don't worry. I'll look after you."

The priest unwound Eunan's blanket from around him and laid it out flat on the straw. He tried unsuccessfully to hide his shock at the damp stink coming off Eunan.

"How can you live like this?"

The priest jerked his head back. He composed himself once more.

"Can you move? I'm going to lay you out on the blanket."

Eunan sat up and, for his efforts, was overwhelmed by a fit of coughs and splutters. The priest half lifted him and helped him to manoeuvre into position.

"Now lie back. I've just the cure for you."

He reached down into his pack and produced a jar. The leeches suckled onto the sides, wondering where their next meal was coming from.

"No!" said Eunan.

But he had neither the energy nor will to resist.

"Don't make any sudden movements," said the priest.

He picked out a rather large leech and attached it to Eunan's chest.

"Now don't move and let it do its thing. These leeches will suck all the illness out of you and you'll feel better in no time."

Eunan could only lift his head to see another leech being produced from the jar. He could resist no more. The bad blood, his father, Odin, and everything rushed back into his head and he blacked out.

CHAPTER TWELVE

ARGUMENTS MET

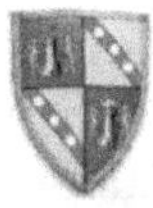

THE BOAT WOBBLED IN the harbour of Desmond's island, its bottom merely inches from the lake bed. Cúchonnacht Óg occupied the middle seat, for it was his young limbs that would propel them to the mainland. His ankle bound, he was determined he would not be a burden on this trip. Desmond sat at the back, red-faced from all the exertions. His bones and old wounds ached. He had the responsibility for steering the boat, more in case of attack than any disturbances in the still waters of the lake. But Dervella waded through the water and gripped the bow of the boat to give herself leverage to climb on board.

"Why do you insist on coming, woman?" said Desmond. "This boat can barely fit two, never mind three."

"And what am I to tell my Seamus, or Eunan, if you keel over and die on the roadside because you got over-excited by the prospect of playing war again? Or worse, that great belly of yours I've done so much to nurture becomes fish food?"

"The only way I'll become fish food is by you capsizing the boat. Now, if you insist on coming, get down here and let us help you on board."

Dervella threw herself onto the side of the boat and the two occupants took an arm each. After much exhilaration and cursing on either side of the port, they were all on board and wobbling across the river. Dervella noticed Desmond looked a little nervous, but she was unsure if it was because of the fear of drowning or of what may come to pass once they reached the shore. Desmond brightened up once he saw the shoreline and Arthur and a bodyguard of MacCabe Galloglass under the cover of the forest, waiting for them. Cúchonnacht Óg helped Desmond to the shore, with Dervella having to make her own way for Desmond was too busy to notice, as he was getting reacquainted with Arthur and some old Galloglass comrades. Desmond noticed Cúchonnacht's wily smile and sensed there was some plotting afoot. However, some of the Galloglass fetched the horses, and they set off for Enniskillen.

Enniskillen could not have come too soon for Desmond. One of the elder Galloglass who had served under him could see the barely hidden pain on his face and went over and helped him dismount when they came to a halt in the courtyard of Enniskillen castle. Caolán Maguire came out as soon as they informed him who had arrived. He also remembered Desmond well.

"What are you doing here, lord? The Maguire did not summon you?"

Respect for his former commander battled with what he knew would be the wishes of his new master.

"Was my hearing faulty when I heard Hugh himself tell me I would be welcome back any time I wished to visit?" said Desmond.

Caolán was silent, for he had no wish to insult his former mentor.

"He is here as my guest, the brother of the Maguire," said Cúchonnacht Óg. "Prepare us some rooms and bring us straight away to see Eunan Maguire."

"But Donnacha said -."

"Donnacha can say what he likes to anyone except the brother of the Maguire. Bring us yourself to Eunan and dispatch a lesser man to make up the rooms. Surely you have a key to the dungeons?"

"I do but -."

"Excellent! To me, you four men. Escort Desmond and me to the cells."

Caolán saw he had no choice.

"This way."

Donnacha watched from the tower. His English and Scottish guests had left, but he had a new guest to entertain. If Desmond wished to hear the babbling of Eunan Maguire, then so be it. It would do neither of them any good in the end.

The stone steps that led down to the dungeon were no less kind to Desmond than the horse's back. They came to the door of the cell. A narrow archer slit in the wall let in some light to the corridor, but the use of torches was obligatory if you were to navigate the pools of water and the slippery slime on the floors of the dungeon. Desmond turned to one guard.

"Fetch me a stool like a good man. I may be here for a while."

They stood back as another guard found the key from his voluminous key chain.

"Stay back," said the guard through the door as he put the key in the lock.

There was no angry assault on the door, only silence. It creaked on its hinge at the pace of the pressure the guard put upon it. The guard, Cúchonnacht Óg, and Desmond stuck their heads in the door.

"Oh God!" said Desmond.

The slime, the straw, the puddles, Eunan's body and face all seemed to be amalgamated into one. Eunan was grey and gaunt, his clothes were damp, his feet were bare and black on the bottom and he did not stir, even though he had an audience at last.

"Check if he's still alive," said Desmond.

The guard bent down and slapped Eunan gently on his cheek. Eunan stirred.

"Get him some water," said Desmond to another guard, then turned to Cúchonnacht Óg. "What's your brother trying to do? Start a civil war? No matter what they accuse him of, and I mean 'accuse' until I hear authoritatively otherwise, he is an innocent man. More so, an innocent man with powerful friends."

Cúchonnacht Óg backed away defensively.

"I did not know he was like this. Hugh would never do this. This is all Donnacha's doing. He is trying to back my brother into a corner and do a deal with the English. They mean to make an example of Eunan."

"Well, get a group of your most trusted MacCabes and get them to guard his door. Much capital could be made either way if someone were to come in and knife the boy."

"Do as he says," shouted Cúchonnacht Óg to the faces in the corridor. "Until I have seen my brother, nobody comes in or out except Desmond and me."

Desmond slapped Cúchonnacht Óg in the chest.

"Get Dervella down here to attend to Eunan and we'll seek an audience with your brother."

Cúchonnacht Óg ignored the indignity of being struck and being spoken to as if he were a boy, for he could see Desmond's fury and knew he was the best hope for Eunan and the Maguires. He waved over his shoulder to his men who disappeared up the stairs.

"Now let us see your brother."

They passed Dervella on the stairs, but she rushed straight past them. Such was her concern for Eunan. They reached the courtyard and Cúchonnacht Óg's bodyguards created a circle around them. They made their way towards the main door to the tower, swift in stride and determined in intent. The guards at the gate sensed their hostility and drew their swords.

"Put them down. He is the Maguire's brother."

Donnacha appeared in the doorway, his arms extended as if he was greeting old friends who had just returned from a long journey.

"Desmond! The Maguire will be pleased to see you. You should have told us you were coming. I could have arranged a nice hunt for you or such the like. Something to keep you entertained in your retirement instead of trying to hold a serious conversation with the Maguire about the ills of the world. Not much politics to speak of on that island of yours?"

Desmond tried to stride past him, but Caolán and his men stood in his way.

"Is that any way to greet an old constable of the Galloglass? Don't let him pour poison in your ears."

But Caolán was not for moving. Desmond realised he would have to engage with Donnacha.

"I was sorry to hear about your nephew. But within the bounds of the law, Eunan has asked me to represent him. In order to do so, I need to meet the Maguire. I'm sure you can arrange that and avoid an ugly scene in his courtyard with a man who served his father so well?"

Cúchonnacht Óg and his men squared up to Caolán and his men.

"Oh, within the bounds of the law? You should have said earlier. If Cúchonnacht Óg would be so good as to show you to your room, I will arrange a formal meeting this very evening. We are so glad to have such an esteemed guest as yourself stay and hope that you don't find your visit too disappointing. I extend to you the hospitality of the Maguire."

Donnacha bowed a little too low for Desmond to take such sentiments seriously.

Caolán and his men parted to let them through. But Desmond had not finished with Donnacha.

"My people are tending to Eunan. I trust they will not be disturbed?"

"As if Eunan needed the attention! The Maguire will take care of him."

"We shall see."

A knock came upon the door. Desmond had barely any time to tend to his appearance after the meagre meal Donnacha had sent up for him.

"Am I a prisoner here also?"

The knock came again.

"Are you ready? My brother will see you now," Cúchonnacht Óg said.

"Come in and don't stand out in the corridor."

"Sorry."

Cúchonnacht Óg shut the door behind him.

"I feel I am the chicken about to be hit over the head and eaten," said Desmond.

Cúchonnacht Óg tried to reassure him.

"My brother has a good heart. He is under a lot of pressure and is the victim of poor advice."

"He has to learn to rule and quickly if the Maguires are to survive. What am I in for?"

"I don't know. I spent my time protecting Dervella in the cells. As soon as Donnacha heard we were tending to Eunan, he was at the prison door trying to force his way in."

"We need to get Eunan out of here or else he is a dead man. He needs you. But I fear the price of the trade to get him at least safely away from Donnacha."

Cúchonnacht Óg put his hand on Desmond's shoulder, but the elder man felt no assurance from such a naïve youth.

"I will offer my protection as the brother of the Maguire. Eunan will stay under my protection until the trial."

"If I can achieve that bargain, I will be happy. Let us have fate wait on us no more."

Donnacha greeted them at the door to the great hall with the smile of a serpent.

"Greetings, both of you. The Maguire will see you now. But please hand any weapons to Caolán there. These are dangerous times."

Both Desmond and Cúchonnacht Óg stared at Donnacha as they undid their swords from their belts.

"I assume that this gesture from us will be reciprocated with the offer of safe passage and our weapons back when we leave?"

Donnacha faked mystification.

"We are all friends here, but at the very least, we are clansmen. Please come this way. I'll not let such inquiries diminish the level of hospitality on offer."

Caolán opened the door and Donnacha smiled and gestured with a sweep of his hand for them to enter.

The room lay before them, warm but uninviting. Hugh Maguire sat upon the seat of the Maguire, a blazing fire to one side illuminating the growing contours on his face. Shadows danced at the edges of the room. It was dark outside now, for the winters of the north closed in quickly, the respite of light from the darkness, wind and rain being increasingly sparse. The Maguire dismissed his guards and only Donnacha, Hugh, Cúchonnacht Óg and Desmond occupied the room. The Maguire appeared melancholy and remained seated.

"Hello, Desmond. It is good to see you again. Donnacha tells me you have some business to discuss with me?"

Desmond was a little confused. The youth he knew so well, who had more or less grown up with him, whom he had taught to fight, with whom he shared his considerable knowledge of strategy, was not the person who sat before him now. Hugh sat like a bird trapped in a cage with all the accoutrements of the Maguire but no freedom to deploy any of the associated powers. Desmond picked up that this was not the place for any reunions, this was purely business.

"Greetings, lord. You have matured into a fine and wise young man. Fermanagh is lucky to have such a wise and just ruler in its hour of need. Surely we are on the eve of the greatest days of the Maguires, an age where legends will be made."

"You must charm those water birds that fly over your island down from the skies," said Donnacha. "I wonder, after such flattery, do they end up in your pies?"

"I have long since left behind the barbed tongues of the court. I am merely expressing my admiration for one who I may have had the faintest of influences over in their youth and was complimenting him on how well he absorbed the lessons of those times. It is only in the court where he may wish that every word uttered was transcribed so he could ponder them for hours trying to discover their true meaning only to realise such efforts are folly."

"Such are the sentiments of one who blows so much hot air. The boy you once knew may have had the time to ponder such ramblings and spy a morsel of truth hidden between the lines, but the Maguire does not have the luxury of so much time to waste. In that spirit, please state why you have troubled yourself to leave your island to dust off your oratory skills?"

Desmond ignored Donnacha and gave a brief bow to Hugh.

"I am here on behalf of Eunan Maguire, for I fear he may have been wronged."

"Wronged?" Donnacha said. "As I bore witness to it myself, he committed the most heinous of crimes. If only we had the brute Seamus on trial with him justice would have the chance of truly being served. The clouds above your island must be very boring for you to compose such tales and have the audacity to come and present them to the Maguire."

Desmond let Donnacha finish talking, for he did not want to appear rude in front of the Maguire as he was asking for favours.

"Lord, I mean to come here to defend Eunan Maguire and the allegations made against him within the bounds of the law."

"Oh, within the bounds of the law, is it?" said Donnacha.

He walked down to the end of the room and knocked on the back of the door. When it opened, he whispered to the guards, who then closed the door behind them.

Cúchonnacht Óg went for his belt to find his scabbard empty. Hugh looked pained.

"I wouldn't do that to you, brother."

He received back sceptical looks from both Desmond and his brother.

Donnacha swept past Desmond and Cúchonnacht Óg and stood once more beside the Maguire.

"How can you sit and not intervene?" said Cúchonnacht Óg. "Does Donnacha do all your speaking for you these days?"

Desmond signalled to Cúchonnacht Óg to be quiet. Now was not the time to witness the Maguire's temper.

The doors at the bottom of the hall opened. A balding man with a generous waistline and a bulging book with protruding loose papers strode towards the top of the hall. Two young boys ran behind him, each overladen with books, and tried to keep up. The man slammed his book down on a table beside the window and continued his stride into the centre of the room and occupied the space with a menace that those clever enough feared; those who did not become victims of his trap. Cúchonnacht Óg looked perplexed. Who was this man who stood before them? He did not look like an assassin, and if he was not, what was he doing here?

Desmond knew exactly who he was. He took a deep intake of breath. He would have preferred an assassin. Much easier to deal with.

"Desmond," said Donnacha. "Assuming your memory does not fail you, you remember Conchobar MacAodhagáin? If you do not, you will soon be acquainted with him."

But Desmond was acquainted with him. Conchobar was the most feared Brehon law expert in the north, maybe in all of Ireland. He was from the esteemed MacAodhagáin family, who specialised in Brehon law, Common law and everything in between. He was known for being the brightest of his family in the interpretation, application and creation of the laws. His cunning had helped create the fortune of the Earl of Clanricard and Desmond estimated that there must be greater forces at work who wanted to see Eunan condemned to persuade the Earl to lend out his greatest legal mind. Desmond now knew that

Donnacha had orchestrated an ambush, and it was not he who he was plotting to kill, but the spirits and will of all of those who opposed him in Fermanagh. Desmond knew he had to escape.

Conchobar bowed. Desmond had twenty years on him, but he knew from the merest twitch of a man's face if he inspired fear in him. He stood in silence, waiting for the twitch. He stared at Desmond and watched the cracks on his face. Donnacha dared not interrupt. There it was. The twitch.

"I am pleased to make your acquaintance, Desmond MacCabe. I may have been a little young to see you in your prime and would hate to ruin your image with the Maguire and make him doubt his judgement by offering you the comforts of retirement on one of his islands. I'm sure the Maguire would forgive and forget if you wished to return there."

Desmond ignored him and turned to Hugh Maguire, who was still seated behind his two representatives.

"Eunan Maguire, no matter what he has done, has always served you well. He does not deserve to rot away in the castle's jail. You should at the very least treat him with the same respect as you would a lord of another clan who was taken prisoner and awaiting ransom or to be exchanged for some other reward. He is held in high esteem in both south Fermanagh and by the men who serve under you. So it would be wise to show to your fellow clansmen that they will be afforded justice and fair treatment from the Maguire."

"I see your pleas are not supported by any facts," said Conchobar. "Have you done any research into the case before attempting to prey on the good nature of the Maguire?"

"I first need to secure Eunan's fair treatment and well-being and then we can decide how to conduct the trial and on what date."

"How do we know whether Eunan or even the Maguire is safe with that brute Seamus MacSheehy roaming the countryside with a band of armed men?" said Donnacha.

"I think you'll find that Seamus MacSheehy is in East Breifne conducting the Maguire's business, having trained men for his service. He poses no threat to the Maguire or to the notion of justice being done but does not yet know of his nephew's mistreatment."

"What will happen if you spread rumours to him?"

"I shall spread no such falsehoods, but your actions, Donnacha, are indefensible and soil the reputation of your master. With the clan so fractious and both Eunan and Seamus held in such high esteem by the O'Donnell and Seamus now working with Cormac MacBaron, the good name of the Maguire has the potential to be diminished in the eyes of his allies if you persist in treating a faithful servant in the manner you have done."

"But if we transfer him to an island, he will just escape," said Donnacha.

"What are you truly afraid of? The Maguires have successfully pulled off many a ransom and hold hostages to this day. Are you attempting to pervert the Maguire's justice for what you perceive as your own personal revenge?"

"But -."

"Enough, Donnacha!" said Hugh Maguire. "I have heard enough. Eunan will be taken to Devenish Island and held there until we set a trial date."

Cúchonnacht Óg stepped forward.

"Brother, I will guarantee both his safety and that he shall stand trial on the appointed day."

"I also ask that I may provide someone to look after him and tend to his ailments after being neglected in the castle jail," said Desmond.

"If I grant these to you, when will you be ready to have the trial?" said Hugh.

Desmond pondered the question.

"I have some distances to travel, witnesses to canvass, and will need to seek some help. About two months."

"Two months!" said Donnacha. "My nephew's memory will have started to fade and hearts will grow faint and waver from true justice being done for his memory."

"I need the time to look into the case and to assemble the resources. No less and the whole trial could be held in disrepute."

"Do you have evidence of independent resources Eunan can bring to bear or a family that can take on such a burden, and it is provable that those resources are theirs and theirs alone and not the result of a benefit gained from the O'Cassidys?" said Conchobar.

"I will cover all your questions when I present my case."

Hugh paused.

"Eunan's trial will be on this day in two months. You must bring evidence to support your case. You must also bring collateral and evidence that such collateral is assignable to Eunan and is independent of the O'Cassidys and are not ill-gotten gains."

"You set high terms, lord," said Desmond.

"We will decide on the jurisdiction of law dependent on what collateral you bring. Donnacha will assign a value for the damages the family has suffered and the court will judge its reasonableness. Once a maximum compensation level is agreed upon, then we will assess it against how much collateral you can evidence. If you can match it or more, Brehon law. If your collateral would be deemed adequate, March law, where either side can refer to English or Brehon law. If the compensation you muster is deemed inadequate, it will be English law, where the court reserves the right to hand Eunan to the Crown. Are you prepared to accept these terms?"

There was no point in contemplating the terms, as they were non-negotiable.

"What of Eunan in the meantime? May your brother be his ward on Devenish Island and may I have access to him?"

"I will be true to my word."

"Then I will bid you farewell, for I have much to do. Thank you for your level judgement."

Desmond bowed, and as he rose, Donnacha and Conchobar grinned at him like a brace of wolves about to descend on some unprotected sheep.

Cúchonnacht followed with a bow of his own, and they hurried out of the room. They scurried down the stairs in silence and made their way to the centre of the courtyard. Desmond looked back at the tower and the smiling face of Donnacha protruded through a window. Desmond turned to Cúchonnacht Óg.

"I need six of your best Galloglass, preferably men already known to me. Neither of us is safe, but at least you have the protection of your brother. I will get the finance and the evidence we require. You take Dervella and protect Eunan with a dozen of your best men. Eunan is only safe as long as Donnacha thinks he is going to win."

"Where are you going to set off to first?"

"The scene of the crime, O'Cassidy house. Whatever evidence is available will be there. I also need to speak to Seamus. I fear only he can save Eunan from this predicament."

Cúchonnacht Óg put his hand on Desmond's shoulder.

"I will get you your men. I know you will succeed, for you have to, for Eunan's sake."

Several hours later, Desmond was on the road once more, this time towards O'Cassidy house.

CHAPTER THIRTEEN

FRIENDS LOOK AFTER FRIENDS

SEAMUS FELT THE NERVES tingle at the bottom of his spine. But O'Reilly paused. Seamus could see him calculating his options on his face. He was not entirely a tool of anger. More like a frightened rabbit that suddenly found himself in charge, but without an escape plan.

"Put down the knife," said Cormac. "It's time to let bygones be bygones while we fight the common enemy."

"No Maguire comes here and insults the O'Reilly," Philip replied.

"No one insulted you."

Cormac stood between Philip and Seamus to calm the situation.

"The O'Reillys rule this part of Leinster and we want our Maguire black rents," said Philip.

His face was getting redder by the minute.

"I want an agreement for my historical rents!"

"You'll get no such agreement at the tip of a dagger," said Cormac.

Seamus laughed.

"He's only humouring you. You may as well use the knife, for you'll get no rents from the Maguires as long as I'm alive."

The rage built in O'Reilly. His Tánaiste Eamon O'Reilly, his designated successor, came over to investigate the shouting.

"Philip! What are you doing?"

That was the ultimate humiliation for Philip. He went for Seamus. He charged and screamed his drunken frustrations into the night and thrust his blade towards Seamus. But this man was not a warrior. He did not have the discipline of a man who had survived to be his age off the back of his prowess in battle. The ease with which he succumbed to his temper and picked a fight meant that it was a testament to his other skills that he had lasted this long. He was more of a rabble rouser, a motivator of men to risk their own lives rather than he waste his. He was the perfect complement to the more cunning and considered John O'Reilly, but the strengths of their partnership had passed away upon John's demise.

Seamus took a step to the side and grabbed the wrist of the knife-wielding arm while at the same time elbowing Philip in the side of the head. Philip went down in a heap and lay motionless. The encircling crowd gasped, and some looked angry at seeing their leader beaten so.

"Nothing to see here. Go back and enjoy your drinks," said Seamus.

He tried to usher them away.

"He just punched Philip O'Reilly," came a call from the back.

"Let's get them," came another.

The crowd gathered and riled itself up.

Eamon O'Reilly stood in front of Seamus and Cormac and addressed the baying crowd.

"This is drunken banter. Philip is fine. Go back to your seats and continue your merriments."

"I saw Maguire punch him in the face. It didn't look like harmless fun to me!" said one O'Reilly.

Cormac thought he should now intervene.

"As the representative of the O'Neill, I can tell you that all of this was harmless fun. Let's all go back to our seats and take it for what it was."

Philip stirred. Seamus went over and stood on his hand.

"Get rid of them. If your people come near us, either way there'll be a massacre. If you ever want to hold a dagger in your hand again, you'll agree."

Philip roared with pain.

"Keep it down. Now decide whilst you can still use your hand."

Seamus applied more pressure and Philip tried to suppress his yelps.

"All right, enough. Leave my hand alone. Let me up."

Seamus dragged him to his feet and made a brief show of dusting him off. Seamus smiled at him, put out his hand, and invited him to address his people. Philip stood before the crowd, looking sheepish.

"Come on, let's all calm down and go back to the revelries. This was fun that got boisterous. Look, we're friends, really."

Philip invited Seamus over and he obliged by putting his arm around his shoulders. The O'Reilly men muttered to themselves suspiciously and cursed the Maguires under their breath but obeyed and dispersed back to their tables and chairs. An O'Neill constable arrived with Cormac's bodyguard and surrounded him. Seamus picked up his cloak and went to have a word in Cormac's ear.

"We have to get rid of him. He's just a liability."

Tempers were calmer the morning after. A light grey fog suppressed the town. A distant sun failed to summon enough energy to dominate the morning, and sore heads searched for water and leftovers from the night before. Nothing so obscured the straight-thinking Seamus. The previous night's experience had shaken off any delusions he may have fostered walking in the shadow of the O'Neill's splendid army. He made straight for Cormac MacBaron's tent. Words were exchanged with the guards, terse but not unpleasant. Seamus made himself comfortable beside the fire in front of the tent as MacBaron dressed. Cormac opened his tent flap to the cold of the morning to be confronted by the sternness of Seamus's face.

"Either you've got an almighty hangover or you are here to talk business?" said Cormac.

"Unfortunately, the latter. Is there anywhere to talk in private?"

Cormac looked to his Galloglass constable, who stood behind him, guarding the tent. They exchanged some whispered words.

"Come, there is a pleasant little wood beside our camp. We can walk and talk. The O'Reillys are too busy nursing their heads."

Seamus followed Cormac and his bodyguards through the camp. The camp appeared orderly. Very few seemed to have joined in the festivities of the night before. Men trained in the fields and searched for provisions. It was more like a professional army from the continent than the motley crew of men that fought for the O'Donnell or the ill-disciplined men of the Maguire. It was like the Galloglass of old, like when he served the Earl of Desmond, but without the poor leadership.

They found a circle in the wood and the MacDonnell Galloglass of the O'Neill formed a perimeter out of earshot to prevent spies from listening in. They both sat on some tree stumps, the remains of part of the wood's contribution to the O'Neill camp. Seamus looked troubled, as if he did not know in which order to let his words out, a position he was not familiar with.

"Let it out, man," said Cormac. "We are two warriors in a wood. What we say in the circle stays within the circle."

"We cannot work with Philip O'Reilly. Were you not there, if that was any other man, his wife and children would be in mourning now."

Cormac chose his words carefully as well.

"If this were any other situation, I would not complain if I heard the tale of how you felled him. But this is Ireland. This is what we are fighting to protect. For my brother to create an alliance capable of beating the English, we must deal with many unsavoury characters, even those of the ilk of Philip O'Reilly. We need to put our petty differences aside, forget the past and work together."

"There wasn't much of that last night. He wanted to stick a blade in me so bad for all these dreams he had of his family's past glories, and I ain't even a Maguire!"

"Both John and Philip approached my brother and the O'Neills need to honour their agreement with them. We need the alliance with the O'Reillys upon which to build a coalition with the remains of the Leinster clans."

Seamus smiled. He knew he could do business with MacBaron. He shook Cormac by the forearm.

"I can give you that alliance, strong and united."

"If you can do that, you are free to create it as you wish."

Seamus smiled once more and the two men set off back to their camp to discuss the campaign ahead.

Several days passed and the sobriety of the O'Neills was passed on to the warriors of the O'Reilly, for Philip now feared for his position and was eager to impress. He gathered together the horsemen of the O'Reillys, for they were both numerous and impressive. Well, impressive when compared to the poorly armed farm boys that made up yet another large body of unorganised and ill-disciplined Kern, which was exactly what the O'Neill did not need. Cormac was as disciplined as ever in the camp outside Cavan town, and he accepted Philip's invitations to inspect his men and nodded his approval as they marched in front of him, and kept his comments concise and polite. Upon his return to the camp, Cormac would ignore Seamus's comments such as: "you'd want to get your hands on some good gun smugglers, for this lot are only good for robbing cattle," and "just what you wanted, another rabble of Kern."

Seamus was not invited to these inspections, for he was barely a couple of categories above the enemy and Seamus had to keep his eye on his men when they mixed with the O'Reillys so that hostilities did not break out. Seamus noticed he was soon involved in a silent tug of war with Philip for the attention of MacBaron, a battle he could not lose.

Seamus had noticed that the much younger Eamon O'Reilly was both pliant and ambitious, a dangerous combination for the possessor of such traits but a gift to those who practised the art of politics on both the periphery and through the battlefield. Seamus knew he needed allies amongst the O'Reillys and noticed Eamon had a good rapport with the O'Reillys of the minor families, be they young or old. Since he would get nothing but animosity from Philip, he knew he had to work on Eamon. He made his move at a dinner for the officers around the campfire of MacBaron. He walked over and sat down beside him.

"Hey, thanks for your help the other night," he said.

"Think nothing of it," said Eamon. "Philip has the powers to motivate men through his enthusiasm and standing in the clan, but no stomach for the drink. I have to watch and see what I need to undo, fix or complete when he is finished with the havoc of his revelries."

Seamus clinked his mug of ale with that of Eamon.

"Well, you're a good man for it anyway. I'm not a Maguire by the way, so there is none of that baggage between us. I'm a MacSheehy, one of the last of the proud MacSheehy Galloglass clan. I mainly sell my services to the O'Donnell. He is a great man of influence and a good friend to have. I am his servant and representative, so what you do for me, you also do for him."

Seamus gave Eamon another toast by chinking mugs. Eamon gave him a nervous smile.

"These are turbulent times," continued Seamus. "It's good to have friends and you need to have allies. These days may be dangerous, but there are opportunities for those who keep their heads and have some good friends. The O'Donnell will be impressed when I tell him how you saved me."

Eamon's curiosity was aroused.

"What about the O'Neill? We heard that the two great lords of the north had split the land in two and Leinster was in the lands of the O'Neill?"

"Am I not here with the O'Neill's brother? Do you not see me ride and converse with him by the day? I have a young nephew who has inherited his family lands which border those of the O'Reillys, a place where Philip dreams about some apparent ancient rights to extort black rents. Pursuing that would be foolhardy. Two new leaders bringing the spirit of rebellion to their clans would make great friends and allies, don't you think? As much as we are grateful to the O'Neill, we must come together so that they can heal our region, be that if the rebellion sets the country ablaze or the Spanish land and liberate the country. But it takes men with wise heads and foresight. Are you with me?"

Eamon nodded and gave him a knowing smile.

"So if I pledge to come to your nephew's aid, he will come to mine?"

"As will my lord, who will swoop down from Tirconnell to aid the O'Reillys should their hour of need come. But my lord will not be pleased if he comes to Breifne on some folly. The O'Reillys need to be led by men with wise heads."

Eamon sat up.

"The O'Reillys will be worthy allies for your master and nephew. I'll make sure of it."

"And I'll leave you to your drink. Stick near me in the campaigns ahead and we can forge a steadfast alliance between two once warring clans."

Eamon raised his mug in salute once more. The wind changed direction, and they became enveloped in the smoke of the fire. Seamus tried to wave the smoke away and, in a fit of coughs, disappeared off into the night.

Word soon came to the camp that Maelmora O'Reilly was touring the towns and villages of south Breifne, rallying all the O'Reillys still loyal to the Crown to his cause. Nothing made Philip's blood boil more than the thought of his rivals, be they O'Reillys or Maguires, prospering and potentially getting one over on him. He took Eamon to one side and amongst the proliferation of curses and flying spittle ordered him to rally the men, for Philip would lead them himself in a pre-emptive strike and rid the land of his rivals. When his temper had subsided enough, Eamon reminded him that the prominent force in the land was that of the O'Neills and he should at the very least consult Cormac before going after Maelmora. Barely had the words settled in his ears then Philip was off to demand a meeting with Cormac.

Cormac heard Philip's protests and pleas for them to attack in measured silence. He then called a council of war, mainly to make the O'Reillys feel as if they were important, not necessarily to listen to what they had to say. Within the hour, the leaders of the various clans stood in the yard before MacBaron's tent and Philip's men brought a crudely drawn map of Breifne for the leaders to ponder over alongside a table to place it upon. Philip took a sharp intake of breath. He had to look the decisive leader. Conviction and force would rule the day. His index finger soared in the air as if it had become an eagle.

"The usurper is here!"

The eagle swooped and prodded the map at several points before swooping up to support his master's decisiveness.

"If we swoop down from both sides -."

The eagle was joined by his mate, and they both swooped down in simultaneous semicircles and met once more on the map.

"We can crush him before he has had time for his masters to join him from the Pale. With the O'Neills on one side and the O'Reillys on the other, he stands no chance."

The O'Reillys rallied around Philip's call and bayed to march on their clan rivals. But Seamus could not resist.

"What about the Maguires?"

Philip almost burst a blood vessel.

"Well, the Maguires can just piss off back to Fermanagh and get me my black rent!"

Seamus just laughed.

"You draw up the battle plans and we'll follow you. Now what formation should we draw up in? Where is the O'Reilly Galloglass? Where shall we deploy the O'Reilly shot when they appear?"

Philip turned purple. Seamus did not move from his seat beside MacBaron and continued laughing to himself.

"That's enough now, Seamus," said Cormac, determined to douse the rising flames of resentment from Philip and the O'Reillys. "If you would be so kind, Philip, to ride with me, the O'Neills will follow your guidance and we shall spring our trap."

Philip went from purple to red and white blotches returned to his face.

"It would be an honour to ride with the O'Neills again and we shall both dominate the lands of Leinster just as our forefathers did before us."

"Then it is agreed. Let us set out whilst there is still light in the day."

But Philip had not finished.

"Once we drive Maelmora from our lands, the O'Neill will have a path straight to the centre of the Pale. Then he shall see the true benefits of having the O'Reillys as their principal ally in the region."

Cormac went up and patted Philip on the back.

"Come. Let us focus on the battle at hand. Only once fate has dealt her cards can we then see what the next move is."

Philip saved his scornful look for Seamus as he was invited into MacBaron's tent. Seamus looked out for Eamon, but he was gone. As everyone left, Seamus took his opportunity to examine the map before Philip's men whisked it away. But Seamus had seen enough. He went to prepare his men and to seek Taighe Maguire and his south Fermanagh shot.

They roamed the fields of south Breifne. All the time Philip was in Cormac's ear as he argued hard for them to march down and defeat Maelmora, which would lead to the O'Reillys uniting and joining the rebellion. He turned over, again and again, the idea that the major advantage to the O'Neill would be to open up a direct route to attack the Pale and threaten Dublin. But all they heard from village to village was that Maelmora had been there a day or so ago but had gone. He had outmanoeuvred them when Philip made the call to march to south Breifne and left for his traditional hideout of Clogh-Oughter castle.

The army of the O'Neills, Maguires and O'Reillys marched back to central Breifne, the land of lakes above Cavan town. The O'Reilly scouts led the allies through the forests and along the lakes of central Breifne. They marched cautiously through one final woodland and encountered no resistance. The scouts reached a clearing beside a lake and sent word back. Philip led Cormac, Eamon, and Seamus to the shore of the lake.

"So where's the illusive Maelmora hiding then?" asked Seamus.

"There," and Philip pointed out onto the islands of the lake.

"Where?"

"Over there. Follow my finger. It is the castle on the island in the middle of the lake."

Seamus strained his eyes.

"How the hell are we supposed to take that?"

CHAPTER FOURTEEN

LOVE LETTERS

Ó ISIN SAT ON A tree stump withering in the cold and looked at the facade of O'Cassidy house and the last vestiges of his confidence left him. It was the depths of winter. The frost crunched underfoot and the gloom of the grey sky cast its shadow over man and beast alike. He picked up several pebbles from the ground and rolled them in the palm of his hand.

His mission had not gone well. He now regretted the destruction his men wastefully wrought upon the house for he was now tasked with returning the house to its original grandeur but afforded no budget to complete the work, except for what funds he could raise himself, nor given any craftsmen to do the repairs except those he could conscript from the surrounding villages on the promise of payment in the future or more likely the threat of facing Seamus when he told them they would not assist. Whilst such methods could throw bodies at the house, none worked with the enthusiasm or skill levels that Óisin expected, and the house repairs were far behind schedule. A pebble skimmed the surface of a nearby pool of muddy water as Óisin mulled his woes.

But all such destruction was not his, well not directly his. He only assumed responsibility after they had been destroyed. The once ebullient fields were now mud, trodden down by hundreds of unskilled men welding an axe, grounding a pike, discovering the weaknesses of their sword fighting skills or firing a musket for the first time. These were worthy pursuits in the turbulent times that smothered the Maguires, but they were surrounded by far more unproductive lands that could have borne these activities and not have affected the potential crop yield, especially in a time of famine. The wedding day massacre started the destruction of the fields around the house and nobody had the sense or foresight to put a stop to it. Another pebble lodged itself in the muddy pool.

But he was no farmer. How could he, an orphan boy from Enniskillen, a dweller on the outskirts of the town, a boy of the woods, a pickpocket, a scoundrel, scum, be expected to take over from a landed gentleman, one of the richest men in Fermanagh, and immediately make his lands as profitable as before? How was he, a boy who could barely count the coin in his pocket, supposed to replace one of the richest traders in the county? No wonder he was failing. He was doomed to fail from the start. Eunan was his friend and would not do that to him. However, Seamus never wanted him to be in charge, so maybe this was Seamus's way of making it clear to Eunan how much of a liability his friend really was. His last stone found its new home at the bottom of the pool. Why should he even try? If he tried, all he was doing was proving Seamus right and providing him with evidence. Why should he -.

"What are you doing here? I told you to stay inside."

Caoimhe stood before him with the sun behind her, so he had to shield his eyes. She looked radiant with the sun enhancing the red of her coat, her long black hair curled down her chest. His nostrils filled with her sweet aroma. She evidently was not running out of perfume. Óisin's heart thumped in his chest. This was all he needed when he felt so down, the enchanting Caoimhe out to revel in his failures.

"I see what you are doing to restore my father's house. You banish me to my room, yet I never see or hear any repairs happening to the house. We sit inside and freeze whilst all you can do is throw pebbles into a pond."

"If I can succeed in one thing, it is to control you. Now get back to your room before I beat you like I beat your servant."

Caoimhe laughed.

"You would be too afraid to lay a finger upon me for fear of what Eunan would say if I showed him some bruises."

"Oh, I'd be careful not to bruise you."

"You may be so, but how is Eunan to know who did what bruise?"

Óisin turned away.

"You're a witch."

"I may be a witch, but I am a cold one, and a cold one that will help you so that she may get warm. Come, take my hand and lead me to the house you wish me to be a prisoner in. You said you wished to inspect the next letter I wanted to write to my uncle and you have your opportunity now. He can help us get the farm up and running again, for they desperately need provisions in Enniskillen."

"You'll help me because I tell you to help me." Óisin stormed past her and strode towards the house.

Caoimhe turned her back to Óisin and slowly removed her cloak to reveal her bare shoulders. Her bare shoulders led to a red dress, the kind that could only be imported through the finest merchants in the Pale. It was far beyond the quality of dress that Óisin could persuade a girl to take off, be it either through his charms or coins. Caoimhe shook her hair behind her to ensure Óisin got a full waft of the combination of her hair and perfume. She laid out her cloak on her bed so the inside was facing up.

"A man as important as you needs somewhere comfortable to sit as he listens to my musings."

She invited him to sit down and Óisin looked confused.

"Sit and let Lasair bring you a drink. Then we can begin the letter writing."

Lasair fetched a drink for Óisin and then sat on the floor, observing him as previously instructed by her mistress.

Caoimhe fetched her quill, ink, and paper. She pondered and then held them out to Óisin.

"Why don't you write the letter since you are in control here? Then you will know exactly what I am saying to my uncle."

Óisin went a little red.

"No, no, no. You do it. If I did it he'd think it was a ransom note."

"We wouldn't want to think I was being held here against my will, even if it was by such a handsome man."

Caoimhe and Lasair both laughed and Óisin went redder still.

"Just write the letter," he said. "I will read it later. No, even better, you read it out to me."

"I bow to the master of the house," said Caoimhe.

She did just that without taking her eyes off Óisin. Óisin's cheeks were now completely red.

"If you ladies are just going to make fun of me, then I shall go. I have much to attend to in the house and do not have time for such frivolities."

Caoimhe knitted her eyebrows and leant towards him.

"But it is a very serious matter writing to my uncle. If he thought I would come to harm, he would send men. Those men may mistakenly go for you. Just as you are my knight and protector, I must, in some small sense, protect you from the harm of mistaken identity. I wouldn't want the men of the Maguire to mistake you for one of Seamus's thugs rather than my protector, would you?"

"Stop your games and just write the letter."

"Your word is my command."

Caoimhe gave a little curtsy to Óisin, still seated on the bed. She sat at her desk and dramatically raised her quill. She glanced at Óisin and wrote furiously. Every thirty seconds, as if she was coming up for air, she would raise her quill, look back at Óisin and then return once more to her frenzied writing.

"Why do you keep looking at me?"

"Inspiration, dear, inspiration."

Caoimhe did not want the redness of his cheeks to go down.

After several minutes she announced: "Finished."

"That was quick. Not much to say then?"

"Oh, plenty to say. I feel so elated to be here with you that the words just flowed."

"I thought you were writing a serious letter to your uncle?"

"It is serious, very serious. I need to protect you from getting killed, my knight."

"A knight is not Irish, it's an English thing."

"If that is not how you see yourself, then you are my heroic hunk of Galloglass, my defender to the death."

By now, Óisin had resorted to hiding his face in his hands. He could escape neither Caoimhe's exaltations nor the overly generous spillage of her perfume on her coat.

"Please, can you just read the letter? I have other things to attend to."

"Do you? Do you really? More important things than attending to the wife of the O'Cassidy Maguire who you have sworn to protect?"

"I didn't do any swearing. Please, just read the letter."

Caoimhe stormed around the room with the letter thrust into her breast.

"Oh, you have hurt my feelings. Read the letter yourself!"

She held out the letter at arm's length to Óisin, as if she was now ashamed of its contents. Óisin trembled, for he was afraid to take it. Such a failure of nerve did not evade the corner of Caoimhe's eye.

"I haven't got time for this. Read it out to me while I think of how to deliver it to your uncle."

"I can't. I'm embarrassed now. You'll consider it folly for a lady to write such things about her protector. It is all right for her to keep it hidden in her heart but to commit it to paper, to her uncle of all people!"

"Please, just read the letter."

"Very well. Let me take up a few more minutes of your precious time that you'd rather spend mucking out horses for Seamus or the like than with me."

Óisin cringed.

"'Dearest uncle, I hope my letter finds you well. Misfortune may have befallen our family, but it has seemed to treat me well. I am still in our family home, still with my Lasair, and have most of my possessions that survived the fire. My 'husband' abandoned me at the first opportunity he got. Lord knows why he would be such a brute to do such a thing to his poor, lonely wife. But I have found myself a protector that will keep me well until we meet again. A handsome, heroic Galloglass has pledged himself to my cause, to help restore our family home and the lands of our fathers. When the Maguire sends soldiers to punish Eunan for his heinous crimes, spare me my Galloglass. He lights my way and protects me from the thieves and wolves of the night. He is all that stands between me and that wicked man Seamus. Write to me, uncle, as I write to you, from the heart, and tell me how you are. Fondness forever, your niece, Caoimhe O'Cassidy.'"

Caoimhe smiled and sought Óisin's approval. Óisin grew ever more uncomfortable in the company of these women.

"Well?" asked Caoimhe. "Can I send it?"

She held it out for Óisin to inspect. He declined.

"It is not up to me how a girl writes to her uncle."

"I am no girl, I am all woman," Caoimhe whispered mischievously in response.

Óisin jumped off the bed.

"Send your letter. I do not care. I do not have time to deal with such things."

"So Lasair can deliver the letter?"

"I do not care." Óisin made for the door.

"Can she have a horse to ride to Enniskillen?"

"Take one from the stables. As long as she does not dilly-dally back."

"Thank you, my love!"

The door slammed shut. The two women struggled to contain their peals of laughter until Óisin was out of earshot.

CHAPTER FIFTEEN

INDEBTED

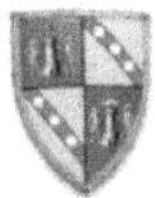

TAIGHE MAGUIRE SAT BY the lakeside with his head in his hands and his feet in the water. The castle on the island in the middle of the lake was lit up like a torch. The O'Reillys were incensed. Their leader was dead. In the camp, an inquisition was taking place about how he got killed. It seemed unlikely that Maelmora's men did it. Anyway, he was now their prisoner. The O'Reillys and the Maguires were now at each other's throats. Taighe was afraid but could not hide, for the woods were the worst, filled with obsessed men searching for traitors and assassins. But Seamus reassured him he would be safe. How did he ever get into Seamus's debt?

The previous day had a dull beginning, camped in a wood besieging an enemy they could not see while a slumbering rival clan rose in the camp beside theirs. At least there was fishing and more food than in Fermanagh, for there seemed to be a never-ending stream of farmers that were declared to be working for the enemy, an enemy of many guises. But the O'Reillys appeared distracted by another matter. It soon became apparent what that was, a summit called by MacBaron.

Seamus wore a wicked smile whilst he pulled on his shoes. He winked at his men and then walked off to meet the other leaders. Seamus returned several hours later, smiling from ear to ear. He called his constables to his tent.

Confidence oozed from his smile as he pointed out at the lake.

"The Maguires have come down to East Breifne and are going to take that island from the O'Reillys. No more will you have to fear their raids. Me and my young nephew will look after you, but only if you stay loyal to us. The O'Reillys will supply us with boats and we'll assault the castle tomorrow. Now I want the constables of the shot to come with me and the rest of you can relax and prepare for the assault tomorrow."

The men dispersed, and Taighe gulped and approached Seamus.

"I want ten of the best shots to assemble here and I want them here quick. Don't try my patience. And Taighe, make sure you are amongst them."

Taighe knew he should be nervous. Being singled out by Seamus was never a good thing.

A short time later, ten of the finest shots in south Fermanagh assembled in front of Seamus's tent.

"Here," said Seamus.

He handed each of them a bow and arrows.

"What did we bring our guns for, then?" asked one man.

"You'll see. Follow me."

He led them into a section of the woods beside the Maguire camp and free from the incursions of the rival O'Reilly clan. The woods seemed eerily quiet, as if waiting for something to happen. Seamus stopped at a clearing and the men looked around them, attempting to work out the significance of this point.

"Look up, men."

Seamus pointed to the trees. Hidden amongst the treetops were ribbons and coloured boards.

"From what the O'Reillys tell us, and I believe them, for they are coming too, they have no cannon in the castle. Therefore, as we row across the lake, all they can do is shoot at us. That is why I have brought you here today. The ribbons and boards represent their musket men on top of the tower. We need to know that we can take them out. We also need to know the distance at which our guns will be effective and whether we need to use bows instead. So split into three groups and fire at your relevant targets. I will come around and assess the results. Taighe, you are with me for I have a special mission for you."

Seamus stood and watched as the men took aim at the targets.

"No, no, no. Take out their muskets or, at the very least, provide cover. Try it with bows."

The men picked up their bows and several minutes later, the boards were like porcupines and the ribbons in tatters.

"Better, much better. We'll stick with bows for this attack."

The men looked a little confused, but they nodded along in agreement, for none of them wished to incur Seamus's wrath. Seamus ordered them back to the camp. Darkness fell, and the O'Reillys called from the woods. The Maguires immediately went for their weapons, but the O'Reillys marched in carrying boats for the early morning raid. Seamus thanked them and sent them away, for he did not want the men on the island to get suspicious. The Maguires vetted the boats for holes, for they did not want to drown in the middle of the lake. It was the end of a sombre evening for Seamus had banned alcohol; he did not want the men to be drunk and fall out of the boats. Fires also suffered a ban, for he did not want the defenders of the castle to know which direction he was coming from. They had little sleep that chilly night.

That morning, a certain fear crept through the Maguire camp. Most thought it suicide to row across a lake with the enemy taking potshots at you, but negative talk earned a slap around the head to enforce the ban. They loaded the boats with their weapons and men as the clouds blocked the light of the moon. The attack was supposed to be timed, so they left in the dark, crossed in the twilight and assaulted in the light. The O'Reilly said the tower could hold only one hundred men, so once they had made it to the island and penetrated the castle, it should be reasonably quick work. Eamon had assured them he had a traitor in the tower who would let them in. Some Maguires were sceptical and said that the O'Reillys were in collusion so they could kill off the Maguires and then attack Fermanagh. No matter what reassurances Seamus gave, he could not dislodge that thought from some of their heads.

Seamus had volunteered them to lead the assault on the impregnable castle in the middle of the lake. Rumour had it that Philip was furious that the Maguires had the potential to steal the glory for liberating East Breifne so had volunteered to go on the assault alongside them as long as they were the first to set foot on the island. The O'Neills put up no protest, for they viewed the assault as foolhardy and were in favour of sitting on the shoreline and starving Maelmora out. Apparently, Seamus had both suggested and insisted on the assault, and Cormac was happy to agree once Philip showed enthusiasm.

Seamus split his men into different boats, each with a set number of oarsmen and bowmen. The only boat with more men was his own, of whom the extra men were himself and Taighe Maguire. Seamus stayed up all night after ordering his men to get some sleep. Seamus watched the stars and for activity on the other sides of the shore. At what he estimated was the allotted time, he went to wake his men, finding most of them already awake. They pushed their boats from the shore and into the lake and jumped on board when momentum alone drove the boats into the water. The oarsmen dipped their oars into the water and rowed as quietly as they could. Soon, one of the four boats lagged behind.

"We've got a leak!" hissed a distant voice in the dark.

"Can you continue?" hissed Seamus back.

"We can, but I fear we would end up at the bottom before we fired a single arrow."

"Turn back, for it is no good us giving away our positions just to save you."

Three boats rowed towards the castle on the lake.

The moon came out from behind a cloud to greet those hoping to make a stealthy assault. It seemed to create a ladder on the rippling waves pointing from the shore to the boats for anyone bothered to look. Seamus ordered the men to pull up their oars and drift away the last of their propulsion. He could see in the distance faint lights in the tower of the castle. That was to be expected, for the defenders knew of the combined army camped along the lake's shores. He also saw the dots of the other boats. To his right was the multitude of O'Reilly boats, which made up the major assault. To the left were two groups of O'Neill boats. They filled the first boats with musket men who had the responsibility of pinning down the defenders so the Maguires and O'Reillys could land. The second had barrels of gunpowder to blow a hole in the walls should the initial assault not breach the castle and fail to bring surrender. There was no sign of any change in activity in the tower. The moon slid behind the clouds and the oars hit the water once more. They came within musket range of the castle and still there was no movement.

"Keep it steady, boys," said Seamus.

The oarsmen kept a steady pace but placed the oars in the water with more precision to create neither waves nor noise. Seamus saw a dim light at the top of the tower.

"Take it easy, boys," he said.

He squinted to see what was happening up there. Three arrows with trails of fire erupted from the tower.

"We've been rumbled," said Seamus. "Row like hell!"

They threw all caution to the wind as they made a dash for the island. But no gunfire or arrows met them on their way. The flame arrows ripped through the sky. One landed near the boats of the Maguires and was extinguished by the water.

"They only fired that to frighten us. If they are not pelting us with bullets or arrows, then they must be short of ammunition."

The second arrow was towards the O'Neills and again fizzled out in the water.

The third was towards the O'Reillys. The three parties rowed on and ignored it. It landed in the water. But something lurked on top of the water that no one had noticed.

"Fire!"

The flaming arrow hit the water and landed in a pool of oil. The pool exploded. Like a tangled beast from the depths of hell, flames shot along its tentacles and soon the rebel ships were surrounded by fire.

Seamus grabbed an oar from the nearest man and forced his way to the back of the boat.

"Break up the water! Break up the water! We have rowed through a line of oil!"

All the oars went to the back of the boat to thrash away any drag they may have picked up from the line of oil. An O'Reilly boat burst into flame. Husks of men jumped from the boat, their backs and heads balls of fire. Their agonised howls pierced the night. The other O'Reilly boats frantically rowed towards the island, for flames blocked their escape route to the shore. Another O'Reilly boat ignited with a roar. More howls of pain penetrated the remaining rebels to their core. The flames tore towards the Maguires and the O'Neills.

"BREAK UP THE OIL! BREAK UP THE OIL!"

Seamus signalled to the other Maguire boats to copy him as he thrashed away at the dark water and the unseen enemy.

The flames ripped down a channel of oil like the horses of Hades. Death echoed in the heads of all who bore witness to them as if they were being ridden down. Another tentacle exploded with fire and hurtled towards the O'Neills. The flames engulfed one of their boats. Minor explosions perforated the night as the gunpowder of the musket men caught fire. The flames ripped onward. A huge BOOM battered the ears of all those in the boats and blinded all that witnessed it as one of the O'Neill gunpowder boats exploded and illuminated the entire lake. The flaming body parts of what were once men and the burning parts of what were once boats showered those who had not yet fallen to the flames. Whilst the men cried and urinated down their own legs, Seamus looked to the island as he had the benefit of light. For all their success with the oil, there were few men out on the shore defending the island.

"FORWARD MEN, FORWARD!" he roared.

The men on the island wheeled out more barrels.

"TAKE THEM OUT! TAKE THEM OUT!" Seamus yelled.

Those rolling the barrels were felled in a hail of arrows. More men came out, this time with shields to protect them, and slowly edged the barrels to the shoreline. The latest line of flames zipped past the rear of the Maguires and on towards the O'Neills.

"I feel the bottom of the lake!" cried one oarsman from the front of Seamus's boat.

"HOW HIGH?" replied Seamus.

The man touched the top of his chest.

"ABOUT THAT!"

"ROW FURTHER!"

The surviving O'Reilly ships were now within reach of the shore. They were about to disembark.

"TO THE RIGHT! TO THE RIGHT!" Seamus roared to his oarsmen.

"BUT THE FIRE!" cried one man.

"TO THE RIGHT!"

The three Maguire ships steered towards the O'Reillys. The O'Reillys jumped from their leading ship. A defender on the shore took out an axe and hacked frantically at the barrel. Seamus grabbed the nearest bowman.

"TAKE THAT BARREL OUT WITH A FLAMING ARROW!"

Defenders on the shore were felled in a barrage of arrows whilst two flaming arrows penetrated the barrel. The heavens roared as the barrel exploded in a ball of flame. Fire engulfed two of the O'Reilly landing boats until only the two shattered burning hulls remained. The side of the castle was doused in flames and they could hear the shrieks of those inside out on the water.

As the fires raged, Seamus could see properly. The men were evacuating the castle. From the intensity of light inside the castle, it was clear the fires were consuming everything flammable they met.

"FORWARD, MEN, AND LAND THE SHIPS!"

The O'Reillys had now come inside to the right to avoid the fires. They were a little ahead of the Maguires whilst on the left-hand side, the remaining O'Neill boats were also closing in. The O'Reillys stood up in their two ships nearest the shore, ready to disembark and attack the island. Seamus recognised Philip O'Reilly's boat as the one closest to him. Seamus grabbed Taighe Maguire by the scruff of his neck.

"Time to pay your debts or die on this island."

He threw Taighe back down and turned to address the rest of the boat.

"MEN, A VOLLEY OF ARROWS TO SUPPORT THE O'REILLYS!"

Taighe held his gun to his chest. He looked over to the O'Reillys' boat and instantly recognised the mop of Philip O'Reilly's grey hair.

"FIRE!"

A volley of arrows hit the defenders on the shore. Philip O'Reilly's head exploded like a watermelon.

"NOW BOYS, DISEMBARK!"

Maguires jumped into the waist-high water and stormed ashore. The O'Reillys realised their leader was dead, gathered around him and lifted his body from the water and back onto the boat. The Maguires waded onto the shore. Defenders tried to retreat into the castle but were blocked by those trying to escape the fire inside. A volley of Maguire arrows and all resistance ended. Seamus charged forward with his axe. The castle was on fire now, along with much of the island and its modest mooring area. The O'Neills landed. Seamus and his men charged towards the mass of men clustered around the castle door. The defenders threw down their weapons and threw up their hands. Seamus elbowed his way through the throng of men and grabbed whoever looked like he may have once been in charge.

"Where is Maelmora? Give him to me and I'll spare your lives."

"There he is."

The man pointed to a plump soot-covered man who had just emerged from the gate, bent over, coughing his lungs up.

Seamus ran up and grabbed him and the Maguire men surrounded him.

"Surrender to me if you'll yield me a decent ransom. Do that and I'll put you on the road to the Pale with an escort of your own men. If you want to fight, I'm sure I can find you an O'Reilly with a grudge against you."

Maelmora clutched at Seamus's sleeve.

"I'll stick with you. You'll be well paid if I see out until the morning and can lay eyes on Dublin town once again."

The sky burned as fragments of fire fell from the castle and the streaks of oil fire still raged. Seamus hid Maelmora in a clutch of his men and smuggled him onto a boat and back to shore.

Seamus had salvaged enough boats to get both his men and Maelmora and three select bodyguards through the remaining oil fires and back to their camp on the shore. They smuggled Maelmora and his men into tents in the middle of the campsite. Seamus emerged from the tent once he had Maelmora settled to find himself surrounded by his melancholic men.

"What is wrong with you? We have come here and won a glorious victory. We were better than both the O'Reillys and the O'Neills. For all their knowledge and weapons, it was us, the boys from south Fermanagh, who took the castle. Find food and ale. Let's celebrate!"

"He's right!" shouted Taighe Maguire. "We have won. Here. Take these."

Taighe handed out bottles of ale and wine that Seamus had forbidden the night before. Soon fires raged and songs were sung, and Seamus could slip out under the cover of darkness.

He made his way keeping out of sight to the O'Reilly camp, which was a much more sombre state of affairs. They had lost many men and had brought back with them the body of their dead leader. They laid him out on one boat and the men surrounded him to see if he was actually dead. Eamon stood amongst them. Seamus knew he had to get to him soon.

"Who are you? A spy?"

Seamus turned to see two angry faces, then the butt of an axe.

They threw a bucket of water on him. Seamus sputtered and wiped the water from his face.

"What shall we do with him? Kill him?" said one man to the other.

The sound of the camp was in the distance.

"We may get some decent money for him," said the other.

"Do you fools know who I am?" Seamus said.

"Shut up, or feel my axe on your head once more."

"If you want money, bring me to Eamon O'Reilly. He will pay handsomely for me," said Seamus.

"How do we know this is not a trick?"

"I assume you are with the O'Reilly? You don't know how much I'm worth, yet I claim to be important? Who else is going to pay you?"

They pondered momentarily, mainly on the risk of their prize being stolen from them.

"This way, and try nothing."

They led Seamus through the camp, past the campfires and the sullen men dragging their dead comrades from boats so they could bury them in a mass grave in the woods. They brought him past the guards and to the fire outside the tent of their former leader, now occupied by Eamon O'Reilly. An ashen-faced Eamon stared into the fire whilst the former leader lay in the boat pulled up from the shore.

"Lord, we caught this spy lurking in the woods. He claims to be important and that you would reward us for bringing him to you," said one man.

Eamon looked up to see Seamus's blood-caked hair and a line of blood rolling down his cheek and meandering around his straggly beard. Eamon rose with the fury in his blood.

"You fools! Do you know who this is?"

The two men backed off, fearing for their lives. Seamus smirked.

"This is Seamus MacSheehy, the leader of the Maguires!"

"We are very sorry, lord!"

"We humbly apologise!"

Both backed away and as soon as they could, turned and ran. Seamus laughed.

"You let them off lightly. I would have at least had them flogged."

"There is enough death and misery here today. We may have taken the burned ruins of the castle, but Maelmora is in the wind. We lost half our men and fear the other half may desert. I hope you have brought some good news to dent our misery?"

"Assemble your captains and we shall go to the tent of MacBaron. From what I have to offer you, I assume our negotiations will be swift and we can end this sorry war."

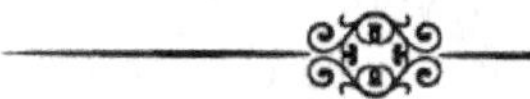

They made their way through the woods to the O'Neill tent on the other side. The guards on the perimeter were familiar with Seamus and Eamon and let them and their men pass. They walked through similar scenes as those in the O'Reilly camp as the O'Neills mournfully buried their dead. No signs of any victory celebrations. The guards woke Cormac, who had gone to rest less than an hour before. Cormac came to them in his nightshirt looking bleary. Seamus was in his body armour looking bright-eyed and bushy-tailed.

"We have come to an agreement that will end this war so we can all go home," said Seamus.

He put his arm around Eamon's shoulders to show they had reached an understanding.

"That is music to my ears," Cormac said. "It was a bad day today to spend so many good men on a clan feud when we could have been fighting the English. Sit and tell me what I need to do."

"We will declare Eamon the new O'Reilly."

"That's easy. Agreed," said Cormac.

"I have Maelmora and get the ransom for him."

"That is not so easy. Many good men died today at his hands. What am I supposed to tell my men? Why did you agree, Eamon? Why would you let such a wily rival live to return another day?"

"Wily?" Seamus said. "He may have been clever enough to ambush us with some slicks of oil, but all his men did was hem us in and force us to attack when he lacked the manpower to finish us. Clever, yes. But also shortsighted and not thought through.

He's exactly the type of enemy you want, one that's easy to beat. If you kill him, then you risk someone more competent taking over."

Cormac smirked.

"What is the fee that Eamon has to pay for your services?"

"Only a little black rent and some food to get my people through the winter. But do not forget that all of this is all part of what I promised you."

"And what was that?"

"The Leinster Alliance. I still need to make good on that promise."

"I'm glad I've not been forgotten in all of your wheeling and dealing. But I am confused. How can you be the key player in declaring the O'Reilly when you are accused of having him killed?"

Seamus shook his head and laughed.

"That is just the O'Reillys looking for someone to blame for their leader's recklessness and incompetence. Easier to blame me than accept their dead leader was a fool."

"A lot of them believe it," said Eamon.

"As I explained to you, we've both seen the body," Seamus said. "A bullet from behind struck Philip's head. As you saw, and all your men that survived witnessed, the Maguires only had arrows. The O'Neills had muskets. If you want to make a big inquiry into his death, then the O'Neills would get blamed. Why would you want to blame your liberators, especially when they have such an enormous army on your land? You know accidents happen on the battlefield all the time. It is up to you if you want to pursue it, but it would be unwise to bite the hand that put you in power."

Cormac gave Seamus a wry smile.

"So, are we agreed on our solution to East Breifne?" asked Seamus.

"Agreed. Arise the new O'Reilly!" said Cormac.

Eamon rose from his seat, and the two rebels embraced him. The O'Reilly captains cheered and Seamus beamed from ear to ear.

CHAPTER SIXTEEN

AN ALLIANCE SEALED

THE MOURNING FOR PHILIP O'Reilly ended before it began. They gave him the honour of a chieftain's funeral but the gentry of East Breifne were too interested in manoeuvring for position under the new O'Reilly and his O'Neill masters to fixate on Philip's death. Eamon saw his former master off into the ground, MacBaron sent a constable, but Seamus had more important business to attend to.

The rain poured down, marking a day not for glory but for transactions. Seamus stood with his bodyguard of Galloglass and Maelmora sat sullenly on a small horse looking every inch the fat drowned rat. Some of Maelmora's men stood behind Seamus, for they saw the changing of power and stuck with the perceived winner. The rest of Maelmora's men stood behind their lord, wishing to take their chances in the Pale, hoping for a quick return as the rebellion fizzled out. But Seamus was the one with the upper hand.

"Well, here we are to conclude our bargain."

He grinned and showed his yellow teeth.

"At least you've been honourable and executed our bargain, as agreed, when you had the advantage. I will reciprocate such a kindness when the English come and chase you back to your holes."

"It's different this time," Seamus said. "You may think of me as an old fool, but I have lived with rebels my whole life. Some were fools caught up in their own dreams, some were opportunists, and some were well-intentioned men whom fate had it in for. But the army of the O'Neills is the finest Irish army I've ever seen and I've seen plenty. It won't be long before they can come down south and beat the English in an open field."

"Now there I thought you were a wise man, and you were just doing this to fill your own pockets. Now that you've been paid and you've struck another bargain with my enemies, I will depart. Thank you for sparing my life and the lives of my men and we'll remember it when we next meet on the battlefield."

Seamus laughed.

"The Pale is that way."

Seamus slapped Maelmora's horse on the rear. The animal reared and bolted. Maelmora's men trudged after him. Seamus patted his pocket.

Seamus returned to Cavan town to find that the O'Neills were preparing to leave. He rushed into Cavan castle to see Cormac, who was busy packing up his things.

"I received a letter from my brother ordering me to return home," Cormac said. "Apparently, the English are getting twitchy in the negotiations and my brother doesn't want to give them any excuse. No raiding by either the O'Neills or the O'Donnells. You'd better go back and report to Hugh Maguire and see where he is at with his negotiations."

Seamus did not look pleased.

"When are you leaving?"

"As soon as we are ready. The next day or so, once Eamon is secure."

"What about the alliance?"

"Your contacts are welcome in Dungannon anytime."

"My scouts say they should arrive here any day now. Can you not wait?"

"You've been saying that for a while."

"How about a compromise? You travel back via West Breifne. There are plenty of secluded spots where we could meet?"

"I will leave when we are ready. If you can arrange something in the meantime, I will consider your proposal before I go."

Seamus was unhappy but from the look on Cormac's face, he knew his mind was made up. He returned to his own men to see if anyone had arrived. His own men had been busy rounding up

Maelmora's cattle and had them sectioned off so they could drive them back to Fermanagh.

"It won't be long before we attract the attention of the O'Reillys and they get brave and think they can steal them back," said Taighe when Seamus turned up to inspect the herd.

"How far away is West Breifne and could you get there and back in a day?"

"It's possible, but you'd be riding your luck going through so much bandit country."

"There are good and bad bandits," replied Seamus. "Many people would call me a bandit."

Taighe held his tongue.

"What would you be wanting to do in West Breifne that would jeopardise the gains you have already made?"

"Seek an audience with Brian Óg O'Rourke."

"You'd have to find him first. Rumour has it he's raiding in Connacht."

"How do you know all of this?"

"The rebellion is all they talk of in Cavan town. They say the English are too weak to wage a proper war, that's why they are trying to negotiate."

"I wouldn't listen to everything you hear. The English will be back soon on the battlefield. They only talk to buy time."

Seamus looked once more at the cattle. To have won so much was far beyond anyone's expectations, but the alliance would cement his position and prop up Eunan's tenuous hold on the title of O'Cassidy Maguire. He knew he had to go for it. He slapped Taighe on the back.

"That village of yours does not know what a debt it owes you. How long will it take to drive the cattle home?"

"Several days, maybe four?"

"I have a mission for you. Tell no one of it and I will reward your village well with the bounty of cattle. If you make it back, I'll even declare you the chieftain."

"What do I have to do to earn such an honour? I know titles with you do not come cheap."

Seamus smiled. The day of bargaining was not yet over.

Seamus returned to the camp and got himself some men and some horses. It was a dry crisp day, and the ground was solid underfoot. It was a good day to ride. His men were preparing to pull out to protect the cattle on the way back to Fermanagh, just as he had ordered. His recently returned scouts had told him that the O'Mores had been raiding the Pale near East Breifne recently and that Uaithne was keen to meet him. He was supposed to be on the way to Cavan town to meet MacBaron, but there was no sign of him. Seamus had also sent scouts to West Breifne to see Brian Óg O'Rourke. Brian Óg said that he would come, but there had been no sign of him either. Seamus had to decide which one he was going to pursue. He rode south.

As Seamus rode through the lands he spotted a hill, one of the few in a relatively flat country, and made for it. He reached the top and looked over the lands of the O'Reillys. The ruptures of the O'Reilly inter-clan war ran deep. Farmhouses burned and refugees took to the road as they fled the violence that one side took out on the other.

Seamus's eyesight was a detriment to him. The smoke and fires of retribution and destruction were as far as his poor eyesight could see. He called forth one of his men, his most trusted scout.

"Can you see south, past the borders of Breifne, to make out smoke caused by raiding rebels?"

"It is hard to see, lord. What are you looking for rather than me just telling you tales you want to hear?"

"I wish to meet the rebels of Leinster and bring them north. But I fear I only have a day's travel to achieve my mission. If you tell me in good faith, I will forgive you for any failure. I always need men of your skills."

The man nodded and looked in every direction and nodded once more as he made his mental notes. He called Seamus over when he had made his assessment. He pointed to the east.

"That way is the Pale. The raiders have made it there, but whom you are looking for is no longer there."

He pointed southwards.

"There is where we should go. The Queen's shires burn and fresh smoke wanders even as far as here. If we had a day to take a chance with, then that is the direction in which I would go."

Seamus slapped him on the back.

"Then that is where we shall go."

Seamus waved his hand and signalled to his men to depart.

They rode south through the wreckage of the countryside, where the scars of years of repression and resentment ran red raw. Farms burned and groups of armed men roamed the land and set upon each other in the name of defending themselves or taking back that to which they laid claim, no matter how tenuous.

Seamus avoided engagement or the taking of lives for time did not give him the luxury of dealing with the consequences. He stopped his scout when he found he knew nothing of these bands of men or their alliances.

"In which direction are we going now? May we veer more towards the Pale, for the men I know would want to wreak their vengeance more directly."

"We have a few hours left where it would be safe to travel. Darkness would merely bring on the chaos. I know of lands of English settlers near here where the men of Leinster love to make merry with fire and sword. Let us go there and then return."

Seamus knew there was little time to delay. He could not risk all that he had gained for this alliance.

"Lead us forth."

They rode until the sun began its daily winter decline. The fires burned with greater intensity upon the lands as the scouts had predicted, and burning houses were surrounded by the bodies of their former occupants.

"The people starve, yet they reap such destruction on next year's crops," said the scout.

"The dividends of war are paid for many years, both good and bad," replied Seamus. "The hour grows dark. We should leave."

They turned their horses around and set off in the other direction. Barely had they set off for Breifne, when they were surrounded by a band of men.

"From whom do you mercenaries take your pay?" said a man who stood before them with his Galloglass axe aloft.

"Your future master, the O'Donnell," replied Seamus.

"We have no masters," said the Galloglass.

"Then do you disgrace the Galloglass class by taking as thieves to the woods?"

The men now surrounded Seamus's party and raised their weapons. Seamus and his men raised theirs in return.

"Leave them, men. I know them," said a rider appearing from behind Seamus and his men.

Seamus turned at the sound of the voice.

"Uaithne!"

The reunion was warm on both sides. Seamus wished that such mutual respect and admiration could exist between Eunan and himself, but he had to make do with what he had. Seamus was glad that Phelim O'Byrne was with Uaithne, even though much animosity remained between them. Fiach MacHugh O'Byrne had seen the sense that since his most able son Turlough was now dead that he should now train up his living eldest son as best he could to replace him.

Seamus embraced him and whispered in his ear,

"Let the past live in the past. We have greater foes than each other and we have the same objectives. I hope we can be friends and allies."

Phelim nodded, but more for the sake of his friend.

They sat beside a fire together and ate. Seamus's self-imposed deadline had long since passed and he was resigned to postponing his return until the next day. Phelim's presence had given him a new sense of purpose, to smooth over relations with the O'Byrnes. He may not have the O'Rourkes, but the O'Byrnes were just as good a prize.

"The O'Neills have the finest army in all of Ireland," said Seamus in between bites of meat from the rabbit bones. "Even better than the English."

"In open battle?" asked Phelim.

"You don't need open battle in the north. It is a waste of the multitude of good ambush spots."

"Well, it's flat down south, at least in the parts we don't already control. If they are to come down south, then they'll have to fight a battle one day. Then we'll see."

"It's the best you're going to get unless you want to tell yourself stories about the Spanish army."

"Let us enjoy our time together and not fight," said Uaithne. "Men like us could die tomorrow, so let's enjoy what we can."

They ate some more until Seamus broke the silence once more.

"We have a hard day's ride ahead of us tomorrow, for I fear that MacBaron, in his impatience, has already left. However, with a little endeavour we can reach him before he enters Fermanagh."

"What has you so confident?" asked Phelim.

"All my cattle will clog up the roads going north," smiled Seamus.

"You'd better hope he doesn't take them for himself and head up north with them," replied Phelim.

"MacBaron is an honourable man."

Phelim kept his next comment to himself.

"Well, I for one look forward to it," said Uaithne. "Here's to new alliances and freedom for all our clans."

Uaithne stood up and raised his mug. "New alliances!"

Seamus echoed him, swiftly followed by Phelim.

"New alliances!"

They rode as fast as the wind could carry them whilst avoiding the fires, hordes of refugees, and gangs of bandits. They arrived on the outskirts of Cavan town at the abandoned O'Neill camp. The fires were still fresh, and the locals told them that the O'Neills had set off back north the day before. Seamus ordered them forward towards Derrylinn, the most likely route MacBaron would take.

They travelled for a couple of hours until they saw the rear ranks of the O'Neill pike.

Seamus and his companions rode past the O'Neill pike and between the woods and bogs, the rest of the army struggling to maintain discipline and formation. It soon became apparent why. One of the O'Neill constables recognised Seamus as he rode by and called out to him. Seamus pulled up his horse and rode back to him.

"You've got a nerve showing up here. MacBaron thinks you did this deliberately. You'll be lucky if he doesn't steal them all and take them back to Tyrone."

"Where is he?" asked Seamus.

"Up top with the cavalry trying to clear the road. You'd better get up there quick if you know what's good for you."

"Thanks. See you on the next battlefield," said Seamus.

He pointed in the direction he thought MacBaron was in and dug his heels into his horse's sides.

They soon came upon MacBaron remonstrating with Taighe Maguire on the dirt road, surrounded by cattle and dung.

"I know why you're here and why Seamus told you to do this. Get these cattle off the road and stop blocking the O'Neill army or I'll charge them with my pike. Then Seamus will hang you from a tree for losing his cattle."

Seamus got off his horse and walked up behind Cormac.

"What's going on here? What's all the commotion?"

"As if you didn't know! You planned this, didn't you?"

"What I did plan for you was to seal the Leinster alliance."

Seamus signalled to the men on the horses.

"Cormac MacBaron, let me introduce you to Uaithne O'More, the most successful raider in central Ireland."

"Good to meet you," said Uaithne.

He went and embraced Cormac.

"Not forgetting Phelim O'Byrne, son of the famous Fiach MacHugh O'Byrne, who has come all the way from Wicklow to meet you."

"Pleased to meet you," and Cormac shook his hand.

"Let us all convene at Derrylinn so we may discuss the future of our rebellion."

The O'Neill constables looked to their master, for they were confused.

"You heard the man," said Cormac. "Forward to Derrylinn."

CHAPTER SEVENTEEN

RESENTMENT IN LOVE

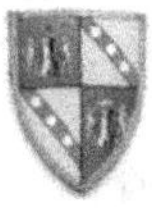

T HE GROUND HARDENED WITH the frosts and the last of the leaves fell from the trees and plants curled up to hide from the harshness of the winter. The ground cried out to be broken by the hoe and the cows echoed the distress from their fields. Even the crows came down from the trees and gathered near the house looking for scraps because the pickings were so poor in the field. Such sentiments hardened the resolve of Caoimhe O'Cassidy to restore her father's lands. Unfortunately, the immovable object needed for the restoration was Óisin.

"You need to get out there and prepare the fields for spring. They don't sow themselves, you know," she told him.

She stood over Óisin as if she were a nagging wife trying to motivate an errand husband.

"I am the man of the house here and you are my ward, so be quiet, woman," he said.

"We may both be your wards, but we are equally neglected. I only harass you so that you will look good in front of my cruel husband so that he does not treat you how he treats me. How I long to be the wife of a real O'Cassidy Maguire who can defend both his woman and his lands with equal rigour, then both would blossom plentifully for him."

The conversation ended as most of theirs did with Óisin attempting to escape to hide his blushes.

"Be the man I need you to be. Be my Galloglass."

Óisin waved her away.

"Go back to the house. Leave me be, woman."

But Caoimhe would not let him be.

"The grey merchants from the Pale will come soon to do deals for the season ahead. We must be prepared for them. How are you going to keep me in the manner I am accustomed to if you don't till the fields?"

"Leave me alone, woman, you are not my wife."

"Only because Eunan keeps us apart. I will leave you now but on one condition. You start work on the fields and come to visit me in my room later."

"Get away from me, woman. I am the one in charge. You'll do as I say."

"There is my Galloglass, taking charge. Now take charge of the fields and then come take charge of me!"

"If it is the only thing that will rid me of your nagging, then I agree. Begone now so I may work."

"I shall see you soon," and Caoimhe blew him a kiss and ran back to the house. "I will watch you from my window as you bend the fields to both your hoe and your will. Then we will see if you will do the same to me!"

She flew up the stairs and to her window since torturing Óisin was now her primary source of entertainment. Óisin stamped around the yard and shouted at the men as he tried to reassure himself that he was in charge. He then sat on a rock and Caoimhe could see the internal debate going on in his mind. He then called out to some men to come and help him. They went to the sheds and several minutes later dragged out the plough for the oxen. Caoimhe watched the clueless Óisin as he assembled the tools, but did not know how to instruct the men on how to use them. They tried to delicately steer Óisin in the right direction. Óisin was having none of it and shouted at all those who tried to contradict him. He had to be in charge.

Caoimhe took to her heels and ran down the stairs to rip control from her slothful puppet. She had seen her father's stewards and tenants plough the fields every season, so knew what to do, but also who to listen to. Caoimhe grabbed her red shawl to be at her most persuasive for Óisin. She burst through the doors and into the farmyard. Then in the distance she saw the returning horsemen of Seamus. Óisin saw her coming and again blushed, for he feared being undermined again. But she turned on a sixpence and ran back into the house. She had to be at her window to see what would happen next.

Óisin turned and saw why she had fled.

"Put those tools away. Quickly, to the kitchens. Have them prepare food," Óisin shouted at anyone who would listen to his instruction.

More riders appeared on the horizon, and those at the front rode ever near. One man worked up the nerve to answer Óisin back.

"We do not have the food to feed a horse such as that yonder. Our stores are nearly empty, and we have nothing to trade."

"Don't listen to the witch in the window. Do as I say and prepare food or you'll be for the whip."

Seamus and his men pulled up on their horses in the yard.

"I am so glad you are well," said Óisin.

He smiled at Seamus, but his nerves betrayed him.

"Why do you pretend to be so happy?" Seamus said. "Tend to the horses. I must inspect the lands for they look as if they have not even been subject to your incompetence."

Seamus dismounted and walked straight past Óisin. He looked up to the window and saw Caoimhe peering out.

"I hope my nephew will not regret leaving you in charge. Get some food and bedding prepared in the house."

Seamus pointed to the window.

"Evict her from her room. We have distinguished guests staying with us. I hope the house is looking better than what I left it for I see the fields and surrounding lands have only been touched by the ravages of winter since I left."

Uaithne and Phelim pulled up and Seamus greeted them and guided them towards the house.

"We may have the misfortune to bear witness to how useless this one really is," he told them, pointing at Óisin. He flung open the door. The scars of the fire had been tamed but not healed. Some paint had reached the walls but in sparse patches and not done by someone with enthusiasm in their endeavours. Seamus scowled.

"I should have you flogged for this," he said.

Óisin gulped, for he knew Seamus was serious. Seamus looked up and saw Caoimhe peering down at him from the top of the stairs.

"Get out of this house, you witch. Get rid of her. Do as I say."

Óisin bowed his head and signalled to his men. They slowly climbed the stairs. Seamus saw their reluctance and signalled to his own men. They ran up the stairs and into Caoimhe's room.

They grabbed both her and Lasair and dragged them down the stairs.

"You're a pig, Seamus MacSheehy."

She spat on his shirt.

"You have chosen your next accommodation," said Seamus. "Bring her to the styes."

"No!" Caoimhe howled.

Seamus's men dragged her to the back door. Uaithne and Phelim came through the front door and witnessed the eviction.

"Her father was the master here and conspired with the English."

Both men nodded their approval. Such evictions were almost a daily occurrence for them. Seamus leant over to Óisin.

"We need to have words later."

Seamus then turned to his men.

"Clear the rooms on the upper floors and prepare them for myself and our guests."

Caoimhe's possessions flew out the window and into the mud of the yard below. There they remained until night fell. Óisin ordered his men under the cover of darkness to gather them up and bring them to the pig styes where Caoimhe and Lasair had found their new homes.

The O'Neill army had passed Derrylinn to camp nearby, but Seamus and Uaithne's men camped on the grounds of O'Cassidy house. They ate what remained of the house's winter supplies and occupied the best green fields with Seamus's newly acquired herd of cattle. Seamus, Uaithne and their entourage made merry whilst Óisin made himself scarce. He wished to avoid Seamus's wrath for at least another day, hoping that it would have either cooled or that he became otherwise distracted.

A terrible guilt over came Óisin, for he feared Caoimhe had suffered because of his negligence and that if he had listened to her and her suggestions for work in the fields and in the house, Seamus would not have been so angry upon his return. He paced the outskirts of the farm, avoiding the fires of the men, deciding on the best way to unburden himself of some of his guilt. He also wished to find out whether in the eviction of Caoimhe's possessions the guilty pleasures he took in her dresses and perfumes had been destroyed in the mud. Her beauty was his winter star. His stomach tightened, his hands shook, and he took in several heavy breaths as he worked up the nerve to check on Caoimhe.

Óisin took a torch from one fire and made his way to the pig pens at the back of the house. It was a sturdy construction with stone walls, a lockable door, and a roof overhead. The pigs were quiet, and a guard stood by the doorway.

"Seamus sent me to check up on her and to get you to take a rest," said Óisin.

The guard summoned up the most nonchalant authority he could muster.

"He told me specifically not to move," he said.

"And now he has calmed down and told me different. You know how his mood changes."

"Aye, that I do."

"They have some spare meat on the fire over there," said Óisin.

He pointed to a fire near the house, some distance away.

"God bless you," the guard said.

He made his way towards the fire.

Óisin's stomach wrenched again as he worked up the nerve to face Caoimhe. He placed his hand on the latch of the door and took a sharp intake of breath to steady his nerves. Óisin lifted the latch. He opened the door and shoved his torch inside.

"Caoimhe, are you there?" he called out into the darkness.

Caoimhe ran from one of the dark corners and embraced him.

"Oh my Galloglass, you have come for me!"

She trembled in Óisin's arms. She may have been covered in mud and stinking like her new housemates, but something triggered inside of Óisin.

"How could he have done this to me?"

The tears washed a small stream through the mud.

"We must get you out of here. Where is Lasair?"

"She has other pigs for company. They saved the dirtiest and most vicious for me."

"I cannot stand it. Such cruelty is undeserved."

"But what can you do about it? An entire army is camped on my father's lands."

"I can release you now and you can run into the woods and into the darkness. If you run in the right direction, then you will be in Enniskillen and with your uncle in a couple of days."

"What about you? When they find out that I escaped, surely they will blame you?"

"I can look after myself. I shall go back to the house, but leave the door off the latch. Shut it behind you and run before the guard returns. I will do the rest. Run towards the woods and I shall see you in Enniskillen one day."

Caoimhe looked at his chest.

"How can I ever thank you for such kindness?"

"Don't worry. I'll think of a way. Run as fast as you can."

Óisin closed the pen door behind himself and Caoimhe did not hear the latch click. She waited for several minutes and then crept towards the door. She gently pushed it so nobody outside would notice. He was true to his word. The door was unlocked. She pushed the door gently with the tips of her fingers. The house was illuminated by the fires of the rebels, and the men danced and sang to their successes in East Breifne. Óisin had disappeared. She looked behind her and the stars peered out from the clouds to show there was at least the distance of a field to cross before the relative darkness of the woods. She knew not what Seamus would do to her, nor if she would get her house back. A faint pang of appreciation for Óisin lodged in her heart. But she soon dismissed it as his action could be revenge for all the times she had humiliated him. He would tell Seamus and they would both hunt her down. She could also be torn apart by animals or raped and murdered by bandits in the woods. She could also be paraded around like a trophy by Seamus, or worse. Worse than getting torn apart by wolves. She ran. She ran towards the blackness of the woods as fast as her legs could carry her.

Óisin returned to the fires of his men and to his seat on the opposite side of the rim to where the smoke blew. He took his ale and his hunk of meat and ate in silence. His mind turned over every permutation of his escape plan, or lack of one. All it would take was for the guard to say that he had dismissed him and Seamus would blame him for her escape. He had thought with his groin rather than his brain. Óisin feared what may happen to him and devised a substitute plan for where there was none before. He noticed the guard had settled down and was making merry. Óisin waited for as long as he could, then he slipped back to the pig sheds.

He looked in Caoimhe's pen. It was empty. He took his torch and covered up her tracks towards the forest. He then went to the other sty.

"Lasair," he whispered.

"Óisin, is that you?"

"It is. I have come to set you free for the exemplary services you have done for your mistress," he said.

"Is this a trick? Are you here to lure me out and then beat me?"

"This is no trick. I am alone. Caoimhe waits for you in the woods. She has paid me well for this favour, if you must know. Run that way to Connor Roe. He will protect us for he wants Caoimhe to marry his other son."

"I suppose I have little choice but to trust you, for if I am caught I know who set me free."

"Don't get too clever for a maid. Get out of here now, before I change my mind."

Lasair stuck her head out of the door. The flames of the torch illuminated Óisin's grim face.

"There is no one here but me," Óisin said.

Lasair froze in the doorway.

"Are you here to rape me?"

"Only to save you. Now see those woods far in the distance?"

"Yes."

"Run towards them and keep running. Caoimhe will be there waiting for you. Now run before I change my mind."

Lasair ran into the dark. Her tears blinded her, and she fell. Óisin ran after her and picked her up.

"You need to run and keep your eyes open. If you fall again, we both could be dead."

Lasair looked pathetic as Óisin dragged her to her feet.

"Go."

He pushed her in the back, but not enough to knock her over. She stumbled and looked back at him, her face a mess of mud and tears. Óisin waved her away. He walked back towards the pen, scattering bones from the feast as he went. Óisin returned to the fires where his men sat. He saw the guard who he had dismissed from guarding the pens.

"Who told you to come up here? Who is guarding the prisoners? Seamus MacSheehy will kill you if the prisoners escape!"

The man dropped his ale and his food and picked up his sword and ran back towards the pens. Óisin leant over to one of his men.

"Follow him."

The guard went back and stood in front of the pens without checking who occupied them. Eventually, his bladder strain overcame him and he went to find a bush. Óisin's spy ran back to the campfire. Óisin and his men stormed down and in the guard's absence flung open Caoimhe's pen. The guard returned to a furious Óisin.

"Where is she? Where have you been?" Óisin said.

"I went for a piss! I was only gone for a minute. She could not have escaped in that time."

"Well, obviously she did! What about the other one?"

One man went and opened Lasair's former pen.

"It is empty too."

"Hold him, men. I don't know what I am going to tell Seamus. Fetch the dogs. We start the search tonight."

Óisin and his men reconvened at the pens about twenty minutes later. Óisin did not inform Seamus of his actions as he wished to deal with it himself. Soon a snarling pack of dogs got the scent of the meat and went off in pursuit, despite their handlers' protestations that the dogs should find the smell of the prisoners from the pens first. However, Óisin had a new occupant for the cells.

"The guard stays in there until we can think of a suitable punishment for his failures. Let him spend his time in there praying for Caoimhe's safe return."

The dogs were let off their leads and began their pursuit. The woods were filled with the barking of dogs, and pursuing men. Lasair made it to the woods across the meadows, but not without falling several times and leaving plenty of fresh scent for the dogs. The dogs picked this up and the men could hardly keep up as the dogs yanked at their leads. The night was dark and the woods darker still, with only periodic bursts of moonlight when the cloud cover permitted. Men stumbled over branches and fell and injured themselves, yet the chase continued.

The commotion in the woods soon drew the attention of Seamus and those cementing their new alliance on the grounds of O'Cassidy house. He did not accept the pleas of Óisin's men gathered around the pig pens who said their master was taking care of it. Seamus ordered some of his men to follow Óisin into the woods.

Meanwhile, several miles away, one of the dog handlers was calling to attract Óisin's attention.

"Look, fresh blood on this branch. She must be near and injured. We'll soon have her."

Óisin slipped his bow from his back, and put his hand into his quiver.

"You come with me. The rest stay here and wait for Seamus. I'll handle it."

The two men disappeared into the darkness with the dog.

The dog was an old reliable hunting dog, a favourite of Cormac O'Cassidy, who did not realise she was changing sides. Once she got a smell of her prey, they rarely got away. The dog stooped to sniff with more frequency.

"She must be hurt," said the dog handler of the pursued. "We'll soon catch her."

"Let us hurry. I don't want to fail in front of Seamus," said Óisin.

The handler urged the dog forward. They heard someone running in the woods, the exaggerated breaths of exhaustion, the moans of pain when an injured foot hit the ground, and the mumbled prayers for direction and escape. The dog rushed to engage her prey. She leapt through the bushes and snarled. Her teeth met flesh and bone and her claws tore at the body to injure and immobilise. The men juddered with the shrieks of pain. Dog and victim thrashed through the bushes as the dog's clenching teeth only deepened their grip no matter how much their victim struggled.

"We are about to be set upon!" cried Óisin.

He let loose his arrow into the bushes.

The commotion suddenly stopped. Then a low growl.

"Come here to me, girl," said the handler, delighted his dog had survived relatively unscathed.

He bent down and hugged his dog and was rewarded with dog slobber and blood all over his shirt.

"So who is in the bushes?" he said.

"Let me see. You stay here with your dog. We don't want her to finish her adversary off."

Óisin put his hand once more in his quiver and loaded his bow. He went back behind the bushes. Before him lay the quivering body of Lasair, mauled in hands, arms and face with an arrow in her chest.

"More's the pity you're still recognisable," and he dispatched his arrow into her face.

Óisin sent the man and his dog ahead and dragged the body of Lasair through the woods, face down so she would be difficult to identify. He met his men by the pigsties.

"Here, take her off my hands," he said as he released the ankles and let them drop in the mud. "Where is Seamus?"

"Up by the fire on the other side of the house. He was going to go after you but some men arrived and he took them to get something to eat."

"Then we will go to him. Take her with us. We need to show Seamus my prize."

They dragged the body around to the other side of the house. Seamus was there by the largest fire, holding court and laughing and joking with his new allies. Óisin ordered his men to drag the body before Seamus. Óisin stood behind them and then over the body as his men moved out of the way.

"I found the wife of Eunan O'Cassidy Maguire in the woods attempting to escape and liaise with the traitor Connor Roe. Unfortunately, she refused to surrender and became a victim of the dogs."

Seamus looked unmoved.

"Well, Eunan must have become far more of a ladies' man than I remember him," said Seamus.

Óisin looked first confused and then nervous.

"For Desmond here was making his way from Enniskillen and ran into a young lady who also claimed to be Eunan's wife and he kindly brought her home. Didn't you, Desmond?"

"I did," said Desmond.

He smirked as he helped himself to a leg of lamb.

"I look forward to asking her what she was doing wandering about in the woods late at night by herself. Why don't we ask her now?"

Seamus's men pushed forward Caoimhe, or a mud-covered, drenched version of Caoimhe with tears streaming down her face.

Óisin's heart sank.

CHAPTER EIGHTEEN

RETURN OF THE MASTER

MORNING BROKE, THE FIRES still burned, and those men with stamina and staying power still ate and drank. Caoimhe had been allowed to wash and change but had been reduced to a scullery maid, cleaning up after the men. Seamus had decided that it was the easiest way to watch her as she cleaned with two of his most diligent men, never letting her out of their sight. At least it was a promotion from the pigsty.

Lasair's body had been dragged away, for Seamus had more important things to do than dredge over Óisin's mistakes. Cormac was pressing him because he wanted to leave for Dungannon to attend to his brother's business. Now was no time for hangovers or regretting the deeds of the night before. Seamus got his men to ready Cormac O'Cassidy's meeting room and call the representatives of the heads of the clans to meet with him there. Desmond had told him he was here on urgent business concerning Eunan, but Seamus told him it would have to wait until the others left.

Desmond was sober, for he had endured a long ride and gone to bed soon after arriving. He was one of the first up and agreed to act as counsel for Seamus. Cormac MacBaron arrived next, and he was eager to leave. They waited for the contingent from down south whose youth had allowed them a greater indulgence than their elders.

They finally arrived and the embraces between those who waited and those who arrived were warm.

Cormac clasped hands with Uaithne.

"Cause chaos. The O'Neills will come down and join you soon. Drive them back to the Pale. We'll supply you with as many men and weapons as we can."

"Thank you, friend. We'll send the English settlers home."

Next Cormac went to say his goodbyes to Phelim O'Byrne.

"The O'Neills will also help you. Make as many of those English soldiers as possible chase you around the Wicklow mountains and we'll do the rest."

"My father has consistently rebelled for the longest time in Ireland. We'll just keep on as before."

"I'll send my agents so we can coordinate. But now I must leave. Seamus's deviousness has delayed me long enough."

Cormac turned to Seamus.

"Try to stay out of trouble and stay alive. The rebellion needs you. If you need any help, the O'Neill owes you. Keep training the Maguires and see you on the next battlefield."

Seamus embraced him.

"The Maguires are with you. I'll make sure of it. I give you my word the Maguires will not abandon the rebellion."

Cormac saluted them and went to join his men to leave for Dungannon.

Seamus turned to Uaithne and Phelim.

"When do you turn south?"

"By the day's end. We have much work to do."

"I may seek your protection on my journey, but must speak with Seamus first," said Desmond.

Seamus came across and nodded.

"Let me speak with Desmond first," he said, offering them the door.

As he watched them cross the courtyard, a horseman rode in, dismounted, and approached.

"I have an urgent message from the O'Donnell for Seamus MacSheehy and only for him."

"That is me," said Seamus.

He held his hand out to receive the letter, broke the seal of the O'Donnell and read the contents.

"This changes everything," he said bitterly.

He stuffed the letter in his pocket, trying not to let its contents cloud his mind. Desmond still sat perched on the edge of his seat in the hall, eager for Seamus's attention.

"It's Eunan," Desmond said.

"It always is. What has he got himself into now? I have heard vague rumours from Enniskillen, but nothing confirmed."

"The Maguire has arrested him for usurping Cormac O'Cassidy, and being implicated in his disappearance and the deaths of his son and the son of Connor Roe."

Seamus laughed.

"I'll say one thing for Donnacha and that is, he sure can spin a lie."

"Why do you say that?"

"We left O'Cassidy on the road to Dublin, penniless but very much alive. Eunan developed too much of a soft spot for Caoimhe, so we left both of them alive. I then let him marry Caoimhe, for I thought it might have done the boy some good. Now I fear I have made a grave mistake."

"You can still make up for that mistake. Eunan is still very much alive and is in the Maguire's custody on Devenish Island awaiting trial. I am going south to hire a Brehon. English spies overrun Enniskillen and are trying to influence the Maguire to either hang Eunan or hand him over to the English. The trial will be a battle for Fermanagh's soul."

Seamus looked directly at Desmond.

"That battle will not involve me."

"You cannot abandon your nephew now. I know he is less than perfect. But we are so near to achieving our aim."

"The O'Donnell has summoned me. I cannot decline his call if we are to continue to build our influence. However, if we are to keep all of our gains in south Fermanagh, pending the trial of course, then I need someone reliable to watch over it for me."

"What about who you have now?"

"Óisin is a liar and a fool, and a lazy fool at that. I need to find out why he thinks dragging a disfigured body before me is supposed to impress me. There is some mischief there which I intend to find out. I had a man sent with Eunan by the name of Sean O'Toole. Do you know his whereabouts?"

"At a guess, in the river Erne. Eunan was the only one of his party taken alive."

Seamus paused and looked at the ceiling.

"He was a good man, reliable too. I need to be gone by the end of the day so I have little time to make appointments and leave instructions."

"I also need to leave today and if I had an escort south, my mission would be more likely to succeed."

"What do you set out to do? Fermanagh, the Maguire all need you. You have a rare combination in these parts of military prowess, sense, and no anchor to the past."

"And what is it that drives you, Seamus MacSheehy? Once a bandit in the woods, then protector of your nephew and now a leader in the rebellion. What are you here to do?"

Seamus looked at him and tried to figure out where this question was coming from. Desmond did not flinch, nor did he look angry or aggressive. Seamus decided he genuinely wanted to know and did not wish to use an emotional response as a tool against him.

"I think you have the best interests of my nephew at heart, so I will answer you truly. All Galloglass, at least the ones that survive to a ripe old age, are brutal men. You know that. You led the Galloglass of the Maguire. My nephew is weak. He lacks the inner resolve in his soul to be a proper Galloglass. Serving a master as a true Galloglass is a brutal business. War is coming, one that will change everything. I wish to end up in Munster and re-establish the great MacSheehy Galloglass once more. Those who survive are bandits or the most cutthroat of mercenaries, if you could be bothered to tell the difference between them. At the end of the day, this trial that he is up for matters little as long as he survives. The O'Donnell would not recall me if there was not something tumultuous going on. Eunan needs to survive that. I can create the power for him to become a great lord in Fermanagh, maybe even one day the Maguire himself, but he needs to have the inner strength to grasp the opportunity. You need to be his wise counsel and ensure that he can take the opportunity when it comes."

"This trial will be the making or death of Eunan. I aim to ensure it is the making. He currently resides on Devenish Island, having been freed from the Enniskillen castle jail where Donnacha was trying to kill him through neglect. Your wife and Cúchonnacht Óg tend to him."

"Thank you at least for all you have done for Dervella, for my feelings for her are true and not confused as they are for the boy. I will speak to Uaithne and arrange your passage and protection. When I reach the house of the O'Donnell, I'll dispatch some men for Eunan's protection. It is a pity I didn't know about this sooner."

"Donnacha is a cunning adversary. I came as soon as it was safe to do so."

"Wait here. I will arrange your passage."

Seamus went and fetched Uaithne, and as they came back into the room he grabbed Uaithne's shoulders from behind and shook him as if he were a proud father.

"Uaithne is the greatest rebel in all of Leinster and the greatest raider," he said.

He released the young man and stood in front of him.

"I have a mission for you of vital importance to both me personally and the rebellion."

"I owe you my life, and my life is for my clan. Name it," said Uaithne.

"Take this man to where he wants to go and escort him back again to Fermanagh. Don't press him on his business, but trust me."

"Of course. I shall treat him as if he were you."

"Good," and Seamus slapped him roundly on the shoulders. "He knows a thing or two of battle and war, even though he looks a little too round and overfond of the mead. He was a great warrior once until time robbed him of his youth."

"That's a little too much of the knocking me there, Seamus. I still have a useful place in the world," said Desmond.

"I will look after you as if you were my father, the great Rory O'More."

Desmond beamed from ear to ear.

"I knew your father. I met him in the court of the Maguire many times. He was a great man and is sadly missed by all of those who have dedicated their lives to ridding us of the English."

Uaithne ran over and embraced Desmond.

"Let us get our horses and depart south. It is best to start our ride in friendly parts whilst there is still light."

Now all Seamus had to do was sort the arrangements of who would manage O'Cassidy house while he was gone. He went out into the yard and watched Uaithne, Phelim and Desmond ride off. His optimism drained away. All he was left with was unreliable O'Cassidys and Maguires, Óisin and Caoimhe. He briefly contemplated a heroic mission to set Eunan free, but quickly deduced that Fermanagh was a tinderbox and it would not take much to start a civil war. He had to leave quickly, and it looked like Óisin was it.

Seamus packed his bag with as many clean clothes as he could gather, which was not much. He added to the bags the papers he thought the O'Donnell may find of interest and inspected the freshly polished weapons left by his horse boy.

There was a gentle knock on the door. A meek Óisin entered when summoned.

"You called?"

"Sit."

Seamus pointed to a chair underneath the window. The shadows played with Óisin's long dirty hair, and Seamus could smell him from where he stood.

"You'll never impress her stinking like that," said Seamus.

"Impress who? All I want to do is impress you with how well I keep the house in your absence."

"What do you think she sees in a man like you? A naive fool who she can manipulate into helping her escape. Then if you meet your death by my axe or that of Connor Roe, she does not care. She would not give you a second thought. It would have been far better to kill the both of them and suffer the consequences than to have this hanging over us. Do you think what you did yesterday in any way fooled me? How many times do you think my men bring me a dishevelled body hoping to claim a reward? How many times do you think I pay? If I find proof you have been in league with her, I'll hang you from the oak tree and her alongside you. That is the only romantic moment you'll ever get with her."

Óisin took a sharp intake of breath.

"I am only here to serve Eunan and yourself. She escaped, and I imprisoned the guard responsible. It was a dark night in the woods and I killed her maid by mistake. You can trust me, I won't let you down."

"You had better not, for against my better judgement, I am going to give you a second chance. I need to go to Tirconnell and will return with a powerful force. Don't make me turn it upon you."

"You will have no cause to be unhappy with me."

"Glad to hear it. Now restore this house to its former glory. We will need food for the people this spring or they will all up and leave. Don't think I won't be watching you, for I will be."

"I won't fail you."

"Good. Go start your chores for I leave today."

Óisin shut the door behind him.

Seamus's horse boy brought his horse into the middle of the yard. Seamus had selected ten of the most trustworthy of the Maguire men to be his escort. He also brought with him Arlo, even though he was the Maguire's man.

"There'll be plenty of men for you to train there," Seamus told him.

"I have a bargain with Eunan for my freedom. I gave you these men and in return he promised me freedom."

"I am not Eunan," replied Seamus.

"You may not be, but underneath the facade you are an honourable military man, a true and proud Galloglass. I have served you well and you should honour the bargain, albeit the one agreed by your nephew."

"If you give me good cause, the bargain will be kept. Now go prepare your horse. I have no time to bicker with you all day."

Taighe Maguire sat to the side of the yard, a little surprised yet relieved that he was not asked to go to Tirconnell. But he got nervous when Seamus strode up to him.

"Come here."

Seamus took him aside, out of the visual and hearing range of the others in the yard.

"Be my eyes and ears here. If you spot anything that you think I would need to know about, send word to the court of the O'Donnell."

"Like what?"

"Like Óisin. Watch Óisin."

Taighe nodded, unhappy at his new role as a spy. But Seamus was already on his horse and on his way to Tirconnell.

CHAPTER NINETEEN

THE DIRT OF THE ROAD

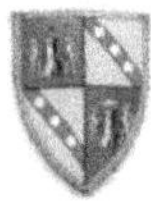

"BE QUIET BACK THERE. We'll be there soon."

Barnard Plunkett was taking no chances. He had a cart full of grain and other goods, and a horse boy to tend to the horses and carry out any other dirty tasks he may have. Completing the party was a young woman called Maeve, who sat hidden in the covered wagon and complained and cursed every time the wheels of the cart jolted over a rock or uneven ground.

Spilled out was the best way to describe Maeve. Her curves and bosoms spilled out of her ill-fitting dress, her auburn hair spilled out from under her winter hat, and curses and joviality spilled out of her mouth.

Barnard could not have been more the opposite. His tunic was a vibrant green with pantaloons and a hat to match, the green only broken up by a red feather sticking out of the top. All well-fitting and neatly tucked in. He would have looked quite dapper on the streets of Dublin, but such attire only made him stick out in the hinterlands. His patchy ginger beard gave away his youth and even he was savvy enough to keep the cross of the Queen's own church hidden in his pocket.

His father had been keen for him to take advantage of the opportunities available in Dublin port, so much so that they turned their back on the Pope and switched to the new Protestant religion. This earned him entrance into the merchants guild even though it was not a profession previously practised by his family. When his father met a man in the merchants guild called Cormac O'Cassidy, who was willing to give young men outside of his own family a chance in the trade, he was signed up.

His first job as a 'grey man', those who travelled the dusty roads of inner Ireland to set up trade with the clans outside the Pale, was to visit a relative of his master and trade with them. He had travelled not even a hundred miles and was yet to be greyed by any dust from the road, for the bitter winter weather had given nothing but rain. But the slightly older but vastly more experienced woman he had in the back of his covered cart disturbed his conscience. He prayed he could resist temptation and return wholesomely to his new bride waiting for him back in Dublin.

"These ears are blessed by the sweet prayers to the Lord, but condemned to hell by your foul mouth. I know not why you are here, but the coin in my pocket has quelled my curiosity if it has not slightly dimmed my soul. If you are quiet, we may just get through this with your virginity intact and my cart still full when we get to our destination."

"Virginity! Ha! You spend way too much time in that church of yours. It doesn't make you pious enough to want to go out and earn a bit of coin."

Such boisterous mockery of virginity and the church sent a shiver down Barnard's spine. He prayed this endeavour would not be too taxing on his soul.

"Our endeavours to make the world a better place and to enhance our own lives are looked on favourably by God. This wagon will feed both the wild Irish in the interior and enrich my own life back in the Pale."

"Where did they get you from at all? You'd better leave the talking to me or the 'wild Irish' will cut you in two."

"I have a mission to complete given to me by my master. I have fended off the rabble of the roads and could have easily discharged the goods under my control for a lesser sum than my master has shown is the market price, and returned safely back to Dublin and been in the arms of my beloved. But I did not. I have been faithful to the trust my master has placed in me. Now, according to his crude maps, we should nearly be upon our destination. Then you can do what you wish, be that perform your duties or run into the wilderness, for I do not care. I will be on the road back to Dublin and away from this forsaken place."

"You had better get used to this if it is your destiny to be a merchant. It is not all sitting at home counting your money and admiring your wife in her lovely dresses. It is hard graft, striking a bargain and then selling those goods on to willing buyers for more. If you survive this trip, it will be an excellent lesson for you."

Barnard gripped the cross in his pocket so hard it made an indent in his hand.

"I think we are here," said Barnard.

Maeve came and stuck her head out of the covered cart.

"It doesn't look like much," said Maeve. "It may well have been a while since your master was here."

"He is not prone to lying," said Barnard.

"I thought you were naive, love, but not that naive."

Barnard cringed as her voluminous bosoms rubbed against his shoulder. He would have to say extra prayers tonight.

Their horses dragged them up the dirt road to the house. The house did not have the benefit of the sunshine of spring, the calling of birds or the sprouting of flowers. It seemed stuck in a perpetual winter, daubed in grey, with black scars, reminding everyone of her battle for survival. The fields were full of puddles surrounded by weeds. The cattle and pigs roamed freely, as if they were the true masters of the land. It did not seem like the destination for a man of commerce who wanted to be on the up.

"Look, try them over there. They might help you fulfil this mission of yours," said Maeve.

She pointed to a man who seemed to be struggling to revive some farm equipment and his wife standing over his shoulder, berating him for his laziness. They appeared rather ill-favoured, dressed in peasant clothes and definitely losing the battle to stay clean in the winter mud. The woman wore a beige tunic with once flowing hair now dirtied and rammed beneath a stained white cap. Barnard directed his horses towards the couple, for there seemed no other destination. He pulled up his cart beside them.

"Excuse me. I'm looking for the master of the house?"

"That would be me."

Óisin put down the broken plough and stood in front of Barnard with his legs apart, firmly rooted into the ground the way he thought the master of the house should meet a stranger.

"Master fool, more like! No one has done more to bring this house to destruction. Not even my brother or my husband!"

Barnard gulped for he lost his nerve a little in the face of the two strangers' aggression towards each other.

"I...I am a travelling merchant. Maybe I have something you may wish to purchase, maybe something to make your wife or lady friend happy once more?"

"The only worse husband I could have than him is my current one! I would happily trade this knave for whatever you could give me."

"Be quiet, woman, and let me think. What do you have for sale?"

"Grain, foodstuffs, cloths. If you have a steady line of payment, be that barter, cattle, or coin, we could supply you with whatever you could wish for from a merchant."

Óisin climbed onto the driver's seat of the cart and scanned the goods within. He nodded to himself in approval.

"How did you know to come here?"

"My master gave me this address."

Caoimhe took hold of Barnard's arm and steered him to the other side of the cart. Maeve thought that this may have some significance to her, so she stood in front of Óisin and distracted him. Caoimhe looked over Barnard's shoulder to see if anyone else was listening.

"Who is your master?"

A fit of nerves seized Barnard, for he felt he may have unwittingly found himself in a hole not of his own creation.

"It is Cormac O'Cassidy, Miss. I barely know the fellow, but from what little I do, he is a man of excellent reputation."

"Did you bring anything for me?"

Barnard took a step back and stared at Caoimhe.

"I have only what is in the back of my cart. Is this a robbery? Do I have to plead for my life? I have barely a few coins in my pocket but would trade the consequences of losing the cart in return for my life."

Caoimhe laughed.

"I'm not here to kill you. I am his daughter."

"Oh, oh, that is a different matter. He asked me to take a passenger with me and didn't tell me why. He just promised me a few extra coins. I was more hoping for a bodyguard for it is dangerous in these parts."

Caoimhe became a bundle of warmth and smiles at the mention of her father.

"Take your cart to the house. You will be reimbursed for all your goods, and be given an order list and an escort back to the Pale. I can see you becoming a rich man soon with such a lucrative trade route."

It was Barnard's turn to smile.

"Oh, thank you. I knew my luck had changed when I met Mr O'Cassidy."

"Indeed, it has. Now go to your cart and get my man to unload it into our stores. Then present me with an inventory and a bill. Let my man check it. In the meantime, I will get to know the passenger you brought here."

Caoimhe led Maeve upstairs into the house to her room. Once Seamus departed, she had straight away got on Óisin's back to have herself restored to her room and had begun slowly to get it back to how she liked it. Most of her jewellery and other valuables had been stolen. Those items of sentimental value that only she would hold to her heart to remind her of glory days past or of her father had been cast out of the window of the room and either trampled into the mud or thrown into a fire. However, her determination to restore the fortunes of herself and her father had only increased.

"When was the fire in the house?" said Maeve as she steered a course up the centre of the stairs. "I can still smell the smoke from the drapes and I've got charcoal stains from the scars on the walls."

"A long time ago now. Laziness afflicts the man who has been left in charge. If my father was here, he would have had him flogged," said Caoimhe. "Here, that door on the right. A ruin or not, I know this house like the back of my hand. We can talk in here without fear of being overheard or disturbed."

Caoimhe invited her in. It was now a sparse room with a blanket for a curtain, a bed worn and battered, a blanket that matched the bed but was an insult to the occupant, and a couple of stools.

"Sit. They have made my once beautiful home into an army camp. Men come and strip the house of anything they can burn to keep themselves warm in this desolate winter. Anything of value that could be slipped into a pocket has found its way to the surrounding villages to be traded for food. And this was once the finest house in south Fermanagh, third only to the two main clan houses, so my father used to say."

Maeve looked around and said nothing. Caoimhe sat down in front of her.

"Don't look at me like that. Don't feel pity for me. Even though my maid was brutally murdered by the man who imprisons me, in an act that he thought would impress me as it allowed me to get recaptured by someone else. I am going to stay here and get my revenge on every one of them who did this to me."

Maeve reached across and touched her knee, hoping that her touch would console her.

"Your father sent me. Well, friends of your father, but we'll get to that. He lives so well in Dublin. He prospers and has many powerful friends. If you wish to leave but cannot, he can send men to rescue you. You could live like a rich lady in Dublin town, far better than you do here, and put all the past behind you."

"The girl he wished to marry off may have taken you up on such a kind offer, but alas, the woman you see before you does not. The O'Cassidys will be restored and I am staying right here to do just that."

Maeve sat back to take the measure of the woman sitting before her.

"These men who hold you captive, they are rebels, yes?"

"They are."

"Do you hold any sympathy for them?"

"I would see them all strung up on the remaining trees in my once plentiful orchards."

"And the Maguire?"

"Connor Roe is the true Maguire."

"What of the Crown?"

"If my father has joined sides with the Crown, I would gladly join him and rid the world of these despotic rebels."

Maeve smiled.

"Then I think we are both of the same ilk."

Maeve reached into a pocket, pulled out a letter, and handed it to Caoimhe.

"It is from your father and only to be given specifically to you."

Maeve folded her hands on her lap as she waited but Caoimhe only dropped the letter and fought the tears in her eyes, not because she did not want to look weak in front of Maeve but because to get through all of this, she would need a hard heart.

"I can do this, if not for me then for my father."

"That is good," said Maeve.

She reached out to touch Caoimhe's knee again as if that was a source of reassurance to her.

"A Captain Williamson sent me here to act as his eyes and ears to work out a way to restore your father and make Connor Roe the Maguire."

"Tell me what I need to do."

"Not a word of this to Barnard. He does not know who I really am and why I am here."

Caoimhe and Maeve returned to the yard as the last of the cart was unloaded. Barnard looked a little unsettled.

"Now that you have taken all of my goods, it is time to arrange for payment. What form of payment do you suggest?"

Óisin's eyes brightened, and he turned and went towards the shed. Caoimhe stepped in.

"I suggest we open a line of credit until the spring when we will repay our debts in full. I have written a letter for your master and a list of goods we need on your next trip. Don't worry, young man. As I said previously, this route will be your most lucrative."

Óisin dropped the axe he had retrieved behind him and went to intercept the letter before Caoimhe could hand it to Barnard.

"Take it. Inspect it. Then hand it to the merchant," said Caoimhe.

She thrust the letter in Óisin's direction. Óisin blushed and declined the offer.

"Then it is done. Read the letter, merchant, and then tell me if your master will accept it."

Barnard hurriedly read the letter, for he had noticed the axe fall to the ground.

"Oh yes Miss, this is most acceptable."

Barnard mounted his empty cart, for he wished to set off back to Dublin as soon as they released him.

"Maeve, are you coming?" he said.

"I have made a bargain with her as well. She is staying with me to be my new maid. My last one died under mysterious circumstances," said Caoimhe.

Óisin shied away from her bitter stare.

"I will take it you agree, Óisin. Now goodbye, dear merchant, and come back to me in a few weeks with a full cart and my list fulfilled."

Barnard saluted her as he turned the cart and whipped hard on the reins.

CHAPTER TWENTY

KEEP IT IN THE FAMILY

DESMOND RODE WITH UAITHNE and his men day and night through Leinster, only slowing to avoid English patrols, armed gangs of English settlers, and to say goodbye to Phelim and the men of Wicklow when they set off for home. The land was in pain, fires proliferated, and Uaithne could point out the English settlements by following the smoke. Uaithne agreed to take Desmond to the castle, wait for him, and then take him back to Enniskillen, for he knew how important the mission was to Seamus and his men could continue the raids without him.

Uaithne noticed how uncomfortable Desmond looked on the back of his horse. He had to ride the English way with stirrups so that he could balance himself properly when his horse picked up speed and had to bear his considerable weight. Desmond frequently looked red-faced and huffed and puffed on the back of his horse as if he was doing most of the work. Yet he declined all offers of help, no matter how subtle, so Uaithne thought of excuses to decrease the pace or have a rest when Desmond looked most stressed. The last thing Uaithne wanted to do was carry the old man's dead body on the back of a horse all the way north to Seamus.

They stopped on a hill just before they crossed into Munster to note where they were. Desmond sat on a rock and gladly drank as much water as he could without making it obvious he was also trying to smooth his saddle sores with his spare hand. But he could get little past Uaithne.

"Not far to go now," Uaithne said. "Just beyond this hill are the lands of the Earl of Ormond. Fiach MacHugh O'Byrne has asked us not to raid their lands as he is trying to prise away the young lords of their clan with a grudge to bear of oversized unmatched ambitions. We have no fear in riding there but do not want to bring about a war that we are not yet ready for."

"Have no fear, do nothing aggressive, and leave the talking to me," said Desmond. "All the clans of Ireland visit to access the knowledge of the MacAodhagáins and the Earl is wise enough to deduct some of the Brehon's fee as his rent. As long as they think there is some juicy legal dispute, they will probably escort us there themselves."

"Can you prove this if we are stopped?"

"I have been there many times, but not for years. The senior MacAodhagáins will know who I am, but wonder why I bypassed their cousins in Connacht and came all the way down here."

"Why did you?"

"Because I have little chance of winning without their help."

They saddled up again and Desmond had to be helped onto the back of his horse.

"Are you going to make it to the castle?" said Uaithne.

"I have to, for all our sakes."

They rode on unhindered for the rest of the afternoon.

They came upon the castle and the guard let them through when Desmond explained he had business with the Brehons. The castle was a prodigious square tower amidst fertile fields, rolling hills, and dense forests. The reputation of the MacAodhagáins, the wealth they had gained as the premier Brehon family in Ireland, only added to the awe of the onlookers. They even had the money to hire the finest MacSweeney Galloglass of the Munster branch of the clan, formidable enough to rival the best men of the Earl of Ormond. But whilst the fields were tilled and productive, it was through their creation and administration of Brehon law and their law school that they made their money.

Having been taken to the main gate of the castle, the visiting party were relieved of their horses and gave their weapons in for safekeeping. The chief steward, who was in charge of the vetting of potential future clients, came out to greet them. His clean red tunic and pantaloons and aloof air only enforced the impression of his masters' wealth. A young note keeper and two bodyguards trailed behind him. He looked nonchalantly at the group of newcomers and dismissed the hungry youthful faces of the majority to settle on the rounded red-cheeked and wheezing face of Desmond.

"And you are?"

"Desmond MacCabe."

"Are you Galloglass?"

"In my better-looking youth."

"And which clan are you from?"

"The Maguire."

"Why have you travelled all of this way when the MacAodhagáins are employed by the Earl of Clanricard? Surely they can resolve your issue?"

"The other side has hired them. The only way you can beat a MacAodhagáin is to hire a MacAodhagáin."

"A very interesting play on words. I shall have to run it past our bards when I have a moment to myself. What is your dispute about?"

"Traitors!" said Uaithne.

"Excuse him, please. Land and succession dispute."

"What is the value of the dispute? In cattle would be the easiest way to quantify it."

"Say eight hundred?"

"To settle a dispute of the nature you imply against a Brehon of the calibre you suggest, it may not be worth our while. It is a long and arduous journey with a herd of cattle of that size and Leinster in flames."

"The outcome of the trial is worth far more than the monetary value that you can assign to it. The repercussions in Fermanagh and indeed the north would be huge."

"Is the man on trial a relative of yours by chance? To make such bloated claims would require evidence. However, we have some aspiring Brehons coming through our school who may deem it a worthwhile risk to take if it meant making a name for themselves."

Desmond saw he was getting nowhere with the gatekeeper.

"I suppose they will if they could get one over on Conchobar MacAodhagáin."

The chief steward's eyes lit up.

"That is a most interesting case you have indeed. There has been a schism in the family as to the development of the law that my master has been most enthused to resolve, and you may have just provided him with the opportunity. Now, I cannot let this rabble into the keep. Select yourself a bodyguard and your men will be treated well whilst they wait for you."

Desmond knew that for all his martial prowess, Uaithne needed to develop some political cunning.

"He'll come with me," said Desmond.

He hooked his arm around Uaithne's shoulders and invited him to enter the castle before him. Uaithne looked around him, a little unsure.

"Sorry, no weapons," said the chief steward.

Uaithne looked back to see if his men were all right, but they were already being escorted away.

The chief steward led them up the back stairs, but also gave them a brief tour as they climbed. They reached the first floor, and the steward nodded to the guard in front of the large oak doors. The guard obliged by opening the door so they could look inside.

They saw two men debating whilst a younger man of about thirty sat in a chair and listened, surrounded by scribes. A more senior man was seated to the right, observing all before him.

"Here we have our young Brehons hearing their first disputes. Normally covering land or theft. We allow the residents of the lands of the Earl of Ormond use of our hearings for a minimal fee as part of our agreement with the Earl and to give our newly qualified Brehons some practice."

Desmond nodded in appreciation. The steward ushered them up the stairs. They came to the next level and again, a nod opened the door. Before them were rows of tables with young men of Uaithne's age or younger copying out the pages of books.

"In here we have the bright young men of the land sent by their families for an education with the MacAodhagáin Brehons. They are copying the Brehon law books such as the Senchus Már and will return to their clans to serve as advisors or diplomats. The first part of their years of training is that they thoroughly familiarise themselves with the law, its rationale, and how the law is constructed. There is enormous prestige in being accepted into this school, as you well know, since you have travelled such a distance to avail yourself of our services."

"Very impressive," said Seamus.

He hoped a sufficient compliment would move them along. They reached the last floor, and the steward ushered them into a small room within the tower itself.

"I apologise for the size of the room, but I assume you wish to discuss your matters in private rather than in the great hall of the house? If you wait here, the Brehon will be with you in a few minutes."

Desmond thanked him and went and sat. The room was sparse with a table and a couple of chairs, two arrow slits and several tapestries dedicated to men of the past whose references Desmond and Uaithne did not understand. They waited patiently until someone arrived, but they brought only an apology and some food and mead.

Desmond paced the room.

"I'm thinking this was a waste of time and that we should have asked Seamus for a solution."

"You don't have the manpower for Seamus's solution," said Uaithne.

The door received a modest nudge, attracting their attention. It creaked open. An unassuming man, thin in body and hair, opened the door with his back, his arms were full of books and paper despite having two novices chasing after him to relieve him of some of his burdens.

"Leave me be, boys. Your time will come when we have to untangle the mystery on the other side of this door."

The door proved less resistant than the force applied. He stumbled into the room. Some of his papers tumbled to the floor and a scurry of youthful hands descended to return them to their owner. Having remembered he had guests, he raised his head from his papers to greet them.

"Good day to you. I am Cairbre Óg MacAodhagáin, one of the chief Brehons here. You may have heard of me and what you may think of me may depend on what side of my judgement you thought correct. But put that aside for now. That I am an Óg yet am old is only the first contradiction you will see."

Desmond stood, mouth agape. Cairbre was one of the most pre-eminent Brehons in all of Ireland. His judgements were legendary. He was the most sought after and expensive of all the Brehons. To prise him away from the business of the Earl of Ormond would be a feat. But why was he so interested in Eunan's case? Uaithne was less impressed. He saw another clumsy old man that he would have to smuggle across Leinster. At least compared to Desmond, there was less chance that he would keel over and die along the way. But the least he could do was offer to help.

"Would you like me to move the table over there so you can put your papers down?"

Cairbre bundled the papers up in his arms and ran across the room.

"No, no, you are our guests. I have boys to do these sorts of things."

Cairbre threw his papers onto the table and took the additional bundles from the boys. He shuffled the papers around for a few minutes, examining one or two and dismissing others. When he finally had them in an order only he understood, he popped his head up.

"Well? Tell me your story, then. Try to stick to facts, for if you want to get all emotional and maybe have a little cry, then I am not the man for you."

Desmond signalled for Uaithne to be quiet.

"It's not that kind of tale. We are like you, rational men of the law. That is why we have come to you."

"It is good that we can start from a basis of understanding. Now summarise your case for me and I will gestate it and come back and dive into the details."

"Let us sit for we may be some time discussing the complexities."

"My apologies. I am a terrible host lost in the excitement of a fresh case. Let us sit. Are you refreshed? Would you like any more food or drink?"

"We are gratefully full, but would appreciate it if you would see that our men are well attended to outside."

"Indeed. I have the opportunity to make up for my previous lapse."

Cairbre clicked his fingers, and one boy ran out of the room. His face shone in anticipation of a new legal dispute to untangle.

"A young man previously under my charge has usurped his uncle," said Desmond.

Cairbre smiled.

"I can go onto the roof and follow the smoke to see a young man that has usurped his uncle for whatever cause fits his purpose. It is an age run by the gun and the sword and the law will sit by the wayside until they are finished and then try to put the pieces back together. What is so special about yours for you to ride all the way down here to offer to pay my exorbitant fees?"

"I am sure you are familiar with the smouldering rebellion in the north?"

"The Crown has been trying to encroach on their lands for years."

"Fermanagh is divided into those who support the Maguire and those who support the pretender, Connor Roe and, by default, the Crown."

"I return once more to my rooftop and look out upon the ever-encroaching smoke."

"That ever-encroaching smoke is coming from Fermanagh. The boy's uncle was about to cement an alliance with Connor Roe, wherein half of Fermanagh would be for the Crown. His cousin is the Maguire's hand who is edging him into a deal with the English to side against the northern lords."

"This is serious."

"Very serious. If the rebels are defeated, then the Crown will do to Ulster what they did to Munster. But this time, they will complete the job and subjugate the lands completely."

"Which means?"

"We would all be Englishmen."

"What a dreadful thought. But we still prosper in Munster. The March law serves us well and there is still a call for Brehons."

"That is because there are borderlands between the two cultures. With no Gaelic culture there are no borderlands and therefore no need for Brehons or their laws."

Cairbre gulped.

"I'll pack my things."

CHAPTER TWENTY-ONE

AN UNEXPECTED REUNION

Eunan awoke and looked at the ceiling. It was familiar, but a distant familiar. As if he had to reach into the back of his brain and drag out the memory. His head throbbed. He felt as if he was in a cocoon of stiffness and pain. Eunan moved his eyes, for they would be the vanguard of returning movement to his body. He followed the shaft of light down the wall to a window. The window framed the light and gulped as much as it could of the light into the room. Eunan felt his nose tingle. It was a long time since he felt his nose properly, for he had spent many an hour in his prison cell praying that he did not have a nose and asking God to take his away. But now he was grateful for his nose and its ability to absorb and decipher the fragrances of the morning. The morning was certainly fresh, but also unfamiliar. But it was a sign. A sign that his senses were returning. A sign that he had woken up to a better morning than the ones that had surrounded him recently. He raised his head.

"Lie down again now. There's nothing to be concerned about."

The voice was familiar, as was the smile.

"Mother?"

His throat felt dry and sore, as if he had not used it in quite a while. It was a strangeness to feel his tongue in his mouth. He became more conscious of his surroundings. He did not know whether he had asked after his mother in his head or out loud. Eunan realised the stupidity of the word and the sentiment it brought once it had left his mouth. He had a mother not worthy of the name.

"There, there. You're lucky you're in good company, a young warrior calling out like that. But at least you're awake again."

He saw the outline of a kindly face and then blurring and then nothing.

"How is he?" said Cúchonnacht Óg.

The weather-beaten posts of the door framed his young, muscular build.

"He'll live," Dervella said. "I can't say he would have lived much longer if he had stayed in that jail. I can nurse him back to a reasonable level of health for the trial, but I would be loathed to do that if your brother is just going to hand him over to the English to be executed."

She mopped Eunan's brow. His face was a picture of illness, hers the epitome of concern.

"My brother will see Eunan all right, considering all that Eunan has done for him. Desmond will return with a solution."

The thought that his brother would cooperate with the English was irksome to Cúchonnacht Óg. He himself had not inherited his father's political skills nor his brother's foolhardy bravery, but he had the vision to see Donnacha knew how to corner him. He could see he was of no use in the house and went outside to inspect the guards. Six old MacCabe Galloglass had volunteered to help protect Eunan against any would-be assassins out of loyalty to Desmond, for they had served under him when he still served the Maguire. Donnacha seemed especially annoyed when Eunan was granted the privilege of awaiting his trial on Devenish Island, and he had posted men on the island especially to watch him. They also patrolled the waters around the house which was granted for Eunan's sole use as he waited.

The sun sank. The moon rose once more and then signed out for its daily leave of absence. Eunan regained consciousness again, but this time it was more sustained. He did not fall down into the emotional trap of calling for his mother, the helpless thoughts of a weak body and an uncontrolled mind. He awoke to a wet cloth lovingly administered to his forehead. The cooling droplets of water rolled down his face, soothing him.

"Dervella."

The sweet smile in return rejuvenated his heart.

"Be quiet, lad. We're so glad to have you awake again. A beastly fever afflicted you, picked up in that horrid jail. How could the

Maguire have turned on you like that after all you have done for him?"

"Where am I now? No, wait. Don't answer that."

He raised himself up on his elbows and looked around. He recognised the cracks on the wall, the missing bricks in the brickwork, the cut of the windows, the breeze that came in from both sides. When the Maguire was at his lowest, when most of his followers had deserted him, he sought sanctuary in this house. In this house he and the Maguire had planned their last stand. They had fought together one last time and were victorious. Hope surged through his veins, only to be suppressed by Dervella's hand on his chest. The softest of touches had him confined to his mattress again.

"There, there. Don't be getting over-excited. There'll be plenty of time for that later, but for now just concentrate on eating something. Do that first and the rest will follow. Here, open your mouth. I have prepared some soup for you. We'll start off slowly."

Several spoonfuls of soup had Eunan coughing and spluttering, and the next spoonfuls ended up all over his tunic.

"Maybe a little slower than that," said Dervella.

She cleaned him up and left him to rest.

A week later, Eunan was up and about and able to leave the house. Cúchonnacht Óg had returned to Enniskillen as he had business to attend to and he also needed to be in the capital in order to influence events as much as he could. Eunan was under strict instructions not to leave the island and to have a bodyguard with him at all times for fear of assassination. By this time he was bored and wanted, at the very least, to explore the island. Dervella agreed, for she knew she could not keep him prisoner, and he needed to regain his strength for the trial ahead. So he set out from the hidden house in the woods.

The islands had many uses for the Maguire and were a source of his enduring power. If you wanted to comprehensively defeat the Maguire, you had to clear out the islands, and to clear out the islands would take a considerable effort and the creation of a river fleet if you could not capture the Maguire's fleet intact. Therefore, the islands had many uses as safe havens for the

Maguire and one of those uses was for prisoners. Besides this, the Maguire had a long-standing arrangement with the O'Donnell that he could make use of the islands to confine his prisoners or those whom he was keeping for ransom. Therefore, dotted around the island were small houses containing the prisoners of the Maguire and the O'Donnell. Some were actual prison cells, while those captives they wanted to treat a little better or who were deemed to not be a threat were given freedom of the island.

Eunan decided he should rebuild his strength and took to running around the circumference of the island as much as the topography would allow. This meant that he could observe the island and see who his fellow residents were. At first, it was to see if any of Donnacha's agents had made it to the island, in case he might have to fend off any potential assassins. Eunan ran for a greater distance each morning. He finally persuaded Cúchonnacht Óg to let him run alone, as he could now make it as far as the modest quay where he had once landed when he arrived from Desmond's island. He went to the end of the pier, sat, and dangled his legs off the edge until the gentle waves splashed around his ankles.

"Hello."

Eunan turned, almost pulling a muscle in his back. Such a sweet voice tickled the hairs on his eardrums and it compelled him to find its owner. He lifted his feet out of the water and looked at the base of the pier. The sun shone out from behind a cloud, temporally blinding him. As he recovered he could make out a mop of black curls dancing on the wind, the curves of a female body and her green dress. He blinked to reset his eyes and when he opened them again she was there in front of him.

"Are you a prisoner too?" she said.

Where once there was a bragger and a swagger came a croak and timidity.

"I am," he said. "I don't know how long I've been here."

"From when I've seen you run across the island, at least a week."

"You've watched me run?"

Eunan automatically went for his side where his throwing axes should be. The girl laughed.

"Only out of boredom. Who are you that's so great they would think a young lady would come to the pier to kill him?"

Eunan did not know whether to answer, but a pretty smile always disarmed him.

"I'm Eunan Maguire."

She did not meet his name with murderous intent or the masked calculation of a bounty hunter, but with a bigger smile.

"Well then, Eunan Maguire, shall I see you here tomorrow?"

"Surely you shall," said Eunan.

However, he said it to the back of her dress and her black curly locks. A few random notes of an indiscernible song drifted in the air as she skipped away.

"What is your name?" he cried.

"Come back tomorrow and find out."

Eunan laughed to himself for the first time in a long time. His heart pounded in his chest and gave him renewed vigour in his legs.

He did not follow her or try to find out where she went, for he thought it better sport to find her the next day. He needed something to occupy the days. He finished his lap of the island and ran back to the house in the woods, then approached more stealthily when he heard raised voices. In front of the house Cúchonnacht Óg stood facing down six heavily armed Galloglass. The dirty chain mail gave away that they had just arrived from the mainland.

"Who are you? Who sent you? How do I know you are not assassins?"

The lead Galloglass laughed. It was a deep cynical laugh, one buried in the bloodshed of battle and the pleasures of brothels. He held his chain mail well on his bulky frame and even made the standard shoulder-high battle-axe of the Galloglass look small.

"Seamus MacSheehy sent us here to guard his nephew and we are going to do that so you'd be wise not to get in our way."

"Do you know who I am?"

The man dwarfed Cúchonnacht Óg, but Cúchonnacht Óg felt confident with his men behind him on their own turf.

"We don't want to fight you, little man, but will if we have to. Now, where is Eunan?"

"I have sworn to defend him by none other than Desmond MacCabe!"

Cúchonnacht Óg displayed some of the well-known Maguire foolhardiness and went for his sword. The visiting Galloglass took a step back into a defensive position. Eunan stepped out of the bushes and held out his hands between both parties.

"Lower your weapons. I am Eunan Maguire. I don't want anyone this day to die on this island, as beautiful as it may be, because of me."

"Let us see if we can live together and make both our masters happy," said the lead Galloglass.

He lowered his axe enough to show obedience to Eunan's plea, but high enough to respond if the other side did not reciprocate. A swirl of emotions overcame Cúchonnacht Óg. He had a burning desire to prove himself in battle, for he had just come of age where a Maguire prince was allowed to risk himself. But he decided that his first battle would not be today. He nodded to his men to lower their weapons.

"Who are you?" said Eunan.

He now stood between both parties and opposite the lead Galloglass.

"Faolán MacSheehy at your service."

He held out his hand, and Eunan met it.

"You bear the same surname as Seamus?"

"I am a son of Aonghus, one of the last great MacSheehy Galloglass, slain in the Desmond rebellion. Only a boy, I was too young to serve. I took to the hills and bogs of Connacht and formed a roaming band of Galloglass for hire waiting for the MacSheehy to reassert themselves and return to their homelands. Alas, they did not. But I heard of the exploits of Seamus and headed to Tirconnell to offer my services. He told me of you, of your heritage, and how you could help your clan. I immediately volunteered to protect you whilst Seamus arranges your release. So, here I am and to you I pledge my axe."

Faolán bowed his head and held his axe out with the palms of his hands and offered it to Eunan. Eunan bowed his head in acknowledgment. Faolán smiled and held his axe upright once more.

"With that settled, I suggest we all get to know each other and then me and the men can reconnoitre the island."

"I am surprised you made it this far because no armed men are allowed on the island without the express permission of the Maguire," said Cúchonnacht Óg.

Faolán smiled.

"We are very resourceful, the MacSheehy."

"What happens when my brother sends his men to the island?"

Cúchonnacht Óg's smile said he thought he had one over Faolán.

"Sure, with the amount of people roaming around this island, how are they going to know the difference? We'll just blend in."

Faolán moved his hand like a wave, and his men laughed.

"Your men can carry weapons and we'll join in when we are needed. Now, where can we set up camp? I saw a little harbour of rocks obscured by trees near here. Does anybody know the way?"

Eunan raised his hand with a smile.

"I do. I know this island like the back of my hand. I know what you're looking for."

"Well, isn't that great?"

He slapped Eunan on the back and they went off into the woods. Cúchonnacht Óg had a face on him like a lake storm. His big adventure had been whisked away from under him.

CHAPTER TWENTY-TWO

REALITY INTERVENES

F AOLÁN TOOK A BLADE to his face, such was his dedication to his new role, and committed order to his beard where there once was none. He had come to an accommodation with Cúchonnacht Óg, leaving the guarding to him and restoring some of his personal honour. He also became Eunan's personal bodyguard and friend and made it his project to restore Eunan to full fitness. They had both taken to completing laps of the island. It differed from the usual methods of Galloglass training, and they had to improvise because of the island's ban on weapons for its guests. Every day they ran, but Eunan did not set eyes on the girl from the pier. He normally set off at quite a pace, for he was competitive in everything he did, but especially with Faolán. They rounded the flat part of the island and Eunan turned and laughed, for he was at least ten paces ahead.

"Watch where you are going. Don't give me the chance to catch you," said Faolán.

But Eunan had visibly slowed. Faolán ran past him and made the rasping sound of an arrow in his ear to signify that he had made a mistake and was now dead, cut down by an archer. But he was far from dead, and very much alive.

"No wonder you wanted to run the same route every day," said Faolán.

The mystery girl from the pier had returned to the lakeside and even Faolán noticed as she washed clothes in the waters of the lake.

She caught Eunan looking at her and returned his gaze with a smile.

"Are you going to stop me?" said Eunan.

"I don't think I could, even if I wanted to," said Faolán.

He smiled as Eunan ran over to speak to her.

"Hello," he said.

His face was a swirl of red where exhaustion collided with embarrassment. She appeared far less concerned, the slight reddening of her cheeks more the result of the wind on the exposed island than the approach of a sweaty man.

"I haven't seen you here in a while," she said.

"Where have you been? I have looked for you."

"And why may that have been? I've been here all along. You mustn't be very good at searching."

More red was added to the flushing of Eunan's face.

"Where's that accent from? You're not from round here."

"Is anyone from round here? The island is being used as a jail for prisoners from all over Ireland."

"You know what I mean."

"South. I'm from down south. I don't know how familiar you are with down south, but that's where I'm from."

"So how did a girl from an unfamiliar place down south end up on a prison island up north?"

Her face bubbled with smiles.

"Well, that's for me to know and you to find out. Now get in the water there and help me load up this washing."

The light, multi-coloured clothes in the baskets, albeit worn and dirty, had turned into soggy beasts needing to be thrashed and wrung to relieve them of their watery burden before they could become usable attire once more. Eunan used the rocks as a base to beat them with.

"I hope you're good at sewing, for if you wreck my clothes, I'll expect you to repair them!"

"Sorry," said Eunan.

He observed how the young woman wrung the clothes.

"If you are not too busy washing this young lady's undergarments, we have to go," said Faolán. "It looks like there's a couple of boats heading to the island and that is always worth investigating."

Eunan stood there dumbstruck up to his knees in water, a soggy dress in his hand.

"Can you put my clothes in the basket on the shore, please?"

"Oh, right."

Eunan obeyed and then climbed out onto the bank. Faolán made pained gestures to him.

"Oh right. Good bye and see you tomorrow?" said Eunan.

"If you're lucky," she replied.

Eunan looked at Faolán to see frustration and spinning hands.

"What's... What's your name?"

She smiled

"Cara."

"Mine is -."

She smiled again.

"I know. Eunan."

"How?"

"You told me before."

Faolán waved at the wavering man.

"Come on, Eunan."

"Goodbye!"

Eunan ran after Faolán and tried to resist looking back at Cara, but could not.

They ran a couple of hundred yards and stood opposite the mouth of the Erne river as it led up from Enniskillen. A large boat with four sets of oars rowed at a steady pace towards the island. Behind it came several smaller ones.

"Are they in pursuit of that main boat?" said Faolán.

"It's hard to tell from here," said Eunan.

The breeze off the lake chilled them, but a cold sun shone in their faces. They shielded their eye Ógs and tried to make out what was happening on the water.

"Those tiny boats definitely look like they are closing in on the larger one. Are you expecting anyone?" said Faolán.

"Well, I am supposed to go on trial at some stage so I would have thought that Desmond would come back for me."

"We must assume it is him, then."

Eunan looked at the sky as if it were about to fall through.

"So what do we do?"

"I am faster. I will run back and get Cúchonnacht Óg. If they make it to the shore, he can drive off the Maguire men if they are to be driven off."

"Well, go then. Run like the wind."

Faolán took to his heels and ran towards the woods. Eunan stared out at the lake and willed the large boat onwards. A crowd gathered by the lake shore for the commotion attracted the attention of anyone who looked out onto the lake. The large boat dipped its oars in and out at a rhythmic pace. The smaller boats thrashed their oars into the waves as if to intimidate the larger one into stopping. But the steady rowing of the larger boat told and as hard as the smaller boats tried, the larger vessel pulled away. Eunan could make out the figures on it a little more clearly now. He recognised the chain mail of Galloglass but saw no Desmond.

"But he wouldn't be at the front of the boat. He is far too heavy for that. Nor would he be at the side, for he is too old to be an oarsman."

He tried to reassure himself. Then reassurance came. A wee warm hand slipped into his. Eunan looked down to his left.

"This is exciting, isn't it?"

Cara shrugged her shoulders and smiled sweetly at him. Eunan squeezed her hand and gave a prayer for Desmond.

"Are they coming for you?" said Cara.

"Not in the manner you think. I will stand trial and win because I am right and do my duty for the Maguire and he will see that and will come round to my side."

"Oh dear. I hope you're not going to die now? We could have had so much fun trapped here on this island. Surely most men die thinking they are in the right?"

"I'm not going to die, for my uncle is my guardian angel. He should really be my guardian devil for his behaviour, but I don't think such a thing exists."

"Many kinds of devil exist, more than you and I want to know," said Cara.

Eunan squeezed her hand until she smiled and then returned his gaze to the lake. The large boat had now left the smaller ones in her wake. Eunan smiled. Cara squeezed his hand.

"Look over there."

From both sides of the lake, more small boats appeared, all with armed men. They rowed parallel to the shore so they could prevent the larger boat from landing. The oarsmen of the large boat continued their rhythmic strokes but were no longer capable of speeding up, for the pursuit had worn them out. The guards of the Maguire now gathered on the shoreline.

"Let them land," said Eunan.

He grabbed the arm of one guard, only to receive the side of his shield in the face.

"Leave him alone, you monster," cried Cara.

She bent over to see if Eunan was all right. He patted her on the arm.

"He was only playing," Eunan said.

He lifted himself to his feet. The large boat came ever nearer. Bowmen on the shore loaded their bows.

"Stop in the name of the Maguire!"

The crowd froze. Cúchonnacht Óg forced himself to the front.

"I am the brother of the Maguire and I order you to stop! If any of those boats attack the larger boat, you are to fire upon them."

The men began to murmur, as if to verify who he was. Cara looked up at Eunan. Confidence rose roughshod over the pain of the squeeze of his hand.

"He is the brother of the Maguire and I swear I know who he is for I have known him since he was a boy."

Eunan went and stood beside Cúchonnacht Óg.

"Men, aim for just in front of that boat."

Cúchonnacht Óg pointed to the most aggressively positioned of the small boats. A volley of arrows made the oarsmen turn around. The large boat had safe passage to the shore.

The boat rowed at a steadier pace now, and the smaller boats withdrew. Eunan went down to the water's edge and stood in the gentle waves. Cara did not leave his side. He could now make out the men in the boat.

"Desmond!"

He called and waved until he got his attention. Desmond stood up in the boat but the unbalancing effect of his sudden movements forced him to sit down again. He smiled and waved at Eunan. The boat pulled up into the shallow water and Eunan joined in with the men who had jumped out of it to haul the vessel to the shore. Eunan then waded over to help Desmond off.

"You'd of got here a lot quicker if you'd gone on a diet," said Eunan.

"And it would have been a far more pleasant trip if Donnacha had not been tipped off as to our movements," said Desmond.

"Bring us to your dwelling, for we have much to discuss and little time in which to do it."

Eunan climbed back onto the shore and walked over to Cara.

"Unfortunately, duty calls me back. I will come and seek you out in a few days. But if you get lonely, come to the woods and ask for me."

"I may take you up on that offer."

She kissed him on the cheek and ran off into the crowd.

"Come on, lover boy," said Faolán.

Eunan took one last lingering look at Cara's back and went back to join the men. They set off for the woods at the north end of the island.

What had once been the Maguire's war room had now become Eunan's. The same dingy four walls within which the Maguire paced had now been made more homely by the efforts and at the direction of Dervella. There was now an abundance of seats and tables, created by bored men in a wood with ready access to axes. There were flowers and a varied diet of food (although a lot of fish) for all that lived in the vicinity, the unwitting beneficiaries of Eunan's rejuvenation. The men had even taken to bartering with the other residents of the island for different foodstuffs and blankets. However, with the new influx, they would be hard pressed for sleeping space.

While Desmond and Dervella caught up, Cairbre Óg MacAodhagáin commandeered the table space and instructed Desmond's men to reconfigure the room so they could hold their case meetings there. It was far too wet and windy to hold meetings outside that involved lots of paper. They sent Faolán out to the people they knew and trusted to arrange for accommodation for the new arrivals. Once Cairbre had everything prepared, he invited Desmond, Eunan, and his junior assistant in for a conference. Desmond's men formed a ring outside the house at a safe distance so no one could overhear what was being said.

The first thing Cairbre did was shake Eunan's hand.

"We have not been properly introduced. Desmond has hired me to represent you in interpreting the law."

Eunan scowled as he grew tired of this entire process.

"I prefer the interpretation of the axe."

Desmond gave him the look a father would give an ungrateful child.

"Seamus would be proud of your last statement, but even he has the guile to know when the law is more powerful than the axe," Desmond said. "Think of Cairbre here as a heroic Galloglass who has travelled across the land, especially to be your champion. He faces his own cousin to save you, just as Cúchonnacht Óg faces his own brother. Listen to Cairbre and do exactly what he says. The time for the axe will come if you survive this challenge."

Cairbre stepped in.

"Thank you Desmond, and yes, I will fight for you in the legal sense and yes, it will be the fight of my life, for yours."

Eunan smiled his apology.

"Sit now, young man, for I have plenty of questions to ask you. Some of these questions may seem obvious to you, and you may have been asked them many times before. But we need to test your story and see how the law would interpret your actions and where the flexibilities are. Now, who are the men you were alleged to have murdered?"

"No one was murdered. Anyone who died did so in the fair game of battle and most of those who died were traitors."

Cairbre looked a little annoyed.

"The cart is going before the horse here. I don't need the bravado, I need the facts. You leave the direction of the trial to me."

Desmond stepped in again.

"It is alleged that he killed his uncle to replace him as the O'Cassidy Maguire."

"And he lives? Where?"

"We left him on the road to the Pale. He was very much alive," said Eunan.

"So note this down, scribe. 'We must find'... What was his name?"

"Cormac O'Cassidy," said Desmond.

"Cormac O'Cassidy and note how he lives. It goes towards mitigation of compensation. If we can prove he still lives, it drastically reduces the honour price. If he prospers, well, we may just have found a chink in their armour."

"I can send spies to track him down," said Desmond.

"Good. My scribe will note down all the tasks and the time we have to perform them."

"That is probably not long."

"Then we must work faster. Eunan, why did you usurp your uncle?"

"Because he was a traitor and he was about to join with Connor Roe."

"Connor Roe is the leader of the English-supporting faction of the Crown?"

"Yes."

"Do you have any evidence?"

"His deeds and actions."

"You need to give me more with your answers, Eunan. I need to point at things and say 'this is irrefutable'."

"Everyone knows his loyalties. He does not hide it."

"So I am thinking at this stage that this whole thing may be more about politics than the law and this entire episode is being manipulated to gain revenge but primarily to advance a cause?"

"That would be how I would see it."

"That makes it difficult since I need to appeal to the Maguire. May I borrow some of your time tomorrow, Desmond, to go through the ins and outs of Maguire politics?"

"My favourite subject."

"Now, what is your uncle's connection to Connor Roe?"

"He wished to marry into Connor Roe's family."

"Not evidence. Surely this Connor Roe is a well-to-do gentleman and every family in Fermanagh would wish to marry into his?"

"Then they too would be traitors."

"I am not asking for your opinion but trying to gauge the standing of the parties."

"The English declared Connor Roe the sheriff of Fermanagh and he was that until the O'Neill subdued him."

"Ah, do you have any connections with the O'Neill?"

"His uncle Seamus does," Desmond said. "He is a very well connected man these days."

"Where is he?"

"Tirconnell. He is on the O'Donnell's business."

"We must speak to him. Is it possible?"

Desmond stroked his chin.

"Potentially, but I would say no. The O'Donnell summoned him on urgent business and that would normally mean some dirty work he cannot do himself. I could arrange for a messenger to go to the court and wait for him."

"If it cannot be, it cannot be. Scribe, note down for me to write to Seamus."

Cairbre circled the room.

"Now we must see what the other side will make their line of attack. If they have no witnesses, they will be on weak ground. Do you have spies in Enniskillen, Desmond?"

"I do, but Donnacha is a cunning enemy. It will be hard to penetrate his inner circle and he will also have the Maguire protected as well. I think the best line of attack would come through Seamus."

Inspiration struck Cairbre like a thunderbolt.

"Ah! I remember now. The Maguire is in negotiations with the English. What do you know of this?"

"Another of Donnacha's secrets. He has kept this from his allies, his nobles and his people."

"In his secrets, we will find his weakness. I suggest, Desmond, that you send out your spies. We will go to the scene of the crime, which I believe is the old house of the man usurped?"

"What do you hope to find there? The house was badly damaged by fire after the incident. I suggest you stay here and compile our defence."

"Thank you for your concern, but there are certain things I need to do myself. You go to Enniskillen and I will meet you back here in a couple of days. If neither comes back in a week, send out the search parties."

"There were a couple more of note that died," said Desmond.

"Who?" demanded Cairbre.

He seemed concerned as the complexities grew.

"The sons of Connor Roe and Cormac O'Cassidy."

Cairbre stroked his chin.

"We must include them in our investigations. We also need to ascertain what access to wealth Eunan has that cannot be attributed to the alleged crimes."

"That will be a swift investigation."

Cairbre frowned at Desmond's inappropriate smugness.

"That could be an issue. We may have to see what monies his uncle can lay his hands on then."

"Leave all that to me," said Desmond. "I know him best and how to deal with him."

They all shook hands in agreement. Everyone had a task but Eunan. But secretly he was glad. He could spend his time with Cara.

CHAPTER TWENTY-THREE

SPANISH SUN

THE SKY COULD NOT decide what to do. It swirled in a morning mist, the wisps of cloud lingering on the sphagnum, intimidating, warning of the dangers to all that trod there. It retreated to its upper reaches and became a blanket of grey clouds puffing and protruding onto one another, daring each to be the first to burst and disintegrate into drops of rainfall. Or would it be glorious grey, thin and scraping the roof of the sky, showing its magnificence to all who dwelt beneath. It could not decide, so it disintegrated into rain which drizzled downwards until it could decisively decide which way to turn.

Seamus rode once more into Donegal town, rain-soaked and windswept with his letter from the O'Donnell firmly in his pocket. The town seemed in the grip of much uncertainty and unrest, with bands of men, some armed, roaming around the streets. The MacSweeney Galloglass did their best to keep order, but with so many bored men with access to alcohol, there was only so much they could do without resorting to violence.

"These men need a war."

Seamus rode to Donegal castle. His letter got him straight inside and he was whisked off into a side room and told to wait. They gave him bread and ale but no word of when the O'Donnell would see him. When Seamus had finished his meal, he sat and admired the tapestries and tried to place the main characters and their dogs in the lineage of the O'Donnells as he knew it. It was difficult, for whomever the O'Donnells glorified on their walls depended on which of the houses was in power. He imagined they must have a large store room of tapestries or, at worst, if they burnt the tapestries of the previous house they must have a ready pool of talented weavers who would look through the history books and find the heroes of the newly elected faction to immortalise in thread. Eventually, the door opened, but it was not to let in the O'Donnell. Instead, Eoghan McToole O'Gallagher walked into the room. He looked tired and as if he had the weight of the world on his shoulders.

"Sorry if you were expecting the O'Donnell. He is off in Dungannon to see the O'Neill for a conference. The negotiations they are having with the English in Dundalk rumble on but the truce holds."

Seamus smiled and shook his hand.

"That's just the way he wants it, isn't it? Negotiate in Dundalk and place his own men in Connacht?"

O'Gallagher pulled up a seat. He meant business, and Seamus knew he wanted something. But here lay the opportunity for a bargain.

"The talks have become more serious now," O'Gallagher said. "O'Neill wants to get a settlement for the north but Red Hugh O'Donnell wants his gains and aspirations in Connacht recognised."

"What about the Spanish?"

"We have sent them many letters, so many that they should have received at least one of them. Our brethren in the Spanish court push our cause and keep on sending positive messages. However, the English are offering generous terms and our people suffer from the repeated famines. The pressure grows on the O'Neill and the O'Donnell to settle before the alliance fractures and the various clans come to their own individual settlements."

"The Maguire started his own negotiations with the English before last year was old."

"The O'Donnell knows."

Seamus laughed.

"That's because I told him the last time we met. See what an excellent servant I am to him?"

O'Gallagher ignored him to play down Seamus's value.

"He has his spies in Enniskillen who keep him abreast of what is going on."

"In every court in Ireland, I'd love to know who is a true patriot, who is there for the clan and not spying for someone else."

"Aye, trust is always in short supply. That is why we have men like you."

"What's that supposed to mean? I'm almost offended. I have always been loyal to the O'Donnell."

"I'm sorry, I misspoke. The O'Donnell employs you because you get things done and are not ideologically encumbered."

Seamus laughed again.

"There's a compliment in there somewhere. But soon I will have to ask my favour of the O'Donnell, which I hope you won't misconstrue as being 'ideologically encumbered'."

It was O'Gallagher's turn to laugh.

"What is it?"

"You're a wise man to ask first. My nephew is going to go on trial for usurping his treacherous uncle. He is a sacrificial lamb to the English law and I fear they will hand him over for execution as part of any settlement."

O'Gallagher looked out the window and mulled over the situation.

"I will raise it with the O'Donnell. The Maguire is our ally but is subservient to the O'Donnell. He should not negotiate a separate peace. We will have to act if the Maguire sides with the English."

Seamus leant forward.

"That is why my nephew is so important to the O'Donnell. Eunan is now in charge of south Fermanagh. We put in place a friendly chieftain in charge of the O'Reillys. The O'Rourkes are with us, as are the O'Mores. We now have a spine that goes through central Leinster, prime farmland. The only weak link all the way to Tirconnell is the Maguire. If he sides with the English, we may need to usurp him and put his brother Cúchonnacht Óg in command. He is a loyal man who realises the long shared history of the Maguires and the O'Donnell and can be trusted by the O'Donnell."

"Let us not get ahead of ourselves, however useful it may be to test out future scenarios. However, this is not why the O'Donnell brought you here."

Seamus sat back again.

"So tell me my mission?"

"Red Hugh is having trouble in Connacht. His choice for lower MacWilliam Burke has not gone down well with some clans."

Seamus shrugged his shoulders.

"There were far stronger candidates."

"All the same, you need to return there and convince them to join us."

"And if convincing doesn't work?"

"The O'Donnell does not want violence whilst he is still in negotiations."

Seamus smiled.

"A hard task as always."

"But one suitable for your skills."

"May I have some men to support me in my mission?"

"You may have your pick of the camps. I hear some good Munster men have come up to join us."

"I knew they'd see sense. Give me a couple of weeks to form a unit and I will venture down to Connacht."

O'Gallagher got to his feet.

"It is always good to see you."

He embraced Seamus.

"And you. Tell Red Hugh I would like to meet him in person on my next visit."

"I will pass the message along."

O'Gallagher made sure Seamus was given an escort to the camps.

Seamus met many a good Munster man in the camps who were willing to serve under his command. He took an instant liking to Faolán MacSheehy who, after a sound testing, was dispatched to guard Eunan. But he did not yet have a person he trusted enough with the right skills to replace Óisin. He feared it was folly to leave Óisin in charge of O'Cassidy house but felt he had little choice given the circumstances. He soon had a good band of loyal men and also set about once more training and organising the veterans from the continent that were in the camps. All seemed well with Seamus, despite the pressure from O'Gallagher to return to Connacht.

However, several days later, he received an urgent message to make all haste to Donegal castle. Seamus dropped everything and set out with two of his men. He thought that war may have come, be it invasion or civil. Both were equally likely. He reached the castle and was guided down corridors thick with tension.

They ushered him into a room where O'Gallagher stood with his foot on a chair, white as a sheet, his face a mixture of confusion and elation. At the back of the room Hugh Boye MacDavitt paced the floor, a whirlwind of excitement, shouting out his joy.

"What happened?" said Seamus.

He did not know who to direct his question to for fear of receiving different replies.

"The Spanish are here," said O'Gallagher.

His voice was but a croak.

"The Spanish are here!" said MacDavitt, and his elated screams reverberated around the room.

"Shut up! We don't want everyone to know. There are spies everywhere," said O'Gallagher.

"Then what do we do? You've been waiting for this opportunity all your life yet you cower in your castle afraid to meet your saviours face to face? What kind of man are you?"

Seamus had not seen MacDavitt this animated since he lost his baggage in Wicklow.

O'Gallagher took a sharp intake of breath and tried to swallow his anger.

"I have sent word to the O'Donnell and have ordered my men to hide the delegation in Killybegs."

MacDavitt nearly exploded.

"You cannot hide a delegation from the Spanish Crown in a fishing village. It is the ultimate insult!"

"Calm down," said O'Gallagher. "We can bring them to Castle Banagh where they can hide until the O'Donnell returns."

"Free me from my duties and let me look after the delegation. I can speak fluent Spanish and know what they want. It is what the O'Donnell brought me here for," said MacDavitt.

He looked like he was pleading for his life.

"You may as well," said Seamus. "It keeps everyone happy until the O'Donnell arrives."

"So be it. Seamus, you need to stay, as you are also familiar with the Spanish. Stay in the castle, Seamus, and I will go to Killybegs with Hugh Boye."

Seamus bowed as he prepared to leave.

"I will fetch my men."

Seamus could not believe his luck. The men of Munster would be in charge of a major castle once again.

Seamus was master of the castle for a couple of days before the O'Donnell returned. His appointment, no matter how temporary, drew puzzled questions from the local O'Donnell gentry and even rumours that a coup had taken place. Seamus had impressed his new men, letting them exercise near the castle, which only encouraged the rumours of a coup. However, the O'Donnell rode back into the castle and the rumours evaporated. He immediately summoned Seamus, Tádhg Óg O'Boyle and Eoghan Óg MacSweeney, the leader of the northern branch of the MacSweeney Galloglass, to his chambers.

When Seamus arrived Red Hugh looked troubled, an amazing reaction for a man who seemed to have gained everything he had hoped for. He sat in his chair, exuding a mood, and said nothing until Tádhg Óg and Eoghan Óg had also entered the room.

"Where are the Spanish delegation now?"

"In Banagh castle," said Seamus.

"Bring them north to Lifford castle. I have arranged a secret conference there with the O'Neill. Eoghan Óg, I need the castle cleared of all people that are not trustworthy. The negotiations with the English are in a very delicate position. We are winning concessions as we think the English have a weak hand. It would be a travesty if we were to throw it all away for a bunch of empty promises."

"Hugh Boye MacDavitt is leading our delegation, lord. He should be able to size up the Spanish."

"He behaves as if he were a prisoner here. What he wouldn't give to jump on that boat and sail back to Spain to his life of luxury as a Spanish officer."

"He had an arrangement with the O'Neill, lord," said Seamus.

Red Hugh glowered.

"And his debt is to me. I have not seen the strides in my army that would lead me to believe that he has repaid his debt. Once he has done that, we can either come to another arrangement or he can offer his services to someone else."

"As we are here discussing other matters, it may have come to your attention -."

Red Hugh threw his hands in the air.

"Enough! Nothing matters more than the Spanish delegation. Once we have concluded, we can resolve other matters. Seamus, go with Eoghan Óg and secure the castle."

"But lord, Niall Garbh owns that castle," said Eoghan Óg. "What are we to do with him?"

"All the castles of Tirconnell belong to the O'Donnell. He is one who I do not trust. I will provide you with a letter sending him on a mission to Connacht. Ensure he is gone before the delegation arrives. Tádhg Óg, you will escort me to the castle."

Eoghan Óg knew Red Hugh had decided and would not change his mind.

"Yes lord, the castle will be secure before you and the delegation arrive."

All three bowed and left to make their preparations.

Eoghan Óg turned to Seamus as they strode across the castle yard.

"Have your men ready at first light tomorrow. We shall march then."

"What are you going to say to Niall Garbh?"

"That the O'Donnell has an important mission."

"When Niall Garbh finds out -."

"The O'Donnell has stored up enough trouble with him already. I would be surprised if he had not asked you to come purely to kill Niall Garbh."

"I am not a common assassin," said Seamus.

"Nor are you an O'Donnell."

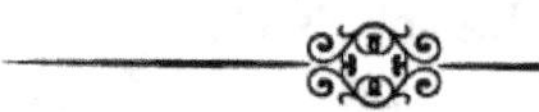

MacSweeney Galloglass secured and populated Lifford castle. Niall Garbh had been insulted to be turfed out of his own castle but resisted the temptation to pick a fight with better trained and better armed men that outnumbered him two to one. He threw the letter from the O'Donnell in the fire and went northwards to solace his ego in one of his lesser homes. They also sent his staff and family packing with him and Eoghan Óg brought down cooks and staff that he knew he could trust from his own castles in northern Tirconnell. The castle was prepared. All they had to do was wait for the conference participants.

The O'Donnell and Tádhg Óg were the first to arrive, swiftly followed by the O'Neill. After a swift discussion, the two lords of the north decided to open negotiations with the Spanish delegation before they informed the other lords of the Confederacy that the Spanish had arrived. They sent word to Banagh castle and O'Gallagher smuggled the Spanish delegation across Tirconnell and safely through the servants' door at the back of the castle under the cover of darkness. The four Spanish delegates waited in a pantry until O'Gallagher reported to the O'Donnell and swore that the Spanish were who they said they were and were not English spies. They were then escorted up to the main hall where the O'Donnell and the O'Neill sat waiting.

The O'Neill and the O'Donnell sat resplendent in their finest clothes that made them at once look rich and agile, very much the splendid rebel lords who were the subjects of the tales their agents told the Spanish King. Alongside them were their bulkiest Galloglass, each over six feet tall with an axe that reached up to the tops of their heads. They also invited their most trusted men, including Seamus, to look intimidating along the walls of the hall. The four Spanish were slender diplomats with dirtier clothes and fresh with colds, for they had experienced nothing like the cold Tirconnell winter. They bowed and turned to their guides, O'Gallagher and MacDavitt.

"They apologise for their lack of knowledge of English never mind Gaelic, and wish me to translate for them."

Hugh O'Neill had brought his trusted advisor Pablo Blanco, who had had his old Spanish uniform repaired and reconstituted to hold his expanded waistline, and he looked to him for approval. Pablo nodded to O'Neill, who subsequently nodded to O'Donnell.

"Please continue," said Red Hugh.

"They send greetings from King Philip, who is pleased to have such esteemed rebels on his side for the righteous cause of defending the Catholic faith and the Pope," said Hugh Boye.

The four Spaniards nodded enthusiastically and looked to the leader of their party, Alonso Cobos.

"We are pleased to have his envoys in our company. We hope the good King has received our letters?"

Hugh Boye turned to the envoys and translated. He received his instructions back.

"The King has received several letters and has in response sent several ships, but it was the devil's own work that drove each ship to the bottom of the sea until our mission successfully arrived."

"We are grateful for the efforts we have made to date. However, we are negotiating a peace settlement with the Queen of England and she has offered us the most favourable of terms, better than any of our forefathers ever achieved. Therefore, we would wish to know what the King has sent alongside the expedition of your good selves?"

The envoys got in a huddle when they heard the translation of Red Hugh's response.

"The King has sent us to measure the strengths of the rebellion and to find out what additional support it would require to ensure it succeeds. The King will give you far more favourable terms than any on offer from the Queen, but he will also give you freedom of worship and supremacy of the Catholic church."

It was the turn of the O'Donnell and the O'Neill to have a huddle. They broke off their whispering and the O'Neill nodded to the O'Donnell.

"We have almost concluded the peace with the Queen of England. We would have to have reassurances from the King how serious his support is and when would it come."

"We implore you not to accept the Queen's terms. The King has sworn an oath to God himself and his representative on earth, the Pope, that he will remove the heathen from the throne. He will give you whatever resources you need to be successful. He will send them as soon as we return."

The O'Neill whispered in the O'Donnell's ear.

"While we welcome your fine words and those of your King, we are reluctant to abandon six months' worth of hard negotiation given what has happened in the past. However, regarding the King and in gratitude for his ongoing support, we will discuss his plans for your mission before we decide to conclude our negotiations with the English Crown."

"King Philip means to back his words with deeds as he has done many times in the past and we are happy to discuss his plans with you."

"We will reconvene with you tomorrow to have our discussions."

"Thank you for the kindness and hospitality you have shown us so far."

"Eoghan and Hugh Boye will show you to your quarters and look after your every wish."

The envoys and their escort bowed and left the great hall, huddled in Spanish discussions. Hugh Boye looked quite animated as he left. Once they were gone, the room turned silent.

"Well?" said Red Hugh.

He leant towards the O'Neill who looked pensive.

"They certainly said all the right things but if they leave us in the lurch, I fear we cannot win on our own."

Red Hugh paused for contemplation.

"I for one have a burning desire to fight on."

The O'Neill nodded in acknowledgement and then went into his own thoughts. Red Hugh waved his hand, and they brought in the food.

The O'Donnell had requisitioned a nearby farmhouse of a loyal supporter near Lifford castle. It was positioned on a slight hill and was relatively exposed, so it had a fair view of the surrounding lands. Red Hugh had the MacSweeney Galloglass draw a ring of steel around it so no one could get in or out. The O'Neill, the O'Donnell and their advisors rode first to the farmhouse followed by the Spanish delegation and Seamus and his men comprised part of their bodyguard. A table was drawn up in the centre of the main room of the house and, as both delegations entered, they took a separate side of the table. Seamus was one of the important and trusted men of the O'Neill and the O'Donnell lining the walls of the room. The O'Neill and the O'Donnell sat opposite the Spanish delegation and Hugh Boye.

Hugh Boye had a freshness in his cheeks that Seamus had not seen since their earliest days together in the Netherlands, before they had both become old and bitter. He had seemed to become reinvigorated by his dealings with the Spanish delegation and placed what appeared to be detailed notes on the table before he sat down. O'Neill nodded to him and Hugh Boye glanced at O'Donnell, who was deep in conversation with one of his advisors. The O'Donnell finished his conversation and gently tapped on the table to bring the room to silence.

"Thank you all for coming today and thank you to the Spanish delegation for travelling through such dangerous seas that have claimed so many lives to get here today. Alonso Cobos will speak today through Hugh Boye during our negotiations. I have invited two scribes from the dominant clans to make notes so that we can evidence the agreements we reach here today. Is that acceptable to the Spanish party?"

Hugh Boye translated, and Alonso nodded.

"Would the party from the King of Spain like to elaborate on why they are here today?" said Red Hugh.

Alonso signalled he would like permission to stand and Red Hugh nodded his approval. Alonso paced up and down and Hugh Boye moved his chair to the side so he could see both what Alonso was doing and address the O'Neill and the O'Donnell without turning his back to them.

"The King of Spain bows only to two persons on this earth, the Pope and God himself. It is with his blessing that he continues the war against the English heretics to claim the throne for both God and the Pope. He has watched from afar your struggle with the heathens and the glorious victories you have won against them. The King has several of your brethren and priesthood as guests in his court that keep him abreast of your heroic deeds for both God and country. He has tried before to help you, but only I have been blessed to make it to your beautiful country. He has sent me here to make a treaty with you, and as a sign of his goodwill has sent with me some military advisors and behind me are two more ships with guns and gunpowder."

Both the O'Neill and the O'Donnell politely applauded the gestures and generosity.

"Now we must get down to the business of negotiation. My kind interpreter has told me he did not have permission to discuss any details of your armed forces or what your weapons requirements would be, but that I should direct such requests directly to the O'Donnell and the O'Neill?"

"That is correct," Red Hugh said. "Hugh Boye has done a magnificent job for us and I assume he has seen that all your wants are met?"

"He has done everything but change the weather. But he said he would put in a few prayers for us."

All the Irish laughed.

"You get used to it eventually or else you patiently wait for the springtime and slightly less rain. The wind never goes away, but it puts the English off too," said Red Hugh.

It was the turn of the Spanish delegation to laugh.

"We can discuss our numbers with you and what we would require, but first we would need to know how many soldiers the King will send," said the O'Neill.

"The good King will send as many men as you require."

O'Neill turned to whisper in O'Donnell's ear.

"We need six thousand men. That is good fighting men with experience of fighting on the continent and capable of defeating the English in open battle. Can the King supply us with that?"

Alonso pondered momentarily and discussed the translation with Hugh Boye.

"Yes, the King can provide you with that."

"We need one thousand to be sent immediately upon your return. Can your King do that?"

"I would have to see what men he had readily available, but it is not an unreasonable request."

"We also need cannon. The type that can take castles. Does your King have any of them to spare?"

"If you tell me how big the castles are, then I can tell you."

Red Hugh was getting excited now.

"Like the one you just came from. That kind of size."

"Oh yes. The King has plenty of cannon for castles like that. He is the most powerful man in the world. As long as he considers you good allies and fighting for the one true faith, he should meet any stipulations you want."

Red Hugh looked expectantly at the O'Neill. However, he controlled his emotions as he had been negotiating for most of his life.

"What does the King want?" said the O'Neill.

"That you become part of the Spanish empire and become his vassal."

"With a ruler of our choosing?"

"I'm sure we could find you a prince who would not agree with your cold and wet climate and prefer to spend his time in sunny Madrid. Then you would be left to your own devices as long as you recognised the King of Spain as your ultimate leader."

"That would be agreeable in principle with the details to be worked out at a later date."

"Of course. We realise that your mind would be on other things such as fending off the English until the King's army arrives. But you have done such a splendid job until now, His Majesty has heard that you could hold off the English army almost indefinitely, hiding in your woods, bogs and mountains."

"Don't let that put the King off. His men have conquered the world. I'm sure they'll get on just fine in Ireland," said O'Neill.

Alonso conversed with Hugh Boye as the translation got caught up in a heated discussion. Hugh Boye pulled his tunic down and sat straight, facing the two northern lords.

"The King would like to know how many men you have, what quality are they and how well armed they are."

Red Hugh tensed up and crossed his arms.

"We need guns, pikes and swords for ten thousand. The King has seen how the Irish fight in his armies on the continent. They fight like dogs until the enemy is dead. That's all he needs to know."

Hugh Boye looked nervously at Red Hugh and hesitated before he turned around to translate. Hugh O'Neill watched as disappointment etched across Alonso's face. He knocked on the table to get their attention.

"Sorry, I fear some of what the learned leader of the O'Donnell has said may get lost in translation. We have many troop types not found on the continent but are especially suited to our bogs and wind and rain."

The O'Neill winked at Hugh Boye and held out his hands and twitched his fingers to impersonate the rain. Hugh Boye laughed and nodded and the laugh was echoed when the delegation heard the translation.

"We have Galloglass and Scottish mercenaries, both well-armed and hardened and used to fighting the English. You may not have the equivalent these days on the continent. But we also have pike and shot trained by Spanish officers left over from the Armada and smuggled into the north over the years. The rebels in all their guises around Ireland could raise and arm four or five thousand men, but could raise twice that. It is hard to get weapons because the English have an embargo on arms sales in Ireland and we have to smuggle everything in or make them ourselves."

O'Neill nodded, instructing Hugh Boye to translate. The O'Donnell made two fists until his knuckles shone white. The O'Neill bent over and whispered in his ear.

"We have a good agreement on the table and I will not lose it on a promise. There's no point in lying to them. They either give us what we want or we make peace. I don't want to waste my time for I have a new young wife at home that I would rather be getting to know than hearing hot air from the King of Spain."

Red Hugh gave a knowing smile.

"Agreed."

The colour came back into Red Hugh's knuckles. Alonso's face brightened up and then grew more serious. He became engrossed in a conversation with Hugh Boye. The O'Neill was patient; the O'Donnell was not.

"He says that some of the delegation can stay and train the men," says Hugh Boye.

"That may not be necessary," said Hugh O'Neill. "This discussion must remain secret and if there are new Spanish officers walking around the north, then it might give away what we are trying to do."

Hugh Boye translated, and Alonso nodded his head vigorously. Red Hugh stood up.

"Now if you'll excuse us, I need to have a discussion with the O'Neill. We'll reconvene here tomorrow to continue our discussions and get to more details of what the King can do for us."

Hugh Boye translated, and Alonso jumped up and shook both their hands and said something in Spanish.

"And God bless you too," said Hugh Boye after receiving the nod from the O'Neill.

Both Hughs pulled their coats around them. They had waved away their guards, who formed a wide perimeter around them. They talked as they made their way back to Lifford castle.

"So, what do you think?" said Red Hugh.

"Even though it is everything we wanted, and he nods along to our every request, I am still cautious. We get sporadic Spanish delegates every couple of years who promise the heavens and the earth, and then we hear nothing. Even if this new one can deliver, we'll have to hold out ourselves for a year or more until they come. I don't know if we could hold out that long. If the Queen throws all of her resources at us, I fear we would be overwhelmed."

Red Hugh stopped and grabbed him by the shoulders.

"I say fight! This is what we have waited for all these years. How many of your forefathers have died at the hands of the English? Shane O'Neill for one. God has given us this opportunity and we should grab it with both hands!"

O'Neill shook him off.

"If we are to do it, we need everyone to agree together. We should first get the basis of an agreement with the Spanish delegation, with as many guarantees as they can give us. Then we must call together all the rebel lords and ensure that they all wish to fight."

Red Hugh beamed.

"Let us do this. I feel in my heart that we shall succeed. The O'Donnells and the O'Neills will reign supreme in the north once more!"

O'Neill smiled at his younger ally and signalled for his horse.

CHAPTER TWENTY-FOUR

THE GREY MAN RETURNS

B ARNARD SAT ATOP A bench cushion with a warm blanket wrapped around his shoulders. Snug shoes protected his feet, and he had a cart full of pre-sold items that all he had to do was deliver. As Mr O'Cassidy promised, this was by far his most lucrative route. He was a young man of means, with a full table at home and a happy young wife with new clothes. He was going up in the world.

Before he departed last time, the lady of the house had given him two letters, both to be handed straight to Mr O'Cassidy. Barnard had received two more letters in return from his master, one a detailed invoice for the goods and a second sealed letter for the eyes of the lady of the house only. But Barnard also carried a more unusual cargo.

He pulled up into the courtyard in front of the house. The rain had given a brief respite, allowing enough time to unload the cart. The sky even displayed a soothing light blue to entice weary travellers to continue their journey so the wind and rain could ambush them later. Barnard handed the invoice to Óisin, who was waiting to receive the fresh supplies.

"I have no time for such things," said Óisin.

He passed the invoice back to Caoimhe.

"See what we can get if you leave the running of the house to me?"

The statement was one of defiance, that she was the rainmaker in a land of famine and pain.

"Ah, you're giving me an ache in my ear. Now what have you got for us?"

He turned to Barnard to inspect the contents of the covered cart.

"What the…!"

He looked inside, and between the boxes and barrels were three men. They got out of the cart and stood beside the wheel. Caoimhe pushed Óisin aside and inspected the men.

"You've all got experience of working on a farm?"

"Yes," one said.

The other two looked at their battered shoes.

"It's backbreaking work. We have next season's crop to sow and few men to do it. You realise this, don't you?"

"For food and board for the winter and a couple of coin when we'll be on our way, we'll do it. Sow your seeds and bring your crops in," said the man.

"I have men to do that, men I trust," said Óisin. "I do not know who these men are and where they're from. They could be spies for all I know."

He tried to push Caoimhe aside, but Maeve came up and pushed him from behind.

"Leave her alone, you bully. You won't drag me out into the woods and set your dogs on me!"

Óisin gave her a murderous look but did not venture his gaze further, for the fist of Caoimhe came down upon him. She let go with all her strength. It did not put him down, but it made him pay attention.

"How many months have you and your layabouts been in charge of this farm? How many crops have been sown and how much of the house has been repaired? If these be good men who can put a seed in the ground and some colour on the walls, surely they will save you from the rope if Seamus returns and you have failed him again? What do you think I've had to do to settle with Barnard here and make sure that he comes back again with a cart full of cargo for us? If they are good men willing to work, it'll be over my dead body before you remove them."

One hand squashed into a fist and the other soothed his jaw. His temper would have goaded him into repaying the punch with interest and then watching Caoimhe writhe around in the mud as she pleaded for mercy to avoid another one. But Maeve stood protectively in front of her and put her arms out so Óisin could not get past. The men looked at the ground for they had no courage, as they had not concluded their negotiations for employment. Barnard hurriedly blessed himself and wondered where his sword was hidden in the cart.

"Leave it there, man," said Maeve. "Let us conclude our business here and then all take a breath. It'll do you no good to take your temper out on this woman."

There was a silence and a tension in the air that paralyzed all but the women. Caoimhe brushed past Maeve and handed a list of required goods for the next trip to Barnard.

"I trust my line of credit is still good with your master?"

"Oh, very good, Miss, very good. We are paid most promptly and my master is glad of your business. May I suggest, Miss, if I may be so bold that you decide on these men's employment, and if you see fit to employ them, they unload the cart? Then I can be on my way."

Caoimhe spun on her feet.

"Men, you'll get food and board and some coin in your pocket after the harvest. If you serve well, we have land to rent that needs to be farmed. Does that sound fair?"

The men grinned and nodded.

"Then, before you is your first task. Unload the cart and I'll direct you where to put everything."

Óisin's temper reared its head.

"I'm the man of the house here," he said.

"So be it. You unload the cart and sow the fields. We need enough food to feed ourselves and pay Barnard. If you can do that, then dismiss the men and I'll retire to the house and inspect what Barnard has brought me. Well?"

Óisin spat on the ground.

"Seamus was right. You are a witch. Men, unload the cart."

"If Seamus is right about what I heard him say about you, then he'll decorate the old oak tree with you if he finds the results of your idleness."

Óisin scowled for he knew he was beaten and took a heavy sack upon his shoulders and staggered towards the store. Caoimhe stayed to supervise and ensure all on the invoice was present and correct.

"Excuse me, Miss."

She heard a timid whisper over her shoulder.

"May I have a moment of your time in private?"

"Of course, Barnard. Let us step over here beside the shed."

Caoimhe stood out of earshot but within sight of the men, for they had not yet earned her trust. Barnard put his hand in his inside pocket and pulled out a letter.

"My employer gave me this to give you. I do not know its contents. He asked me to wait for a reply and if the response was to his liking, he will give me a bonus."

Barnard smiled as if he was holding his cap out, but only in the politest way possible.

"If you stay in the yard, supervise the men and help Maeve ensure that all the goods go to the right place, then I will read the letter and write you an instant response."

Barnard nodded in agreement. He returned to the cart where Óisin was still attempting to assert his authority over Maeve, but her tongue repelled every clumsy contention. Caoimhe ran up to her room and shut the door behind her. She went to her restored table to retrieve her fire-scarred letter opener and prised open the seal. The letter was all she thought it would be. Functional, angry, vengeful, but with an actionable plan. She had to read into it love and reassurance for the compositions of her father rarely strayed into such realms, and as she held the letter to her chest, she thought of her brother. It was funny how her father's admonishments of her brother would bring out comparative affection for her. Was that affection genuine or just to harden the rebuke? It did not matter now for her youth had been ended by the brutes Seamus and Eunan and vengeance drove her on. She penned a response to her father and ran down the stairs to give it to Barnard so he could leave. She openly held out the letter and handed it to Barnard.

"What's that?"

The only part of this scenario Óisin could control was his anger, but he was too old to master that now.

"It is a letter to his master outlining how good our credit is."

She waved the letter in front of him.

"You can come and inspect it if you want. You can even rewrite it as you are the man of the house."

Óisin snarled and spat.

"It better be right what you wrote. I'll believe you for now, as the merchant did well for that last round and the goods keep rolling in. But you and me'll have words later on unless you keep me abreast of everything."

Caoimhe nodded at Óisin until he turned to take hold of one end of a trunk to take into the house. She smiled at Barnard.

"I wrote something nice about you in the letter so you should get a bonus."

"Why thank you, Miss. I'm very grateful."

"If you come back quickly with what I asked you, there'll be plenty more where that came from."

A thud came from the other side of the cart where Óisin had dropped a chest secured with a large chain into the mud of the yard.

"Good bye, Barnard," said Caoimhe.

She turned her attention to Óisin.

"That is my chest you dropped in the mud. It better not be damaged!"

"What have you got in here? Rocks? I almost broke my back trying to lift it."

"You should be more careful then, shouldn't you? They are clothes from Dublin. They are to replace the ones that Seamus destroyed when he cruelly evicted me and sent me to the pigsty. We'll say no more of what happened after that."

Óisin had taken up an end of the chest with one of the new men at the other. But in his frustration he dropped it once more into the mud.

"Hey! Watch my things. Fish it out of there at once."

"Where does all the money for this come from?"

"From all the crops you are going to sow and harvest. You don't want the lady of the house to look like a dowdy tramp all covered in mud and hair in a tangle. If you do, then you should just get me with child and leave me in the house and wait for Seamus's repercussions."

Óisin blushed as he tried to ignore her comments.

"What am I supposed to tell Seamus?"

Caoimhe put her hands together in prayer.

"Please don't kill me Seamus, sir. I have sown all the crops and fixed and painted the house. I have even raised some money for you. I have made sure that Eunan's wife looks beautiful for him when he comes home. I haven't touched her, I swear, because I am not man enough to take the title O'Cassidy Maguire even though you are both fully preoccupied elsewhere."

Óisin growled again.

"Seamus was right. You really are a witch."

"Leave the chest in my room and I will follow you up."
Óisin's face was puce again.
"I want to see everything in that chest."
"Oh, I fully intend for you to see everything. Let me bathe first and relieve myself of this mud, and I will call you."
"You'd better be quick about it."
He picked the chest out of the mud and cursed at the hired hand. Maeve ran over to Caoimhe and they both burst out laughing.

The chest was delivered to Caoimhe's room after the bottom of it had been cleaned of mud. Óisin stood in the doorway brooding in the shadow.
"I want to see what is in that chest."
"All in good time," said Caoimhe.
She ushered him out of the doorway.
"They are womanly things, a surprise for you. Once I am washed and out of this oppressive garb which saw my mind drawn to the trivial and mundane, we can be lord and lady of the manor and enjoy our beautiful house. You'd like that, wouldn't you?"
Óisin's silence was betrayed by the glint of lust in his eyes. He managed a mumble and Caoimhe returned his glances.
"All in good time, my handsome prince, all in good time. Why don't you go out and organise the men to plant the crops and I will send Maeve to get you when I am good and ready?"
"But, but -."
"You don't need directing to the sheds, do you?"
"No."
"Then the sooner you start the work the sooner I will be ready."
Óisin had no response, so Caoimhe slammed the door in his face.
She giggled to herself as Maeve stood over the chest and yanked on the chain.
"So how do we get it off?"
"Barnard slipped me a key."
Maeve gave the sly grin of a person well versed in intrigue.

"Does he know you are his master's daughter and a prisoner here?"

"He may suspect but is too polite or well-paid to mention it."

She then turned to Maeve with a playful sternness.

"How can I be a prisoner in my own home? I am the resistance to wicked invaders. Each will pay a mighty price for usurping the rightful O'Cassidy Maguire!"

They both laughed.

"Check at the window to see if that lazy lout has actually gone to do some work whilst I open the chest."

Maeve looked out the window, and Caoimhe fiddled with the lock.

"He has gone into the shed. Whether that means he intends to do any work whilst there is anyone's guess."

The lock clicked, and Caoimhe's spirits soared.

"As long as he is not here will do for now. Come here, Maeve, and let us see what my father has sent."

The two women knelt beside the chest, and Caoimhe opened it. The waft of entombed perfume escaping into the atmosphere filled their nostrils. Caoimhe sat back and closed her eyes. Such a surge of happiness had not been hers since the thoughts of marriage and her wedding day filled her mind before colliding with reality, be that meeting the groom or the actual events of the day. Maeve put her warm hand on Caoimhe's.

"You'll be free one day soon. You need to keep persevering."

Caoimhe shook the thoughts from her mind and returned to the chest.

"My father can hire good staff," she said.

She put her hands in the chest and delicately lifted out a neatly folded green velvet dress. She stood up and unfurled it and held it to her shapely body. She spun in elation.

"My beautiful dress. I may not have you back, but my father remembered!"

"Óisin will be no match for you when you put that on," said Maeve. "What else is in here?"

Caoimhe delved her hands into the box and took out dress after dress, setting them out neatly in their folded state on her bed. Dresses of many colours in her favourite velvet and some of brocade with exquisite floral designs. They were a wonder to behold for any young woman looking to keep up with the fashions of the streets of Dublin or what the merchants brought in from overseas. With this attire, she would surely outshine any woman in the hinterland who would shrivel up into a dowdy ball beside her. She radiated youthful joy.

"You are once more the lady of the house, Miss," said Maeve.

Caoimhe slipped into seriousness once more.

"It is but one small step to restoring my father. We have much work to do. The chest is not yet empty."

There were some small boxes in the chest. Caoimhe carefully removed them and opened them. They were full of her favourite perfumes and also some more exotic smells seldom obtainable in rural Ireland. She placed the boxes with great care on her table with a grace that far exceeded the goods' value.

The floor of the chest was covered in sheets. Caoimhe put her hands in to gather one up. She felt the weight. She looked at Maeve, who immediately picked up the surprise mixed with a dash of fear. Caoimhe dived into the box and enveloped the contents of the sheet and lay it on the floor. She carefully unfolded the edges of the sheet. Nestled inside were a couple of swords and four daggers. She quickly covered them up again. She gathered them up and shoved the package beneath her bed.

"We need to find a better place to hide them than that," said Maeve.

"If Óisin finds me with weapons, it will be a strain on my womanly ways to get me out of that," said Caoimhe.

She went to put the chest away.

"Hold on, there is more. There are two letters here."

She bent over and picked them out. She sat on the stool she had acquired from one of the other rooms, a poor replacement for the grand chair she used to sit upon to look out over her father's fine estate that was stolen by the rebels and used for firewood. Maeve began to neatly hang the dresses in Caoimhe's fire-damaged cupboards from which they had worked hard to remove the smell of smoke.

Caoimhe sat somewhat uncomfortably upon her stool and read the first letter and then the second. Her face jumped between beaming smiles and angry frowns. She put down the letters and made an announcement to Maeve.

"I know now what we need to do. We must make haste, for we have little time."

CHAPTER TWENTY-FIVE

A TUG ON THE HEART STRINGS

O VER THE NEXT COUPLE of weeks, Óisin did not find out what was in the chest, no matter how much he demanded. Caoimhe told him he had to wait until he earned the right to come into her room. She gave him tasks to do, such as repairing the house, painting the interior rooms, preparing the soil for the next harvest and visiting the locals who prepared cloth for sale by the O'Cassidy Maguire. Upon receiving no visible results to her allocation of chores and that Óisin had previously waved away all threats that Seamus would hang him upon his return, she decided upon a change of tactics.

He once more became her Galloglass and her knight, her protector against Seamus. She pleaded with him to save her from the wrath of Seamus and to fix the house and lands so they could live together in peace as lord and lady. He did not respond in public, but Maeve, who was sent to spy on him, noticed he had organised the men to prepare the fields. Caoimhe had made sure she washed every day and was free of mud and not dressed like a scullery maid. She tried to avoid Óisin, but every time they met, she would try to wear him down with her compliments.

In the meantime, Maeve had made herself acquainted with the three men that Barnard had brought. She had done so under the instruction of Caoimhe, who told her parts of the letter when she needed to know. After hearing about how Lasair was killed by Óisin, she agreed what she did not know she could not tell. The only person who Óisin could not torture without Seamus's permission was Caoimhe. The men had been sent for Caoimhe's protection and the weapons in the chest were theirs. The weapons remained hidden under the bed until the opportune moment came when Óisin left to go hunting for the day. They had proved themselves to be adept craftsmen and set about repairing the house. Óisin protested but Caoimhe persuaded him it was better to pay them to do that than pay them to be idle. The house began to slowly transform.

Maeve also joined in working on Óisin by telling him how much time Caoimhe spent talking about him and how handsome and brave he was. She also said that Caoimhe wished he were her husband instead of Eunan. Óisin waved away such talk, but Maeve saw his head was turning.

Then one fateful day a rider came escorted by two Galloglass. He asked for Óisin and one man helping around the farm went to look for him in the fields. Óisin returned cold and covered in mud. Caoimhe rushed to her window but kept out of sight.

"Maeve," she hissed.

Her maid came running.

"Get down there now and listen in. I need to know what they are saying."

Maeve ran down the stairs and looked around. She grabbed a broom idly leaning against a wall and swept around the doorway, edging into earshot of the strangers. Óisin brushed himself off and stood in front of the house.

"What are armed men doing calling here? We are faithful servants of the Maguire and are sworn to keep his truce."

"Greetings, lord. I believe you must be Óisin guarding the lands of Eunan the O'Cassidy Maguire?"

"I am, and who are you and what is your business?"

The youngest of the men answered his question.

"My name is Sean and I am an apprentice Brehon working for Cairbre Óg MacAodhagáin, the Brehon defending your master. Eunan has given me permission to come here and gather evidence for his trial. He says that you are a great friend and will assist me in any way possible."

Something twitched in Óisin's mind. He did not know how to react. He liked the present and this could change everything for the worse. Yes, he wanted to save his friend, but he relished being the man of the house, and if he tried hard enough, he reckoned he could get with Caoimhe. In a distant dream, he would take her for his wife. He needed to preserve his position.

"How do I know you are who you say you are?"

"Here is a sealed letter from Desmond MacCabe for anyone who wishes to see it."

Óisin brushed it away.

"I was expecting you to appear at some stage. When is my friend to appear on trial?"

"They say it will be at the week of Easter. Enniskillen will prepare for the holy celebrations, so there will be a large crowd in the town. All the better for them to show their justice being done."

"How long do you intend to stay and what help do you need?"

Sean got down from his horse and handed the reins to one of the farm hands.

"I can only stay a couple of days. I need to see the site where the battle took place, any papers relating to Cormac O'Cassidy, and speak to any witnesses. You should be the first person I speak to."

"All that can be arranged. Consider the house your own. Now come and let us feed you after your long journey and we'll get to business afterwards. One of my men will show you to a room in the outhouses from where you can conduct your investigation."

Sean and his Galloglass scraped off the visible mud from their clothes and entered the house. Caoimhe signalled to Óisin from behind the banister at the top of the stairs to come up urgently and visit her. Óisin saw the men to the kitchen and then trudged up the stairs. He feared he would get his ears filled by her nagging. She stood in her doorway with her back to the slightly ajar door, tempting him to enter.

"Who are they? I'm not speaking to them. How could you give the lackeys who evicted my father the freedom of the estate?"

"Eunan is the O'Cassidy Maguire now," said Óisin.

He stood at the top of the stairs and tried to look past Caoimhe and into her room. Caoimhe gave him a coy smile, glanced behind her, and then returned her gaze to Óisin with the added hint of an invitation to explore the mysteries of her room. Óisin smiled like a dumb beast compelled to compete with his rivals at the annual ritual for procreation.

"You could come in here anytime you wanted if you were master of the house, but you're not. Give all the evidence to Eunan's men, watch them all lie to the Brehons and then sit at the bottom of the stairs like a good little boy as Eunan returns and strides up the stairs to have his way with me."

Óisin stopped, his brain overwhelmed. He shook his head free of the thoughts of Caoimhe's room and her laid out naked on the bed, waiting for him to do as he wished. But he could not. She was Eunan's wife. He turned and went down the stairs again.

"If you loved me, you wouldn't let Eunan do this to me," said Caoimhe.

She gripped the rail as if she had been cast into the sea, with each wave large enough to engulf her. Her eyes became large pools of deepest blue ready to drown any sailor foolish enough to answer her pleas. Óisin wavered, then slowly edged down the stairs, afraid to look back. Caoimhe wailed as if the waves had finally got her and she let go of the banister and fell to the floor. Óisin turned, and upon seeing her distress, ran up to the landing and picked her up.

"No matter what happens, I'll see that you're all right," he whispered.

"Thank you, my knight."

The meekness warbled in her voice, as if life and hope ebbed away. Óisin held her in his arms and once more did battle with temptation. Caoimhe lay as helpless and still as a rag doll.

"Lord!"

A cry came from the door to the house.

"The Brehon wishes to speak to you."

Caoimhe lifted her head.

"Don't throw me to the wolves."

Óisin could barely think.

"I will do my duty."

He laid Caoimhe's head gently on the floor and stood up. The pads of his fingers lingered on her soft black curls and she smiled back at him. He shook his head to clear it and went to speak to the Brehon.

Óisin's mood darkened as it seemed the walls were moving in to crush him. The Brehon was becoming more and more frustrated with the answers he was giving. Óisin needed to think faster since he had only had the time it took to walk from the stairs to prepare.

"No, I did not set fire to the house of my own accord. Eunan told me to do it. He was furious with his uncle. Angry enough to kill him? I think yes. They found him with the body of his own cousin at his feet."

The scribe threw his pen onto his page. Excess ink splashed everywhere. The scribe did not care because he would have to dispose of the page anyway.

"This does not correspond with anything that Eunan told us. In fact, it contradicts most of it."

Óisin shrugged the young scribe's assertions away.

"The fault belongs to me? How do I know what Seamus told him to say? Eunan is stuck in some prison somewhere. How do I know what he will say to save himself?"

The young scribe shook his head. He was not expecting such obstinacy.

"It is not what he will say, it is the search for the truth. We both, or at least I hope we both, believe that Eunan is innocent of a crime and had sufficient justification for what he did so that the Maguire would view his actions as being in the best interests of the clan. Therefore, I am in search of witnesses willing to speak on his behalf and evidence to show that his uncle was in collusion with the English. Is there any such evidence available in the house? Can you introduce me to any witnesses?"

Óisin got up and grunted.

"I don't know how much money he is paying you, but it is bound to be a lot. I'll say whatever he needs me to say. Just tell me where and when. Most of the witnesses have returned to their homes or are out in the field or are serving under arms for various lords. You have the freedom of the house to find evidence, but the rain has been heavy, and the fire ravaged the house, so you'll not find much. I suggest you stay a sufficient time so you can tell your master you tried, but I would think he has better ways of employing you. There will be an evening meal prepared for you, some bedding in the outhouses, and we will give you food for your journey. Just send me the details of the trial and I will come with some witnesses to defend my friend."

Óisin nodded and walked to the door. The scribe hurriedly gathered his papers and ran after him.

"If I have the run of the house, please can you show me the tree beneath which the wedding took place and also where Cormac O'Cassidy conducted his business? Then may I make use of your dinner invitation to ask you a few questions about what I find, if anything?"

"It is a busy time of year, what with the fields needing tilling and the animals needing tending. But I shall spare you some time before I retire to bed. One of my men here will tend to you. Stay here and I will fetch him."

Óisin returned with one of his trusted men, but took him aside before they reached the room.

"Taighe, this is your chance to be rid of Eunan and Seamus for good. Think of that before you do anything."

Taighe nodded, but his mind was awash in a sea of confusion. He considered Óisin as Eunan's greatest friend and being on the wrong side of Seamus was an unwanted position for any of the men. But could this be the chance that he was waiting for? Would he be left to deal with Óisin if he filled the vacuum? He took on the task with a heavy heart and a tumultuous mind.

Óisin pushed open the door but did not venture into the room.

"This is Taighe. He'll be your guide. Taighe has known Eunan since he was a boy and was at the wedding. He will show you what you want to see and tell you his account of what happened. Tomorrow he will escort you to the edge of the O'Cassidy lands. He will fetch me if I am needed, but I am a busy man, so only call me if I am required. I bid you good luck in your mission."

Óisin walked off across the yard, leaving Taighe standing in the doorway.

"When you gentlemen are ready, shall we go to the oak tree?"

Sean the scribe gave a sceptical look to his Galloglass bodyguards and returned his attention to Taighe.

"Please, lead the way. Your master has granted me precious little time."

They stood under the oak tree and the only thing to observe was the way the naked branches gathered raindrops and compiled them into globules to pour on their heads. The ground was a mire of mud, stick and acorn, only good for the creation of an ailment of the foot, not for the yielding of leads and clues. Taighe poked a pool of water with the bottom of the shaft of his six-foot axe.

"There's been a lot of rain since that faithful day. Seamus made us clean up just in case Donnacha sent the Maguire's men to investigate. Cormac's son died here," said Taighe.

He stood with one foot resting on the gnarled knot of a root.

"Some say they killed him in a hail of arrows fired by Óisín's men. But he's done his best to suppress that story under pain of death. He has tried to tell everyone that Eunan killed him in single combat. He is under the spell of the lady of the house. We all think that Seamus will hang him from this very tree when he returns."

The young scribe's face brightened, for it was the first time in his trip that he had encountered anything that resembled honesty.

"Thank you for being so candid. I can see that I must leave here as soon as I can. Why would you put yourself in danger to protect me and save Eunan?"

"I served under Seamus for a short time in Breifne recently. The rebellion is gaining strength. It may not be for the likes of me, for I will always have a similar master taking my crops and inflicting hardship on my family for his own gain. But for the Maguire and our way of life, it is the last stand. The English will come and occupy our lands and only God knows what will happen then. I may have only contempt for Seamus and pity for Eunan, but Óisín is rapidly becoming a cruel man who wants to lead this sept. Unfortunately, cruelty is his main leadership strength, for God omitted to grant him any other abilities. If I have a brief opportunity to select my master, I would like to take it."

"The Brehons are here to make sure you are fairly treated under the law. If you tell me what evidence survives, then I can confine my search to just that and then I can leave whilst I still can and you can surely come with me."

Taighe considered for a moment. He thought of his family and the village and what was best for them in the future. He concluded he was the right man at the wrong time and no matter what he did, he would probably end up dead.

"Some of Cormac O'Cassidy's papers survived in his office. I cannot read them, but if you want evidence, that is probably where some remains if anywhere."

"Then let us not stand out here in the rain when we have work to do. Please, lead the way."

Taighe turned and trudged back towards the house.

The grey clouds with their grey speckled water offspring that were the constant companion of anyone caught out in the open, barely diminished the prettiness of the knoll beside the oak tree. But the bushes on the knoll rustled with the sound of deceit and a dark figure rushed towards the opposite side of the house, determined to beat Taighe and his guests inside. Maeve had to warn Caoimhe of Taighe's treachery.

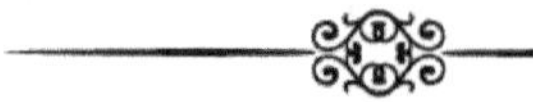

Maeve flew up the stairs, and knocked on Caoimhe's door at the same time that Taighe came in through the front doors. The guards inside the door stopped him until he informed them he had freedom of the house granted to him by Óisin. The guards parted and let him into Cormac O'Cassidy's old office.

Maeve wheezed for breath as she leant on the back of Caoimhe's closed door.

"What has you up those stairs in such a tizzy? I have finally persuaded that oaf Óisin to do some work in the fields and you come to me in this state?" said Caoimhe.

"He has failed you," said Maeve between breaths.

"If there is one thing I am certain of it is that. But we must make do until our circumstances change."

"No, he has told Taighe Maguire to deal with the Brehon and Taighe is showing the Brehon what he wants to see."

Emotion drained from Caoimhe's face to leave a sheer cliff of pragmatism and determination.

"If all else has failed, then it is time to give the knight Óisin a dragon to slay. But first, we need his damsel in distress."

Caoimhe sat at her dressing table and handpicked her war paint and odour.

"Place my green dress on the bed. The velvet one, yes, my favourite and most expensive dress. There is no room for error here if my father and uncle's plans are to be a success."

Maeve had the kitchen staff bring up pail after pail of hot water and her mistress bathed and washed her hair. She then sat as Maeve combed her hair out and it regained its black curly lustre. Caoimhe put on her green dress and then sprayed herself with perfume. She laid a blanket out on the bed for Óisin to sit on, which was also liberally doused in perfume. Caoimhe then stood in front of her mirror for a last inspection.

"The poor man won't know what hit him," said Maeve.

Caoimhe smiled with smug satisfaction and a measure of curiosity, for she wished to gauge just how persuasive she could be. She smiled once more, satisfaction having won the battle of the mouth and cheek muscles.

"Fetch him. Then assign one of my father's men to watch the Brehon."

Maeve nodded and bowed on her way out and then dashed down the stairs again.

CHAPTER TWENTY-SIX

CREATING THE DRAGON

TAIGHE BROUGHT SEAN AND his men into Cormac O'Cassidy's old office, where his papers were stored.

"Whatever papers survived the fire will be in those boxes over there."

Taighe pointed to a corner of the office surrounded by bookshelves with unordered boxes shoved into the corner, stacked haphazardly, one on top of the other.

"Anything received after the fire the mistress guards zealously in her room."

This pricked Sean's interest.

"By chance does our freedom of the house encompass her room?"

The failing hope at the end of sentence gave Taighe ample room to decline.

"The master of the house gave you freedom out of lip service only. He means only to give you enough permission so that he can present an argument in his defence when you accuse him of being obstructive."

Sean sighed and eyed the boxes as his only source of hope.

"I thought so. Has anyone been through these boxes?"

"Few men that Seamus left behind can actually read. To my knowledge, the mistress and her handmaid are the only ones. Óisin certainly can't."

"That may present us with the slightest of advantages in our limited time here. Men, you search the room and the surrounding house and I will search these old papers."

Taighe helped him drag the boxes across the floor and set them in some kind of order beside the main table almost in the centre of the room. Sean sat at the table and read the letters as fast as his knowledge of the written word would allow. He would read until he had the gist of the subject of the letter and would then either discard it into another empty box to his right-hand side or pile them by subject upon the table. He soon had several piles that warranted further investigation.

Maeve ran out into the fields as fast as her feet would allow her to navigate the mud and the freshly tilled soil. It seemed such a waste to disturb Óisin now when her mistress had invested so much time in trying to persuade him to do the farm chores and he was finally doing something.

She shouted at Óisin to come back to the house, but he either did not hear her or else wilfully ignored her. She shouted some more, but slipped as she shouted. Her misfortune certainly got Óisin's attention, for he did not shirk an occasion to have a laugh at Maeve's expense.

"What is so important that you have to throw yourself in the mud to get my attention?"

A fuming Maeve lifted herself out of a puddle.

"Some gentleman you are, not helping a lady in distress. I hope you'll be more charitable to my mistress?"

Óisin by now had stopped laughing.

"It depends on what your mistress wants, how she asks for it and what she is willing to do to get it."

Maeve swept the lumps of mud from her skirt.

"She wants you to avoid getting the rope."

"That's kind of her. Is that all you came to tell me?"

"She wants to see you right now."

Óisin turned his back and walked off.

"She nagged me so much to till the fields and now she wants me so urgently it can't wait. Well, she'll have to."

"The Brehon your master invited in is in her father's office going through all of his letters you should have disposed of."

Óisin stopped and threw the spade he held into the mud. He muttered some curses as he strode past Maeve, not caring where he stepped or that he covered her once more in mud. Maeve ran behind him.

"She wants to see you first. Don't see the Brehon with an axe in your hand."

Óisin turned, and Maeve almost ran straight into him. His face was a knot of tension, a hotchpotch of pink and red channelled down the lines of his face to his mouth, a pit of hellish fury.

"What can she tell me to do that I can't think of myself?"

Spittle flew and nestled on Maeve's already muddy dress.

"Just see her first," Maeve cooed. "It won't be bad."

Óisin cursed again and changed direction.

Maeve ran up and hooked Óisin's arm when he reached the house before he could run up the stairs.

"Nothing is so urgent that you should wish to upset my mistress by bringing the mud of the field into the house. I would advise a change of clothes, something suitable for a man of business."

Óisin yanked his arm back and directed his anger at Maeve, but she just stared back. Óisin bent down and removed his boots and climbed the stairs. He had been brave enough only after Seamus left to occupy one of the bedrooms on the upper floor near Caoimhe's room. He went and changed into pantaloons and a shirt and tucked a sheathed dagger into his belt for good measure. That was dressing for business for him. He walked intrepidly across the landing to Caoimhe's room and gave a polite knock on the door. Maeve stood at the bottom of the stairs out of sight laughing to herself waiting to bound up the stairs to press her ear to the door once she heard Óisin close it behind him.

A voice from behind the door cooed like a morning songbird.

"Come in."

Óisin twisted the handle and gently pressed on the door. The perfume wafted up his nostrils and his longing returned. His previous bravado melted away. He opened the door and what he thought was Caoimhe stood before him. A silhouette of a long dress, the shape of a young woman in her prime and long luscious curls stood in front of the window as if an angel had come down to visit him.

"Sit, my Galloglass."

The words mingled with the sweet smell of perfume in the air, and he was mesmerised. He sat down on the blanket and became immersed in the perfumes liberally applied to it. This was not Caoimhe, a picture of mud and drabness, a whip protruding from her tongue, always wanting, wanting, wanting. This was Caoimhe as an angel, as he liked to imagine her, and she wanted him, and only him.

She threw herself to the floor and landed with a sway just beyond his knees.

"Oh, my Galloglass."

She sat there smiling at him. His thighs instantly went rigid. She had powdered her face, eliminating every blemish. He tried not to stare. Her black curls framed her face, the picture of Irish beauty. But Óisin was just a tangle of muscle and hormones. He could no more pick out a dimple on her face or a curl out of place than he could lift her off him and escape out of the room and shut the door behind him. She placed her hands on his knees as if they were two pillows and laid her head on one side to rest on her knuckles. She could feel the tension in his body. If ever there was a time, it was now.

"Oh my Galloglass, we have both been wronged."

Óisin shook his head to free himself from his daydream.

"How so?"

His voice croaked with as much anger as he could muster, but being careful not to move Caoimhe's head or to upset her, for he would do anything for this moment not to end.

"I received a letter from my uncle the other day."

His legs stiffened once more, but he held them in place and Caoimhe smiled to herself.

"It was in the pile of papers I showed you the other day, but you were too busy to read. I try to help the best I can and repay you for how you look after me and also my father's house."

"Yes, yes. I remember now. I had some very important things to attend to that day. But since you mention it and deem it so important to mention now, please tell me what the letter contained."

Caoimhe raised her head from his lap to his visible disappointment and her face wore a picture of sadness. Óisin leant forward and placed his coarse hands gently on her shoulders.

"What is it, my love -."

He shook his head clear and Caoimhe looked sadder still.

"What was in the letter?"

Caoimhe released herself from his grip, stood up and went to the window.

"It was a sad story, a sad story indeed. He is high in the court of the Maguire and hears many such sad things, but even he was compelled to put quill to paper to tell of this story."

Óisin now pulled himself off the bed. He did not know what made him angrier, that his intimate moment had to end, or that this story had upset Caoimhe so.

"It is the story of a boy and his mother."

Óisin clenched his fist and went to the window to hide his anger from Caoimhe.

"I barely remember my mother. How does your uncle know of this supposed story?"

"He has to do many of the dirty jobs for the Maguire. The jobs the Maguire cannot be associated with."

Óisin's eyes flashed, and he turned on Caoimhe.

"How do I know your story is not a lie?"

Caoimhe spread her hands upon his chest and felt his muscles.

"Because we are alike. We have both been grievously wronged."

"I knew it, I knew it."

In a torrent of rage he flew across the room, spreading curses and spittle with every stomp. Caoimhe ran after him and attempted to soothe him resting her hands on his back.

"Sit, my love, and let me tell you the story. Once you know, then we can seek our revenge."

He took Caoimhe in his arms and leant down with his eyes closed to kiss her. She wriggled out of his grip.

"There will be plenty of time for that when we are man and wife."

She danced across the room and stood beside the bed.

"Sit, and let me tell you the story. It may sadden you at first, but then I will bring the light of a solution into our lives. It will be hard, but you have truly been wronged."

Óisin breathed out and in once more and tried to calm himself enough to listen.

"Very well. I shall sit and let you tell the tale. But if I am in a murderous mood afterwards, do not stand in my way."

Caoimhe guided him to the bed and Óisin obeyed and sat. Caoimhe resumed her position with her arms on his lap. She stared into his eyes and saw only rage and anger, a tumultuous, never-ending storm. He looked into her deep blue eyes and into what he imagined was her soul, and he melted. Caoimhe felt the tension drain from his thighs and knew it was time to begin.

"Your mother knew Cúchonnacht Maguire, Hugh's father, well. She was his part-time concubine."

Caoimhe looked up and saw only blankness and decided that now was not the time to be subtle.

"She was his prostitute."

Óisin winced and held his head in his hands.

"The story has barely started, my love. Be strong, for me."

Óisin fought back the tears in his eyes. The smell of the perfume on the blanket had brought him to a place he had seldom been and had run away from at every opportunity, his youth.

"Cúchonnacht had many concubines during his life, but your mother was his favourite. He had set her up in a nice little house in Enniskillen town, and she was a frequent visitor and resident of the castle. It was even rumoured that he secretly took her for his wife. The only obstacle was that she was low-born and a man normally as wise as Cúchonnacht knew he had to reserve his married status to build alliances for his clan. There was no time for love."

Caoimhe stared up into his eyes again and saw that he was about to well up.

"Then it came the time for Cúchonnacht to find himself a proper wife. They banished your mother to the town, for the advisors to the Maguire did not want her around as a distraction. They put the word out to the other lords of the north and a parade of eligible young ladies came to the castle one by one. But Cúchonnacht rejected each one for what seemed trivial or over picky reasons. Then your mother found herself with child. She sent messages to the Maguire swearing her undying love and asking him to follow the Brehon law traditions and for him to adopt the child as his bastard son and let her into the castle so she could give birth in comfort and peace. But it was not to be.

"His advisors had found him the perfect wife, or most say they had the perfect wife thrust upon them. Mairghréag, daughter of Seán O'Neill, the O'Neill at that time, was arranged to be his wife. They had little choice as the O'Neills had overlordship of the Maguires and it was deemed wise to get closer to them.

"In the meantime, your mother had given birth. You were born in secret in a house outside Enniskillen. But rumours of the child soon reached the castle. They did not want a recently low-born child to impede the marriage and wished to forgo the tradition of adopting bastard children. The MacCabe Galloglass, under Desmond MacCabe, came for her. She saw them coming and hid you in a cupboard. Someone found you and you ended up on the streets of Enniskillen as an orphan. Your mother disappeared and was never seen again. Some say she was murdered and you can see on a clear night her body floating in the loughs to remind the sons of Cúchonnacht of what he did."

Tears streamed down Óisin's face as he blubbered like a child. Caoimhe held his hand and did her best to empathise.

"Do you know what your mother's name was?"

"No," said Óisin between sobs.

"Bé Bhionn. Her name was Bé Bhionn."

Óisin howled and threw his head into his hands and sobbed. Caoimhe hesitated and then held his head to her chest.

"There, there. I told you we had something in common."

Óisin pushed her off his knees, howled to release the choking clutches of pain, and beat his chest. He pulled himself off the bed and staggered around the room as if drunk.

"I will carve the name Bé Bhionn on the lips of all those who have wronged her."

Caoimhe crawled after Óisin and grabbed for his hands.

"Come sit, my love. I have more to tell you."

"What else can you tell me now after you have ripped my heart from my chest? There is barely any more of me that can hurt."

"But your hands can get revenge. Sit a moment and let your anger be properly directed rather than blindly lashing out. I can help you get revenge on all of those who have hurt you and try to heal some of your wounds at the same time."

Óisin looked at her like an injured wolf looking for an escape.

"I can listen but my wounded heart won't let me rest for long."

"Come sit."

She invited him back onto the blanket. The wafts of perfume took on special meaning now. Once they meant a mother to be longed for, the dream of what could have been. Now she was a woman brutally wronged. Óisin took a corner of the blanket, inhaled deeply, and closed his eyes.

"Tell me now of my vengeance."

"My husband, the one who imprisons me, goes on trial at Easter in Enniskillen. I wish to give evidence."

"You can speak to the Brehon who is downstairs."

"I do not wish to feed the one who works for him with a defence. I wish to disown my husband and condemn him for his actions."

"And you wish me to bring you there?"

Caoimhe now gently took his hands and stared into his eyes.

"I wish to declare you as my husband to be."

Another storm was cast into the tumultuous seas on Óisin's heart. He once more cast his head in his hands.

"If this had been mere moments before you told me the story of my mother, I would have been the happiest man alive. But with such depths to sink and such skies to scrape, my heart knows not whether to beat for joy or sink down to the pit of my stomach and die."

Caoimhe grabbed his hands again.

"Once you have fully gained your revenge and rid your heart of such woes, when your mind is free, then we can become man and wife. But first, we must prepare for the trial. I will divorce Eunan in front of the crowd and then announce you as my new husband. But if we are to be man and wife and live together in this house, we must ensure that justice is done for my father and that Eunan Maguire is found guilty. For you, being the O'Cassidy Maguire, getting revenge for the death of your mother will only be the start. But the first thing you need to do is take care of that Brehon downstairs."

Óisin pushed her aside and strode towards the door with renewed determination.

"Pack your bags and prepare to leave. Do not come downstairs until you hear the end of the commotion. It may be dangerous."

She reached down into her pocket and took out a heart-shaped locket. It was old and worn and the latch to open it with was faulty. Óisin's eyes lit up.

"Is that a token from you of your love for me?"

"Alas, no. But it may be even more valuable."

Óisin took it in the palm of his hand and gently rolled it over with his finger, admiring its craftsmanship.

"How so?"

"It was a gift from Cúchonnacht to your mother. It goes some way to proving who you are and the wrong that has been done to you."

Óisin's face went a putrid shade of red and he scooped the locket up and put it in his pocket. He strode towards the door without a word.

"Goodbye, my love," said Caoimhe.

The door was already shut.

CHAPTER TWENTY-SEVEN

TAKING SIDES

S EAN HELD ANOTHER LETTER up to the light from the window to see if it was another contribution to unravelling the past.

"How long were you in the service of Cormac O'Cassidy, Taighe?"

Taighe scratched his head as he thought it obvious that Sean should not direct such a question to him.

"I was never so much in his service the way I think you are asking. I know nothing of his business or his letters, if that is what you mean. I was just one of his distant tenants, a man who would give him a couple of bundles of barley, or maybe the odd pig when his men came to the village looking for their rent. But we mainly dealt with the MacCabes."

Sean shot him a glance, a rebuke for avoiding his question. When he was met with a blank stare, he decided a different type of prodding was required.

"Would you say that O'Cassidy was an ambitious man?"

Taighe pondered momentarily.

"Aye, definitely. No matter how you define it, he was. But it was measured way more in the coin than by the axe. He had little interest in the raising of cattle but was obsessed with the market and sending his goods here, there and everywhere."

"Was he a big supporter of Connor Roe?"

"Sure we all were. Connor Roe may be stronger across the other side of the lough, but he was always canvassing for support over these parts. For every time he'd appear over this side of the lough, O'Cassidy would not be far behind trying to lick his arse."

Sean stood up and surveyed the different piles of letters he had assembled on the desk.

"So, if you had to put money on it, who would you say the largest pile of letters is addressed to?"

Taighe rubbed his chin, hoping this was a real wager.

"Well, most would be letters of commerce, but I am assuming they wouldn't count as you are looking for letters to one person."

"Correct. And?"

"You'd have an enormous pile to the Maguire about his taxes."

"Correct. Is that your guess?"

"By the smile on your face, it's got to be Connor Roe?"

Sean punched the air. He was onto something.

"Now, would it be beyond the realm of possibility that O'Cassidy was plotting to make Connor Roe the new Maguire and change the clan allegiance to the English?"

Taighe laughed.

"Beyond the realm of possibility? What? That's like asking, does the devil like fornication or do all good Catholics go to mass on a Sunday? Plotting against the Maguire is like a pastime around here. Eunan's father died in a fight between the different factions. He definitely was plotting against the Maguire and you don't need letters to tell you that."

Sean beamed from ear to ear.

"You may not need evidence here, but you need it in the court of the Maguire. Let me pack up the letters and then we shall eat. We should see if that Óisin fellow is friendlier once his work is done."

Sean tied his letters up in different bundles, sorted by author or recipient and by subject. He was sure that his master would heap praise upon him when he returned for such a diligent job well done.

The door of the room slammed against the wall.

"I want you to leave. Now!"

Óisin stood in the doorway, a surly, brooding monster. Sean immediately dropped everything in his hands and edged towards the door. His two Galloglass prepared to unsheathe their swords.

"I have the permission of the master of these lands to be here," Sean said. "I have been given freedom of the house and the surrounding lands by both yourself and him. What has happened to you that you renege on that permission now?"

Óisin stepped into the room, and two of his men, who followed behind him, occupied the doorway. He prowled around the room like a wolf herding sheep. Sean, Taighe and the two Galloglass centred themselves in the room.

"I do not need to give you a reason to ask you to leave. I am the master of this house," said Óisin.

Sean steadied himself.

"If you are, then you are a usurper. Eunan Maguire awaits trial and until that trial is over he is the master of the house."

"Brave words for one that hides behind a pen. What conspiracies and lies have you thought up whilst you took advantage of my hospitality? I was going to give you food and shelter, but now I shall cast you out into the storms."

"How would you know what I have been up to unless you are stricken by paranoia or you have a spy who whispers lies in your ear? What I have is enough to free your friend and master and for you to share in the bounty of his freedom when he returns to his home."

Óisin stalked the room, making Sean and his men's circle ever smaller. Sean knew that if he was to escape, he needed to do so quickly.

"Either set upon us or set us free. I am tired of watching you walk around us in your infernal circles."

Óisin stopped opposite the doorway.

"Leave your weapons and your cloaks behind and you will be allowed safe passage. I do not want you to take anything you have found here back to Enniskillen."

"I may be young, but don't take me for a fool. As soon as we drop our weapons, you'll set upon us. Leave us with our weapons and our horses, and we'll say nothing of this to Eunan and Seamus. I will tell them all the evidence was destroyed or has gone."

"How do I know you have not hidden any of those letters on your person to smuggle them back?"

"What has created such mistrust since our last conversation?"

"I saw the light. Now remove your cloaks."

Sean nodded to his men.

"Remove your cloaks."

One of the Galloglass turned to whisper in his ear.

"Then they will have us with our weapons down."

Sean stepped forward, stood in front of Óisin, and dropped his cloak to the floor.

"You may search me if you wish."

"That won't be necessary. Now put your cloak on and leave."

Óisin, his face a slab of sternness, pointed to the door. Sean looked back at his comrades in anguish. One of the Galloglass stepped forward and dropped his cloak, but not his axe.

"Satisfied?" he sneered.

"Get out."

Óisin pointed once more at the door. The second Galloglass did the same and was dismissed to the door. Only Taighe was left standing in the middle of the room.

"Do you not trust me either?" he pleaded.

"You have chosen your side. Now remove your cloak."

"You chose it for me."

"Remove your cloak."

Taighe took his cloak off and, like the Galloglass, kept his weapon in his hand.

"Leave and never darken my door again."

Taighe edged away, ensuring his back was protected by the wall. He stopped and raised his weapon when he reached the doorway, for Óisin's men still lingered there. Óisin waved them aside.

Taighe now found himself in the courtyard. His new comrades were in the centre of the yard, surrounded by men with an assortment of weapons, from pitchforks to axes.

"You are all right?" said Sean. "You can come with us to Enniskillen. I will find you gainful employment."

Taighe went and joined the group's defensive square in the middle of the courtyard. The smell of roasting mutton from what was once to be their dinner filled the courtyard and proved a bitter relish to hungry men who were once invited to this feast.

"Would you spare us one kindness and give us our horses so that we may leave?"

Óisin nodded and some of his men ran to the stables. Óisin stroked the locket in his pocket. Caoimhe appeared in an upper window of the house. She smiled down at Óisin and then she nodded.

"Weapon!" shouted Óisin.

He threw his axe at the defensive square and one of the Galloglass deflected it away with his shield. Óisin's men ran in to engage. The two Galloglass stood in front of Sean and edged back, fending off their attackers and trying to create the opportunity for Sean to make his escape. Taighe flailed his axe to either side of the Galloglasses to provide extra cover. They edged towards the perimeter of the yard. Óisin looked up at the window to see Caoimhe's scowling face. He grabbed an axe from one of his men and gave out a yell. He charged straight between the two Galloglass and drove a wedge between them. His men then set upon them.

Sean saw he was doomed and ran. He barely got three yards before his back became like that of a hedgehog, bristling with arrows. The first Galloglass fell to his knees under a storm of blows. Taighe's nerves went. He took to his heels. He saw the open fields and his freedom. He saw the face of a grateful Seamus when he told him of such treachery. He saw the village fields once more filled with an abundance of cattle and the sun shimmering on the waters of the lake. He felt a heavy thud between his shoulder blades, then another, then another. His legs fell away beneath him, his vision became blurry. His head suddenly became very painful as it met the ground. All he could feel was pain and his life drain away. Then there was nothing.

CHAPTER TWENTY-EIGHT

THE DECISION

T HE O'NEILL AND THE O'Donnell waited a week in Lifford castle as their messengers travelled to all the northern lords that were deemed suitably loyal and that could keep a secret. In the meantime, they would return to the farmhouse every day to hold talks with Alonso Cobos and his delegation. The lords of the north would put a proposal to Alonso, he would agree to it and note it down saying that he would present it to his King. The next day they would put a proposal to Alonso that built on the discussions of the day before and, again, Alonso would note it down and agree to everything. Then they brought in maps of the coast of the north and examined them for inlets and bays where a substantial force could land. But this time Alonso was more resistant.

"The Spanish Armada lives long in the memories of the nervous at home," he said. "Yes, we suffered substantial losses, more to the wind and storms than to the English navy. But the tales of the jaggedness of the Scottish and Irish rocks loom large in the memory. Some say the heathen Queen cursed them. But even if I overcame such superstition and fits of nerves, there is no landing bay that I could convincingly point to other than Lough Foyle, but that would be too far into the devil's teeth and we would have to sail all around the island through the storms of the Atlantic Ocean to get to it. I would very much doubt that the King would commit so many of his men to such a journey when we have lost so many already trying to support you with little to show for it."

O'Neill shoved the map into the centre of the table.

"Well, that's that then. I have good terms from the Queen on the table. Tell me why I shouldn't accept them?"

O'Donnell mistook the brinkmanship for anger and took out his dagger and stabbed the table top with it. He stood up in a flurry of curses and stormed out. Eoghan McToole O'Gallagher and Seamus abandoned their posts by the wall and ran after him. Red Hugh stomped up the hill towards the castle, leaving a trail of bodyguards and advisors behind him.

"Lord, wait," said O'Gallagher.

He undid the buckle of his sword and let it fall to the ground so he could run faster up the hill in pursuit of his master. He eventually caught him before Red Hugh could get too far.

"Stop, lord, please. I am old and my bones feel it when I try to match you stride for stride up a hill."

The O'Donnell's fury dissipated enough to stop propelling him up the hill and to engage in a conversation, albeit one punctuated by spittle and curses.

"All is lost. I don't know why you bother to run after me. The O'Neill, pompous old fool that he is, just wants to be a vassal and an Earl for his Queen. Why doesn't he just jump on a boat and go to court her and see if he can become King? The O'Donnells should never have trusted the O'Neills. We can fight alone. Once Connacht falls to me, I will be the power in Ireland. The Spanish King can't ignore me then!"

"Come back to the table, lord, and negotiate. The Spanish reluctance is understandable. How many have we lost to the treacherous seas? Let me send back to the castle for the maps I ordered my men to bring along. I cannot vouch for their quality, but the ones of Connacht and Munster were made by Godly Irish scholars and the ones captured from the English have been verified to be of a reasonable quality by Irish allies of ours from those regions."

"But I don't want to negotiate anymore. I want to fight! All we have done with the Crown this half year is circle each other like serpents waiting for the other to bite."

"Eoghan is right lord," said Seamus. "We must keep clear heads if victory is to be ours. Let me bring you back and Eoghan can arrange the maps."

Red Hugh cursed and shook his head.

"Damn it, my forefathers would have me do this. There's nothing like a good negotiation to give you something to stab each other in the back over. If we must, we must. Let's go."

Red Hugh set off down the hill at a similar pace to which he climbed up it. His bodyguards and advisors caught up with him one by one but backed away to give his temper space and followed him down at a distance. He came back into the room without a word and retook his seat. O'Neill had been to enough negotiations with him to know to leave him his space to cool down. Alonso spoke, but Hugh Boye did not translate until Red Hugh signalled his approval for talks to continue.

"Our King means you no disrespect and only wants to see success for our venture."

"But we are strong in the north. We know the lands, the English fear treading here."

"Again, no disrespect, but from what I know of your topography, the north is easy to defend while to conquer the whole of Ireland you will have to travel south and defeat the English in open battle."

Red Hugh scowled and leant to his left to whisper in O'Neill's ear.

O'Gallagher arrived with two men carrying a large chest. He bowed at the end of the table.

"Lords, I bring you the finest maps of Ireland we have in Tirconnell. First, I will lay out the maps of the coasts of Tirconnell and Connacht."

He snapped his fingers and the two men delved into the chest and rolled out two small maps. Their size did not impress O'Gallagher's master.

"Sorry lord, but these are the two that the men from the region vouched were the most accurate."

"No matter. Hugh Boye, examine the maps with Alonso and make us a proposal."

They pored over the maps, conscious that the O'Neill and especially the O'Donnell were looking over their heads, expecting a concrete proposal. With the detail on the maps so small and the maps unhelpfully ornamented by sea monsters, it was difficult to get Alonso to decide. The pressure was mounting on Hugh Boye for with every translation he adopted and owned more of Alonso's words.

"Lords, in order not to delay you, for I am sure you have very important business to attend to, may I suggest that Alonso and I present you with a proposal tomorrow?"

Red Hugh looked displeased, but O'Neill was ready to leave.

"We shall see you here at the same time tomorrow. Hugh and I have some other matters to discuss."

"May we have access to the whole plethora of maps in that yonder chest?"

"You may have access to anything you believe may bring you success. Come on Hugh, I for one am starving."

The room emptied except for Hugh Boye and the Spanish contingent.

Both parties returned to the farmhouse the next day and the Tirconnell winter weather, with its swirling grey clouds, biting winds and sheets of rain, did little to dampen the spirits. Red Hugh had decided that this was to be a decisive make or break day, whether to continue the rebellion or whether he would take the peace offer and enhance his hold in Connacht independent of the O'Neill. His servants were in the farmhouse to take everyone's wet coats and hang them up to dry so their masters could concern themselves with matters of state. Both sides exchanged greetings in their different languages and took their seats.

"Well," said Red Hugh. "Are we to have our rebellion?"

"You are to the point today," said O'Neill. "I would prefer a revolution for they are a tad more successful."

Hugh Boye smiled but did not translate.

"I'm glad I amuse you so. I only want us to draw a conclusion," said O'Donnell. "Let the rain not wear away your skin. Now Hugh Boye, think of something apt to say to our Spanish friends that will convince them to send a large army."

Hugh Boye tried unsuccessfully to hide his discomfort, but he did his best and members of the Spanish team unfurled several maps across the table.

"We talked long into the night and we think we have come up with several points where a large army can be quickly and successfully deployed."

Hugh Boye pointed at several spots across two maps, one of Connacht and one of Munster. Red Hugh cursed.

"I know you are not a stupid man, for a stupid man would not have a reputation such as yours. But you know that everywhere you have pointed is in hostile territory and our lands are in the north?"

"Excuse me, lord, but the only way that this rebellion is going to work is if the entire island rises up simultaneously. It is too risky to travel all the way around the country. The safest way is through the Irish Sea and the English navy would see you coming all the way past Brittany. Remember when you hired three thousand Scottish mercenaries, and they sailed too near to the English navy? If that happened, the Spanish may give up on us. They have promised to scout the shorelines along the Atlantic coast to see where it would be best to land and then give you ample notice of where you can prepare the landing."

Red Hugh slammed his fist on the table.

"Leave us!"

Hugh Boye signalled to the Spanish contingent to move towards the door.

"All of you! The O'Neill and I need to have a conversation."

A choke point developed at the door, for no one wanted to be seen to be dilly-dallying on the O'Donnell's instruction. The door slammed shut to emphasise the room was clear.

The O'Donnell struggled to contain his fury in the face of the more powerful lord.

"This is not what I agreed to. We wrote on many occasions to the Spanish King and told him what we needed. We sent some of our best men to him to explain our requirements. And they now turn up here and say they cannot land in the north? The Queen's terms look more attractive by the minute."

The O'Neill leant forward. The number of years he had on Red Hugh had greyed his hair and rounded his belly but wised his head.

"Have you not spent much of the last year trying to extend the O'Donnell influence in Connacht?"

"I have."

"Have you been successful?"

"I would count half the province as vassals and the other half ready to be toppled."

"What would topple the other half in the name of the O'Donnell? A Spanish army landing on her shores, perhaps?"

Red Hugh's eyes lit up.

"You have put so much good work in already that it would only be if they landed in Munster that we would have much to do. The island is a tinderbox. Years of famine, the suppression of our religion, the laws against our culture, the corruption of the English state, never mind the near century of war. It would not take much to light up the country."

"How would we do it? Which one of us would be High King of Ireland as in tales of old?"

"If men would not turn out for us, they would turn out for the one true religion. For all the efforts of the English monarch to impose their false religion on us. Men will turn out in their droves if they know there is a realistic possibility of being a Papist country once more."

"I cannot think of a nobler cause."

"Then it is done? We are agreed?"

The O'Donnell broke into a smile.

"It is."

Red Hugh hugged the O'Neill as if he was his father.

"Then send them back in again!"

It was a strange concept, the finest feast, yet it was to be kept a secret. It was hard to hide the hunting parties being sent out to the mountains to track down deer and wild pig. It was equally hard to hide from a spy, the finest cows from the O'Donnell herd being singled out and slaughtered. One by one, the loyal lords of the north came, each with a retinue of bodyguards and advisors, and rode into the confines of Lifford castle. The castle was too small to hold them all, and it was too much of a security risk, so they gave some lords residence in the surrounding farmhouses.

But Seamus was concerned. The Maguire had not arrived yet, and it was his opportunity to speak to him before Eunan's trial. However, he first needed to secure the support of the O'Donnell. He could not secure an audience with the O'Donnell so he had to resort to sending messages via O'Gallagher and he was still waiting for his response. The more lords arrived, the busier the

O'Donnell got. Seamus attempted to slip through the guards, but he was caught. Every time he was in the room with the O'Donnell he was busy talking and planning with the O'Neill. He needed to know if he had the O'Donnell's blessing before he made any moves on behalf of Eunan.

However, O'Gallagher was far more accessible, and Seamus finally cornered him. He was in the corridor beside the pantry, issuing instructions for the grand banquet. His cheeks were red and his brow furrowed and decorated with beads of sweat, but Seamus was unconcerned. He took him by the elbow and whispered in his ear.

"We have business which I raised previously that we need to discuss."

"In there. Give me a few moments."

He pointed to a room across the corridor. Seamus nodded and walked into the room and stood out of sight of the corridor.

O'Gallagher followed him in, confused, for he could not see him at first.

"Oh, there you are. I have not much time. Red Hugh is anxious that this should all go according to plan, and he takes his nerves out on me. What do we need to discuss?"

"My nephew, Eunan, of whom I told you before?"

"Oh yes, I remember. But remind me of what you wished me to do."

"He goes on trial for being a usurper in a week in Enniskillen. Before Easter."

"Yes, and what do you want me to do? Is he guilty?"

"Only of being loyal to the rebellion and loyal to the O'Donnell. I have hired the finest Brehons who will prove that the man he usurped was a traitor."

O'Gallagher shrugged his shoulders.

"So, where's the problem?"

"Connor Roe and his supporters. The man usurped was an ally."

"Once the lords declare for the rebellion, then no more rebels will be executed in the lands of the north. The O'Donnell knows of Eunan and remembers his service. He will be seriously offended if the Maguire takes this action. I will see that the O'Donnell gives his blessing that you may speak with the Maguire and mention the unhappiness of the O'Donnell should your nephew be proven innocent and still be killed."

Seamus scowled.

"I would have preferred it if the trial was abandoned altogether."

"The O'Donnell cannot be seen to be interfering in the justice meted out by other lords with whom he is in alliance."

Seamus looked away.

"I suppose I can work with that."

"You are a man of legendary resource. That blessing should be more than ample for your needs. I will see what I can arrange given your service of the past and present."

Seamus sealed the agreement with a handshake. Now he had to find the Maguire.

The Maguire arrived in Lifford castle that afternoon. He came surrounded by his horsemen, made up of the young nobles of the Maguire, some of whom were familiar to Seamus, some were not. The men and horses were streaked with mud, for the winter weather had not let up for the entire journey. Maguire hollered to the gate who he was and to let him in. The doors opened to reveal his guide standing, waiting for him.

"Seamus MacSheehy," said the Maguire. "I should have known it would not be long before I met you again."

"I am pleased to see you as well, lord. The O'Donnell has assigned me to ensure you have a pleasant stay on his lands. Unfortunately, his castle is small, so his hospitality is not all that he would wish it to be. But he has set aside a farmhouse nearby that you can occupy whilst you are here. I will ensure that you are secure at all times and will be your escort whilst you are here."

The Maguire smiled.

"I'm sure that you'll also bend my ear off about your nephew's impending trial?"

It was Seamus's turn to smile.

"I always like to keep up with what is going on in Fermanagh."

"Well, let me rest a while for I have had a long ride."

"The feast is this evening and if it goes as the O'Donnell plans, then you will return to Fermanagh in the morning."

This did not sit well on the ears of the tired Maguire.

"How cruel to bring us all this way on the pretext of a feast and then to spare the ale! We can talk on the way from the farmhouse to the feast. I don't have the energy to discuss politics now."

Seamus went and fetched his horse and an escort of men. They rode for about a mile with the castle still in view in the distance. The rain did not let up and the Maguire and his men were relieved to dismount and take off their wet clothes. The residents of the farmhouse stayed for they were obliged by the O'Donnell to show his guests hospitality. Seamus left them to recuperate as he returned to the castle to give them some space.

He returned later in the afternoon to bring them to the feast. The residents of the house invited him in. The Maguire was sleeping in the master's bed and one of his men went and woke him. He dressed and readied himself for an important night. The Maguire could only take one advisor with him and the escort was Seamus and a contingent of MacSweeney Galloglass. The rain had relented and whilst the ground underfoot was still soaked, the path back to the castle was free of another drenching. The Maguire's men fetched his horse whilst Seamus and his men stood waiting for him.

"Why don't we walk and talk?" said the Maguire. "I assume we have enough time and we can barter information, for I need to be prepared for tonight's feast and you want to know about your nephew."

"Seems fair. We have time."

Seamus spread his men in a circle around them but out of earshot. Two of the men walked behind them with their horses.

"It is a difficult time in Fermanagh, Seamus. We could do with a man of your abilities," said the Maguire.

"It doesn't seem like it from where I'm standing, lord. If you'll excuse the insolence."

"It is better we speak as two warriors in a bog. It is not a conversation I will have in company or in Fermanagh."

"I'll try not to abuse your favour. My nephew goes on trial soon."

"Within the week. We will know his fate before Easter is over."

"What will you do with him?"

"Me? Nothing."

"Then why have this farce of a trial?"

"It is not a farce. I have separated myself from Eunan because of our past."

"You mean all those times he served you so faithfully? When he stood by you when most had left?"

"It is just such emotional arguments that make me vulnerable. How can the Maguire be publicly seen to do a friend a favour? Fermanagh is such a divided land. It is a very tricky balance. I only keep Connor Roe at bay or avoid an endless civil war by the good grace of the O'Neill. That is why I have given Eunan's fate to the Brehons. Donnacha has hired maybe the finest Brehon in the land and Desmond has countered by hiring the best up-and-coming Brehon. It should be quite a contest and attract a large crowd from around the region. If there is any silver lining, if you excuse the pun, it should be good for the coffers."

"You realise Eunan is a usurper and therefore guilty as charged. But he did it for you and the greater good of the Maguires. If Cormac O'Cassidy's daughter had married Connor Roe's son, then half the territory of Fermanagh would have been under Connor Roe's supporters, greatly increasing the threat to you."

"It is this same set of supporters that I have to placate, hoping if the rebellion continues and the Spanish come, they will then side with me in the coming war. I do not have enough support to hold the Maguire together by just appealing to my own supporters."

"What of Donnacha? You know he is just a stooge of Connor Roe?"

"I was foolish when my father died, maybe overcome with grief, but definitely not mature or experienced enough to take over from him. I just wanted to charge out on my horse and fight the English. I changed nothing because I thought it worked, not realising that my father held it all together. Donnacha could see me coming from over the hill. By the time I realised it he was entrenched and trying to force my hand to reach an accommodation with Connor Roe that if I died, he would be my successor and then when he had little luck with that he tried to get me to reach a separate peace with the English saying that everyone else is conducting their own negotiations and that I'd be a fool not to."

"He's not all wrong."

"But he is far too emotionally entangled in Eunan's trial and if he loses, it gives me good reason to be rid of him."

"We would all be better off seeing the back of Donnacha."

"That would leave a position open as my advisor."

"If that is an offer, I would have to kindly decline, lord. I am much more a man of the axe. Whilst I can negotiate the intrigues of a court, you and your public may not stomach the body count. It would also be difficult to prise me permanently out of the service of the O'Donnell. He is a possessive man and less sensitive to the obligatory body count my work would bring. You'd be far better off persuading Desmond to come out of retirement, at least for the duration of the war. At that point reassess your position."

"We shall see what happens this evening and then at Eunan's trial. We would be fools to think we are masters of our own circumstances."

"What if my nephew were to survive his trial? What would you do with him then?"

"It would all depend on the circumstances and the political balance of power at the end of his trial. I would hope to be in the position to give him a command and make him one of my top men."

"What if I were to take leave to go down and influence those circumstances?"

"If such interventions were for the good of the Maguire and the Maguires, then you would have his blessing, albeit only in private. The rewards at the right time would be material. But I would frown upon such interventions if they should go wrong, end in a bloodbath and favour Connor Roe."

"I understand and our business is, therefore, concluded. You will meet a Spanish delegation tonight that will promise you the world. The O'Donnell will be giddy with joy and the O'Neill more restrained. They will pressure you into pledging to rebel and add your name to another letter to the Spanish King. If you ever want to be free of the English, now is your best chance while they are weak. Or else they will slowly grind you down until you get absorbed like the lords of Munster. I can't tell you which way to vote, but a young man like you will be a rebel by the end of the evening."

"You impress me with your wise words, yet you turn down my offers to serve. I may just do a deal with the O'Donnell for your services."

"See my nephew all right with a role in Enniskillen and the title of O'Cassidy Maguire and you'll be seeing a lot more of me in Fermanagh when I am not out on the battlefield. Look, lord."

The castle loomed up ahead and they could see other parties making their way up the hill.

"Destiny is before you," said Seamus. "The decision you take in there will set the direction of the Maguire forever. May your name live in legend rather than you be remembered as the last Maguire."

Hugh Maguire rested his hands on Seamus's shoulders.

"You certainly know how to heap pressure on the shoulders of a young man."

"You will be fine. You will probably not see me until after the trial. I will seek the permission of the O'Donnell to take my leave. Let us hope that our next meeting is a joyful one."

"Good luck, Seamus MacSheehy. Let's hope some of your luck rubs off on me."

Seamus waved to him and watched him enter the castle, then went to look for O'Gallagher to seek permission to leave.

CHAPTER TWENTY-NINE

DONNACHA'S CURSE

"OW!"

The needle pricked Dervella's finger instead of penetrating the cloth.

"The least we can do is have you looking your best before the trial."

Eunan tried to balance himself on top of his stool.

"Would you like me to get that girl you like to spend so much of your time with to sit on a stool opposite you?" Dervella said. "Then you can stay still for a few moments and let me adjust your clothes."

Eunan shied away from the mischievous glint in her eye.

"I can stay still myself, thank you."

Dervella smiled as she measured.

"It's good to spend some time with her. It helps get your mind off things. Are you going to invite her to Enniskillen with you?"

"How should I put that to her? 'Would you like to come with me to Enniskillen and watch me be humiliated and then executed?' No thank you."

"But you are coping much better now than when you were a child. You don't seem to harp on your mother so much, nor have those blasphemous dreams you used to get lost in."

Eunan became animated, stepped off the stool, and used it as a seat.

"I know so much more about my mother now than I did when I had those dreams. No longer is she the cruel tormentor who, for some mysterious reason, would take out all of her regrets and misgivings about life on her child. She was a victim. A victim of her brother's ambition, a victim of the role in which the clan cast her. She was like me, always pondering why is life so cruel to me, why is life so unfair? But almost starving to death in a jail cell really gave me a much greater perspective. Why must I jump at every perceived provocation from Seamus? He is a great distance from being a perfect and decent man, but he is a man of his time. He was created by times like these and is the best hope for us to navigate them. Believe me, I don't say that because you are his wife. I say that because you are like a mother to me. The nearest thing I ever had to a proper mother and I suppose Seamus is the nearest I ever had to a father who looked out for me, albeit only when his own interests aligned."

Dervella trembled and took his hand.

"Thank you for those kind words. They mean the world to me and it warms my heart to know that you appreciate my efforts. You are like the son I never had, for I would have no better son if Seamus himself sired him. If one good thing has come out of this trial, it is that you have gained a maturity and sense of perspective that you'll need to get you through those hard times. Seamus is a selfish man, but he was a good man in his youth when I met him first and fate dealt him a cruel hand. Like you, his circumstances forged him. Having you as his nephew, along with the rebellion, has seemed to renew his sense of purpose, given him something to strive for. Think of what he put himself through and the efforts he made on your behalf. Think of the men he sent to protect you on this island. You would have been dead without them. Remember that the next time you see him."

Eunan rose and took Dervella by the hands.

"I remember all the sacrifices that people have made to protect me around this trial. I mean to repay them all. Especially to you, Seamus and Desmond."

He leant forward and gave her a tender kiss on the cheek. But Dervella was a woman from a hard life with only occasional sentiment.

"Now get back up on that stool and let's get you measured up. The Brehon will not let off any oul' scruffy beggar."

Desmond returned to the island from Enniskillen. He was late and had to be found by Cúchonnacht Óg's men. He made his way from the harbour to the house under escort, for as the trial drew nearer, the threats to his life grew. Cairbre was waiting for him in the main room of the tiny house which was now surrounded by tents of the retinue of guards that Eunan had assembled. Cairbre was assembling the main strands of the case together to come up with a strategy to defend Eunan. The enormous shadow at the entrance irritated his already frayed nerves.

"Don't just linger in the doorway, Desmond. Come in. What news from Enniskillen have you?" he said.

"I could find nothing beneficial to our case."

He came in, threw his bag to the ground and almost flattened the stool as he flopped down to sit. Cairbre rushed to the table to protect the integrity of his carefully constructed piles of paper.

"Be careful, please! A lot of work has assembled these documents in a very particular order."

"Is there enough in there?" said Desmond.

"I can cast doubt, but any Brehon worth his salt should be able to cast doubt with merely thin air."

"So what do you think will happen to him?"

"God only knows. It depends on many things. What case they put, the mood of the crowd, Eunan's demeanour. Impossible to predict, impossible."

"Then we are lost."

Cairbre threw his hands in the air as if they had brought him here for nothing.

"How so?"

"Donnacha's curse is all over this," Desmond said.

Cairbre shrugged his shoulders.

"What's that? This is no time for superstition."

"He is a wily political operator, is our Donnacha. He always stacks the deck before playing his hand. The streets and surrounding countryside are full of his men, probably to ensure that Seamus doesn't show up to free his nephew. The Maguire has conveniently left town, leaving Donnacha in sole charge at the time of the trial. It is even rumoured that Connor Roe will show up in force to ensure the trial goes the way he wants it to."

It was Cairbre's turn to sit.

"Well, we are now all prisoners here. There is no escape from this island for any of us. We have no choice but to win the trial."

"Do you have enough to do that?"

"Without young Sean bringing me back something from the O'Cassidy house, I'd be saying a few prayers if I were you."

A faint warmness kissed the land, but the relentless wind continued its quest to rid the countryside of its touch. The white fluffy clouds hid in the upper echelons of the sky. Little daisies poked their heads out of the dew-laden grass. The woods were filled with the sound of chirping birds. It was a beautiful spring day.

Eunan got dressed in one of several outfits that Dervella had prepared especially for the trial. The mood was sombre in one and all.

"It would be far more honest if we were all going into battle. At least we'd have some control over our own fates," said Eunan.

"Aye, you're not wrong there, but we can't all choose our own fates," said Faolán.

He and his men had been ready for hours, watching out for the boats that would take them to Enniskillen and ensuring there were no dirty tricks along the way. Cairbre, his assistant and Desmond packed the trunks with the various papers they would need for the trial.

"It is almost time," said Desmond.

He rested his hand on Eunan's shoulder, but there was no reassurance in his touch.

"No, I cannot go yet," said Eunan.

He ran, but Faolán blocked his way.

"You can't do this. You've got to face up to this, for all our sakes."

Eunan tried to force his way past him, but to no avail. If Faolán did not block him, one of his men did.

"I only want to see Cara one last time. If I am to die, can I not see her one last time?"

Desmond sighed and waved Faolán away.

"Let him go, but follow him. Don't let him out of your sight. He must be back when the Maguire's men come for him."

He took Eunan by the arm.

"You must return or we will all pay for it with our lives."

Eunan nodded and brushed past Faolán. Faolán nodded to Desmond, signalled to some of his men, and they followed Eunan.

They followed at a distance. Eunan quickly noticed them, but that did not deter him from his task. As the trial grew nearer, every time Eunan left the confines of his house, he attracted attention, usually that of Donnacha's spies. Today was no different, but no sooner had the unwanted watchers followed him than they noticed Faolán and his men and they kept their distance. Eunan went to the other side of the island to the pier and sure enough, she was sitting on some nearby rocks dangling her feet in the water. He went and sat beside her. Eunan did not say a word. He took off his shoes and laid them beside hers. He planted a kiss on her lips.

"Is today the day?" she said.

Eunan nodded. He looked into her eyes and drowned in the sadness.

"Don't look at me like that. I have to be strong and for more than just me."

"I wish you would let me come with you."

"I don't want to let you see me just die."

"You won't die. I feel it in here."

She took his hand and placed it on her beating heart.

"How much better would things be if I was there beside you, to help you, to comfort you, rather than pacing around this island worried sick, not knowing if you were alive or dead?"

Eunan was torn. His mind and heart were already a storm of emotions, but sitting here, holding her hand, was comforting. As if everything had paused mid-action and he could take a few moments to breathe.

"Why are you on this island? Are you free to leave?"

Cara smiled back at him.

"Why have you not asked me this before?"

"I was just enjoying the moments. It never seemed real that we could leave together, so I never asked. A condemned man doesn't want much to do with reality."

Eunan smiled, for it was the nearest to a joke that he could muster.

"Don't worry about me. I am a refugee from Munster feeding myself through doing chores for whoever will pay."

Eunan juddered back.

"Not those kinds of chores. My heart is only for you. Take me with you. All I require is board and lodgings."

Eunan looked out onto the lake. This was too much for him to think about, too much pressure.

"Come on, Eunan. The boats are crossing the lake."

Faolán had walked across from where he was sitting with his men. Eunan put on his shoes and ran over to him.

"Can Cara come with us?"

"No."

Faolán walked off. Eunan ran after him.

"Why not?"

"We do not know who she is."

Cara put on her shoes and ran after Eunan.

"I want her to come," said Eunan.

"I don't care. She could be a spy."

"Along with all the other spies we have in our ranks? At least she would provide me with some comfort."

Faolán stopped and turned to face Eunan.

"And how are we supposed to take her with us? Donnacha's men are coming to take you and a very limited set of named people with you and they won't have made room for your mistress."

"How are you getting to Enniskillen?"

"I will sneak off the island when you've gone. You are by far the most important prisoner on the island. With you gone it should be a lot easier. All of Donnacha's men will have followed you to Enniskillen."

"Then you take her with you."

"No. Far too risky."

"Do you think I'll win the trial?"

"By fair means or foul, yes."

Eunan smiled.

"Then I will see it a huge favour to me and I will ensure that you are well rewarded by either Seamus or myself."

Faolán pondered for a minute.

"I'll make no promises -."

"Thank you, my friend!"

Eunan ran back to Cara and kissed her goodbye with all his heart.

"Follow Faolán. He will bring you to Enniskillen."

Eunan turned and ran towards his entourage, and they made their way out of the forest to meet the boats. His heart was suddenly full of joy.

CHAPTER THIRTY

TRIBULATIONS

THE WIND BLEW FROM the west and the clouds made their journeys with haste across the sky, guided by the white-yellow dot that appeared to be a sun without heat. Flowers appeared from between the clumps of mud and grass, their petals reaching upwards to cling on to every ray of sun, no matter how cold. But most got trampled or covered by cold mud as from every road, river and dirt track, people came to Enniskillen for the Easter market. Cows, chickens and pigs also made their way to Enniskillen but under duress, driven by kicks and sticks.

Eunan joined these farmyard animals for when he touched mainland soil he was immediately set upon by Donnacha's men and put in chains, and then cast into a cage cart to be brought to Enniskillen. Caolán Maguire had posted a ring of MacCabe Galloglass around the cart so no one could get near. When they set out on the road to Enniskillen, the cart passed by the jeering crowds followed by Cairbre and Desmond who berated Caolán every opportunity they got.

"This is a disgrace," said Desmond.

His face was so red with anger it brought concern to his men.

"We have already agreed to be bound by the rulings of the Brehon and Eunan has surrendered peacefully. The only reason you would parade him in chains would be to prejudice the trial in front of the people and make him appear guilty before one shred of evidence is presented."

Caolán was unmoved and did not even turn around to receive Desmond's concerns.

"I suggest you take that up with Donnacha when we get to Enniskillen. He is acting as Maguire as the Maguire is away. I have my orders and do not try to prevent me from carrying them out or I will be forced to defend myself."

"This is most irregular. I have never come across such pre-trial behaviour in any territory," said Cairbre.

"Welcome to Fermanagh, I hope you enjoy your stay," said Caolán.

The MacCabes marched on and Desmond and Cairbre followed at a distance.

As they came closer to Enniskillen, they noticed that the Easter festivities had already started.

"The crafty oul' fox," said Desmond. "No wonder they threw him in a cage. Everyone's out on the streets celebrating and seeing him being paraded like a caged animal."

Desmond and Cairbre redoubled their efforts to persuade Caolán to let Eunan go, but they could not get within earshot because the guards held them back.

They walked behind this macabre spectacle and onto the streets of Enniskillen. They saw everyone was happy and carousing. Some even took the time to throw rotten food at the cage. The Easter passion plays had started. The castigation of Judas called from every street corner. Every street player that Donnacha could hire asked for his thirty pieces of silver as Eunan came past in his cage.

"And Donnacha has his Judas," said Desmond to Cairbre.

By the time that Eunan arrived at the gates of the castle, they had so covered him in the juices and fragments of rotten fruit and vegetables that he had as much food gathered at the bottom of his cage as Donnacha fed him the last time he was incarcerated there. The castle guards surrounded the cage and forced the crowd back. The gate opened, and the castle swallowed Eunan.

Donnacha was waiting for him inside. He was in the full garb of the Maguire's advisor, red pantaloons with a cloth cap to match, white socks and a heavy black coat. Guards surrounded him. Galloglass also lined the way to the cells beneath the castle. He walked up to the cage to gloat at Eunan's predicament. He stood out of Eunan's throwing range.

"Greetings, young Eunan. It will not be long until it is all over. We have your cell waiting for you where you can wait overnight for your trial to begin. All of Fermanagh and maybe even all of

Ireland will see you pay for your heinous crimes. I look forward to telling my story about how the advisor of the Maguire had to flee your onslaught for fear of his own life. Indeed, the sheriff of Fermanagh appointed by the Queen herself looks forward to giving evidence about the affray you caused and the assault on his person, not to mention the other charges that will be covered in great detail tomorrow. What have you to say to all of that?"

Eunan leapt up from his seated position and grabbed the bars, and shook with all his might.

"I shall see that at the end of this trial, it is you called a traitor, and it is you that is behind bars."

Donnacha laughed and turned away.

"Don't waste your energy, boy. We have some nice leeches waiting for you in your cell to make sure you can face the trial tomorrow. There is no Maguire here to help you as he has had to leave on urgent business, so I am in charge of your trial. May the Lord bless your soul as you face the full wrath of Maguire justice."

Donnacha walked back to the door of the tower of the castle as his men unlocked the cage and tried to extricate Eunan from it.

Desmond battered the doors in the castle gate with his fists.

"This is scandalous. Let me in or the Maguire will hear of this!"

A head popped over the parapet.

"Get away from the gates, old man, or I'll release the slops of the castle upon you."

Desmond went a peculiar shade of red.

"I'll have your head for this! Don't you recognise me?"

"Should I? Donnacha is in charge now and he ordered us to shut the gates. Now, if you don't stop making a ruckus, one of my men will shoot an arrow at you. Now go into the town and console your importance with some ale."

"You'd better not be here when the Maguire returns."

"Neither should you. Now be off with you."

Cairbre took him by the arm.

"Come. We're getting nowhere here except maybe to get ourselves killed. Do you know anyone in the town?"

Desmond glared at the top of the wall.

"Some of my old comrades live in the surrounding districts. We may need both their hospitality and their swords."

They set off into the town with their assistants guiding the horses that carried their law books on their backs.

Another cart from the countryside queued to enter Enniskillen. Óisin sat in sullen contemplation with the reins of the horses in his hands. His memories of Enniskillen had changed irreparably now. No longer was it the colourful town of his youth, where his pick-pocketing and fighting skills saw him pull himself out of the gutter and filled him with pride as he was not dead, a menial labourer, or bowing his head to a lord. Instead, it was where he was wronged, where he had his life stolen away from him and his mother killed. His grim mood told of his determination to right those wrongs and to get back what should have been his - the tale of many a young lord born on the wrong side of the sheets up and down the island of Ireland.

The cart was covered and contained some fine produce supplied via Barnard to sell at the Easter market. The bills were yet to be paid, but Caoimhe's father had extended an unending line of credit. She sat just to the rear of Óisin and she wore one of her fine dresses, enough for anyone on the streets of Enniskillen to know that a lady, if not from Dublin but with wonderful connections, graced their streets. She had also brought her three guards to protect her. Óisin still did not know they were secret agents of Captain Williamson and soldiers in the English army. He only knew they were both skilled craftsmen and handy with an axe. They did the work Caoimhe asked them to do competently, and that kept Caoimhe off his back. Óisin put up with it for Caoimhe told him he had a lot to learn to keep up with the demands of a fine lady, and she was taking the time to teach him these things for his own good. He would have many demands on himself that he was not used to when he was restored to his rightful position.

He had arranged for lodgings in a tavern on the outskirts of the town, a modest house with room for all of them if you counted the outhouses. Óisin had not even brought the cart to a halt before Caoimhe protested she would not stay there.

"He is a friend of mine from old, used to run with me on the streets. I can get many an interesting piece of information out of him."

Caoimhe slapped him on the back.

"Nothing our Maeve couldn't get out of him in the back alley and him not even spill a drop of ale from his mug. And it would save me the indignity of staying in that pit. How will the court view me and my multitude of wrongs if I arrive having come from that decrepit house? I need to appear as a lady who has been deeply wronged by Eunan Maguire, not some harlot that is bitter because he turned his back after he had it away with her in a bush. My uncle has arranged for us to have some much grander accommodation where we will meet the Brehon before the start of the trial and he can help us and especially you with what we are going to say."

Óisin cracked the whip with extra bite, and the horses reared.

"Why didn't you tell me any of this? I'm supposed to be your fiancé, pending, of course, on your husband's demise."

Caoimhe climbed up onto the driver's seat and cupped his head in her hands.

"I didn't want to worry you about any of the arrangements, my dear. Spend the time coming to terms with the stories of how your mother and yourself were wronged. Now don't argue in front of the hired help. It's unbecoming of a man who is going to be the O'Cassidy Maguire in a couple of days' time."

Caoimhe smiled and patted him on the shoulder.

"Maeve will show you the way. Now I'm going to sit back there. Keep the horses steady, for there are many stones on the streets and we don't want them to go lame or any of the goods to get damaged. We can talk later before I retire to bed."

Óisin nodded his head. He felt like a little boy. But a whiff of Caoimhe's perfume lingered on the tip of his nostril. Anger took over again. He shook the reins of the horses and Maeve took her place alongside him.

CHAPTER THIRTY-ONE

THE TRIAL OPENS

DESMOND BREATHED IN THE cold. Once the frigid air had penetrated to the bottom of his lungs, he remembered where he was. Desmond coughed and rose from his bed. He had been one of the lucky ones to get some sort of bed, for he was surrounded by his bodyguards sleeping on the floor. Word had quickly spread of Desmond's arrival, and several of his old comrades rallied to his cause. The room smelt of dampness and sweat and a dirty haze rose from the men as they slept. Frosty morning air quickly penetrated his lungs, and he sat and coughed up all sorts of phlegm and soon, the men joined in the dawn coughing chorus. He staggered over the men and outside to the laneway so he could relieve himself, and then he went back inside to prepare for the day.

The only water to bathe his face was cold, and the only clothes to wear were dirty with yesterday's mud. He sat at the end of his bed and tried to scrape it off. He was left with clothes with scrape marks still covered in mud. They had not been allowed to take any baggage with them since the Brehon could take his books, as this was custom, but Caolán said that these books had used up all of their weight allowances so they were left with little but the clothes on their backs.

An assortment of groans came from the bundles of aching limbs as the men lifted themselves up from their restless night. Desmond ordered them to clean the house as a measure of appreciation for the occupants. They cursed as they held their backs and rubbed their knees and wished for a better retirement. Cairbre came in through the back door as they had given him accommodation in another house. He was still half asleep and Desmond pulled him up a stool so he could sit and wake up properly.

"Donnacha knows a trick or two all right," said Desmond. "He is trying to set the place and time where the battle will be fought and is harassing us until we get there."

"You're an old soldier and more than used to this," said Cairbre. "And I am a much experienced Brehon and used to someone trying to place a stone in my shoe to influence my decision making. I have directed some of my young Brehons from my school to meet us here. They will bring us suitable attire for this street trial and also stand in the crowd to assess the mood for no Brehon is going to come to a verdict that will get him lynched."

Desmond smiled.

"We'll need someone there who is on our side. I have spoken to my friend and he will attend alongside some of my retired former men, so at least we'll see some friendly faces."

There was no reassurance but concern.

"Will these men be armed?"

"Now you are being naive. All this trial needs is a spark and it will all go off. Nothing would please Donnacha more than to have the excuse to set his men upon us and have us all killed. We must be at our most vigilant. See how he incites the people with tales of Judas before the trial even starts? Of course the men will be armed."

"The life of a Brehon is expensive, as it is a direct rejection of the law to kill one of us. I must make that clear when we reach the court."

"You'd better get ready then. We start at the midday sun."

An escort arrived for them, led by Caolán. Desmond nodded to them. He was nearly ready, freshly washed with new clean clothes supplied by the young Brehons, ill-fitting around the edges. Maybe Cairbre had been too polite to tell them how fat he was. But Desmond looked fit to go to court. A line of young MacCabe Galloglass formed before him in respect to his status as it was an official Maguire function with all the nobles there up to but excluding the Maguire himself. The young men had clean chain mail shirts, polished cabasset and morion helmets and decorative ceremonial axes, but no less sharp or lethal for it.

"Have you come here to execute me?" asked Desmond.

Caolán did not see the humour in the question.

"I have been sent to summon you to the trial as you are here to represent Eunan Maguire, are you not?"

"I am here to represent a young man called Eunan O'Cassidy Maguire, who rightfully holds the title of O'Cassidy Maguire. Are you sure you are in the right place?"

Caolán ignored him.

"We need to go now. You must dismiss your own private bodyguards, for armed men are not allowed near the trial. These men are here to escort you and are at your disposal for the duration of the trial. They are afforded to you out of respect for your position as former head of the MacCabe Galloglass. Don't think that such privileges will not be withdrawn, dependent on what happens in the trial."

"Do I have the pleasure of your company for the trial as well ?"

"I have other duties. These men will escort you to and from the trial, transport whatever baggage you have, and ensure your safety during the trial. Questions?"

Desmond gave him a withering look.

"It seems clear to me. Wait here whilst I ensure we are ready to go."

Cairbre had ignored the Galloglass and had been going through his books and notes and making final decisions about what he needed to bring with him. Cairbre stacked his notes and books in a pile, and his young apprentices stacked them into boxes.

"You are either very optimistic or are planning on boring us to death," said Caolán.

"The time is nearly upon us where we all take sides," said Desmond.

"Some of us already have," Caolán said.

Desmond went and thanked his friends, who had dutifully guarded him that night, and arranged to see them later.

The trial was to be held in the main square of the town. They had cleared it of the local market and street performers who had gathered there in previous days in the run-up to the Easter celebrations. They had, however, left up the flags and Easter images of the betrayal of Jesus and his subsequent death on the cross as a reminder of Donnacha's interpretations of the underlying themes of the trial.

A ring of guards surrounded the square with concentrations of Galloglass around the main entrances. Upon the roofs were archers, their eagle eyes combing the crowd, looking for troublemakers. A certain number of people could congregate around the periphery as they needed to leave room for the prisoner, witnesses, and Brehons to plead their cases. At the end of the square nearest the castle was an elevated platform upon which were placed several grand-looking chairs designed to enhance the status of those who sat upon them. This was for Donnacha and the other dignitaries that would be in attendance. Below this were two tables on either side of the platform for both the prosecution and the defence respectively to sit behind and make their cases when it came to their turn. At the other end of the square was a gallows ominously looming in the background, should the relevant sentence be passed.

People from all over Fermanagh and the surrounding districts flowed through the streets to congregate around the perimeter of the central square. There was a festive atmosphere, as this trial was supposed to be the highlight of the Easter celebrations. Caolán threw Desmond and Cairbre into the maelstrom of the people clamouring to reach the square. The guards tried to guide them through, but they were not dedicated to their task and the party split and got lost in the crowd and suffered in the currents of elbows and impatience. Cairbre found himself thrown into the square. What clean and respectable clothes his apprentices had given him suffered in the carnage of the crowd and he tried to brush himself down with the low-level jeering of the crowd ringing in his ears.

"Is this all my learned friend has to bring with him today?"

Cairbre turned around and saw that the seats on the elevated platform had been occupied. Cúchonnacht Óg sat on the right-hand side, Connor Roe on the left and a grinning Donnacha in the middle, obviously the provider of the comment.

"My young apprentices have become lost in the crowd but will soon find their way here," said Cairbre.

He examined the crowds around the main entrances, searching for familiar faces. None were forthcoming.

"I hope your tardiness is not a reflection of your preparations for your case," Donnacha said. "I have drawn many of the nobility of the Maguire to this trial and I hope you will not waste too much of their time in trying to prolong the life of your client. We could have had him hanged long ago, such is the weight of evidence against him, but he insisted on his right to a trial. I hope it does not backfire on him or his relatives will have to live with his inflated infamy for the rest of their natural lives."

"You will hear my defence when the trial starts. If it would please the representative of the Maguire, I would appreciate it if he had his men search for my apprentices, for I fear they have lost their way."

"I thought you were saving the theme of your defence until later? I fear being misled will spread as if it were plague this very day. Eunan misled you, you misled the court. But you cannot fool the people of the Maguire and I warn you they do not take kindly to being misled themselves so you may wish to reconsider your defence and your client's pleas whilst you have a few moments to reflect."

In the meantime, Conchobar MacAodhagáin had taken his time setting himself up in front of the elevated platform, and once he had laid out his books, he and his assistants had the time to sit and listen to Donnacha ridicule Cairbre. Cairbre stood and waited. Finally, some of his apprentices were spat out from the crowd, hauling some of Cairbre's bags behind them. Cairbre crouched over them as they tended their bruises and opened the boxes to see what had survived the mauling of the crowd.

"Where have you been?" hissed Cairbre.

"Those soldiers were worse than brutes," replied one. "They dragged us down back alleys and tried to rob our bags. We took what we could get our hands on and fought our way through the crowd with the soldiers encouraging the rabble to kick and spit at us as we passed."

"If I had known I would have been treated with such disrespect, I never would have agreed to this. Set up over on the table to the left of the platform occupied by those savages. Let me distract them for a while."

Cairbre strode up to the platform and past the table of his rival, Conchobar.

"I must protest. I must protest at the appalling treatment that has been meted out to my assistants and me. To grant us an escort that leads us to the trial the long way round and then tries to steal some of our baggage!"

Donnacha gave a smug laugh.

"I hope your defence is better than this litany of unsubstantiated complaints. It is up to you to organise yourself. I assume that Desmond, who is probably stuck in some alehouse somewhere, never saw you in action before he hired you? If you are ready to proceed, then may I bring in the accused?"

With that, Desmond fell out of the crowd and into the empty square. He huffed and puffed as he got his breath back.

"Those young Galloglass you have are a disgrace to the MacCabe name," he hollered up at the platform.

Donnacha smiled at Connor Roe, who smirked back.

"I suppose everything was better in your day? Are we also to hear as a defence today the unsubstantiated claims of the poor memories of the old? Can you please get your shambolic team together so we may get on with this trial? My Brehon actually wants to earn his fee and not have an easy victory assigned to him because of your ineptitude. I will give you a minute to sort yourselves out before we begin."

Desmond went as red as a beetroot and staggered over the ten yards to the table of Cairbre amid the sniggers and jeers of the crowd. Cairbre took him aside and whispered in his ear.

"We are being set up to fail. You never told me it would be this hostile. I have never been disrespected so much nor heard of any other Brehon being subjected to such treatment."

Desmond put his hand on Cairbre's shoulder.

"Thank you, my friend, for all that you have done and put up with. But we have come too far to give up now. We have to believe the truth will overcome."

"I never took you for a foolish man."

Cairbre turned to address the court.

"I can now start. But we must come to far better arrangements for my treatment as the trial continues. The Maguire may not be here in person but it sullies his reputation that a representative could treat a Brehon and therefore the law in such a manner."

"I want better treatment myself for the death of my nephew and the death of the sheriff's son," Donnacha said. "In light of the allegations against the defendant, your complaints are trivial. Surely you have drawn a crowd to your trials before? Surely you can lay on such a spectacle for the people? Take it up with the man who pays you, who organised everything for the defence of Eunan Maguire. Do not seek recompense for how you have been treated by those who are the victims in this case when you are about to lay out such a shallow defence for the perpetrator. I have had enough of your delays to sabotage the trial. Bring out the prisoner."

A murmur went through the crowd, and it parted at the entrance opposite the raised platform. Those that could see down the street saw a throng of guards force their way through the crowds, with the top of a cage cart bobbing between the tops of their axes. Donnacha's smile was so wide it was as if an axe had inflicted it. The cage and its escort slowly forced their way through the narrow streets, eventually reaching the bottom of the town square. The cart broke the skin of the crowd and was propelled into the square, where it found its freedom of movement and quickly assumed its assigned position. Eunan looked every inch the guilty man, dressed in rags, dirty and sullen. The cage had been pelted with rotten fruit and Eunan spat upon continually. It looked as if he had been dragged through bushes, both physically and emotionally.

"I must protest!"

Cairbre's eyes bulged, his chest puffed out and anger overcame his normally sallow cheeks. Donnacha smiled at him, which only wound him up more.

"Please tell me, what have you to protest about?"

"You cannot treat a nobleman of the Maguire in such a contemptuous manner. To cage him, dress him in rags and parade him around the streets without convicting him first is an absolute disgrace! This spectacle is purely prejudicial."

Donnacha sat back in his chair and dramatically threw his hands up.

"I see we are going to have some trouble with you today. First, you complain about the escort given to you and how you got lost and your assistants got assaulted. So then we provide a proper escort and protection to the accused and you complain about that as well. These disruptions to the court and your unruly complaints and behaviour will just have to stop. The only thing prejudicial to the defendant's case is his actions that led to the death of my nephew and the sheriff's son. If you continue behaving in such a manner, we'll disband this trial and let the Queen's appointed sheriff dispense justice.

"We have come here to show fairness in the trial's conduct for these most heinous crimes. Part of our decision is whether to pursue the case under Common, Marsh or Brehon law. But I would put it to the court that both these Brehons, and I say both so I cannot be accused by one of being biased, both are from the MacAodhagáin family. The MacAodhagáin family is the premier and by far the most dominant Brehon sept in all of Ireland and therefore has a monopoly on both the creation and dispensation of Brehon law. The MacAodhagáins will profit from this trial no matter the outcome.

"But despite all of that, we have settled on leaving the case open for interpretation as to which branch of law by which it will be prosecuted in the name of fairness. All of this over the simplicity of leaving the judgement of the crime to the voices of the hue and cry and to the rightfully appointed sheriff of Fermanagh. In the name of fairness, we subject the trial to such tribulations and deny the simplicity of giving a father the chance to revenge his son, cruelly struck down on his own wedding day."

Cairbre turned to argue, but Desmond got off his chair and grabbed his sleeve.

"Let's just start the trial. This is all a trap," he whispered.

"I assure you that the people of Enniskillen revel in the sight of justice being done. But I will indulge you once more and obey your instruction."

Donnacha bowed and scurried backwards to his chair, doffing an invisible cap to Cairbre, much to the amusement of the crowd.

Eunan was released from the cage and was escorted to a chair beneath the elevated platform where he was surrounded by guards. The bowmen on the rooftops ensured he was within their range.

"Does he have to be dressed in the rags of a prisoner?" said Cairbre.

"Do you wish me to indulge you again? Are you not satisfied with your monopoly on the creation and distribution of the law that you also need to dress everyone up as props to support your flimsy case?"

Unlike the crowd, Cairbre was unamused. Donnacha rose once again.

"We have released a violent and dangerous man from his cage so that it does not look prejudicial. I only hope it is not to all of our detriment and he kills someone else and escapes. However, to show fairness, I will indulge you one last time. You can make the defendant your prop when we have a break, but I look forward to the case you present. You have done your utmost to disrupt and delay so that you don't have to present it. Now, may we please continue?"

"As long as the trial is conducted in a fair and transparent manner and my client is not deemed or treated in a manner that implies guilt until the court reaches its decision."

"If you MacAodhagáins so wish to come onto the territory of the Maguire by his invitation and take over our legal process for your own ends, then who am I, the mere humble representative of the Maguire, to object."

"Please refrain from trying to direct the court and leave it to the Brehons as your master agreed."

"Very well, I shall sit down now. When you MacAodhagáins have decided amongst yourselves the affairs of the Maguire, let me know."

Conchobar sheepishly got to his feet whilst keeping one eye on Donnacha to see if he had stopped speaking. Donnacha signalled to him to proceed.

"Would the ward of the Maguire please announce the charges to be brought against Eunan Maguire?"

Donnacha looked around himself to the amusement of the crowd.

"Oh, that'll be me then if you MacAodhagáins don't mind."

He took from his pocket a scroll and slowly unravelled it.

"The accusations brought before the court today are that Eunan Maguire committed two murders of men of distinction. The first, was Art Maguire, the son of the current sheriff of Fermanagh. The second was Cillian O'Cassidy a brave constable in the service of the Maguire who served with distinction in the cause of the Maguire and greatly inflated the ranks of the army of the Maguire with men he trained and led, who also served with distinction.

"Eunan Maguire is also accused of usurping Cormac O'Cassidy, who rightfully had the title of O'Cassidy Maguire, which title

Eunan Maguire stole from him along with his house, lands and other worldly possessions.

"In the act of usurping Cormac O'Cassidy, Eunan Maguire caused an affray, leading to the unlawful deaths of at least fifty men. Charges relating to this are also breaches of the peace and incitement of rebellion.

"During this affray, Eunan Maguire also assaulted the sheriff of Fermanagh, meaning to cause serious injury or death.

"As a result of this cowardly sneak attack on the lawful wedding of the son of the sheriff of Fermanagh and the daughter of Cormac O'Cassidy Maguire, the accused also forced Caoimhe O'Cassidy over the dead body of her fiancé to marry him so he could unlawfully claim the title of O'Cassidy Maguire.

"In committing the previous offences but specifically relating to the accusations of assault on the sheriff and his men and a breach of the peace and incitement of rebellion, Eunan Maguire is also accused of treason against the Crown.

"With the accusation of treason, the point is also raised that if he were found guilty, he should be condemned as an attainder and his relatives would be blocked from obtaining any honorary title given to them or any of their relatives by the Queen.

"The first point of order is assembling the witnesses and deciding which jurisdiction to try him under, be it Brehon, March or Common law. Would the Brehons please state their cases?"

Conchobar stood and spoke first, as that was the tradition.

"I would like to thank you all for inviting me here today, but wish it were under more pleasant circumstances. I think both sides can swiftly conclude that Eunan Maguire committed these crimes for the hue and cry has travelled far through the land and I will present to you many witnesses of both lofty and low status that will attest to the fact that Eunan Maguire committed these crimes. In fact, I do not think my fellow Brehon will contest these facts for the two young men mentioned are both indeed dead and Eunan Maguire has been all too eager to tell whoever would listen that he is the new O'Cassidy Maguire and taken Caoimhe O'Cassidy to be his wife to gain himself some cloak of legitimacy. My fellow Brehon will try to claim that there was some shadowy plot instead of love that brought Art Maguire and Caoimhe O'Cassidy together in marriage, but will have no evidence to support it except the ravings from Eunan Maguire's imagination. When the testimonies have been heard, I will ask that Eunan Maguire be handed over to the sheriff and hanged."

The crowd roared its approval, and Desmond looked nervously at Cairbre. Eunan stared straight ahead and gave no reaction to the accusations, for Cairbre had given him strict instructions to be silent unless asked to speak.

"We have been waiting a long time for your defence, Cairbre. I hope you will not disappoint us," said Donnacha.

Cairbre stood up and ignored Donnacha's comments.

"I do not live in Fermanagh and have not spent long here," said Cairbre.

"The lakes are beautiful at this time of year," said Donnacha. "I hope you have time to see them after the trial and not be run out of town."

Cairbre ignored him and paced up and down in front of the crowd, and then walked up to the elevated platform.

"But even I have noticed that Fermanagh sits on a powder keg. The biggest shock of this trial so far is that Connor Roe Maguire has shown his face in Enniskillen, whilst also noting that he has brought a heavily armed group of Galloglass to protect him and the Maguire himself is not in the county. These two have been at each other's throats since Hugh Maguire was elected and it is only through the intervention of the O'Neill that Connor Roe has been pacified and both branches of the family are on the same side no matter how reluctantly. To say that Connor Roe is plotting against the Maguire is not even an accusation, it is a statement of fact!"

Connor Roe shot out of his seat.

"How dare you accuse me of such a thing! I can barely stand the insult of a learned Brehon defending the murderer of my boy but do not test my patience!"

Cairbre continued.

"The prosecution apparently depends on proving what you all already know, take as fact and use as a fundamental truth by which to run your daily lives: that Connor Roe and the Maguire are mortal enemies and are continually plotting against each other. Also, any marriage into either branch of the family has to be seen as a political move and a signal of support or subservience to the side you are marrying into."

"This is outrageous!"

Connor Roe's chair flew back, a victim of his rage.

"The matter that is outrageous is that all actions between the two parties and the alliances they try to create are political, but the union of the senior branch of the Maguire and the family of the most prominent family in south Fermanagh is not!"

Connor Roe pointed at Cairbre, his finger shaking, his hand on his sword handle and his cheeks a dangerous shade of red.

"If this man continues to insult my dead son with his egregious claims, then I will have to assert myself as the sheriff of Fermanagh and have the court cleared."

Cairbre smiled and stood below Connor Roe on his platform, being careful to avoid the spittle.

"Which leads me nicely to my next point. The sheriff of Fermanagh. Why is such a respected member of the senior branch of the Maguire family so proud of this title? Who bestowed such a title on him? Why would he be so keen to hand the accused to the English to be hanged? Do the proud Maguire family who has owned Fermanagh for so many hundreds of years dispense their own justice?"

Murmurs rippled through the crowd. Desmond sat back as a smile danced across his face. He had never seen a mouse roar so. Donnacha could also sense the change in mood.

"Now that is enough oratory," Donnacha said. "You are not trying to get elected. Stick to the facts of the case."

"I am sticking to the case. What Eunan did was a political act and needs to be shown in its true light."

"You will get plenty of time to do that once you can call your witnesses. Have you finished your introductory speech?"

"Not yet."

"Please hurry, and while you're about it, try not to stir up the crowd too much with your wild stories and accusations. We have no wish for this trial to end in a riot."

"I will attempt to put your mistreatment of both myself and my client and your clumsy and obvious attempts to make him appear guilty out of my mind during my speech. May I continue?"

"If you must."

Donnacha sat down in a heap and looked bored. Connor Roe had not the guile to contain his fury.

"What authority does someone claiming to be the sheriff of Fermanagh actually have in your beloved county?"

"The authority to hang you!" shouted Connor Roe from his seat.

Donnacha signalled to him to calm down.

"Either you control this debacle or I will!" hissed Connor Roe.

"Let him have his say and vent his anger. Let me assure you, it will not be the last word," said Donnacha.

Cairbre looked up at the men seated on their platform.

"May I continue?"

Donnacha waved at him nonchalantly.

"All the sheriffs who have been imposed on the people of Fermanagh have stolen your property and killed everyone who stood in their way. They have acted to their own benefit and that of the Crown. How was Eunan Maguire to know that this sheriff was going to be any different when you had to call on the O'Neill to evict the first sheriff and call on him again to subdue this one?"

The crowd erupted. They pushed on Donnacha's ring of Galloglass, punching and kicking them. Donnacha leapt to his feet.

"Clear the square! Clear the square! Do not use violence. Take the prisoner back to the castle."

Cairbre signalled for his assistants to pack up. Some old comrades of Desmond broke through the disintegrating lines and surrounded Cairbre and himself.

"We are here to protect you, lord," said one.

"Thank you, men, for your enduring loyal support," Desmond replied.

Desmond bent over and took Cairbre by the elbow as he leant over a box of books.

"I didn't know you had it in you," Desmond said.

Cairbre winked back.

"Gentlemen. Please follow me to the castle. We need to talk about the future conduct of this trial."

Donnacha stood behind them with a phalanx of guards. He was not taking no for an answer.

CHAPTER THIRTY-TWO

INTERLUDE

THE RAIN PELTED DOWN upon them, so Desmond, Cairbre and their assortment of escorts ran to the castle gates. They were quickly ushered through, the rain having done more to avert the mini riot than the stand-off tactics employed by Donnacha's men. The streets quickly emptied as the mud took over. The guards separated Desmond and Cairbre from their escort and hustled them up the stairs to the great hall. Donnacha sat in the Maguire's chair whilst Connor Roe paced the room. Their Brehon had not been invited.

"You've wanted to sit in that chair a long time, Donnacha," Desmond said.

"I would only keep it warm for Connor Roe here," said Donnacha.

All Connor Roe could manage was a curt nod.

"I have laid on some food."

Donnacha clapped his hands, and the servants brought out a hot beef meal and laid it across the large table in the centre of the room. Neither Desmond nor Cairbre moved.

"Well, you can't just stand there dripping on the floor. Sit and eat."

They still did not move.

"I want to know why you have brought me here against my will?" said Cairbre.

"This is not a time for making a show, this is a time when men can sit and talk. You almost caused a riot out there and we brought you here for your own safety."

"You can't fool me, no matter how much you try. I am your prisoner," said Cairbre.

"If you won't sit, then listen. We need to get this trial over with as soon as possible. As you saw out there today, it doesn't take much to light the fuse."

"If you wanted the trial over quickly, you could have passed me off to the sheriff there, or got one of your men to knife me down an alleyway and say I was robbed. But you can't kill a Brehon, can you? You know your powers are limited and the sheriff there will run off at the first sight of the Maguire. So why are we here? Concede the trial and it is all over and we can all go home."

"We all know that Eunan Maguire killed those boys and unless the people see that justice is done, then it will fester like a sore," said Donnacha.

"Ireland is about to explode," Desmond said. "Do you think that any secret deal you do with the English will last? They are weak and if there was ever a time to strike, it is now."

"If we do that, we'll all swing from the trees as traitors," Connor Roe said. "Those who wish to rebel get support by perpetuating the myth of the Spanish sailing to the rescue. I'll bide my time in Lisnaskea, thank you very much and God help anyone who has crossed me when the English arrive in force to douse any remaining embers of rebellion."

"I can see that we are at an impasse," said Cairbre. "If you have nothing to offer us but empty threats and childish intimidation, then I suggest you release us and we'll see you in the square tomorrow."

"Once the witnesses come, and there are many, it will not look good for Eunan Maguire," Donnacha said.

"Then there is no need for this. Let us go to prepare our case unless you think your own is so weak."

"Enniskillen is so factionalised that I fear the trial may lead to a civil war," said Donnacha.

"This is a path of your choosing. You chose the battleground to fight upon and now you feel you are losing. Release us and see you in the square."

"Is there no sum of money or land, women or cattle that I can offer you to end this now for the good of Fermanagh? We are men of means and of much influence in all the power spheres of Ireland."

"All a Brehon is required to do is to see that justice is done. I will make my case and Fermanagh will see that I am right. What Fermanagh needs is truth and justice and I mean to supply them with it."

Donnacha pointed to the door.

"Then you are free to go."

Cairbre and Desmond looked at each other in confusion. But Donnacha's hand did not waiver. They walked cautiously to the door and did not look back.

Seamus never got permission to leave early. O'Gallagher thought the security of the conference to be too important to let any of his best men go. Therefore, Seamus sat outside the castle and waited but sent word to his men in Donegal town to be prepared to ride at a moment's notice. It was a black night with fires dotted around the castle as Seamus waited for news. O'Gallagher strode out to the largest fire where most of his men and Seamus sat.

"It is done. To the rebellion!"

O'Gallagher raised his sword to the sky, to the shouts of his men. The celebrations died down and O'Gallagher crouched down to address them.

"Now, not a word of this to anyone. There are spies everywhere. We must act in secret until the O'Donnell is ready to strike. We need to be vigilant and make sure that no spies can leave the castle, so I want patrols every couple of minutes. Now I must get back to the castle and join the celebrations."

O'Gallagher turned to walk back to the castle, but Seamus leapt to his feet and hooked him by the arm. O'Gallagher glared at the insult of being manhandled so.

"I'm sorry, lord, but I must speak with the Maguire urgently," Seamus said. "It is a matter of the life or death of my nephew Eunan. I need to speak with him at once."

O'Gallagher contemplated the request against any deemed threat to the security of the northern lords.

"As it is you, follow me. But you are using up much of the credit you have built up with the O'Donnell."

"From your announcement, it sounds as if I'll have plenty of opportunity to build it back up again."

"This way," O'Gallagher growled.

Seamus ran behind him.

"When can I leave?"

"You are really pushing your luck."

"I'm trying to save my nephew from the rope and Fermanagh from potential civil war."

"You're full of yourself."

"They will probably hang my nephew in the middle of Enniskillen."

O'Gallagher stopped and turned to Seamus.

"I'll take you at your word. You do what you must with the Maguire and I'll secure your absence with the O'Donnell."

"Thanks. I owe you one."

"As you said before, you'll have plenty of opportunity to pay me back."

The celebrations in the hall were in full swing. It was as boisterous as any of the campsites around the castle but the alcohol was more abundant and the revellers far better fed. The Maguire was deeply embedded in the celebrations with his arm draped over Alonso Cobos. Maguire was amongst the younger lords congregated near Red Hugh as they were all of similar ages. The O'Neill showed his age and his restraint.

Seamus wriggled his way past swaying lords, clumsy elbows and endless toasts until he was within touching distance of the Maguire.

"Lord, may I have a word?" he said, and he gently touched the Maguire on the elbow.

"Who's that? Oh, it's you!"

The Maguire evidently was well inebriated.

"Lord, Eunan is about to be hanged in Enniskillen. If you are going to join the rebellion, you need your best warriors at your disposal. No matter what Donnacha has convinced you Eunan has done, he did it for the good of the Maguire."

"When this rebellion takes off, I'll send Donnacha packing off to Lisnaskea where he belongs. That is, if I let him live."

"That is good to hear, lord, but I need you to sign a pardon for Eunan before it is too late. If you sign one for me now, then I can ride straight to Enniskillen and save Eunan. What do you say?"

"I say yes," and Hugh Maguire raised his mug in another toast. "Yes, let's save Eunan. Get me a secretary and I will sign a pardon."

"Wait there. Wait there, lord."

Seamus stood in a panic with one eye on the Maguire to see that he did not wander off and with one eye on the periphery of the room to see if there was anyone who could write this pardon. He saw a secretary just as the Maguire went to embrace the O'Donnell. Seamus ran over and grabbed the man who was holding a book.

"Can you take notes right now?" Seamus asked.

"I can do that, but you must give me a moment whilst I get a quill."

Seamus danced like a cat on a hot tin roof whilst the man went away to fetch himself a quill. The Maguire was now embroiled in a conversation with the O'Donnell but Seamus knew he would not get a better opportunity. He grabbed the man by the arm and forced his way through to where the Maguire was standing.

"Lord, I need your help now," pleaded Seamus.

"Oh yes. Hugh, do you know that my man Donnacha is going to hang Eunan Maguire?"

Red Hugh seemed genuinely taken aback.

"Why would you allow such a thing?"

"He twists my arm with threats about Connor Roe. I thought that if I gave into the idea of this sham trial Eunan would easily get off and it would undermine him and give me the chance to be rid of him."

"Be strong," said Red Hugh, getting very animated. "If someone is going against you, act decisively."

The Maguire, even in his drunken state, knew what he meant.

"Send over the secretary and I will dictate a pardon."

He then turned to Seamus.

"Then you come and be one of my commanders."

Seamus froze.

"You need to ask the permission of the O'Donnell for I am bound to him."

The Maguire looked quizzically at the O'Donnell.

"We may come to some arrangement for you to borrow him, but I need him as one of my chief organisers of men. The

O'Neill has twisted my arm to hand him over Hugh Boye, so this conference has been quite costly to me."

Seamus saw he needed to offer something.

"If Eunan lives, give the position to him. He has served you well in the past. I will mentor him, so you will benefit from my skills as well. Is that enough to earn Eunan a pardon?"

"I cannot let Eunan die, and I can easily use this as an excuse to be rid of Donnacha. You shall have your pardon."

The Maguire turned to mutter in the secretary's ear. Seamus now turned to Red Hugh before he wandered off.

"May I take my leave, lord, to go to Fermanagh to save my nephew?"

Red Hugh put his hand on Seamus's shoulders.

"Do what you must and take as many men as you need. But when you are ready, hurry back for I have much work for you."

"Thank you, lord, thank you."

Seamus bowed and walked backwards until he was once more in the company of the Maguire.

"Now where is a table? Oh, there."

The Maguire set the dictated pardon on a table and signed it.

"Now take it and with God's speed I hope you are not too late."

"So do I, lord, so do I."

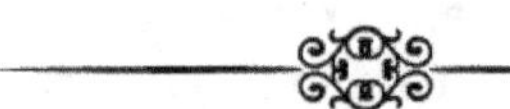

Desmond and Cairbre were reunited with their escort and released from Enniskillen castle. They wandered through the emptied streets of Enniskillen, wondering why Donnacha had made them go there if he was going to release them so easily. They turned the corner to reach the house of Desmond's ex-comrade who had taken them in. They now realised why Donnacha had delayed them so. The house burned and a line of neighbours snaked down the street passing buckets of water along to douse the fire. In front of the house were the bodies of Cairbre's assistants and Desmond's friend, obviously having been bludgeoned to death. Cairbre broke down in tears and Desmond tried to console himself in a more practical way by organising the efforts to put out the fires.

"What happened here?" cried Cairbre to the crowd.

No one spoke until an old man came forward.

"Soldiers came, soldiers of the Maguire. Under the command of that constable, Caolán. They killed everyone they could find, set the house on fire and threw in the dead men's baggage. Then they ran off to contain the riot. It all happened so quickly."

"Would you be willing to stand up in the town square and swear on the Bible to what you saw?" said Cairbre.

The tears by now could barely douse his anger.

"I may be old, but I don't want to die. I'll give you my story right here and now and you can do with it what you will. But I'll go no further."

As angry as he was, Cairbre could barely blurt out a "thank you". He went and joined the line of bucket-bearers for he had to do something with himself to take some time to think. Eventually, the fire went out, and some locals shared out bread and ale with all of those who had helped. Cairbre and Desmond were grateful for the sustenance, for they had not eaten since the morning. They sat and rested as it began to rain.

"Well, curse the heavens, it could have started to rain earlier and saved us all that work," said Desmond.

"Don't bring down more bad luck on us. I lost all my notes and books in the fire. This was deliberate," said Cairbre.

A bitterness simmered within his words.

"Will you be able to continue tomorrow?"

"What choice do I have? I can stay up most of the night to recreate my notes but I must get some rest for no matter how exhausting today was, tomorrow will be worse."

"Well, in amongst the disaster that was this evening, I have a sliver of good news. I have a friend who can take us in for the evening and claims that he can smuggle us to the trial in the morning and avoid this morning's debacle."

"As long as he has paper and a quill for me and a bed for you, his offer will be welcome."

"I think he can manage that. Come this way."

CHAPTER THIRTY-THREE

THE HUE AND CRY FOR TRAITOR MAGUIRE

T HE NEXT MORNING THE crowds had swelled in and around the central square of Enniskillen, for the stories of what happened the day before had travelled far and wide. Donnacha, Connor Roe, and Cúchonnacht Óg took their seats and waited. They pulled Eunan into the square in his cage cart to howls of derision, but Donnacha noted they were far less pronounced than the day before. The crowd had kept their rotten vegetables to themselves. They waited and waited whilst Connor Roe got more and more agitated. He leant over and whispered in Donnacha's ear.

"Can we either start these proceedings or else get them declared forfeit for the actions of their Brehon? I hear Seamus MacSheehy has left Tirconnell with a band of men and is heading this way. The sooner Eunan Maguire is hanging in the square, the sooner I can leave for home."

Donnacha winced.

"Be patient. Give our Brehon a little more time. There is still a distance to travel before we can carry the population with us. Don't worry about Seamus. Captain Williamson has assured me he will keep MacSheehy away for the duration of the trial."

"He better had. If he doesn't, we'll be plunged into a destructive war."

A cheer came from a distant section of the crowd. Cairbre and Desmond entered the section reserved for the court. They were escorted by Faolán and his men, who had arrived the night before and had acquired arms and armour through Seamus's connections in the town. Donnacha could see the fury in Cairbre's eyes as he strode across the empty square. Yet he was undeterred. He stood up and walked to the edge of the platform.

"Are you going to apologise to the court for your tardiness?"

Cairbre did not reply. He continued walking until he was directly beneath Donnacha, and he could look up and address him.

"I wish for the court to record why I am late and the mistreatment and insulting behaviour I have had to endure since the trial started."

"We have no time for your attention-seeking for another day," Donnacha said. "Are your complaints to do with the riot you caused yesterday because of your wild and insensitive accusations? Therefore, if the suffering you have endured is because of the riot you instigated then we will record your complaints but I will reserve my right to a rebuttal to place your comments in context so that it will not be seen as a flagrant attempt to influence the outcome of the trial."

"Then you leave me with no choice."

Cairbre did an about-turn and addressed the crowd.

"Nothing I have said in this court has been meant to provoke, merely to establish the truth and the circumstances around why these events happened and to place them in context. If it causes an affray, I can merely speculate that it is because the people of Fermanagh think that a grave injustice is about to be done."

"Address the court! Please come and face the court," shouted Donnacha at Cairbre's back.

"After being taken against my will to Enniskillen castle, I returned to my lodgings to find it set on fire. But worse than that, my host was slain, along with all my assistants and my books and notes were cast into the flames."

"Sit down and wait your turn to speak," Donnacha said. "When you speak, address the court and not the crowd. If you continue to bait the crowd, I will have you arrested and hand the prisoner over to the sheriff."

Cairbre turned from the crowd and walked back to beneath the stage once more.

"I came here under the written agreement signed by both sides that they would abide by the judgement and law of the Brehons and, by default, the rules devised by the Brehons in how to conduct the trial. So far you have broken every rule and then some."

"You are well within your rights to argue with your fellow Brehon and MacAodhagáin about the conduct of the trial, but only when it is concluded. Now please will you sit down before I have to send in my men to sit you down?"

Cairbre stood defiantly, and Donnacha sat and signalled to Caolán. Cairbre was soon seated with two guards beside him.

"Now that all the disruption is over, Conchobar, please would you present your case?"

Conchobar stood up, almost surprised that Donnacha had allowed him to speak. He shuffled his papers, consulted his notes and took up Cairbre's former position in front of the stage.

"It is well known in all of Fermanagh that Eunan Maguire was responsible for the deaths of the two men for whom we seek justice. I will present to you members of the hue and cry that has rung out from Derrylinn to Enniskillen which told of the crimes of Eunan Maguire. May I present my first witness?"

A parade of random people whom neither Desmond nor Cairbre knew stood up and testified that they either saw Eunan kill the two men or they had heard that Eunan had killed the two men.

"So what do you have to say to that, Cairbre?" asked Conchobar.

"We do not dispute that the two men are both dead, that Eunan was involved in the affray, but no consistent evidence is given to say that Eunan killed both men with his own hand. However, I could go into any village or wood in South Fermanagh and offer coin to the starving and they would repeat anything that I told them if they had no fear of repercussion. Their testimony is useless."

"Well, I, for one, am glad to know that you hold the opinions and observations of the people of Fermanagh in such contempt. I'm sure you'll be glad to leave when the trial is over and return to your MacAodhagáin school of Brehon law and dictate to us from your lofty towers the rules by which we should live our lives."

That earned a tremendous roar from the crowd and a broad smile from Connor Roe.

"Since the evidence of the common man is not to your liking, let me ask a noble woman who has been grievously wronged by Eunan Maguire, the woman whom he forced to be his wife. Please, may I have Caoimhe O'Cassidy?"

Caoimhe let go of Óisin's hand and emerged from the crowd to the right of the platform. She let her cloak fall to the ground, which Óisin scurried to pick up after her. Caoimhe was wearing her green velvet dress and wore flowers in her hair. She looked the epitome of Irish beauty but with an aftertaste. On second glance, was this the personification of Maguire beauty or that of a lady of the Pale? The crowd cheered as she positioned herself in front of Donnacha. She smiled coyly at the crowd and cowered as she passed Eunan, the perfect picture of victim and woman wronged. She made much of pretending not to be able to look Eunan in the eye. Eunan, for reasons only known to himself, looked wounded because his wife was here to testify against him. He looked at Desmond, who nodded in reassurance. Eunan searched the crowd for Cara, but could not find her. He felt all alone.

"I curse the day I ever laid eyes on Eunan Maguire and that I took pity on him, for he looked a little boy lost," said Caoimhe.

"That's a lie!" cried Eunan.

Cairbre glared at him, for he had broken their agreement that he should be silent for the duration of the trial unless directly addressed.

Eunan mouthed a "sorry" to Cairbre.

Caoimhe looked as if she was going to cry.

"From my days as a little girl, I always dreamed of my wedding day and never in my worst nightmares did I think it would turn out the way it did. I was to be married to the man of my dreams and met him under the tree which I played under as a child, and we were about to exchange our vows until a flying axe brutally felled him. The blood and brains of my beloved flowed down my dress."

Then she cried, and the crowd booed. Donnacha smiled. He had played his ace card, and it was working.

"So we know how your fiancé was brutally murdered. How did you end up married to Eunan Maguire?" asked Conchobar.

"I fled to the house and my new husband-to-be, Óisin Maguire, tried to hide me. But Seamus MacSheehy found me in the house and dragged me back to the tree. He said that since I had my wedding dress on, I may as well get married and if Eunan married me, it would make it harder to argue against him being the real O'Cassidy Maguire."

Conchobar approached the platform and then turned to address the crowd.

"It is obvious to me that Eunan Maguire killed Art Maguire in a callous attempt to legitimise his usurping of Caoimhe's father and taking his title."

A hush came over the crowd.

"What is your situation now?"

"I was kept prisoner by Eunan and his wicked uncle. I could not leave my room except if they wished to degrade me and force me to do menial chores in front of my former servants. They killed my maid when she tried to run to make an example of her."

"If that is your situation, how are you able to testify here today?"

"One of Eunan's, hopefully former, men has a kind heart, and we fell in love. He protected me, helped to restore somewhat my father's lands and smuggled me here today. Once Eunan Maguire has seen justice, we will be married and then see my father returned to his home."

She then shed a couple of tears, and the crowd began to murmur.

"Cairbre, you may question the witness if you can avoid making your comments too incendiary," Donnacha said.

Cairbre stood up from his seat and Caolán took a step forward and stood beside him with his hand on the grip of his sword.

"I hope your scribes are noting how I am being treated, Conchobar, for all mine are dead."

Donnacha laughed.

"Please keep your comments on the case at hand. You can discuss with your fellow MacAodhagáins how to hide the transparency of cases once you have left Fermanagh."

Cairbre ignored Donnacha and walked over to where Caoimhe was standing.

"Did you see who threw the axe that killed your fiancé?"

"It was Eunan Maguire."

"That is who you think and want to have thrown the axe. But you were standing face forward with your fiancé on your right-hand side. You were about to exchange vows. Your fiancé was struck square in the back of his head and fell forward, covering you in both blood and brains. Would you have us believe that when you were about to exchange vows, you were looking behind you and saw Eunan Maguire actually throw the axe?"

"I...I cannot be sure. It was a very traumatic moment for me. I saw Eunan Maguire but it may have been in the melee afterwards."

"So that is no. You did not see Eunan Maguire actually throw the axe. You merely assume that he did for whatever reasons you have."

Caoimhe gritted her teeth.

"Please do not badger the young lady, she has obviously been through a lot," said Donnacha.

"Don't worry, I'll be gentle with your niece," came the reply.

"You are very well dressed for a captive?" Cairbre said.

"I have to appear in front of the clan to get justice for both myself and my father. It gives me confidence to look my best. My father was a well-respected man in the clan and I am here to restore him to his previous good fortune."

"Did your father survive the affray at your wedding?"

Caoimhe paused and became coy at this line of questioning.

"Does my father's survival make Eunan's crime any the less wicked?"

"Please answer the question."

"He fled, eastwards, I think. I was a prisoner. I couldn't exactly visit him," she said, her voice tinged with defiance.

"Where eastwards?"

"I do not have a map in my meagre possessions. If you wanted to speak to him, you could have summoned him here instead of asking me."

"We both know he now lives in the Pale. We both know that he is now a successful merchant hand in hand with the English. Where did you get that splendid dress that you illuminate the court with today?"

"I made it," she hissed.

"One day the Maguire will return and he will implement Brehon law and he will hold you to a breach of that law by lying to a Brehon."

"Do not dictate what the court can and can't do," said Donnacha.

"It is a Brehon law court that implements Brehon law!"

"Again, do not come here to dictate MacAodhagáin laws to the Maguires. We have our own customs."

"Since I cannot pursue this line of questioning, I will make the court aware of my conclusions."

"Please keep these conclusions factual and do not waste the court's time with idle speculation," replied Donnacha.

"Your father is now a well-to-do merchant in the Pale, having been admitted to the exclusive and Protestant merchants guild. I wonder how he negotiated that?"

"This is hearsay, mere speculation," cried Donnacha.

"Well, I could provide evidence, but I sent one of my assistants to O'Cassidy house with a substantial bodyguard and they never returned."

"Perhaps he lost his virginity to some south Fermanagh girl and absconded leaving the bookish life behind?" suggested Donnacha.

He smiled as the howls of derision from the crowd signalled the comment had won their approval.

"I would hope that the battle-hardened MacCabe Galloglass that escorted him were not that hard up for such a dereliction of their duties for they did not return either."

"Do not incite a riot as you did yesterday. The MacCabes' honour is beyond repute."

"If that is so, then I wish to give evidence to the court as to Eunan's motivations," said Desmond.

He got off his seat and stood directly behind Donnacha.

"It's time that the people of Enniskillen knew what really goes on."

A bead of sweat fell from Donnacha's forehead, despite the crisp coolness of the day. He looked to Connor Roe for reassurance, but Connor Roe mouthed "no".

"I am surprised at my fellow Brehon's silence throughout this trial," Cairbre said. "It may be easy to sit there and say nothing and earn his eleven per cent fee, but by the way this trial has been conducted it may be his last for his own reputation and that of Brehon law will have been ruined."

Conchobar's fury at being ignored finally got the better of him.

"If the witness can add further colour to the defendant's case, then it is allowable under Brehon law. We can hear his testimony tomorrow if the other Brehon agrees?"

"I do," said Cairbre.

He smiled. His cousin had finally come to life.

"If we agree, then I suggest we adjourn for the day," said Conchobar. "We can then meet up in the morning to discuss the conduct of the trial before it concludes. I fear that if the trial continues in the present manner, then the reputation of Brehon law will be sullied in Fermanagh forever."

Donnacha leapt out of his seat and stormed off the stage without another word. Connor Roe signalled to the MacCabe Galloglass to secure the prisoner and then followed Donnacha.

Cairbre walked over to his fellow Brehon and placed his hand gently on his shoulder.

"We must sort this out and retrieve some semblance of justice from this sorry mess."

"I apologise for my negligence. I now see the damage I have done. I will speak with Donnacha and tomorrow will be different or not happen at all."

Caoimhe had been in the centre of the square but slipped off when Cairbre had started to debate with Donnacha. She made her way back to Óisin through the restless crowd. She came back to a little boy suffering the contorted rage of a monster.

"Is Eunan going to get away with it? Is the murderer of my mother going to have the ultimate word and save the man who did all of this to you?"

Caoimhe stroked his face and held his hand.

"Calm down, my love. Have faith in my uncle. He will see Eunan hanged before tomorrow's sun is set."

Óisin pulled his hand away.

"It didn't look like that to me. He will not take you away from me as well. I will not let that happen."

"ÓISIN," Caoimhe cried.

But it was too late. He had already vanished into the crowd.

CHAPTER THIRTY-FOUR

THE RECKONING

Ó ISIN WANDERED THROUGH THE backstreets of Enniskillen, searching for a way to quench the burning hole in his chest. It was dark by now and the streets buzzed with discontent as tales from the trial were retold on every street corner and from the doorway of every tavern. Some argued for Eunan Maguire and some argued against. The arguments were all hotly contested, some ending in shouting matches and some in brawls. The MacCabes kept to the shadows and only interjected when the fights threatened to get out of control. Óisin wandered from tavern to tavern, taking drinks as he went. He soon came to one that was very familiar to him, one where the landlord would have set upon him if he showed his face. He sat at a table and hid his face, resisting the urge to join in until he heard that someone knew where Eunan Maguire's Brehon was staying.

"Those bastard MacAodhagáins have come here to fix this trial. They'll let Eunan off and we'll be back to the coign and livery of the Maguire and the O'Neill and rising and rising rents. They should hang Eunan for his treachery and make the peace," said one man.

He slammed his tankard on his table in drunken contempt.

"Eunan Maguire is one of the Maguire's greatest warriors. I don't believe a word that liar Donnacha says," cried another with equal fury.

Óisin stood in the middle of the floor and slung off his coat.

"I served with Eunan Maguire in many battles, helped to recruit his men and was also involved in the assault on O'Cassidy house. You know me, I am Óisin Maguire who spent his youth crawling around these gutters worshiping the very mud the Maguire walked upon and put my life in danger for him so many times. I say that Eunan murdered those two men for his own enrichment and I'll fight any man that says different here and now."

He produced a knife from his belt and prowled the room for any takers. One man in the crowd piped up.

"I know you, Óisin. We used to run together in the fields as children."

He came forward and Óisin looked at him and hesitated until his memory returned. He took his friend by the shoulders.

"I remember you now. It is good to see you. You remember when we used to dream about how it would be us living in the castle looking down on those below? Well, now it is time. Let us take back this town from the rule of the Brehons, from coign and livery and from corrupt sheriffs. Let us show these lying Brehons what we think. Who knows where the Brehon and his companion the traitor Desmond are staying? Who is with me?"

A tremendous roar came from the tavern. Óisin had chosen well, for these had been the men he grew up with and he could read them perfectly.

"I know where he is!" cried one man from the back.

"Then let us go. Lead the way!"

The landlord slipped out the back to alert the Galloglass.

Cúchonnacht Óg had arranged for Cairbre and Desmond to stay in a farmhouse outside of Fermanagh down by the river. He could not risk appearing biased and offering armed protection, but he had ensured that Faolán and his men were fully armed. He could not approach them directly at the trial, but sent one of his men to guide them.

The farmhouse was isolated but had a good view of the countryside and, therefore, anyone that approached them. They also had a boat by which they could take to the river if needs be and travel to Enniskillen castle to seek Cúchonnacht Óg's protection. They arrived and were given a warm meal by the farmer and his wife. Faolán and his men set up watch around the perimeter of the house, allowing Desmond and Cairbre to retire for the evening. The day had been long and hard and neither wished to dwell on what had happened. They were given beds in a room at the back of the house and the farmer pointed to a stack of firewood pointed towards the castle, which was to be lit should they encounter any distress. They were asleep as their heads hit the pillow.

The unrest continued that evening in Enniskillen and the surrounding districts. The air was a concoction of smoke, fire, and noise. It was difficult for Faolán and his men, for there was always something to be alert about. But gradually their senses dulled, and they became immune to certain levels of noise.

Óisin and his men reached the perimeter of Enniskillen, split into groups and fanned out across the countryside so they could approach the farm from several angles. They had paused after they rolled out of the tavern in their drunken state to arm themselves. Óisin persuaded the men that it was safer to plan the assault rather than storm the farmhouse, given what had happened the previous evening. They surrounded the house and remained undetected. The night was in their favour, having provided a blanket of cloud and ensuring it was as dark as possible for that time of year. Óisin raised his hand in the air and when he lowered it, they filled the sky with flaming arrows.

"We are under attack! We are under attack!" cried Faolán as the first of his men fell to Óisin's rabble.

He ran inside to ensure Desmond and Cairbre were safe.

Desmond was out of bed, but barely dressed.

"Take Cairbre and our host and his wife to the boat and row down to Enniskillen castle," he ordered. "Those fools have accidentally lit the beacon, so Cúchonnacht Óg will be here soon. I can help hold them off."

"You get in the boat, lord. I am here to fight."

"Don't argue with me now. The boat is too small for all of us. The most important thing now is that Cairbre is safe as he is Eunan's best hope. I'm nothing but a sick old man. I'd much rather be taken by an axe or a sword than die in my bed, feeble with fever. Go now! You are here to obey my orders."

Faolán looked at him but saw his mind was not for changing.

"Goodbye, Desmond. See you in the next world if not again in this."

Desmond waved him away.

"Get out of here, you sentimental fool. This is a time for fighting, not crying."

Faolán ran out, and Cairbre was already struggling with the boat with the aid of the farmer. Faolán grabbed the end and with one more heave, it was in the water. They jumped inside and Faolán pushed it off the shore. His strength was absorbed in the oars and as he rowed, they saw the perimeter of the farm being overwhelmed by Óisin and his men.

Desmond stood in his room with his sword. He just had time to pull on his clothes and his boots before he heard the men in the house. In the doorway of his room appeared a man with a toothless grin and alcohol on his breath.

"He's in here," he cried.

Desmond raised his sword and prepared to die.

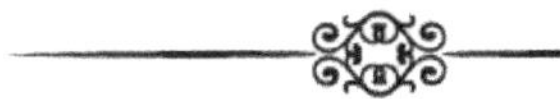

Seamus gathered his men and rode south. He had twenty men, all of whom had served in the Low Countries and all of whom shared his love for Munster. They rode as fast as they could until they reached the borders of Tirconnell. They stood on the top of a hill in the fading light and surveyed the path before them. Upon the hills in front of them were the silhouettes of a group of horsemen.

"Lord, we have been followed for at least half a day and now more men appear in front of us," said one of Seamus's scouts as he came back to report to him.

"I was not expecting such an easy ride until now. I should always remember that secrets are always short-lived. Take the main body of men and ride south. Draw them away so that I can make it to Enniskillen."

"Yes, lord. We'll shake them off and meet you there the day after next."

Seamus picked two of his men and rode down behind the hill whilst the main body of men made themselves visible on the hilltop and rode in a more direct route to Enniskillen. Seamus found himself a place to hide in a nearby wood and sat and waited for the enemy to be drawn away.

Desmond braced himself for what was about to come through the door but another face appeared.

"Óisin! How did you get here? Never mind that. How are we to make our escape?"

But the curl of Óisin's lip was cruel.

"There is no escape. I have come for you."

Desmond was both confused and afraid. Both were feelings that had made themselves known to him with age.

"It is me, Desmond. What has happened to you? Have you been overcome by drink? Whatever anyone has told you is not true and we can sort it out once we have made our escape."

"There is no escape for you."

"Tell me what is wrong. But hurry for we have little time."

"Do you remember Bé Bhionn?"

Desmond looked confused.

"I do. It was certainly a low in the reign of Cúchonnacht. What of it?"

"I am her son!"

Óisin ran towards him, and Desmond parried him away with his blade. He did not go in for the kill, for he still wished to reason with him.

"Put down your dagger and fight our real enemy. Such things are deep in the past."

"Not for me, they're not!"

He thrust his dagger and wounded Desmond's sword arm. Desmond knew Óisin would get him on his next pass.

"I am old and wounded and whatever you think you are doing, your mother wouldn't have wanted this."

"Never speak of my mother again for you are her murderer."

Óisin swung and plunged his dagger into Desmond's chest. Desmond wrapped his hands around the grip of the blade and Óisin sliced his hands as he withdrew the blade. Desmond fell to his knees and then keeled over onto the floor. His breathing became slower and heavier and his blood pooled beneath him on the floor.

"Whoever... told you... you are the son of Bé Bhionn is a liar. It is an old wives' tale she was murdered and her son taken away. Yes, I took her, but I took her to Tirconnell. She had MacSweeney blood in her, so I took her north to her distant family. She met a tragic end as both she and her son died of plague."

Óisin fell to his knees and lifted Desmond's head. His face was by now a mess of spittle and tears.

"You're lying to me!"

"What's the point of that? I'll be dead in a couple of moments. What you have to think about is what would anyone have to gain by telling you this lie and by killing me? Was this Caoimhe's lie?"

"Yes, yes," he yelped.

"You'll more likely be dead at the hands of Donnacha's men before you exchange any vows with her. Eunan was always your friend. Save him before it is too late for both of you."

The thundering sound of horses was heard outside.

"Go, before you are caught over my body. Make this right."

Óisin laid the old man's head gently on the ground, tears streaming down his face.

"Go."

Óisin wiped his knife on a cloth lying on the ground. He ran through the house and out the back door. The men he had brought were being run down by men on horseback. The shrill cries of their last moments ran through his head. He leapt into the river Erne.

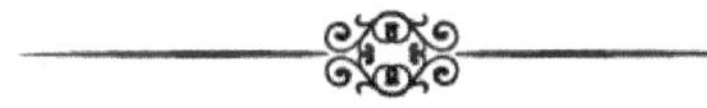

The next day, Seamus emerged from the woods. The air was thick with fog and an unfriendly drizzle. With visibility poor, it was the perfect time to travel if you knew where you were going.

"All we've got to do is get to the lake and then get a boat down to Enniskillen. We can't miss the lake, boys, it's massive," said Seamus.

"Which direction do we go in, lord? We can't see the tops of the mountains from here."

"Well, if we can't follow the mountains, then we can follow the streams. We are far enough away from the river Derg so that all rivers should flow south into the lake."

Seamus climbed a boulder and listened for the sound of flowing water.

"Over there. I hear a stream. If we follow that, we should run into the lake."

They picked up their gear and led their horses towards the sound of the water. The going was slow as the ground was covered in rocks and thick with bracken and the fog was unrelenting. The water did indeed flow downwards and appeared to point in the direction Seamus wanted it to. They walked alongside the stream for several hours until they came across a group of armed men watering their horses.

"Should we approach with caution?" asked one man.

"Have your weapons to hand but don't appear unfriendly."

One warrior had a pointed metal helmet on which both openings for the eyes met below the nose and remained open at the mouth and down to the chin.

"Excuse me strangers," called Seamus to the helmeted man. "We seem to have got lost in the fog and are seeking the great lake. Do you know where it is and how long it should take us to get there?"

The helmeted man turned to Seamus and then laughed.

"You don't recognise me, do you? I've been out here looking for you all day."

Seamus looked at the man again as he raised his axe to a combat position.

"Men! To arms!"

He still didn't recognise him.

"This is for my boy!"

Shea Óg plunged down his axe, only to be parried by Seamus.

CHAPTER THIRTY-FIVE

THE VERDICT

THE CROWDS ASSEMBLED FOR a third day and what was strongly rumoured to be the ultimate day of the trial. Donnacha's men had been busy the night before, for they had built a platform and a hangman's noose at the far end of the square, replacing the one damaged earlier in the riot. The crowds surged around the square, swelling to almost twice the size of the day before. Eunan was once more brought out in his cage, but the howls of derision were more muted than they had been on the two previous days, with no vegetables or spittle cast at him on his journey. Donnacha and Connor Roe took their seats. Their grim anticipation was reflected in the majority of the crowd.

"Do we have to wait for Eunan's Brehon again?" said Connor Roe in Donnacha's ear.

Donnacha signalled to him to be patient and stood up to address the crowd.

"Good morning, everyone, and I must once more apologise for the delay. We will again wait for the Brehon for Eunan Maguire out of respect for the law. However, we have had enough of the delaying and incitement tactics from Eunan's side and mean to move to deliberation and sentencing today. We will tolerate no violence from the renegade supporters of Eunan Maguire."

Donnacha sat down to wait whilst the decidedly mixed reaction from the crowd rang in his ears.

"Where is Cúchonnacht Óg?" asked Connor Roe. "I hope he has not chosen today to show his true colours."

Donnacha once again signalled to him to be patient. He preferred to spend the time granted to him surveying the crowd, trying to read their mood and the limitations they may place upon him that day. A body of armed Galloglass marched down one of the prominent streets that led down to where the trial was being held. They formed a hollow square with their axes slung over their right shoulders. Donnacha and Connor Roe rose from their seats and their constables prepared for violence. The top of the square opened up, and the men peeled away and lined the perimeter of the square. Cúchonnacht Óg stepped into the square in full battle uniform and stood in the middle and raised his sword. Some in the crowd nearest the square began to wail. Connor Roe waved to his men, and they formed a line in front of the raised platform.

Out from the centre of the hollowed square came a body held aloft by six MacCabe Galloglass. The body was that of their former leader, Desmond MacCabe. The six men marched up to in front of the platform, and on Cúchonnacht Óg's instruction, they laid him down in front of the platform. Desmond had been cleaned up, dressed in the battle dress of the MacCabe and laid to rest on a bed of shields. Cairbre then entered the square, having been in the back of the hollow square. He stood behind Desmond and bowed his head in reverence. Eunan could barely speak from behind his wall of Donnacha's guards. He welled up and began cursing to himself.

Donnacha stepped up behind his guards on the platform.

"It is a sad day. A great servant to the Maguire has died."

"You have no right to speak about him," shouted Eunan over the heads of his guards. "You are not worthy to speak of him."

"And you are?" bellowed Donnacha. "A boy up before us for two cowardly murders? I'll see you hang here today. It would not surprise me if you had anything to do with this!"

Eunan's guards wrestled with him to silence him. A punch in the jaw eventually did the trick.

"Given your conduct during the trial, it would not surprise me if this was your handiwork," Cairbre said, staring straight into Donnacha's eyes. "Twice my lodgings have been assaulted, leading to the death of my companions during a three-day trial."

The small man was now a fearless bundle of rage.

"Watch your accusations, Brehon. You may think you are the law, but you are in Maguire territory now. One more comment from you and it will be the castle jail and the justice of the sheriff for you."

Conchobar had been watching from the sidelines but has decided that his reputation had taken enough of a drubbing. He walked out for behind the cover of Connor Roe's men and stood beside Cairbre.

"Lord, I retire. I have held my tongue for two days now as this so-called trial has descended into farce. It is time to say enough is enough. I hereby close this trial and ask that my fellow Brehon and I be given an escort to at least out of the county, but preferably to our places of residence. You should release Eunan Maguire given your conduct here. There is no evidence to say that his actions were not justified."

"If you abandon your duty at the first sign of adversity, then you are no longer worthy of the name Brehon and therefore rescind all your privileges. Therefore, I will grant you a meal, a horse and a boy for directions, the same as we would any other wanderer to which we play host. As the acting Maguire, I will take your place and hope I perform with the minimal amount of skill you have shown whilst you were here."

Conchobar called his assistants together and they began to pack his things.

"Are you still going to perform your duties?" Donnacha asked Cairbre.

"These proceeding never descended above farce from the beginning. I will join my fellow Brehon and apologise to Eunan Maguire, for I can do no more for him, even if I ever thought I could."

Cairbre turned and started to collect his by now meagre possessions together. Conchobar instructed one of his assistants to help him.

"So my reward for preventing the MacAodhagáin Brehons from fixing the trial is they abandon their duties as the instruments of the law? Cowards, both of them."

The crowd jeered and goose pimples went down both Brehons' backs. They looked to Cúchonnacht Óg, for he seemed the only reasonable person in command of armed men.

"Then so be it," Donnacha said. "As acting Maguire, I shall take control of this shambles. We have heard enough from the hue and cry for traitor Maguire to be assured of his guilt. I would go through the Brehon rigmarole of seeing how many cows the two dead men were worth and how much the traitor could afford to pay but Brehon law has been placed into such disrepute by the Brehons in this case that I am forced to set it aside.

"Next I would consider whether to declare Eunan an attainder which would prevent himself or any of his offspring, should he have any, of holding any titles. However, he had no right to the title of O'Cassidy Maguire in the first place being common-born and his parentage not proven. Therefore, to sentence him as an attainder would be to strip him of a social standing that he never had. Therefore, I condemn him to hang, the sentence to be carried out immediately. Men, take him to the rope!"

The guards seized Eunan and quickly overpowered him. They dragged him down the square. Only the MacCabes could stop them, for they had formed a line across the square in honour of Desmond. Cúchonnacht Óg froze.

"Step aside," called Donnacha from the stage. "We don't want to dishonour Desmond's death by having this turn into a riot."

The men looked to Cúchonnacht Óg. He looked like a frightened rabbit. To fight could be the start of a civil war and the end to his brother as the Maguire. To step aside would dishonour both Desmond's death and Brehon law, condemn his friend to death, and be against everything he stood for. He shook, for he knew not what to do.

Caoimhe and Óisin had been standing in the crowd watching the proceedings. This was to be the day of Caoimhe's great revenge against Eunan and she had worn a grand bright red dress in celebration. Needless to say, she was the only person in the crowd in such attire but she wished to stand out, for once Eunan was hanged and her uncle and Connor Roe were in charge she would be a lady and wished to show everyone what she was about to become. She had the men her father had sent to act as her bodyguards, and Óisin would be beside her until they choked the last life from Eunan's neck. However, Caoimhe could see the emotions of the sentencing play out on Óisin's face and sensed he still kept feelings for his former friend. She cupped his hand in hers.

"Don't worry, it'll soon be over. Then we can be married."

She smiled sweetly up at him, but Óisin did not have the emotional energy to respond.

"I know things are bad in Enniskillen now, but I have arranged with my uncle that we shall both go to Lisnaskea under the protection of Connor Roe and be married there."

She smiled up at him again, but he let go of her hand.

"I've got to save my friend."

"Óisin! Don't be a fool. Óisin!"

Óisin pushed his way into the crowd, elbowing away Caoimhe's bodyguards and then wrestled with the guards on the perimeter until some of his fellow town residents came to his aid and created a hole in the wall of bodies. Óisin spilled out into the open square.

"Who is this? Guards, get rid of him," said Donnacha.

Óisin puffed his chest out to give himself bravery and strength. He strode wide-legged towards the stage. The two Brehons got out of his way and stood by Cúchonnacht Óg.

"I am the wedding day massacre witness you never heard from."

"So what do you have to say that is relevant now?" Donnacha said. "We have heard an overwhelming weight of evidence against Eunan Maguire, and he has already been found guilty and is about to be sentenced. Get back in the crowd before my men make an example out of you."

"I have had to live with my guilt for too long. I cannot live a lie any longer. It is me that should face the rope, not him."

Donnacha shook with anger, for Eunan still struggled with his guards in the middle of the square and the crowd were growing increasingly agitated while the thin wall of his men rippled with the pressure.

"I was one of Eunan's commanders at the wedding day massacre. I led the attack on the wedding itself. Eunan instructed me on where to attack and it was my bowmen that killed everyone at the wedding and my men that set fire to the house despite Eunan's explicit instructions not to damage it."

Óisin bowed his head, expecting his punishment and his friend to be released.

"It is commendable that you would wish to join your former commander on the scaffold and I'm sure that we can accommodate you. However, nothing you have said exonerates Eunan Maguire. Cúchonnacht Óg, please step aside and let the court conclude its punishment."

"I killed Desmond MacCabe."

The square went silent and everyone stopped.

"You did what?" asked Donnacha, barely believing his ears. "Why would Eunan want you to kill Desmond?"

"I was under the influence of that sorceress Caoimhe O'Cassidy. She told me that my mother was the mistress of Cúchonnacht Maguire and that he instructed Desmond to have her killed. In a fit of rage, I went to murder him. As you can see today, I succeeded."

The shock around the square was audible. Donnacha went crimson, incandescent with rage. Caoimhe tried to slip through the crowd but the extravagance of her clothing made her easy to identify as she had made herself known to everyone the previous day with her evidence. The crowd surrounded her and tore at her clothes. Connor Roe rose as he lost sight of her. He ordered one of his constables to fetch his men and retrieve her.

Donnacha saw the crowd wrestle with his men. Eunan's guards tried to force their way past the line of Cúchonnacht Óg's men, but to no avail. He knew he had one last chance.

"But you killed the man who killed your mother?"

"She lied."

The MacCabes went for Óisin and in their haste the line broke. Eunan was bundled towards the hangman's rope. Cúchonnacht Óg rallied his men and pointed his sword.

"Free Eunan and hang the slayer of your former master!"

Connor Roe was handed his sword, shield, and helmet and leapt from the stage.

"As the sheriff of Fermanagh I order you all to disperse or face my men."

With that, all hell broke loose. MacCabes fought to free Eunan and battled Connor Roe and his men. The line of Donnacha's men also fractured, and they fled back towards the stage. The crowd broke into a charge and swept all before it. Donnacha jumped off the back of the stage and ordered the reserves of men forward. They took position on the stage and swept the square with arrows which flew indiscriminately into men, women and children and Galloglass, friend or foe alike.

"Hound down the traitors!" shouted Cúchonnacht Óg.

He thrust his sword into the belly of one of Connor Roe's men and was rewarded with a jet of warm blood all over his hand and sleeve. For the crowd, being swept with arrows was the final straw, and they took Cúchonnacht Óg's side and stormed the stage. Connor Roe's men were overwhelmed and broke and ran. Connor Roe himself was surrounded but fought his way out, for there were poorly armed commoners around him, easy victims for his sword. The men surrounding Eunan became isolated and broke and fled. Eunan was burning on pure adrenalin and he picked up an axe and charged towards the stage.

Óisin was bundled towards the scaffold amidst all the fighting as the crowd ran past him to attack the tribunal. Despite his confession, he still had some allies among the street people of Enniskillen and they set upon the Galloglass trying to drag him to the hangman's noose.

Connor Roe fought his way to behind the stage to where the chaos had spilled over.

"Lord," a familiar voice called. "I have your horse."

Connor Roe thrust downwards and into the chest of a Maguire peasant armed only with a pitchfork and relieved him of his life.

"Rally the men. It is time to go."

The houses and buildings surrounding the square had caught fire and smoke billowed in the air. It got more difficult for the participants in the riot to either see or breathe. The townsfolk began to disperse.

Eunan fought his way onto the stage. The remains of Donnacha's men were in full retreat. Eunan saw Donnacha running down a backstreet. He looked around and recognised some of Cúchonnacht Óg's men that fought alongside him.

"To me, men!"

He raised his axe and charged after Donnacha.

The crowd drifted off, leaving the dead, wounded and trampled to lie or groan in the backstreets.

"Here, Miss. Take my hand."

It was a kindly voice, but not enough to drown out the shrieking and the hands that had grabbed at her before. She was hurt but could walk. She took the stranger's hand without looking to see who it was. Her life was in the hands of God now. She had survived the punches, scratches, and taunts. Surely she would not get murdered now? She opened her eyes. It was Caolán, Donnacha's constable of his Galloglass.

"Quickly. It is not safe."

Caoimhe looked around, and found her three former bodyguards were all dead. They had fallen trying to protect her.

There was no sign of Maeve. This hand was all she was going to get. They wound their way through the houses and past the rabble of the streets.

Óisin's friends were no match for the MacCabes and had little remaining stomach for the fight. Óisin stood on a stool as the MacCabes placed his head through the noose.

"This is for Desmond MacCabe," a voice in his ear sneered.

Óisin inhaled the man's foul-smelling breath as he had the stool kicked from under him. His legs kicked until the life drained out of him.

"Clear the streets of Connor Roe's men," cried Cúchonnacht Óg.

Donnacha's men had started to defect, and the crowds melted away when they found themselves no match for the heavily armed Galloglass.

Connor Roe had rallied his men behind the stage. They were gradually being forced back by the weight of Cúchonnacht Óg's men, who were also using their superior knowledge of the town and attempting to outflank them.

"We must leave, lord," said one of Connor Roe's constables.

"Where are Donnacha and his niece? I gave my word I would protect them."

"The girl has not been seen since the murderer confessed. Donnacha is presumed to have fled."

A few more of his men fell and Donnacha's forces were deserting. He saw it would be impossible for the line to hold much longer.

"Then we must leave. I have no intention of dying for nothing. Retreat, men. Retreat!"

Caolán led Caoimhe by the hand towards one of the piers beneath Enniskillen castle.

"We can escape south and follow the river until we reach the upper lake. Connor Roe controls the north shore and we can get to Lisnaskea within a couple of hours. You'll be safe there."

Caoimhe stopped and bent down to tend to her ankle.

"I don't know if I can make it that far."

"You must. Your uncle will be there waiting for you. He asked me to take care of you. He has arranged for boats to be there just in case something went wrong."

"I will try but you need to help me."

Caolán threw her arm over his shoulder, and they limped towards the boats.

"There she is!"

Óisin's friends had witnessed his hanging, but could do nothing about it. They roamed the streets looking to relieve their anger. The tattered remains of Caoimhe's red dress had stood out on the darkened streets as a beacon for their revenge. They pursued Caoimhe and Caolán down the street to the pier and trapped them in front of one of the houses cutting them off from the river. The rabble of Enniskillen formed a semi-circle around Caoimhe and Caolán and closed in. Caolán drew his sword and pointed it at whoever came nearest.

"I am a constable in the Maguire's Galloglass. Those who hinder me will feel the tip of my sword. Those who aid me will be richly rewarded when the Maguire returns and restores order. Which is it to be?"

The mob edged closer and Caoimhe leaned against the wall of the house. A woman hidden under a hood came out from the crowd.

"That witch cast a spell on our friend and now he swings from a rope and Desmond MacCabe lies dead, all because of her. If she lives then she'll curse us all."

The mob advanced forward.

"Get away from here while you can old woman or I'll slice you in two," replied Caolán. "My men are on their way and will make short work of you all. Now be gone before you all die because of some rumour spread by an old woman."

Indecision hung in the air and a bead of sweat rolled down Caolán's face as he fended off the mob. The sound of the street fighting in the town came nearer.

"Listen," said Caolán. "That is the sound of my men coming. Flee while you still can."

"Not while she still lives," said the old woman.

She turned from the crowd and picked a pebble up from the street. She threw it towards Caolán and it hit him in the side of the head. His sword dropped and his brain went numb as a torrent of rocks struck him in the head.

Donnacha still had a couple of men with him and some last tricks up his sleeve. He estimated that if things fell apart, the castle would fall and he would need another escape route. He had strategically placed some horses on the outskirts of town, and arrived to find the horse boys had all fled except for the body of one laid before his means of escape. Donnacha blessed himself and gestured to his guards to prepare themselves.

"That won't save you."

Donnacha turned around and his two guards raised their weapons.

"Seamus MacSheehy! How long have you been here?"

"Long enough for your horse boy to tell me what has gone on."

Seamus reached into his pocket and pulled out a letter.

"I have returned with a reprieve for Eunan signed by the Maguire himself. I hope I'm not too late to use it, for your sake."

Donnacha looked behind Seamus for he did not believe that he would face him alone.

"If you go back into town, you'll find that Eunan is very much alive."

"I'd prefer to bring you with me whilst I make sure."

"You know it is a crime to lay a hand on a counsellor for the Maguire?"

"Given what your horse boy told me, I doubt you'll be counselling anyone when the Maguire returns."

"That is not for you to say. Step aside or face the wrath of my men."

Seamus looked at both the guards. They did not look like they wanted to fight.

"Hand over your master and I'll spare your lives. I'll only make this offer once."

The guards lowered their axes as they contemplated what Seamus said.

"I can pay you, Seamus. A reprieve for your nephew, land in Fermanagh? What will it take?"

There was the sound of a whoosh swiftly followed by the splash and thud of Donnacha's severed head landing in the mud below his body.

"That is for Desmond MacCabe!"

Eunan slowly lowered his axe, too tense to wipe his blood-spattered face. He stood and watched Donnacha's body fall to the ground. Donnacha's two guards fled. Seamus held up the letter.

"I got you a reprieve from the Maguire but I don't think it covers this."

Eunan wiped his face, put down his axe, and took a sack from his belt.

"Hold this."

Seamus took hold of the rim of the sack and Eunan carefully picked the head out of the puddle with Donnacha's face opposite his. He placed it in the sack.

"When the Maguire returns, I'll present him with the head. Then whatever happens, happens. I no longer care."

Seamus slapped him on the back.

"You're a real MacSheehy now."

Eunan shrugged him off.

"Does it really matter? Am I even the O'Cassidy Maguire anymore?"

"Come, we need to go back to the castle. All I know is that change is coming. The Maguire will return, eager for war. You have your soldiers. I have my connections and alliances. If ever the Maguire needed us, it is now."

They walked through the streets and passed by the piers to the south of the castle. Eunan had time to think and was now curious.

"Show me the letter from the Maguire."

Seamus obliged, and Eunan took it and read it.

"What took you so long getting here?" said Eunan.

"I ran into our old friend Shea Óg, and it took me a while to escape. I should have killed him, but his men proved too plentiful. One day I will rid myself of that stone in my shoe."

They walked towards the castle only to hear a scream from one of the side streets up ahead. They looked at each other with a sense of duty.

"Come on," said Seamus.

They drew their axes into a defensive position as they made their way to where they thought was the source of the noise. The mob spilled out onto the street and cheered when they recognised Eunan. A flash of bright colour caught Eunan's eye.

"What is that you have there?" he demanded, catching a woman by the arm.

The woman looked at the jagged piece of red cloth in her hands.

"'Tis part of the dress of the sorceress who bewitched poor Óisin. We killed her guard and drowned her in the river like you should all witches. She can haunt the lake forever now. If you look out on a dark night, you will hear her calling for Óisin to do her bidding, but he'll never come for we're going to get the priests to bless his body so he can't be bewitched ever again."

Eunan looked at Seamus, and he did not know whether to be tearful. It had been a long emotional day in what had been several long emotional years. They went down the side street to see if what the woman said was true. The pulverised body of Caolán lay surrounded by bloodied pebbles and rocks. Another piece of the red dress clung to a post of the pier.

"What a way to go," said Seamus for even he was tinged with emotion. He put his arm around Eunan. "Come on, she's gone."

They walked up to the main street.

"Eunan!"

Cara ran up the street, threw her arms open and embraced him. Eunan tensed then gave way and took her in his arms.

"It's good to see you are with a good Munster girl now," said Seamus winking at him. "She even looks a bit like Caoimhe."

"How did you know -?"

But Cara looked up at him and smiled, and for that moment everything was all right.

Also By

Scan the QR code to purchase these books on the online retailer of your choice.

Bad Blood

★ ★ ★ ★ ★

"a tale that is filled with twists, including stabbings-in-the-back, and one that puts readers on the edge of their seats," – The Book Commentary

Uprising

★ ★ ★ ★ ★

"Fully action-packed, this pulls you further into Eunan and Seamus' story; making you question who to support the whole way through," – Reedsy Discovery

*Coming soon
- Exiles book
4*

About Author

QR code for the C R Dempsey newsletter mailing list.

C R Dempsey is the author of 'Traitor Maguire', 'Uprising' and 'Bad Blood', three historical fiction books set in Elizabethan Ireland. He has plans for many more, and he needs to find the time to write them. History has always been his fascination, and historical fiction was an obvious outlet for his accumulated knowledge. C R spends lots of time working on his books, mainly in the twilight hours of the morning. C R wishes he spent more time writing and less time jumping down the rabbit hole of excessive research.

C R Dempsey lives in London with his wife and cat. He was born in Dublin but has lived most of his adult life in London.

C R can be found at:

https://www.crdempseybooks.com/,

https://www.facebook.com/crdempsey,

https://www.instagram.com/crdempsey/,
Twitter: @dempsey_cr

Acknowledgments

Thank you to all my family and friends and all of those who helped to create this book.

Special thanks to Mena (endless patience and support), Eoin (advice and inspiration), Justin Moule (feedback and support).
   Thank you also for the professional support of:
   Book cover: Dominic Forbes
   Editing: Robin Seavill

Both these individuals can be found on www.Reedsy.com